THINGS WE DO IN THE DARK

ALSO BY JENNIFER HILLIER

Creep
Freak
The Butcher
Wonderland
Jar of Hearts
Little Secrets

THINGS
WE DO
IN THE
DARK

JENNIFER HILLIER

MINOTAUR
BOOKS

NEW YORK

Content Warning:

Please note that this novel contains references to murder, child abuse, sexual violence,
suicide, mental health, addiction, racism, body shaming, and misogyny.

This is a work of fiction. All of the characters, organizations, and events portrayed in this
novel are either products of the author's imagination or are used fictitiously.

First published in the United States by Minotaur Books,
an imprint of St. Martin's Publishing Group

Designed by Steven Seighman

ISBN 9781250763167

For Mox

you are my sunshine
and the air that I breathe
and the reason for everything

PART ONE

She can kill with a smile, she can wound with her eyes

—BILLY JOEL

CHAPTER ONE

There's a time and a place for erect nipples, but the back of a Seattle police car definitely isn't it.

Paris Peralta didn't think to grab a sweater before they arrested her, so she's only wearing a bloodstained tank top. It is July, after all. But the air-conditioning is on high, and she feels cold and exposed. With her wrists cuffed, all she can do is clasp her hands together and hold her forearms up to cover her breasts. It looks like she's praying.

She's not praying. It's much too late for that.

Her head throbs underneath the butterfly bandage one of the EMTs stuck on before they put her in the cop car. She must have slammed it into the rim of the bathtub sometime last night, but she doesn't remember tripping or falling. All she remembers is her husband, lying in a bathtub filled with blood, and the screaming that woke her up this morning.

The blond-ponytailed detective behind the wheel glances at Paris again in the rearview mirror. Ever since Jimmy signed a streaming deal with new Netflix competitor Quan six months ago, people have been staring at her a lot. Paris hates it. When she and Jimmy got married, she expected to live a quiet life with the retired actor-comedian. That's the deal they made; that's the marriage she signed up for. But then Jimmy changed his mind and *un*-retired, and it was about the worst thing he could have done to her.

And now he's dead.

The detective has been keeping an eye on her in the back seat the entire time, her eyes shifting from the road to the mirror every few minutes. Paris can already tell the woman thinks she did it. Okay, fine, so it looked bad. There was so much blood, and when the detective arrived on the scene, there were already three officers in the bedroom pointing their guns straight at Paris through the bathroom doorway. Soon there were four pairs of eyes staring at her as if she'd done something terrible. Nobody seemed to be blinking or breathing, including her.

"Mrs. Peralta, please put the weapon down," the detective had said. Her voice was calm and direct as she unholstered her pistol. "And then come out of the bathroom slowly with your hands up."

But I don't have a weapon, Paris thought. It was the second time someone had told her to do that, and just like before, it didn't make sense. *What weapon?*

Then the detective's eyes flickered downward. Paris followed her glance and was shocked to discover that she was still holding Jimmy's straight razor. And not just holding it, but *clutching* it in her right hand, her fingers wrapped tightly around the handle, her knuckles white. She lifted it up, staring at it in wonder as she turned it over in her hand. The police officers didn't like that, and the detective repeated her demand again in a tone louder and more commanding than before.

The whole thing was so absurd. Everybody was overreacting. Paris wasn't holding a weapon. It was just a shaving tool, one of several straight razors that Jimmy owned, because her husband was an old-school guy who liked straight shaves and cassette tapes and landlines. He wasn't even allowed to use his straight razors anymore. The worsening tremor in his hand had rendered them unsafe.

So why the hell was Paris still holding the ebony-handled razor he'd bought in Germany decades ago?

Everything happened in slow-motion. As the detective continued to speak, Paris once again took in the blood spattered across the white marble tile floor, diluted pink from mixing with the bathwater. It was Jimmy's blood, and she knew that if she turned around, she would see her husband behind her, submerged in the deep soaker bathtub where he'd bled out the night before.

Paris did not turn around. But she did manage to catch a glimpse of herself in the mirror above the sink, where she saw a woman who looked just like her wearing a tank top splotched with blood. Her hair was tangled and her eyes were wild, the side of her face covered in blood that had oozed from a gash over her right eyebrow. In her hand, Jimmy's old straight razor did look like a weapon.

A *murder* weapon.

"Mrs. Peralta, drop the razor," the detective commanded again.

Paris finally dropped it. The steel blade landed on the tile with a dull clang, and the uniformed officers moved in on her in a swarm. One of them slapped the cuffs on her, and the detective informed her of her rights. As they led her out of the bedroom and down the stairs, Paris wondered how she would possibly explain this.

Years ago, the last time this happened, she didn't have to explain it at all.

"I'm sorry, but would you mind turning down the air-conditioning?" Paris's nipples are pressing hard against her forearms like ball bearings. Though she'd lived in Seattle for almost twenty years now, the Canadian in her still can't break the habit of apologizing before asking for something. "I'm sorry, it's just really cold back here."

The officer in the passenger seat pushes a button on the dashboard repeatedly until the cold air eases up.

"Thank you," she says.

The officer turns around. "Anything else we can do for you?" he asks. "Need a mint? Want to stop and grab a coffee?"

He's not asking real questions, so she doesn't respond.

On some level Paris understands that she's in shock and that the full extent of the situation hasn't hit her yet. At least her self-preservation instincts have kicked in—she knows she's been arrested, she knows she's going to be booked, and she knows she needs to keep her mouth shut and call a lawyer at the first opportunity. But still, it feels like she's watching all this happen from the *outside*, as if she's in a movie where someone who looks like her is about to be charged with murder.

This feeling of *disassociation*—a word she learned as a kid—is something that happens to her whenever she's in situations of extreme stress.

Disassociation was her mind's way of protecting her from the traumas that were happening to her body. While this isn't what's happening now, the feeling of separation between her brain and physical form tends to happen whenever she feels vulnerable and unsafe.

Right now, the life she knows—the life she's built—is being threatened.

Paris can't float away, though. She needs to stay present if she's going to make it through this, so she focuses on her breathing. As she tells her yoga students, whatever is happening, you can always come back to your breath. Constricting her throat just a little, she takes a slow, deep inhale, holds it, then exhales. It makes a slight hissing sound, as if she's trying to fog up the car window, and the detective's eyes dart toward her in the rearview mirror once again.

After a few ocean breaths—*ujjayi* breaths—Paris is more clearheaded, more *here*, and she tries to process how the hell she ended up in the back of a cop car, on her way to jail. She watches enough TV to know that the police always assume it's the spouse. Of course, it hadn't helped one bit that Zoe, Jimmy's assistant, was the one pointing the finger and screaming herself hoarse. *She murdered him she murdered him oh my God she's a murderer!*

They think she killed Jimmy.

And now the rest of the world will, too, because that's how it looks when you're led out of your home in handcuffs with blood on your clothes as news of your celebrity husband's death ripples through the crowd of onlookers snapping photos and recording videos of your arrest. The irony is, the crowd was already conveniently in place outside the house well before Zoe called the cops. Paris and Jimmy live on Queen Anne Hill, right across the street from Kerry Park, which boasts the best views of Seattle. It's a popular spot for both locals and tourists to take photos of the city skyline and Mount Rainier, and the crowd today was like any other, except the cameras were pointing toward the house instead of the skyline. And just like there hadn't been time to put on another shirt, there had been no opportunity to put on different shoes. Paris heard someone yell, "Nice slippers!" as soon as she stepped outside, but it didn't sound like a compliment.

The neighbors on the street were all outside, too. Bob and Elaine from next door were standing at the end of their driveway, their faces filled with shock and horror at the sight of her. Since they didn't call out or offer to help in any way, they must have already heard what happened. They must already think Paris is guilty.

They're supposed to be her friends.

She can imagine the headlines already. JIMMY PERALTA, THE PRINCE OF POUGHKEEPSIE, FOUND DEAD AT 68. Though Jimmy's highly rated sitcom had ended its ten-year run more than two decades earlier, he would forever be known for his starring role as the son of a bakery owner in *The Prince of Poughkeepsie*, which won over a dozen Emmys and propelled Jimmy into movie stardom until he retired seven years ago. Paris doesn't have to be a publicist to predict that the news of her husband's death will be even bigger than the headline-making multimillion-dollar deal Jimmy signed with Quan when he decided to make his comeback. Even Paris would think this was a juicy story if it wasn't happening to her.

She continues to focus on her breathing, but her mind refuses to settle. None of this feels right. While she had no illusions that she and Jimmy would grow old together, she thought they had more time. In the two years they'd been married, they'd established an easy routine. Paris worked at the yoga studio six days a week, and Jimmy always had things going on. But Sundays were their day together. They should be having a lazy brunch right now at the nearby diner, where the owner always saved them a table by the window. Pancakes and bacon for Jimmy, waffles with strawberries for Paris. Afterward, they might head into Fremont for the farmers' market or take a drive to Snohomish to do some antiques hunting. More often than not, though, they'd head home, where Jimmy would putter in the garden, trimming this and weeding that, while she cracked open a paperback and sat by the pool.

But this is not a normal Sunday. This is a fucking nightmare. Paris should have known it would end like this, because there's no such thing as happily ever after when you run away from one life to start a whole new one.

Karma has come for her.

A feather from her ridiculous slippers tickles the top of her foot. When she received them for her birthday last month—not her real birthday, but the one that's listed on her ID—they were funny and cute. Her instructors at the studio had all chipped in to buy her the pair of seriously expensive Italian designer slides made out of pink ostrich feathers. They were supposed to stay at the studio so she'd have something to walk around in between classes, but she couldn't resist bringing them home to show Jimmy. She knew he would laugh, and he did.

The slippers aren't funny now. All they'll do is play into the narrative the media keeps trying to create, which is that Paris is a rich, self-entitled asshole. She managed to fly under the radar for nineteen years after she escaped Toronto, only to have it all undone when Jimmy's trusty assistant Zoe included their wedding photo with the press release about the streaming deal. Zoe couldn't understand why Paris was so upset, but until that day, most people hadn't even known that Jimmy Peralta had gotten married again. Paris had been living in blissful anonymity with her retired husband, and then it all went to hell.

As Zoe would say, the optics are terrible. Paris is Jimmy's fifth wife, and she's almost thirty years younger than he is. While the age difference was never a problem for Jimmy—why would it be?—it makes Paris look like a gold-digging bitch who was just waiting for her husband to die.

And now he's dead.

CHAPTER TWO

The desk clerk at the King County jail asks for her phone, but Paris doesn't have it with her. As far as she remembers, it's still on the nightstand in her bedroom, in the house that's now a crime scene.

"All personal items need to be bagged and placed in the bin," the clerk informs her. Like the detective that brought her here, he hasn't stopped staring since she was brought in. "That includes your jewelry."

All Paris has is her wedding ring. Jimmy had offered to buy her an engagement ring, too, but she declined, insisting she would never wear it while teaching yoga anyway. In the end, he talked her into an eternity band crafted with fifteen fancy pink oval-shaped diamonds. The retail cost was an astounding $250,000, but the jeweler had offered Jimmy a discount if they were willing to have the ring photographed and publicized. Paris declined that, too.

"I don't want the publicity," she told Jimmy. "I'm really okay with a simple gold band."

"Not a fucking chance." Jimmy had a short conversation with the jeweler and slapped down his black Amex. Because he was Jimmy Peralta, he got the discount anyway.

"Paris Peralta." The desk clerk says her name with a smirk as he types on his keyboard, drawing out the syllables. *Paaarrrisssss Peraaaaalta.* "My wife's gonna shit herself when I tell her who I booked today. She was a big fan of *The Prince of Poughkeepsie.* Never liked the show myself. I always thought Jimmy Peralta was an ass."

"Have some respect, Officer." The detective is standing beside her, elbow to elbow, as if she thinks there's a chance Paris might bolt. She tosses her head, and the tip of her ponytail flicks Paris's bare arm. "The man is dead."

Paris pulls off her wedding ring and passes it through the window. Beside her, she hears the detective mutter under her breath, "Jesus, it's pink." The desk clerk examines the ring closely before sealing it in a small plastic bag. He then drops it into the plastic bin, where it lands with an audible *smack*.

Inwardly, she winces. *The value of that ring*, Paris thinks, *is probably triple what you earned last year.* Outwardly, she maintains her composure. She's not going to give anyone a story to sell to the tabloids. Instead, she makes eye contact with him through the smudged plexiglass window and stares him down. As she predicts, he's a weasel, and his gaze drops back to his computer.

"Sign this." He shoves her inventory list through the window. There's only one item on it. *Ring, diamond, pink*. Paris scrawls her signature.

Another officer comes out from behind the desk and waits expectantly. The detective turns to Paris. She probably did introduce herself at the time of the arrest, but her name eludes Paris now, assuming she even heard it in the first place.

"We'll need your clothes," the detective says. "Slippers, too. They'll give you something else to put on. And then I'll come and talk to you, okay?"

"I'd like to call my lawyer," Paris says.

The detective isn't surprised, but she does seem disappointed. "You can do that after you're processed."

A buzzer sounds, and Paris is led through a set of doors and into a small, brightly lit room. She's directed to take her clothes off in the corner behind a blue curtain. She undresses quickly, removing everything but her underwear, and puts on the sweatshirt, sweatpants, socks, and rubber slides they've given her. It's a relief to get the bloodstained clothes off and change into footwear that doesn't resemble a cat toy. Everything is stamped with the letters *DOC*.

She's fingerprinted and photographed. Her hair is a matted mess, but it's not like she can borrow a hairbrush. She looks straight at the camera and lifts her chin. Jimmy once said that it's near impossible to not look like a criminal in a mugshot. He would know. He was arrested twice for driving under the influence and once for assault after shoving a heckler in Las Vegas after a show. In all three mugshots, he looked guilty as hell.

The processing done, she's led to an elevator for a quick ride down one floor. The young officer escorting her shoots furtive glances in her direction from time to time, but he doesn't say a word until they get to the holding cell. In a voice that squeaks (followed by a quick throat clear), he directs her to go inside. As soon as she steps in, the bars close and lock with a clang.

And just like that, Paris is in jail.

It's both better and worse than she always imagined, and she has imagined it many times. It's bigger than she expected, and there's only one other person in here, a woman who's currently passed out on the opposite side of the cell. One bare leg hangs off the edge of the bench, and the soles of her bare feet are filthy. Her tight neon-yellow dress is covered in stains from an indeterminate substance, but at least she wasn't forced to change her clothes. Whatever she's being held for, it's not murder.

Though the cell appears clean, the harsh fluorescent lights show smears from whatever was recently mopped up. Based on the lingering odors, it was both urine and vomit. The walls look sticky and are covered in a dingy shade of beige paint the color of weak tea, and there's a camera mounted in one corner of the ceiling.

At the back of the cell, right beside the telephone anchored to the wall, is a plastic-covered sign that lists the phone numbers of three different bail bond companies. With any luck, she won't need them. She picks up the handset and punches in one of the few phone numbers she has memorized. *Pick up, pick up, pick up* . . .

Voice mail. *Shit.* She hears her own voice encouraging her to leave a message.

"Henry, it's Paris," she says quietly. "I'm going to try your cell. I'm in trouble."

She hangs up, waits for the dial tone, and calls the second number she knows by heart. This, too, goes to voice mail. A few feet away, her cellmate sits up, her greasy hair falling around her oily face. She regards Paris with bleary, mascara-smeared raccoon eyes.

"I know you." Her words are thick and slurred. Even from a few feet away, Paris can smell her, an aroma like rotting food in a whiskey distillery. "I seen you before. You're, like, a famous person."

Paris pretends not to hear her.

"You're that chick who married that old guy." The woman blinks, trying to focus. When Paris doesn't respond, she says, "Oh, okay, I get it, you're a fucking princess, too good to talk to me. Well, fuck you, princess." She lies back down. Ten seconds later, her face is slack and her mouth falls open.

There's a schoolhouse clock on the wall outside the cell, and Paris waits exactly four and a half minutes before picking up the phone again. This time, someone answers immediately.

"Ocean Breath Yoga."

"Henry." Relief floods through Paris at the sound of her business partner's voice. "Thank God."

"Holy shit, P, are you okay?" Henry's voice is filled with concern. "I just heard about Jimmy. Oh, honey, I'm so sorry. I can't believe it—"

"Henry, they've arrested me." She can't believe she's saying the words. "I'm in a holding cell at the King County jail."

"I saw the arrest. It's such bullshit—"

"You saw? It's on the news?"

"On the *news*? Honey, it's on TikTok." She hears some background noise and then hears a door shut, which means Henry has taken the cordless phone into the office. "One of the tourists at the park filmed your arrest and uploaded it. It's currently the number one trending video."

Of course this isn't surprising, but hearing Henry say it makes it all the more real. Paris swallows down the panic and reminds herself that there will be plenty of time to fall apart later.

"Henry, listen," she says. "I need you to call Elsie Dixon for me."

"Jimmy's friend? The lawyer who sings showtunes at all your parties?"

"That's the one. I don't have my phone, so I don't have her number."

"I'll google her law office."

"She won't be in, it's Sunday. But if you look in the desk, there might be a business card with her cell. Ask her to come down to the jail right away, okay?"

"I don't see a card." She can hear Henry rifling through the drawers. "Don't worry, I'll figure something out. I thought she was in litigation?"

"She started her career as a public defender," Paris says. "And she's the only lawyer I know."

"God, P . . . ," Henry says, sounding genuinely stunned. "I can't believe you're in jail. Is it like in the movies?"

She looks around. "More or less. But bleaker."

"Can I bring you anything? A pillow? A book? A shank?"

He's trying to make her laugh, but the best she can manage is a snort. "I love you. Just track Elsie down, okay? And maybe you could let the instructors know what's going on."

"P, they're saying . . ." A pause. "They're saying you killed Jimmy. I know that's not possible, because I know *you*. You're not a murderer."

"I appreciate that," Paris says, and after saying goodbye, they hang up.

Henry has always been a supportive friend, and he's loyal to the core. But he doesn't know her, not really.

Nobody does.

CHAPTER THREE

Thanks to the wonders of sensory adaptation, Paris has gone nose blind and can no longer smell the various odors that assaulted her when she first entered the holding cell. Unfortunately, she can't say the same about the noises.

She sits on the bench with her hands in her lap, doing her best to ignore her cellmate's snores mixing with the random chatter wafting in from the other cells. Everything is going to be fine. Elsie will be here soon, and she'll know exactly what to do, because Elsie Dixon is a lawyer, and that's what lawyers do.

Except she's not just a lawyer. Elsie is also Jimmy's best friend. The two of them met in high school fifty years ago, which makes their friendship eleven years older than Paris. There will be no question where the woman's loyalties lie, and if she believes there's the slightest chance that Paris murdered her dearest friend, Elsie will not show up today, or ever.

She hopes Elsie shows up.

In the meantime, there's nothing to do but wait. And without a phone or a book to distract herself, all there is to do is think. And the longer she thinks, the more the pain of Jimmy's death tries to fight its way in. Paris doesn't want to feel it. Not here and not now, because she doesn't know how to feel the depth of her grief while also saving herself from the mess she's now in. She closes her eyes. Even if she didn't kill her husband, it sure as hell looks like she did.

The part that nobody could ever seem to accept is that Paris actually loved Jimmy very much. But it wasn't necessarily *romantic* love, and that's the part that bothers people. Apparently you're only supposed to marry someone you're head over heels for, someone you can't get enough of, someone you can't imagine your life without. By that definition, what she and Jimmy had wouldn't be considered love at all. Their feet were always on solid ground. They probably spent more time apart than they did together. And *of course* they could live without each other. *Please.* Jimmy had lived a whole sixty-five years before he met Paris, achieving a level of success most comedians would never reach. Paris was thirty-six when she met Jimmy, and was fine being on her own. She was an old soul; he was young at heart. Their relationship worked.

And yet, all anyone could see—the press, Jimmy's friends, and especially Elsie—was the twenty-nine-year age difference.

"We're good together, don't you think?" Jimmy had said to her during lunch one random Wednesday. They'd been seeing each other for about nine months. "Have you ever thought about getting married?"

"To who?"

"To me, you dope."

She almost choked on the pastrami-on-rye they were sharing. Jimmy wasn't capable of eating a sandwich that didn't include deli meat.

"Are you proposing?" she asked.

"I guess I am."

It wasn't romantic. Jimmy wasn't built that way and neither was she. They were two adults making a decision to do life together, and that was enough for both of them. They got married in Kauai three months later, at sunset, in an intimate ceremony on the beach. Jimmy's good friend, a big-time Hollywood director whose own wife was younger than Paris, flew the small group there on his Gulfstream. Elsie was there—she came solo, as she'd never found anyone special after her second marriage ended a decade earlier—and so were Henry and his longtime partner, Brent. Bob and Elaine Cavanaugh from next door were invited, too. And, of course, Zoe.

The thought of Jimmy's frizzy-haired assistant makes Paris want to stab something.

"Peralta. Your lawyer is here."

She opens her eyes to see the same young officer from earlier unlocking the doors to the cell. Somehow, three hours have passed. Considering that Jimmy's oldest friend only lives twenty minutes away from the courthouse, Elsie sure took her time getting here.

But at least she's here. And the officer said *your lawyer*, which hopefully means Elsie is here to help.

"Garza," the officer says in a louder voice. Hearing her name, Paris's cellmate wakes up again. "You made bail. Let's go."

Yawning, the woman stands and waggles her fingers at Paris. Her nails are painted the same tennis ball yellow as her dress. She still seems drunk, and she nearly collides with Elsie, who steps aside just in time. Elsie's nose wrinkles at the other woman's smell.

"Bye, princess," she says over her shoulder before disappearing down the hallway.

Finally, the lawyer is permitted to enter. Elsie Dixon is only five two, but she has the personality of someone six feet tall. Her silver hair is cut in a chin-length bob, her signature style, and she's dressed as if she's on her way to a ladies' brunch—if the brunch was on a tropical cruise. Her pink pumps match her drapey pink blouse and floral skirt, and her chunky turquoise statement necklace complements her blue eyes. This is a normal outfit for her.

Elsie's eyes are red-rimmed and swollen. She doesn't say hello or ask Paris how she's doing. She flicks a speck of dirt off the bench before taking a seat.

"I asked for an interview room, but they're all full." The older woman speaks briskly. "So we'll have to talk here. Even though we're alone, keep your voice low and your head down at all times. You never know who's listening."

"Thank you for coming," Paris says quietly.

Elsie doesn't answer. Instead, she opens her briefcase and takes out a lined notepad, her reading glasses, and an elegant black-and-gold pen with the name of her firm stamped on the side. Elsie is a partner at Strathroy, Oakwood, and Strauss, and while she's no longer a criminal defense attorney, she used to be. She got her start working as a public defender for a few years before switching over to private practice. She's now in litigation, and Jimmy has always said she's fierce in court.

Paris isn't sure how much Elsie can help with her situation, but she's grateful the lawyer at least showed up. The other woman has always been fiercely protective of Jimmy, and she was suspicious of Paris from the beginning. The night she and Elsie first met, Elsie had asked outright whether Jimmy's new and much younger girlfriend was just in it for the green card. The woman was on her third glass of chardonnay at the time, but still.

"It's like it didn't even occur to her that I'm already a US citizen," Paris had fumed to Jimmy later. "Would she have asked me that if I was white?"

"She asked you that because she's jealous." Jimmy moved a lock of hair off her face. "Full transparency—she and I dated back in high school. I was the class clown, she was the school valedictorian, and I broke her heart when I moved to LA after graduation. She's never nice to any of my girlfriends at first. But she'll come around. She always does."

Over time, Paris and Elsie learned to tolerate each other, especially once they discovered they were on the same page about two important things: both were concerned about Jimmy's comeback at the age of sixty-eight (though for very different reasons), and both completely blamed Zoe for the fact that it was happening. If Paris can get Elsie to believe that she didn't kill Jimmy, she might have a shot at getting everyone else to believe it, too.

"I didn't murder Jimmy," she finally blurts, unable to stand the silence any longer.

"If I thought you did," Elsie says calmly, "I wouldn't be here."

Paris exhales, slumping back against the wall with relief. But her hair catches on something sticky, so she straightens up again.

Elsie clicks her pen, tests the ink. She checks her reading glasses and uses the hem of her blouse to wipe away a smudge. Her hands won't stop moving, as if she's channeling everything she's feeling into them, as if she's afraid to be still because it will force her to fully process that something terrible has happened.

Because something terrible has.

"Elsie, I'm so sorry—"

"We don't have much time, so let's talk about all that later, okay?" Unlike her hands, Elsie's voice is steady. "Right now, I need you to answer all my questions as accurately as you can. We're meeting with Detective Kellogg in ten minutes. Has she tried to question you without me here?"

"I asked to call a lawyer as soon as I got here," Paris says. "Elsie, Jimmy had—"

Elsie puts a hand up. "Save it for later. Just let me do my job. I need you to answer all my questions."

Paris shuts up.

"Have you talked to anyone since you were arrested?"

"No."

"What about since you were brought in?"

"No."

"What about Little Miss Sunshine, the woman who just left?"

"I haven't said anything to anyone."

"Good." Elsie's voice turns brisk again. "Okay. You've been arrested on suspicion of murder, but that's not a formal charge. The case is too high-profile, so they can't afford to make mistakes. From what I've read in the arrest report, everything they have is circumstantial. You were married to Jimmy, you live in that house; it's normal and expected that you would be in the bathroom and . . . touch things. Now, I want you to think hard. When did you discover Jimmy was dead?"

"Last night," Paris says. "I had just gotten back from Vancouver—"

"What time?"

"Uh, two . . . maybe two thirty in the morning. Very late."

"Did you drive or fly?"

"I drove."

"So you crossed the border around midnight?"

"That sounds about right."

Elsie scratches notes into her pad. "And then what?"

"When I got home, I noticed the alarm wasn't set. But that's not un-usual, as Jimmy can't be bothered half the time. You know how he is."

Elsie nods without looking up.

"I went straight upstairs to get ready for bed. Jimmy always wants to know when I'm home, no matter what time it is, so I went down the hall to his bedroom."

"*His* bedroom?"

"Yes, his bedroom."

Elsie raises an eyebrow. "You sleep in different rooms?"

"We do."

"When did that start?"

"It's what we've always done," Paris says. "Neither of us sleeps well with another person in the bed. He gets hot, so he's constantly shifting around, and the slightest movement wakes me up."

Jimmy would be mortified if anyone knew their sleeping arrangements, but it wasn't a big deal. What she'd just told Elsie is true—they both preferred sleeping alone. It didn't mean anything, but people will assign meaning to everything.

"So you went into his bedroom," Elsie says. "Was the door open or closed?"

"I can't remember."

"Think."

Paris has never seen Elsie in lawyer mode, and frankly, she's a little scary. It's hard to reconcile this version of her with the one Paris usually sees. At Paris and Jimmy's anniversary party a month ago, the woman was draped across a grand piano with a glass of wine in one hand and a microphone in the other, singing "If Ever I Would Leave You" from *Camelot*.

"The door was slightly open," Paris says. "I don't think I turned the knob. I just pushed."

"Continue."

"I saw the bathroom light was on—"

"Wait, back up. Had the bed been slept in?"

"I—" Paris stops. "I didn't look at the bed. I saw the bathroom light and headed straight there."

"Was the bathroom door open or closed?"

"Open, about halfway. When I got closer, I saw him in the tub."

"And what, exactly, did you see?"

Paris takes a breath and closes her eyes. She can see Jimmy lying in the bathtub. He's wearing shorts and a T-shirt, his head leaning to one side at an awkward angle. His eyes are open. One arm dangles over the rim of the tub, which is half full of red water. Except it's not just water. It's blood. So much blood.

"He was in the tub." To her own ears, Paris's voice sounds distant. "It looked like he was dead, but I couldn't be sure. I rushed over and pressed on his wrist, and then his neck. There was no pulse. His skin felt cool to the touch."

And there was screaming. So much screaming. Coming from her.

Elsie closes her eyes briefly. "Could you tell how he died?"

"No. There was too much blood in the tub to see."

"And then what did you do?"

"I tried to lift him up."

Elsie looks up from her notepad. "Why?"

"I know it doesn't make sense, but . . . I didn't want to leave him in there." Paris looks away. "But he was so heavy, and I couldn't get a good grip. When I tried to pull him out, he slipped, and the bathwater splashed everywhere, all over the floor, all over me."

"What did you do then?"

"I felt my foot touch something, and when I looked down, I caught a glimpse of something shiny. I bent down to pick it up . . . and then I must have slipped, because I don't remember anything after that."

"The report says you hit your head."

"I guess so." Paris touches the butterfly bandage on her forehead. "All I know is that when I woke up, my face was on the floor, and the sun was up. There was blood everywhere. Someone was screaming, and I heard my name. I sat up, and saw that there were police officers standing just outside the bathroom. When I tried to stand, the officers immediately drew their guns."

"The report says you were holding a straight razor."

"I didn't realize it until they told me." Paris looks at Elsie. "One of the officers said, 'Mrs. Peralta, please put the weapon down,' and I looked down and saw the razor in my hand. I tried to explain that it wasn't a weapon, that it was just one of Jimmy's straight razors, but the words wouldn't come."

"The report says you were waving it around." Elsie raises an eyebrow. "The word they used was *brandishing.*"

"For God's sake, that wasn't my intention," Paris says helplessly. "I understand that's probably what it looked like. My head was pounding, and I was having a hard time hearing them because Zoe wouldn't stop screaming. When they said, 'Drop the *razor,*' I did. But they were still staring at me, like I was something out of a horror movie. That's when I saw myself in the mirror. I looked like Carrie at the prom."

"What happened next?"

"One of the officers told me to turn around slowly. He handcuffed me, read me my rights. When they led me out of the bedroom, Zoe was at the bottom of the stairs, still screaming at me, asking how I could have done it, how I could have murdered Jimmy. And then the detective said, 'Mrs. Peralta, did you murder your husband?'"

"And you said . . . ?"

"I said, 'I don't remember.'"

Elsie sighs, the lines in her forehead deepening. "Not the greatest choice of words."

"It's just what slipped out." Paris can hear the desperation in her own voice. "Elsie, I think Jimmy killed himself. I know that probably sounds crazy, but—"

"It actually doesn't." Elsie puts her pen down and meets Paris's gaze. "I just never thought he'd try it again."

Paris's mouth drops open. "*Again?*"

"He never told you?"

No, he did not. "He only ever told me about the overdoses."

"It was a long time ago, about a year after *The Prince of Poughkeepsie* ended. Not long after his mother died." Elsie's eyes are moist. "He left a suicide note and everything. I'm actually not surprised he didn't tell you. He was deeply ashamed of it. He was hospitalized for a week. We managed to keep it out of the press. That was . . . a rough time."

"I didn't see a note."

"I'll make sure the forensic team knows to look for one." Elsie's face is impossible to read as she jots it down on her pad. "But I'm going to level with you, Paris. It looks bad. Without witnesses or a suicide note, they can probably make a case for murder. His femoral artery was severed. They're going to say that's an unusual place for him to cut himself, because it is."

Paris slumps.

"But we do have one good thing on our side," Elsie says, but before she can tell Paris what that is, the officer is back.

Both women look up as the cell door opens again. "Detective Kellogg will meet you in room three," he says.

Elsie packs up her briefcase. "Answer all her questions unless I direct you not to. In which case, you stop talking. Immediately."

"Got it."

As they follow the officer down the hallway, Paris's hands begin to shake. It's finally beginning to sink in. Jimmy is really dead. He won't be home when she gets there. He won't ask her if she's in the mood to cook anything for dinner, or whether he should grill salmon or steak. He won't kiss the top of her head and say, "I'm good with whatever you want, babe."

Paris's husband might not have been her greatest love—that honor still belongs to someone she knew years ago, in a different life, when she was a very different person—but Jimmy Peralta was the love of *this* life, the one she built from the ashes of her old one.

She chokes back a sob just as they reach room 3. A voice floats through her mind then, always the unwanted intruder, forever the snake in her brain that uncoils at the worst possible times.

You're absolutely useless. Stop your crying before I smack the shit out of you again.

CHAPTER FOUR

Now that they're sitting across from each other, Paris notices that Detective Kellogg is pretty, more like an actress playing a detective on TV than an actual detective. Her long blond ponytail bounces when she nods her head. Which is often.

"I'm surprised you're representing her," the detective says to Elsie. "You were good friends with the deceased, weren't you? You must really believe she didn't do it."

"Because she didn't," Elsie says.

"You know, before we get into all that, where were *you* last night, Ms. Dixon?" Kellogg's voice is amiable. Like Elsie, she has a notepad open in front of her, but it's small, something that would fit in her back pocket. Her pencil taps the table.

"You're asking *me* where I was?"

The detective smiles. "I'm asking everybody who knew Jimmy Peralta. You might be Mrs. Peralta's lawyer, but you were Mr. Peralta's best friend. Or so we've heard."

Elsie exchanges a look with Paris and sighs. "I was out to dinner with friends until about nine. Happy to give you their names as well as the name of the restaurant. Got in about nine thirty and went straight to bed."

"When was the last time you saw Mr. Peralta?" Kellogg is still directing her questions to Elsie.

"Last week. Monday, I think."

"It was Tuesday," Paris says to Elsie. "I was leaving to teach a morning class as you were pulling up."

The lawyer nods. "That's right, Tuesday. Jimmy and I went to breakfast."

"Okay." Kellogg seems satisfied. "I'm just asking because we heard your voice on the cassette tape we took out of Mr. Peralta's portable stereo in the bathroom. It wasn't easy to find a tape deck to play it on here, but yes, it did catch you saying something about having plans."

"Jimmy likes to practice his jokes in the bathroom in front of the mirror," Paris says. An image of her husband gesturing madly at his reflection pops into her mind, and a pang of grief hits her. "He uses his old boombox to rehearse."

"He single-handedly keeps cassette manufacturers in business," Elsie says.

"Every phone has a voice-recording app now," Kellogg says. "Wouldn't it be more convenient to use that?"

Paris and Elsie both snort at the same time.

"What?" the detective says, looking back and forth between them. "Why is that funny?"

"Jimmy was an old soul, Detective," Elsie says. "He had a flip phone up until four years ago, and he still has a VCR in the living room. So, am I a suspect?"

"Not at this time, but anything can happen." Kellogg smiles, then turns to Paris. "So. Your turn. According to your husband's assistant, Zoe Moffatt, you were scheduled to be away for the weekend. Where'd you go?"

Paris glances at Elsie, who nods.

"I drove up to Vancouver," Paris answers. "For the International Yoga Convention and Expo."

"Who went with you?"

"Nobody."

"Where'd you stay?"

"The Pan Pacific."

"How long were you there for?"

"Thursday afternoon to last night."

Kellogg opens the manila folder beside her notepad and thumbs through the documents. "And what time did you leave Vancouver?"

"I got home just after two a.m., maybe closer to two thirty."

The detective smiles. "That's not what I asked. I asked you what time you left Vancouver. According to the hotel, you booked the room for three nights. Why did you leave early?"

"There weren't any more panels I wanted to attend."

"What does this matter?" Elsie snaps. "I'm sure border patrol can send you pictures of her car the moment she crossed back into the US. Or you could just check the CCTV cameras for the park across the street from their house."

"The park is more like a lookout, and there are only two cameras nearby. One of them doesn't work, and the one that does points toward the city, not the houses behind it."

"You're kidding," Paris says.

"Don't worry about it," Elsie says to her, but she's focused on the detective. "This is a pretty clear-cut case of suicide, Detective Kellogg. Jimmy Peralta had a long and well-documented history of addiction and depression, including a suicide attempt years ago."

"Maybe he did," Kellogg says. "But here's what bothers me: Zoe Moffatt, who has her own code to the front door keypad, let herself into the house this morning because she and Jimmy had a meeting scheduled at ten a.m. When Mr. Peralta didn't come down at the scheduled time, she called up the stairs, and when nobody answered, she checked the garage to see if his car was inside. It was, but it was right beside Mrs. Peralta's, who was supposed to still be in Canada. Ms. Moffatt called up again, still no answer. Concerned that neither of them were answering, she went upstairs to check, and that's when she found her boss dead in his own bathtub, with Mrs. Peralta on the floor right next to him, covered in blood, the murder weapon in her hand."

"Except it's not the murder weapon, because it's not murder," Elsie says. "And it hasn't been confirmed yet that the straight razor is what actually caused Jimmy's death. You're only assuming it was because it was in the bathroom. The medical examiner's early estimation is that death occurred between nine p.m. and midnight. My client was nowhere near the house at that time. Again, why don't you just ask border patrol to send you photos of the time she crossed so we can all go home?"

"Apparently, US Border Patrol experienced some kind of technical glitch last night, so they can't confirm anything just yet." The detective speaks to Elsie, but she's observing Paris. "And until they figure it out, we don't know where your client was at the time her husband was killed."

"Check her phone records," Elsie says.

Shit.

"We tried." Kellogg leans back and addresses Paris directly. "But it appears the whole weekend you were gone, your phone never left your house."

"I forgot it at home." Paris works to keep her voice even. When telling a lie, it's always best not to rush or overexplain. "I was almost at the border by the time I realized I didn't have it."

"So you went the whole weekend without a phone?"

"Yes." Another lie. Paris doesn't blink.

The detective smiles. "Well, that makes you the unluckiest person in the world."

"You're really going to hold her on this?" Elsie's either a great actor or she truly is flabbergasted. Paris is betting on the former.

"I've held murder suspects on a lot less," Kellogg says. "Because it's *murder*, counselor. Your client is almost thirty years younger than her husband, who happened to be a very famous and very wealthy man."

"And? Jimmy's will leaves nearly everything to charity. I would know." Elsie crosses her arms over her chest. "I was the one who drafted it. My client had no motive to kill her husband."

"That we know of. We've only just begun our investigation, and rest assured, we will leave no stone unturned." Detective Kellogg gives Paris another small smile. "You're a little mysterious, you know that? It makes me want to . . . dig."

A bonfire of fear ignites in Paris's stomach, and it takes every ounce of willpower to not let it show.

"Let's also not forget the interesting thing she admitted after the officers arrested her," Kellogg adds.

"You mean the few meaningless words she said after she hit her head?" Elsie scoffed. "That's not admission, that's confusion. Let her go home so she can properly mourn her husband."

"Yeah, about that." The detective cocks her head, her ponytail swaying behind her. "Are you even sad, Mrs. Peralta? Because you really don't seem like it."

Elsie puts a hand on her arm. "Don't answer—"

"How I grieve is none of your business," Paris snaps, ignoring her lawyer. "I'm sorry that I don't fit how a grieving widow is supposed to act a few hours after she's been accused of murdering her husband. Next time, I'll read the memo in advance that details the appropriate behaviors and be sure to rehearse first."

The tiny smile from Kellogg remains, and she taps on her notepad. "Walk me through exactly how you found him."

Paris repeats the same story she told her lawyer, and finds it's much easier the second time around.

"Tell me, Mrs. Peralta," the detective says when Paris finishes. "If your husband took his own life, as you both are so certain he did, why do you think he cut his leg? Why not his wrists? That's what most people would do."

"I can answer that," Elsie says confidently, and Paris turns to her in surprise. "When Jimmy attempted suicide before, he did cut his arm. Obviously he didn't die. But the scar, which ran halfway down his forearm, forever bothered him."

"*That's* how he got that scar?" Paris says to Elsie. "He told me he fell through a plate-glass window while he was high."

"He did. But that's not how he got *that* scar."

Paris sits back in her chair. What else doesn't she know about Jimmy's past? It seems her husband had just as many secrets as she does.

"To me, it makes sense that he'd choose a spot on his body he could easily hide." Elsie turns her attention back to Detective Kellogg. "It would have been his way of protecting his future self, in the event that he survived."

"If I didn't know otherwise, I might have thought *you* were his wife, you know him so well," Kellogg says to Elsie. She turns back to Paris. "Anyway, we have lots of time to put the pieces together. You never know what might turn up in the next day or two."

Paris's stomach burns.

"We're done here," Elsie says.

"I figured," the detective says.

Elsie gets up to bang on the door. Detective Kellogg stays seated, continuing to stare at Paris thoughtfully, as if trying to figure her out. Well, Detective Frosted Flakes can try as hard as she wants, but so far, nobody ever has.

"How much longer do I have to stay here?" Paris asks Elsie as they follow an officer back to the holding cell.

"They can hold you for up to seventy-two hours, at which point they have to formally charge you or let you go."

"Three *days?*" Paris grips her lawyer's arm. "Elsie, I can't stay here that long."

"It won't be that long." Elsie pats her hand. "I'll be back later. For now, just sit tight. And remember, not a word to anyone. We'll prove what happened soon enough."

They reach the cell, and looking through the bars at the dingy walls, Paris feels a sudden stab of claustrophobia. She would give anything to not go back in there, and if she feels that way now, how will she ever survive prison? She can't bring herself to step inside until the officer places a hand on her back and pushes her in. The door locks.

"Paris," Elsie says, her voice catching, and Paris turns. "Why didn't Jimmy tell me he was having a hard time? He always told me everything. How did I not pick up on it? If I'd known, I could have . . ." She chokes up.

Paris reaches a hand through the bars. "You knew Jimmy better than anyone, and you know how difficult it was for him to admit when he needed help. Zoe was at the house nearly every day, and even she didn't know. So how could you?"

Elsie nods and gives her hand a brief squeeze before letting go. Paris knows that what she just said made the other woman feel better, and for the most part, it's true. There's no way Elsie and Zoe could have known Jimmy was struggling.

Because Paris didn't know, either.

* * *

After Elsie leaves, she calls Henry again.

"I don't know how long I'll be here," Paris tells him. "I'm sorry, I know that puts you in a bad spot."

"I can handle it," Henry says, but she detects more anxiety in his voice than there was earlier. "The staff all support you. A few members have asked me questions because of the arrest video, but I've been reminding everyone that an arrest isn't the same thing as being charged."

"I doubt most people will understand the difference. But thank you."

They say their goodbyes again and hang up.

He's a good man, that Henry Chu, and Paris knows how lucky she is to have him as her business partner and studio manager. Ten years ago, he walked into Ocean Breath for the first time, stressed and exhausted from a programming job at Amazon that was driving up his blood pressure. She was still in the Fremont neighborhood then, in a tiny studio on the second level of a low-rise commercial building that housed a bead store, a private investigator's office, and a psychic who only worked on Fridays. Henry took to yoga like a fish to water, and he practiced five days a week. After a few months, noticing that Paris was struggling to attract new members, Henry suggested she do a Groupon, and Ocean Breath's clientele began to grow.

He eventually left Amazon with a generous severance package. When the studio's booking system crashed, he offered to come in as a partner and build her a better one. Paris jumped at the opportunity to bring him on board. It took a huge load off the studio's finances and allowed Paris more time to teach. They then moved Ocean Breath to its current location, a gorgeous space near Whole Foods, which attracted an entirely different level of clientele.

The new location is where she met Jimmy. At least that's the story they agreed to tell people. Nobody questioned it, because nobody cared. Retired comedian marries yoga instructor? Not exactly *Entertainment Tonight*–worthy. Jimmy hadn't been considered "relevant" for a while, which was just fine with Paris.

And then Zoe fucked it all up.

Somewhere along the way, Jimmy's longtime personal assistant had started acting more like his manager. Zoe had worked for him in Los Angeles for years, and when Jimmy finally decided to leave the industry for good, she helped him sell both his California properties and find a new house in his hometown of Seattle. She was only supposed to stick around for a few weeks to get him settled, but Zoe never went back to LA. She just . . . stayed. And so Jimmy kept her on the payroll. She answered his phone, managed his website, and handled all his emails and fan mail. She scheduled the house cleaners and repairs, paid the utility bills, and took his car in for maintenance. She also did the grocery shopping, ran his errands, and even took out the garbage and recycling every week.

When Paris met Jimmy, Zoe was at the house maybe two days a week. But ever since Quan first reached out, she'd been at the house nearly every damn day, coming and going as she pleased, leaving her granola bars in the cupboards and her kombucha in the fridge and driving Paris absolutely nuts.

"You gotta ease up on the kid," Jimmy said, when Paris complained about the assistant's constant presence. "She does all the shit that I don't want to do. If I could pay her to go to the dentist for me, trust me, I would. And you think I know anything about this streaming shit? I need her."

Zoe isn't a kid. She's thirty-five. And she wanted Jimmy's comeback to happen even more than he did. All Jimmy wanted was to tell jokes again; it was Zoe who took it next-level. Quan released his first comedy special in more than a decade a couple of months back. It did so well, they asked for a third, even though the second show wasn't scheduled to stream for another month. Jimmy didn't want to do a third. But Zoe did, and she was pushing for him to sign off on the contract.

"How much material do you think you have?" Zoe had asked Jimmy a few days ago.

The three of them were in the kitchen. Paris was leaving for Vancouver soon and hoping to have a quiet lunch with her husband before the long drive. But Zoe was still talking to her boss at the kitchen table as Paris reheated leftovers on the stove. Pork adobo, Jimmy's favorite.

"Right now, enough for half, maybe two-thirds of a show," Jimmy answered.

"Can you stretch it to an hour?"

"Not if you want it to be funny."

"That's fine," Zoe said. "We've got time. I can tell them you'll be ready to film a third in, say, six months? You could do it in Las Vegas.

The Venetian is interested, but MGM wants you pretty bad. I think it should be the Venetian, since it was built where the Sands used to be."

The Sands was where Jimmy did a five-year residency back in the late eighties, before he became a sitcom superstar. It's also where he overdosed. The first time.

"Thanks for the history lesson, kid." Jimmy's voice was dry. "But if there's going to be a third, it's gotta be next month, here in Seattle. The Showbox."

Paris brought two plates of food over to the table and sat down. Jimmy leaned over and gave her a kiss.

"Jimmy." Zoe sounded frustrated. She took off her glasses and rubbed her eyes. "You said before that you were open to a Las Vegas show. Your original Vegas run was your heyday as a stand-up comic, and they want to see you back there. I already spoke with the entertainment director at the Venetian. They can start promotion immediately with billboards—"

"Is it my heyday if I was too bombed every night to remember it? I have no intention of setting foot in a Vegas casino. Nowhere in the original contract did it say that I would." Jimmy spooned a mouthful of adobo and rice, and gave Paris a thumbs-up.

"We agreed in good faith—"

"Fuck that," he said, chewing. "Good faith means letting me do my show where I'm comfortable. I nearly died in Vegas."

A long silence.

"I'm sorry," Zoe said. "I understand. But it can't be the Showbox."

"Jesus Christ—"

"*Jimmy.* You know Quan wants a minimum seating capacity of eighteen hundred. They want the show to have energy. They don't want a tiny audience and a brick wall behind you. They want you on a big stage, with big laughs."

"Then I'll do the Paramount. What is that, two thousand seats?"

Zoe typed in her laptop. "Twenty-eight hundred and seven. Perfect. But it looks like they're booked up for the next two months, and we need at least three nights to tape."

Paris learned that most hour-long comedy specials recorded for HBO,

Netflix, Quan, and the like are actually a blend of several live perfor- mances. That way if a joke falls flat one night or the comedian doesn't deliver a certain segment perfectly, the best of each performance can be used.

"Call them. I'm a hometown kid. They'll make it work. Any day next month is fine. The sooner, the better."

"But you don't have enough material—"

"I'll be ready."

Paris looked at her husband. "Jimmy," she said quietly. "That's a lot of pressure."

"I'll be fine." He gave her a pointed look, and she shut up.

After they finished eating, Zoe remained in the kitchen while Jimmy carried Paris's weekend bag to the car.

"I don't have to go to Vancouver, you know," she said to him. "I can stay."

"No, I want you to go." Jimmy spoke decisively as he put the bag in the trunk. "I know you've been looking forward to getting out of here for a few days. Don't worry, I got stuff to keep me busy. I got that charity thing on Saturday night, and I'm going to try out some of the new jokes."

"Jimmy," she said, "I don't feel right leaving you alone."

He lifted her chin and looked right into her eyes. "I'll be here when you get back. I promise. I love you. Drive safe, okay?"

They looked at each other a while longer. Jimmy wasn't handsome, not exactly. He looked his age, his face full of the lines and creases that told the stories of his life. But it never mattered. She was attracted to his kindness, and his acceptance. Unlike every other man Paris had known, Jimmy Peralta had never asked her for anything.

Except, of course, to sign that airtight, nonnegotiable prenup. What- ever the police are thinking she did, at least they can't say she did it for the money.

CHAPTER FIVE

Dinner in the holding cell is a sandwich and an apple. The small Honey-crisp is fine. The sandwich is two slices of white Wonder Bread, a slice of ham, a Kraft single, and a swipe of mustard.

Paris examines it. No mold, no strange spots; it's safe to eat. If she learned one thing growing up, it was to never, ever take food for granted. As a kid, a sandwich like this would have been a treat. She takes a bite. It tastes like her childhood.

Her new cellmates, however, are less than thrilled with their meal.

"What is this?" one of them says, poking through the brown paper bag. "I wouldn't feed this shit to my dog."

"Disgusting," the other one agrees. "I can't eat this."

Oh, the privilege of being a picky eater. Jimmy liked aged tenderloin, hand-picked truffles, and sushi so fresh the hook was still in it. Paris, on the other hand, was considerably less discerning. Cheddar in the fridge too long? Scrape off the green bits. Bread's gone stale? Toast it. If you were hungry as a child, you never really get over it. The idea of wasting food makes Paris feel physically ill.

There was a shift change before dinner, and the officer now in charge is an older man with heavy footsteps and a wheeze. The keys jangling on his belt serve as warning bells for his imminent appearance at the bars, and all three women look up when they hear him approaching.

"My lawyer here?" one of her cellmates calls out. "Because I need to get the fuck home. I got kids."

"It's her lawyer." The officer points to Paris. "And you shoulda thought about your kids before you assaulted your neighbor."

"*Allegedly.*"

"Peralta," he says, "you getting up or what?"

Paris moves toward the bars as her cellmates talk in low voices about her. They were brought in separately for unrelated reasons, but the two women recognized each other right away. It turns out they move in similar social circles, and they both dated a guy named Dexter, who they agree is a loser. But now they're tittering about Paris, and their continuous snark mixed with cackles of laughter makes her think of the two hecklers, Statler and Waldorf, from *The Muppet Show.*

". . . killed her husband . . ."

". . . gold-digging ho, but I respect that . . ."

". . . I do like those slippers, though . . ."

". . . Netflix show is funny as shit . . ."

". . . not Netflix, it's on Quan . . ."

Elsie finally appears, looking worn. The bright skirt and blouse have been replaced by leggings and a tunic top, and she looks like she's had a longer day than Paris has. She passes a white paper bag through the bars.

"I brought you a late supper. I can't stay long."

"They fed us already." Paris peers into the bag. Another sandwich, pulled pork on a freshly baked baguette from Fénix, the Cuban place in Elsie's neighborhood. "But this is much better. Thank you."

"That smells good," one of the Muppets says loudly. "Where's ours?"

Elsie glares at them with a look that could melt steel, then motions for Paris to come closer. She doesn't begin speaking until their faces are inches apart through the bars.

"I just got a look at the toxicology report." Elsie's tone is a hair above a whisper. "They found cocaine and amphetamines in Jimmy's system. Did you know he was using again?"

"No," Paris says, unable to conceal her shock. "Of course not."

"He was clean for seven years." Elsie's voice hitches. "I told Zoe months ago that the Quan deal might be too much pressure for him. She insisted he was fine."

"He did seem fine," Paris says. "But Elsie—" She hesitates.

"Spit it out. This is not the time to withhold anything from me."

"There was something going on with Jimmy's memory," Paris says. "He was starting to . . . forget things. Not all the time. But every so often, he'd forget something completely random."

Elsie stares at her through the bars. "Example?"

"I once caught him staring at an orange for a whole minute. An *orange*. When I asked him what he was doing, he asked me what the name of the fruit was. Then he tried to laugh it off, saying he was just kidding around. When something similar happened a couple of weeks later, I said I was concerned. He got really angry and said he couldn't believe he married someone who couldn't take a joke. It was the first time he ever spoke to me that way."

She was understating it. Jimmy hadn't just been angry, he'd been enraged. And mean. *Are you fucking kidding me right now? How can you be my fucking wife and not get that it's a joke? Either you're stupid, or you have zero sense of humor. I can't decide which is worse.*

"That wasn't anger, that was fear." Elsie sags against the bars. "He watched his mother waste away from Alzheimer's, not long after *The Prince of Poughkeepsie* ended. I don't know if you've known anyone with the disease, but the end stage is absolutely brutal. Jimmy was there every day during her final year. He always said his biggest nightmare was that the same thing would happen to him." She gives Paris a look. "Why didn't you take him to the doctor?"

"He wouldn't go," Paris says. "I made two appointments for him, and he canceled both without telling me. He finally promised to go once the second show was recorded, but when I reminded him, he brushed it off, saying he was too busy doing press. He told me I was turning into a nag and to get off his back. He got angry every time I brought it up."

"Why didn't you tell me?" It's clear from Elsie's controlled tone that she's furious. "He would have listened to me. I could have made him go."

Paris meets her gaze. "That's why he told me not to tell you. He was my husband, Elsie. What was I supposed to do?"

"You were supposed to watch out for him, is what," Elsie snaps. "That's the deal you make when you marry a man three decades older than you. You're supposed to give a shit that he's getting sick, and you're supposed to notice that he's using drugs again. For fuck's sake, Paris. How self-absorbed are you that you missed these things?"

Paris's face is hot. There's nothing she can say to this, because Elsie is right. She *has* been completely focused on herself the past few months, trying to figure out how to keep her own life from imploding. She wasn't paying attention to Jimmy's health. In fairness, neither was Zoe, but Zoe wasn't his wife.

"Your arraignment is tomorrow at ten," Elsie says. "That's when the prosecution has to show the judge they have probable cause to charge you. I'll give you a heads-up now—you will probably be charged. But so far everything they have is circumstantial, so it doesn't necessarily mean we're going to trial. And trust me, with all the publicity, they can't afford to get it wrong."

"How bad is it? The publicity?"

"Considering you're all over the news, I'd say it's pretty bad. One of the junior associates texted me a picture from Instagram. It's a side-by-side of you and one of the Kardashians wearing the same furry slippers. You look guilty *and* rich, and that's a bad combination."

"It's not fur, it's feathers," Paris says, pointlessly.

"Eat your sandwich," Elsie says. "I'll be back in the morning. Remember, no talking. Especially not to Dumb and Dumber over there. Try to get some rest."

Paris isn't hungry, and she can't imagine how she'll fall asleep in here. Her cellmates are once again trading stories about their mutual ex-boyfriend, Dexter, who apparently smoked too much weed, cheated on them both, stole one woman's money, and crashed the other woman's car. What a prize.

She'd never had to worry about any of those things with Jimmy. He wasn't a taker; he gave. The day after they agreed to get married, they had a brutally honest conversation about money. Jimmy didn't want any surprises. He told Paris exactly how much she'd get if their marriage ended.

"Whatever happens, whether it's death or divorce, you'll get a million dollars flat," Jimmy said. "I'm not as rich as people seem to think, and I want you to know what you're walking into. A lot of my money went to bad investments, a shady manager, up my nose, and in my arms."

A million sounded like a lot to Paris. It would pay off her condo and her car and provide a nest egg for retirement. She'd still have to work, and that was fine. It just seemed weird to be in a relationship where a prenup was even necessary. Because he's nosy, Henry had Zillow'd Jimmy's house as soon as Paris began dating him. The "Zestimate" was around seven million because of the location and the views. She understood why Jimmy would want to protect himself.

"I've been burned before," Jimmy said. "Four wives. Three rehabs. The bankruptcy in the eighties. Shit, we don't need to rehash, you know all this. Elsie put the prenup together after wife number two. So it's kind of, you know, boilerplate. But it protected my dumb ass when the last two marriages went south."

"We don't have to get married, you know," Paris said. "I'm fine on my own. I've been taking care of myself my whole life."

"I know you have." He touched her face. "But I figure I got twenty years left, and if I'm lucky, at least ten of them will be good. I want to spend them with you. What can I say? I like being married."

She kissed his hand.

Jimmy leaned forward, his blue eyes piercing hers. "But I want you with *me*, kid. *Me.* Not the Prince of Poughkeepsie—"

"Never seen it."

"Or the Vegas guy—"

"Never been."

"Or the winner of thirteen Emmys, a Golden Globe, an Oscar nom—"

"Awards are overrated."

He finally laughed. "I get it. You really don't give a shit. And that's what I dig about you."

"Send me the paperwork," Paris said. "I'm a realist, I know this might not last. But tell me when you want to get married, because I'll need to find coverage for my classes."

She signed the prenup, but it didn't take long before she began to suspect that Jimmy actually had more money than he'd let on. His insistence on her quarter-of-a-million-dollar wedding ring was the first clue. But then as a wedding gift, he paid off the balance of the mortgage on her condo, encouraging her to rent it out and bank the income. And then he bought her a Tesla, a pair of diamond stud earrings, and a Birkin bag. He had money. And after signing with Quan, he had a whole lot more.

She never did ask him about it. Everybody was entitled to their secrets, and if she demanded to know his, he might demand to know hers. She'd lived a couple of different lives before the one she shared with Jimmy. And both those lives had ended with someone murdered.

And now here she is again.

You can run all the way from Toronto, away from the dead bodies and into a whole new life with a whole new name, and it still doesn't matter. Because while you can reinvent yourself, you can't outrun yourself. As a woman once reminded her a long time ago, the common denominator in all the terrible things that have happened to you is *you*.

Everywhere you go, there you are.

CHAPTER SIX

When Paris wakes up the next morning, Statler and Waldorf are gone, and so is her Cuban sandwich.

A new person is huddled in the corner where the Muppets used to be, her small body drowning in an oversize hoodie pulled up and over her forehead. It's hard to tell if her eyes are open or closed. Either way, she doesn't acknowledge Paris, and that's fine, because Paris is in no mood to talk. The problem with falling asleep is that when you wake up, you get a fresh dose of reality.

Jimmy is dead.

The pain threatens to stab its way in, and she needs to move her body before it can pierce too deeply. She stands up and practices a simple sun salutation flow to stretch her muscles and get the blood flowing, which will help clear her head. Beginning with *tadasana*, also known as mountain pose, the flow normally takes ten minutes. She completes all the postures except for upward and downward dog, which would require her to place her hands on the floor. Instead, she opts to finish with *malasana*, garland pose, which is a full squat with her hands in prayer position. It feels good, so she stays here for a while, creating space in her spine and allowing her hips and groin to open up. When she's ready, she stands up slowly, then takes a seat back on the bench. She closes her eyes, breathing in through the nose and out through the mouth. Inhale, exhale. *Namaste.*

"I knew it was you," a voice says from the corner. Paris opens her eyes.

Her cellmate has uncurled herself, but her face is still obscured. "I used to be a member of your studio back when you were in Fremont, before you changed locations."

"Oh." Paris isn't sure what to say to this. Ocean Breath has had thousands of members over the years, and she can't exactly say *nice to see you again* if she has no idea who the woman is. Also, it's not like they're bumping into each other at the coffee shop. "That's . . . great."

"I saw the video of your arrest." The woman pushes the hood off her face. "Did you do it?"

Paris jolts at the sight of her. She remembers the woman. Charlotte . . . something. She attended class every Saturday morning for a couple of years at the original location, just as she said. In her current state, Charlotte is almost unrecognizable. One of her eyes is swollen purple, there's a bandage on her cheek, and her upper lip is split. She didn't trip and fall. She didn't get into a fender bender. Someone beat this woman, and badly. Paris knows how she feels, and she knows it must hurt like hell to even talk.

"Are you okay?" Paris asks, concerned. "You should be in the hospital."

"I'm fine," Charlotte says. "It looks worse than it feels."

Paris is familiar with this line, having used it herself many times in the past. "What happened?"

"I killed my husband last night."

"Don't say that." Alarmed, Paris glances up at the camera.

"I don't care, I already gave my statement." Charlotte leans back against the wall and gives the camera a little wave. "It was self-defense. Nigel beat the shit out of me for years, but last night, when he went after our daughter, I did what I had to do. I don't regret it, and I'd do it again."

Paris crosses the cell and takes a seat beside Charlotte on the bench. "How did you kill him?" she asks in a low voice.

Charlotte looks at Paris with her one good eye. "He was beating on me, but when he hit Olivia, I just . . . snapped. I pushed him without even thinking. He fell backward down the stairs. Broke his neck." Her eyes are moist. "I didn't mean to kill him, I just wanted him to stop. But I'm not sad he's dead. It was always going to end with one of us in a casket. I just wish my daughter hadn't seen it, you know? I'm worried it's going to mess her up when she's older."

"How old is she?"

"Six."

"There's a good chance she won't remember," Paris says. "At this age, their minds are so malleable. Just tell Olivia every day that you love her, that it's not her fault, and that she's a good girl. Over time, she'll understand that you slayed a monster. For her."

A small smile, followed by a wince. Charlotte's lip is still raw. "You must have slayed a monster yourself at some point. That, or you have kids."

"I don't have kids," Paris says. "But I remember what it was like to be a kid. And these were the things I would have wanted to hear."

The woman nods, her tears beginning to flow freely, though she makes no sound. Paris understands this, too. It's always best to cry silently, so you don't make things worse. *Stop those fucking tears God I hate your face when you cry.*

They both turn their heads as an officer appears at the cell.

"Peralta," he says, unlocking the door. "You're being transferred to the courthouse. Your lawyer will meet you there."

"Good luck," Charlotte says, and touches Paris's arm.

"You too," Paris says.

They'll both need it.

* * *

The elevator ride is quick, and this time they go up instead of down, stopping a few floors above the main level. There's a walkway that connects the jail to the courthouse, and since Paris's wrists are cuffed, the officer holds her elbow as they pass through.

When they arrive on the other side, Elsie is waiting. No tropical colors for the older woman today. For her court appearance, the lawyer has chosen a pinstriped navy skirt and matching jacket paired with a crisp white blouse. Standing beside her is an attractive young woman in a dark pantsuit, platinum hair in a sleek bun, holding a Nordstrom bag. This must be the junior associate Elsie mentioned the day before. The young woman appraises Paris through her trendy, oversize glasses.

"This is Hazel," Elsie says.

The two women shake hands, and Hazel hands Paris the bag. "I couldn't go into your house to get you anything from your closet, but your friend Henry gave me your sizes. You should find everything you need to freshen up in here."

Elsie fingers a lock of Paris's hair and grimaces. "Did you bring her a hair elastic, too?" she asks Hazel.

"Oh, I didn't think—"

"Give her the one in your hair."

The young associate takes out her bun and hands over the elastic without argument. The officer escorts Paris to a nearby bathroom. Once alone, she carefully peels off the bloodstained butterfly bandage from her forehead, then rinses her face and brushes her teeth. In the bag, she finds a hairbrush with the price tag still on it, and does her best to comb out the tangles in her hair before securing it in a loose bun with Hazel's elastic. She then locks herself in a stall and sprays her armpits generously with deodorant before putting on her new outfit. Hazel has great taste. The conservative knee-length dress is dove gray and a perfect fit. The modest heels are less comfortable for someone who spends most of her day barefoot, but they'll do. At the bottom of the bag, she finds a brand-new lipstick. She has the same one at home. The shade is called "Orgasm," a bold name for a universally flattering color. She swipes it on her lips and then, impulsively, dabs a little on her cheeks.

When she comes back out of the bathroom, Elsie nods her approval. With Hazel in tow, they make their way over to the assigned courtroom, where the lawyer pauses just outside the double doors.

"Whatever happens in there, do not react." Elsie's voice is low and firm. "You are quiet, you are serious, you are well-mannered, and you are sad because your husband just died. Got it?"

Paris nods. She doesn't have to pretend, because she is all those things.

The security guard opens the door. The courtroom is packed, every seat in the spectator area full. It doesn't look anything like the fictional New York City courtrooms Paris sees on TV, which always appear so opulent, with ornately carved wood and high ceilings. This courtroom is modern and understated, with mid-toned paneling and natural light.

All eyes are on her as she heads down the aisle with Elsie, who keeps a hand on her elbow until the three of them reach the table on the left side of the courtroom. On the other side is the prosecutor's table, where a man in a well-tailored suit glances over with an expression of mild interest. Quiet conversations hum from all different directions behind them.

Elsie leans in to talk to Paris. "There's been a new development that the prosecutor believes will cement their argument for probable cause. They won't tell me what it is, but if there's anything at all you haven't told me yet, now is the time."

There's a lot Paris hasn't told Elsie, but now is definitely not the time. "You already know everything."

"Good." Elsie squeezes her arm.

Paris and Hazel sit quietly while Elsie reads over her notes. The judge isn't here yet, so Paris turns around for a quick scan of the courtroom. She has no idea who all these people are, but their conversations pause briefly at the sight of her face. She spots Detective Kellogg at the very back. A few rows away, she sees Henry and waves. The sight of her friend and business partner helps loosen the knot in her stomach, but it tightens again when she catches a glimpse of frizzy brown hair that could only belong to Zoe Moffatt. She and Jimmy's assistant make eye contact briefly before the other woman averts her gaze.

"All rise." The bailiff's voice projects through the wall-mounted speakers.

The room falls silent, and everyone stands as the judge enters. Paris works to settle herself. She can't let her mind disconnect today. The prosecutor is about to publicly accuse her of murdering her husband, and everyone sitting behind her is here for the show.

The judge's robes are black and flowy, which does resemble what she's seen on TV. Paris can't help but think that this would make a perfect ripped-from-the-headlines episode of *Law & Order: SVU*. Ice-T and Mariska Hargitay are sitting in the back of the courtroom, waiting to see if the dead celebrity's trophy wife will be officially charged with murder. Diane Keaton could guest star as Elsie. Ed Harris could play Jimmy in flashbacks. And the role of Paris Peralta could be played by . . .

She feels a pinch on her elbow.

"Wherever you are," her lawyer hisses, "come back to earth. *Now.*"

"Be seated," the judge says tersely, and they all sit.

The judge speaks to her bailiff, one hand covering the thin microphone in front of her. Judge Eleanor Barker is in her early fifties with bright ginger hair, and she looks stern but not unkind. A full minute passes as she skims the folder the bailiff has given her. Finally, she turns her attention to the prosecutor's table.

"You're up," the judge says.

The prosecutor stands, fastening the button on his suit jacket. "Nico Salazar for the prosecution, Your Honor." He's younger than Paris originally thought, a trim man with perfectly styled black hair. "We believe Paris Peralta should be charged with murder in the first degree for the death of her husband, James Peralta. The cause of death is exsanguination due to a laceration to the femoral artery. We believe his murder was made to look like a suicide, but Jimmy Peralta had no reason to end his own life. He just filmed two comedy specials where he earned fifteen million dollars each, and he was in contract negotiations for a third. We believe Paris Peralta murdered her husband for his money."

Beside her, Elsie snorts. The judge turns to her. "Counselor?"

Paris's lawyer stands. "Elsie Dixon, Your Honor, defense counsel for Mrs. Peralta. Nothing Mr. Salazar said here is true. What happened to Jimmy Peralta is tragic, but it's not murder. My client is not set to inherit anything but a boilerplate sum of money specified in the same prenuptial agreement that Mr. Peralta asked his last two wives to sign. While it's a significant sum at one million dollars, it's nowhere near enough to keep my client in the lifestyle she enjoyed during the marriage. With her husband dead, Mrs. Peralta's financial circumstances will not be enough to keep her in her marital home indefinitely. The monthly upkeep alone exceeds her current income."

Elsie told her not to react, but it takes a Herculean effort for Paris to hide her shock. She knew a million dollars wouldn't be enough to allow her to continue living as she'd been living, but it never occurred to her that if Jimmy died, she'd be homeless. The condo she owns is currently rented, and the tenants have a year to go on their lease. If Paris can't afford to continue living in the house, where is she supposed to go?

Then again, they don't charge you rent in prison.

"In addition," Elsie continues, "having known Jimmy Peralta person-ally for fifty years, I can attest to his struggles with addiction and depres-sion. He's had multiple trips to rehab, has overdosed twice, and attempted suicide once before. The toxicology report shows he started using drugs again. He was also experiencing memory lapses, which we believe would have negatively affected his mental health. We can provide medical re-cords for all of this, Your Honor. As difficult as this is to say, we do believe Jimmy Peralta died by suicide."

There's a low buzz in the courtroom. The judge turns back to the pros-ecutor. "Mr. Salazar?"

"Until we can confirm what state of health Jimmy Peralta was in at the time of his death, here's what we do know." Salazar speaks confidently. "Jimmy Peralta was clean and sober for seven years. While there were drugs found in his system, the tox report cannot determine whether there was regular use of illegal narcotics, or even that he ingested those drugs willingly—"

"Which also means there's nothing to support that he *didn't* take them willingly," Elsie fires back.

"—so it's possible that Mrs. Peralta either encouraged her husband to use, or forced him—"

"Your Honor, I can stand here and make up wild theories, too," Elsie says, her arms extended in disbelief. "This is ridiculous."

The judge raises a hand. "Stick to the facts, Mr. Salazar."

The prosecutor nods and makes a show of checking his notes. "Mr. Peralta was right-handed. The slash to his right inner thigh that ulti-mately severed his femoral artery doesn't fit with a self-induced right-handed slash—"

"Your Honor, Mr. Peralta was diagnosed with a benign tremor in his right hand last year, which made it difficult for him to grip things," Elsie interrupts. "He was learning how to use his left hand for many things. We have medical records for this, too."

Salazar ignores her. "And when the police arrived, Mrs. Peralta was in the bathroom with her husband, who was lying dead in a tub filled with his own blood. She had the murder weapon—a straight razor—in her hand. And when asked if she killed her husband, she uttered three words: *I don't remember.*"

Behind her, the buzzing in the courtroom grows louder. The judge smacks her gavel. *Bang.* But the prosecutor still isn't finished.

"Last, we've just learned that Paris Peralta is set to inherit a significant sum of money. While the prenuptial agreement was still in place at the time of Mr. Peralta's murder, he updated his last will and testament six weeks ago." Nico Salazar holds up a document. "In keeping with his philanthropic nature, thirty percent of his estate will be left to various charities he supported. Five million dollars will go to his assistant, Zoe Moffatt—"

A gasp from the back. Paris doesn't need to turn around to know that it's Zoe.

"—and another five million is directed to Elsie Dixon, the defendant's lawyer."

Beside Paris, there's a sharp intake of breath.

"The remaining amount, which makes up more than half of Jimmy Peralta's estate," Salazar says, his cadence slowing down just a notch, "is to go to his wife, Paris Aquino Peralta. This is a considerably larger amount than the boilerplate sum Ms. Dixon was referring to earlier."

The buzzing in the courtroom starts up again. As instructed, Paris does her best not to react. The prosecutor seems to be implying that Paris will inherit more than she originally thought, but half of Jimmy's estate is . . . what? She doesn't know what Jimmy was worth, and there's no way to do the math without the numbers.

Again, the judge reaches for her gavel. *Bang.*

"I don't know what document Mr. Salazar is looking at," Elsie says, shaking her head in disgust, "but as the attorney who personally drafted Jimmy Peralta's last will and testament, I can say that Mr. Salazar is absolutely incorrect. The amount Mrs. Peralta is set to receive upon her husband's death is the exact same amount specified in the prenup. One million dollars, no more, no less."

"As I said, Your Honor, this is a new will." Salazar holds it up again. "It was drafted by a different firm than Ms. Dixon's, and it supersedes everything before it."

"May I see it?" Elsie is annoyed.

"I'd like to see it, too," the judge says.

"We've made copies for you both."

Salazar hands two documents to the bailiff, who brings one to the judge. The other he hands to Elsie, who puts on her reading glasses. A few minutes pass as both women scan the document. Paris glances over at Elsie, but the lawyer's face gives nothing away.

"What is the current value of Jimmy Peralta's estate?" The judge directs her question to Salazar.

"The estimate is eighty million, Your Honor." The prosecutor pauses and clears his throat. "Which means that Paris Peralta is set to inherit approximately forty-six million dollars. Give or take a million."

Paris's jaw drops.

Behind her, the courtroom erupts, louder than all the previous times. The judge bangs her gavel, asking for order, but the noise begins to drift away as Paris attempts to understand what she just heard.

Jimmy was worth *eighty million*? That can't be right. If it is, that means Jimmy was already worth tens of millions *before* his comeback. While she did suspect that Jimmy actually had more money than he was telling her, she never imagined it would be this much. It was one thing for her husband to underestimate his net worth, and a whole other thing to blatantly lie about being filthy stinking rich.

Zoe's dry voice floats into her head. *Optics, Paris.*

This is a disaster.

"Anything to say, Ms. Dixon?" the judge asks.

Elsie's face is stone. "No, Your Honor."

The judge looks directly at Paris, taking off her own reading glasses. "Paris Peralta, please stand."

Paris stands. On either side of her, Elsie and Hazel stand, too.

"Paris Peralta, you are charged with murder in the first degree in the death of James Peralta. How do you plead?"

The courtroom is quiet. Paris doesn't realize she hasn't answered until she feels Elsie's elbow in her ribs.

"Not guilty," she says, her voice faint.

"We request remand, Your Honor," Nico Salazar says. "Mrs. Peralta is obviously a flight risk. She's a very wealthy woman who has friends with private jets."

Jesus Christ. That was *one* friend, and it was Jimmy's friend, who sure as shit won't be lending Paris his G280 if he actually thinks she murdered his buddy.

"We request reasonable bail, Your Honor." The wind has been knocked out of Elsie, and the strength in her voice sounds forced. "My client cannot inherit anything from her husband's estate if she's found responsible for his death, and any funds she's entitled to receive will be withheld until she's acquitted. That being said, there's no reason Mrs. Peralta can't await trial at home, where she can be monitored by ankle bracelet. She will surrender her passport."

"Bail is set at five million, cash or bond."

Bang.

CHAPTER SEVEN

Unlike what Paris has seen on TV, you can't just get in the car and go home because the judge says you can. Calls must be made, funds must be transferred, paperwork must be signed.

It takes the rest of the day for her to arrange the bail amount. She doesn't have five million dollars of assets she can guarantee to the court, so her only choice is to pay a bond company a 10 percent premium, which she'll never get back. Her condo—for which she has clear title, thanks to Jimmy—is worth around seven hundred thousand. Her bank allows her to borrow against 80 percent of that, so she's able to transfer half a million dollars directly to the bond company.

The jeweler agrees to buy back her wedding ring for half of what Jimmy paid for it, and the car dealership will take back the Tesla for 15 percent less than the current blue book value. She doesn't have to sell either just yet, but it may very well come to that if her legal situation isn't resolved in the next few months. If her calculations are correct, she'll be right back to where she was financially when she met Jimmy.

It feels strangely full circle.

And after all this, Paris can't even go home. The house on Queen Anne Hill is a crime scene, and there's no word on when it will be released. A married couple with a baby is living in her condo. Henry offers her his spare bedroom, but he and Brent live in a very small house, and the quickest way to ruin a friendship is to impose.

Luckily, the Emerald Hotel is only ten minutes away from the court-house. Elsie drives her over and doesn't speak to her at all until they get there. When she finally does say something, her tone is clipped.

"Jimmy's corporation has an account with the Emerald." Elsie doesn't pull up to the front doors of the boutique luxury hotel. Instead, she drives to the back of the building and parks her Mercedes right in front of the doors designated for deliveries. A tall, thin man dressed in a green blazer with the hotel's insignia appears to be waiting for them. "You can stay here as long as you need to. It's all been arranged."

"Elsie, you have to know I didn't make Jimmy change his will," Paris says as they both get out of the car. Out of habit, she reaches for her purse, only to remember she doesn't have it with her. She doesn't have anything. "We never talked about money. Could we all . . . contest it somehow?"

"Why would any of us contest it?" Elsie looks at her, and it's clear Paris just asked the world's stupidest question. "You inherit, I inherit, Zoe in-herits. Jimmy had no children and no other family than you, so there's no one to contest the will, because we all benefit."

"But I never even knew how much he—"

"We'll discuss it later."

The manager of the Emerald greets them with a frosty smile, offering them both a cold, limp handshake. Paris has met him before, when she and Jimmy spent a week in the hotel's Rainier Suite while they had their hardwood floors refinished. He'd been warm and accommodating then. Now he seems . . . put out.

"It will be a few more minutes for the room." The manager leads them down a hallway to a small office with a plate on the door that reads THOMAS MANNION, GENERAL MANAGER. With his small, round, gold-rimmed glasses and his elbows resting on the table, hands in prayer position, Mannion re-minds Paris of the villain in the first Indiana Jones movie, the one whose face melted at the end. His long fingers tap together. "Had we been given more notice, the room would have been ready for your arrival. Might you have some idea of how long you'll be staying?"

"Mrs. Peralta will be here at least a few days," Elsie says. "We certainly appreciate your ability to accommodate our last-minute request."

A fake smile flickers across the manager's face and then disappears.

Elsie turns to her. "I asked Zoe to make sure you'll have everything you need. Do not leave the hotel for any reason. Stay in your room at all times. And don't forget this." She hands Paris a small plastic bag.

Paris is amazed that Zoe would be willing to help with anything. "But when are you and I going to talk?"

"I'll call you later." Elsie gives her a look that shuts her up. The manager is three feet away, and he's not even pretending not to listen. "In the meantime, have a shower, order room service, take a nap. And remember—"

"I know. Don't talk to anyone."

There's a soft ping. Mannion checks his phone.

"Your room is ready," he announces. "Mrs. Peralta, if you'll follow me."

Paris says goodbye to Elsie and wonders if she should start looking for a new lawyer. The woman is so angry with her that it's hard to imagine she'll be back.

The manager escorts her to an elevator reserved for staff. The true depth of Mannion's dislike for her becomes clear once they reach her room. Which turns out to be the Rainier Suite.

It looks exactly the same as it did the last time she was here. Fourteen hundred square feet, nine-foot ceilings, with a foyer, two bedrooms, two bathrooms, a living room, a dining room, and a fully stocked bar. Floor-to-ceiling windows showcase perfect views of the snowcapped mountain the suite is named after. A gigantic basket of fruit is on the coffee table, and beside it are several shopping bags and a large cardboard box.

The only thing missing is Jimmy.

"This is way more than I need," Paris says. "I'd really be fine with a smaller room."

"Ms. Moffatt requested an upgrade to the same suite you and your husband stayed in the last time, to ensure your optimum comfort." The manager's voice is flat. "We were happy to honor that request. All of us here at the Emerald are—were—huge fans of your husband."

She waits for him to offer some kind of obligatory condolences, but he doesn't. Instead, he plucks a business card from his breast pocket and sets it on the foyer table.

"Jimmy Peralta was a loyal, valued guest of our hotel," Mannion says.

"If there's anything you need, you may contact me personally. As Ms. Dixon mentioned, it's best you stay in the suite at all times, so as not to attract the attention of the other guests. It also makes it easier for my staff to ensure your safety." He glances down at her ankle, where the little light on her monitoring bracelet is flashing green. "We hope you're not here too long."

Polite rudeness is a difficult skill to master, she'll give him that. As soon as he leaves, she presses the button for the electronic DO NOT DIS- TURB sign and engages the deadbolt.

The plastic bag Elsie handed her in the manager's office holds a wall charger and an extra battery from the GPS monitoring company. She plugs it into the living room wall, then plops down on the sofa with a heavy sigh. It feels good to sit on something not made entirely of metal, but the ugly black band around her ankle feels strange. She can only take it off for fifteen minutes a day to shower, and the mere thought of constantly having it on makes her skin itch. If Jimmy were here, he'd say something funny, make some kind of joke to lighten her mood.

She looks over at the door, half expecting him to be there. It feels like he could let himself in at any minute, wearing his palm-tree swim trunks, a towel around his neck, his hair wet from the hotel pool as he tosses his key card onto the table. *Babe, hurry up. The breakfast buffet ends in thirty minutes, and they got an omelet station.*

The sadness radiates throughout Paris's whole body, filling her up and hollowing her out at the same time. She might feel some relief if she could just cry, but the tears refuse to come. *You don't stop with that baby shit I swear to God I'm going to punch you in the face.*

She breaks off a banana from the basket and pokes through the shop- ping bags Zoe has left for her while she eats it. She has to admit, Jimmy's assistant has come through. She bought Paris a new iPhone, still in the box, with her new cell number scrawled on a sticky note. There are also T-shirts, leggings, pajamas, underwear, and all her regular toiletries and skincare products. She even went to the post office and picked up Jimmy's fan mail, which is what's in the large cardboard box.

Everything but the fan mail is great.

Paris is confused. Zoe was the one who called her a murderer and screamed for the police to arrest her. So what the hell is all this? An apology?

She hears a soft *ping* coming from the box with her new iPhone in it. Zoe must have set it up already, which shouldn't surprise her, because this is the exact kind of thing Jimmy paid her to do. Her job was to anticipate Jimmy's needs, and now she's doing the same for Paris.

She plucks the phone out of the box. There's one new text message.

Hi Paris. I hope you have everything you need. I know I made things worse yesterday, and I am so sorry. Jimmy would be disappointed in me. Please call or text me anytime if there's anything I can do for you. I'm still on the payroll, and Jimmy would want me to help you. Stay strong.—Zoe

Aha. Finally, that explains it.

Zoe, who's technically an employee of Jimmy's corporation, doesn't want to lose her job. After all, she can't get her five million dollars until the will is probated, and Elsie explained that won't happen until after the trial. In the meantime, she still has bills to pay, and she must think Paris has some kind of say in her employment. She'd be wrong. Paris has never been involved in any part of her husband's business, and she has no idea what will happen to Jimmy's corporation now that he's gone.

But Zoe doesn't know that.

Paris starts typing, then rereads her text to make sure it's worded exactly right. Short and sweet. She hits send and allows herself a small smile. Oh, this feels good.

Hi Zoe. Thanks for the phone. You're fired.

* * *

After a room-service dinner and a long, hot shower, Paris puts on her new pajamas and turns on the TV in the living room. She's managed to avoid the television up until now, but she's too tired to read and too anxious to sleep. A movie might take her mind off things. She flips quickly past the news stations, afraid she'll see herself, only to realize that it's not just the news she needs to worry about.

It's Kimmel.

Despite her brain screaming at her not to watch, Paris stops on *Jimmy Kimmel Live!* and turns up the volume. The talk show host—her Jimmy's favorite Jimmy—is showing the audience Paris's arrest video from TikTok as part of his monologue. It looks even worse than she feared, especially when Kimmel freezes the video and zooms in on her slippers, with their stupid pink feathers blowing around in the breeze.

"*Three hundred dollars* for a pair of *Fraggle Rock* slippers," Kimmel crows. "That's *insane*. If a crime has been committed, it's on the ostriches who are walking around naked."

Big laughs from the audience. The irony is, Jimmy would have found the joke hilarious. Things like this never bothered him. *It's a compliment when they roast you. It means they give a shit.* If that's true, then Paris is a few days away from being a *Saturday Night Live* skit.

She turns off the TV and looks out the window. The lights of the city are pretty, but the view is nowhere near as nice as the one she has at home. It's too dark to see Mount Rainier in the distance, but it's comforting to know that it's there. Just like Jimmy used to be.

"I'll be here when you get back," he'd said to her a few days ago, the morning before she left for Vancouver.

There is so much she regrets.

Earlier that morning, she had caught Jimmy trying to shave with one of his straight razors. She was immediately upset, because the benign tremor in his right hand had worsened, and they'd agreed a year ago that it was best to switch to an electric shaver, or at least safety razors. But there he was, the stubborn ass, attempting to drag a goddamned straight razor across his throat with a shaky hand.

They'd gotten into a nasty argument. Paris had yelled at him, asking if he had a death wish, which of course was a terrible choice of words, in hindsight. Jimmy yelled back, accusing her of trying to change him, saying that she had forced him to do something he never wanted to do, and that she was treating him like a child. He told her to get the fuck off his back.

Twenty minutes later, when they both cooled off, Jimmy apologized. As a peace offering, Paris offered to shave him. It turned out to be a surprisingly intimate experience for them both. She had never shaved anyone before, and the straight razor was beautiful, one of several Jimmy owned. The one he was trying to use that morning had been a gift from Elsie the day he finished shooting the final episode of *The Prince of Poughkeepsie*. The inscription on the blade read: IT'S A CUTTHROAT BUSINESS, BUT YOU SLAYED IT. LOVE, E.

The blade was steel, but the handle was wood, and it warmed in Paris's hand the longer she held it. She skimmed the blade lightly across Jimmy's throat, and the little scraping sound it made was satisfying. And then he asked her about Canada.

"Are you looking forward to your trip?" he said, looking up at her, his blue eyes bright.

Her hand jerked then, and she nicked him. It could have been worse. She could have sliced his jugular.

CHAPTER EIGHT

Paris is jittery enough, but she pours herself a second cup of coffee anyway from the small carafe that room service brought with her breakfast. It's time to open the box of Jimmy's fan mail, and while she's dreading it, it has to be done.

The fact that he still receives so much snail mail is a testament to the median age of his fan base. When she first met Jimmy, he was only receiving a few letters a week. But once the first comedy special started streaming, the post office told Zoe that her boss would need to rent a bigger PO box.

"You know, you wouldn't get so much mail if you'd just let me set you up with Facebook and Twitter," Zoe had said a couple of months back.

The three of them were working through all his letters, one by one. They had a system: Paris would open the letters and read them out loud. Jimmy would sign a 5x7 black-and-white headshot with a Sharpie, his signature illegible due to the tremor. Zoe would address the return envelope, pop the photo in, and seal it. They would work like this until Jimmy's hand started cramping, but he enjoyed it.

"You wouldn't even have to do anything," Zoe said. "I'll manage all your accounts."

"I'm an old dog with old tricks," Jimmy said. "And my fans are as old as me. They don't give a shit if I'm on social media, so why should I?"

"Uh, because of your *new* fans?" Zoe, exasperated, turned to Paris for help. "Is that not the *entire* point of doing a streaming deal? Come on, Paris, tell him."

Paris shrugged and opened the next letter. She had no online profiles, either, so she was the last person to convince her sixty-eight-year-old husband to do anything. Jimmy could barely tolerate emails, and he despised texting.

"Kid, that's not the point at all," Jimmy said. "They're paying me money to tell jokes. I can't control what the fans like, and I learned a long time ago not to worry about it."

"Think about it, Zoe," Paris said. "Do you really want Jimmy on Twitter? He's impulsive enough with the things he says."

"I'll write all the tweets." Zoe looked back and forth between them. "A Twitter account could help build Jimmy's brand."

"Nobody writes for Jimmy but Jimmy," said Jimmy. "And my brand is I don't want to be on fucking Twitter."

Paris had come to like reading her husband's fan mail, which provided a glimpse into the parts of Jimmy's life that Paris was least familiar with—his work, the history of his work, his legacy. She once asked him how he knew it was time to walk away from show business. He told her that his creative well had run dry for several reasons: burnout, life stress, age, mental health challenges, nearly dying. But the biggest reason was that he got sober.

"The only thing that ever brought me joy was drugs," Jimmy said.

"You're not serious."

"Wish I was, kid."

He'd been clean for four years when they met, and he was committed to staying that way. He said he felt great . . . but he missed being funny.

"I try to tell myself it's okay," he said with a shrug. "But I'd be lying if I said I didn't miss it every goddamned day."

"The drugs or the comedy?" she asked.

"Both. I've never had one without the other."

Being funny—razor-sharp funny, the kind of funny that can make an audience double over with laughter while cringing at the same time, the kind of funny that hurts as much as it entertains—was Jimmy's gift. The only thing he'd ever wanted to do was make people laugh.

According to friends who'd known him for decades, he'd always been hilarious. But the business of being funny was a whole different animal than just cracking your friends up at parties. The pressure of being "on" night after night, whether he felt like it or not, was hard. He started doing cocaine as a young comedian to give himself energy onstage and to make his brain work as fast as his mouth did. Some of his funniest milestone moments—his first appearance on *The Tonight Show Starring Johnny Carson*, for example—he was too high to even remember. At the height of his fame, he was taking cocaine and Adderall to perform, Xanax to calm down, Valium to sleep, and heroin just because it felt good. Without the drugs, the funny came slower, and the humor was diluted. And all his attempts to get clean, with rehab and without, were followed by periods of depression that would last for months.

When he got clean for the last time, the funny was gone. He could still tell a good joke, but the thing that made Jimmy Peralta *Jimmy Peralta* had left the building.

And then it came back. By accident.

Jimmy always donated a lot of money to charity, and he was often invited to local events. A few months into their marriage, Paris went with him to a black-tie fundraising dinner at the Fairmont, where he was awarded a plaque for his generous contribution to a charity that supported mental health services in underserved neighborhoods. When he went onstage to accept it, he said a few words of thanks, then impulsively threw in a dirty joke about one of the presidential candidates . . . and a donkey. The laughs and applause he'd received in the hotel ballroom that night buoyed him for days. And that's when it all began to change.

Someone caught the joke on video and uploaded it to Twitter, hashtagging it #ThePresidentsDonkey and #JimmyPeraltaLives. Within a day, it was retweeted over two hundred thousand times. Chrissy Teigen even tweet-quoted it with a cry-laugh emoji, saying "I fucking love you Jimmy Peralta."

And that's when he realized he might once again have something to say.

Over the next few weeks, he wrote some new jokes, testing them out on both Paris and Zoe, the two people he spent the most time with. The two women, who didn't agree on much, could agree on this: Jimmy Peralta was still very fucking funny, and the material he was writing was relevant to everything that was currently happening in the world.

When he had about twenty minutes' worth of material, he tried it out at a couple of local comedy clubs. Eventually, he was invited to perform at other venues across the US, even making a surprise appearance at the legendary Comedy Cellar in New York. Audiences loved this new Jimmy. He was older, yes, but he was also wiser, more sensitive, more self-aware, and somehow funnier in 2017 than he'd been twenty years earlier. The older fans were glad to see him back. The younger fans were delighted by his no-bullshit takes on politics. And Jimmy took shots at *everybody*, political affiliation be damned. A two-minute clip of one of his jokes about a democratic politician caught in an affair ended up on YouTube, where it garnered over twenty-five million views.

In early 2018, Netflix competitor Quan called, and that's when everything changed. Jimmy decided that at sixty-eight, he was ready for a comeback. Worse, he was doing it big. The first special was called *Jimmy Peralta Lives*. It debuted a couple of months ago to huge numbers, and cemented Jimmy as a star once again. The second one, scheduled for release in a few weeks, will be called *I Love You, Jimmy Peralta*.

There was publicity. Interviews. Their wedding photo made Page Six.

"This could be an opportunity for you to capitalize on, Paris," Zoe said. "People want to know who you are, too."

"No, they don't. I'm not famous."

"But you're famous-*adjacent*." Zoe thought for a moment, then perked up. "What if you started making short videos demonstrating yoga poses? I could get you a collaboration with an apparel company. You could have your own line of yoga wear."

Paris couldn't think of anything she wanted less. "No thanks."

The publicity wasn't all good. When the news got out that Jimmy's fifth wife was of Filipino descent, it rekindled some of the controversy from his past. A couple of weeks after the Quan deal was announced, TMZ unearthed an old stand-up video of Jimmy's from 1990. It showed the comedian making fun of Asians . . . except "Asian" wasn't the term he used. A clip of the offensive joke was posted on TMZ's site, and was trending on Twitter within a few hours.

The next day, Paris made the mistake of answering a call on her cell from an unknown number. It turned out to be a journalist asking her how it felt to be married to a man who'd once made fun of Chinese people.

"I'm Filipino," Paris answered. "Do all Asians look the same to you?" Before he could answer, she hung up.

When she told Jimmy about it later, he laughed. Zoe was horrified.

"Jesus Christ, Jimmy, if you made that same joke today, you'd be canceled," Zoe said. "*Instantly*. You need to issue an apology. Right away."

"Don't you dare apologize," Paris said to Jimmy. "*Please* get canceled. Maybe then they'll leave us alone."

Jimmy did not get canceled. He referenced the old joke at the beginning of the first special, owning up to it in a way that was funny, yet still sensitive. People forgave him. They *wanted* Jimmy Peralta back. But it was only a matter of time before someone from Paris's old life saw photos of her in her new life.

The first blackmail letter arrived a month later.

Paris reaches for the cardboard box and opens it. Ripping off the tape, she begins pulling the letters out, a few at a time. A quarter of the way through, she sees it.

Lavender-colored, birthday-card-size, two Canadian stamps in the top-right corner, mailed all the way from the women's prison in Sainte-Élisabeth, Quebec. It's from an inmate currently serving a life sentence for the murder of her lover in the early nineties. Her name is Ruby Reyes, and the media back then had nicknamed her "the Ice Queen."

She's also the woman whose daughter Paris killed nineteen years ago.

CHAPTER NINE

Of all the people Paris thought might track her down, she never thought it would be Ruby Reyes.

But of course they have TVs in prison, with access to shows like *Entertainment Tonight*, and magazines like *People* and *Us Weekly*. Sainte-Élisabeth Institution is a women's correctional facility, not a bunker. The assumption that Ruby wouldn't be the one to find her was Paris's first mistake.

Her second mistake was not paying her.

When the first blackmail letter arrived, it was sitting innocently in the box with the rest of her husband's fan mail. Jimmy was busy signing photos, Zoe was sealing and stamping all the return envelopes, and neither of them noticed that Paris's heart nearly stopped when she plucked the lavender-colored envelope from the box and saw who the sender was. Neither did they notice when she slipped it under her shirt with shaking hands before excusing herself to go to the bathroom, where she locked the door, read the letter, tore everything into pieces, and flushed it all down the toilet.

Paris rips open the new envelope and pulls out a photo and a letter handwritten on matching lavender notepaper. It was dated a week ago, which means that when Ruby wrote and mailed it, Jimmy was still alive.

Dear Paris,

I have to admit I've been disappointed every time the mail arrives and there's no response from you. I understand how famous Jimmy is, now more than ever, and he must receive mail from fans all over the world. I'm looking forward to watching his new comedy special on Quan as soon as I'm out of prison, once someone teaches me how to do it (ha ha).

And yes, you read that correctly. After a whirlwind hearing filled with so much drama, the Parole Board of Canada has decided that I am no longer a danger to society. After twenty-five years in this hellhole, I'm being released from Sainte-Élisabeth at the end of this month.

In light of this wonderful change in circumstance, I think it makes sense to increase the original amount I requested. I'll need somewhere to live once I'm back in the regular world, and I've heard Toronto real estate is very expensive now. I feel an amount of three million dollars is appropriate for a fresh start.

I have several interviews lined up in the coming weeks, and what I say to those journalists will depend entirely on whether you've paid me what I'm owed. It's the least you can do, considering what you've taken from me.

In my next letter, I will send you the information for the bank account where you can wire the money.

My warmest regards,
Ruby

P.S. I sent you a photo. Thought you might like a reminder of the life you decided to destroy.

P.P.S. Perhaps, once our transaction is complete, you'll tell me the story of how you became Paris. In particular, I'm dying to know whose ashes are in the urn with your real name on it.

Paris drops the letter onto the coffee table. *No. It can't be true.* Ruby Reyes cannot actually be getting out of prison. The Ice Queen received a life sentence for the brutal murder of her wealthy, married lover, a crime that made headlines back in Toronto in the nineties. In what fucked-up world could someone like that make parole? And in what fucked-up world would any journalist want to hear what Ruby Reyes has to say about *anything*?

With shaking hands, Paris grabs her new iPhone. The woman is a liar, after all, and until she sees it for herself, she won't believe a word Ruby says. Opening Safari, she googles *Ruby Reyes Ice Queen Toronto*.

But, oh God, it's true. There it is, in the *Toronto Star*. Everything after the headline and first few sentences is behind a paywall, but there's enough of the article showing to confirm that Ruby isn't lying. They really are letting her out, and in all the ways Paris's mind permutated the possibilities of what might happen once she left Toronto, Ruby Reyes being released had never once occurred to her. The woman was convicted of first-degree murder. The Ice Queen was supposed to die in prison.

In her first letter, Ruby asked Paris for a million dollars. A few months ago, that had seemed utterly ridiculous. What does an inmate serving a life sentence need a million bucks for? How much can commissary snacks cost? The only logical reason Paris could come up with for an ask like that was that Ruby wanted to fuck with her, to see if Paris would pay *something* to keep her quiet.

But now Ruby wants *three* million. And if Paris doesn't pay her, *everyone* will know who Paris really is. And it won't just be Jimmy's death she'll go down for.

The only thing worse than a murder charge? *Two* murder charges.

Paris closes her eyes and focuses on her breathing until she feels her heart rate beginning to slow. She reaches for the photo Ruby sent with the letter. Scrawled on the back in faded blue ink is *Humber Bay Park, Toronto, 1982. Joey's 3rd birthday.*

The greenish-tinted photo is a perfect square with rounded edges. Ruby Reyes is sitting with her daughter, Joey, at a picnic table covered with a red-and-white-checkered cloth. There's so much food—a bucket of Kentucky Fried Chicken, Styrofoam containers filled with bright green coleslaw and macaroni salad, a large bowl of white rice, a tray of fried *lumpia* with dipping sauce, and a cooler filled with cans of Tab and cream soda. There are also balloons, a birthday cake with three candles and pink icing, and a modest stack of brightly wrapped presents. Ruby's sister and brother-in-law are in the background, laughing.

Ruby and her little girl are wearing matching yellow sundresses, each of them eating one half of a banana Popsicle, the kind you could split apart and share. They're smiling at each other, their faces beaming with happiness in the sun. The love between mother and daughter in that moment is obvious, and it hurts Paris to look at it now. She runs a finger lightly over the little girl's sweet face. Joey was so small in this photo, which was taken in better times.

It wasn't like Paris planned to kill her. But neither was it an accident.

She places the photo back on the coffee table and brings the letter with her to the bathroom. Standing over the toilet, she rips it up into tiny pieces. It looks like purple confetti swirling around the bowl until it finally disappears.

Paris soaks a washcloth in cold water and presses it to her face, staring into the mirror. It was a risk not paying Ruby right after the first blackmail letter arrived. But she didn't have the money, and asking Jimmy for it was not an option. Instead, she'd tried to fix things on her own, but her plan to retrieve the urn filled with the ashes that everyone assumes are hers did not go as she'd hoped.

If she doesn't pay Ruby the money, all her secrets will come out.

She's worked so hard to shed her old identity and become Paris. Most days, it feels like she's succeeded, that she has reinvented herself. But at night, in her dreams, it's nineteen years ago, and she's back in Toronto, in that dingy basement apartment with the checkerboard floors, staring at the ravaged body and bloody face of the young woman who was her best friend, her eyes pleading and desperate, her voice raspy and weak.

She had begged at the end.

Please, she had whispered. *Please*.

Paris walks back out to the living room and picks up the photo once again. She thought she'd left this picture behind on the night of the fire, the night she stepped out of one life and into another.

She thought she'd left this photo to burn, along with the girl in the urn.

PART TWO

What a life to take, what a bond to break, I'll be missing you

—Puff Daddy and Faith Evans, featuring 112

CHAPTER TEN

RUBY REYES, #METOO VICTIM, HAS BEEN GRANTED PAROLE
AFTER SERVING 25 YEARS FOR MURDER

Drew Malcolm assumed the article was a joke at first, because it sounds like something written for a satire news outlet like The Onion. But it's not a prank, it's really happening, and the headline is so absurd that he has to read it several times before it finally sinks in.

The Ice Queen, a *victim*? If it wasn't such an insult to actual #Me-Too victims, Drew might have laughed. But there is nothing funny about Joey Reyes's mother getting out of prison. And he's so mad about it, he's decided he's finally going to break the vow he made to himself after he landed his first real job as a journalist, not long after Joey died.

He's going to talk about the Ice Queen on his podcast. Ruby Reyes may be getting out of prison, but if Drew has anything at all to say about it, she will never be free. Because not only is the woman a murderer, she was an absolute horror of a mother.

Fuck that psychopathic bitch.

* * *

They arrested Ruby Reyes on a hot, sticky June night in 1992.

It was a quiet affair, even with the two police cars, the ambulance, and the woman from child protective services. The flashing rays of red and blue from the first-responder vehicles cut through the darkness, lighting up the trees in the lakeside park across the way, illuminating the dirty brick exterior of the run-down low-rise apartment building where Ruby and her thirteen-year-old daughter, Joey, lived.

The neighbors stepped out onto their balconies to see what was going on. Police vehicles in this neighborhood were common, but usually they were called because of the activities that took place in Willow Park after dark. Drug deals. Sexual transactions. Teenagers doing what teenagers do when they're out past curfew. Fights between homeless people with nowhere else to go.

This, in comparison, was tame. Ruby didn't protest or struggle. If anything, she seemed inconvenienced as she was led out of the building's lobby in handcuffs, as if being arrested was a minor misunderstanding that would all be rectified soon.

"Mama," Joey said, leaping down from the back of the ambulance where a paramedic was tending to a cut above her eyebrow. It didn't hurt too much, but her ribs were sore, and she knew from experience that her torso would be blue and purple in the morning. She ran to Ruby and threw her arms around her waist, pressing her face into her mother's chest. "Mama, I'm sorry."

The social worker who was standing behind Joey removed her gently. Ruby glanced down at her daughter, the lights flashing across her face. Even in her old, stained nightgown, with her hair stringy and unwashed, Ruby was beautiful.

"Oh, Joey." Her voice was soft, almost tender. But behind her dark eyes, there was nothing. They were two black holes, sucking in the light, sucking in everything. "What have you done?"

The officers escorting her tugged Ruby's arm, and Joey's mother continued on, chin up, head high, somehow managing to look magnificent despite the circumstances. One of the officers placed a hand on her head, and she sank into the back seat of the police car as gracefully as anyone could.

Deborah Jackson, the social worker assigned to the case, managed to catch Joey just as her knees buckled. Strong arms wrapped around the young girl as her whole body began to shake. It wasn't because Joey was cold. There was a heat wave in Toronto that week, and even here by the lake at eleven at night, it was 30 degrees Celsius, with a humidity index of 37. Worse, the heat felt grimy. This part of Lake Ontario always stank in the summer, the heat trapping the smells of shit and garbage and pollution from the factories not far away.

The social worker wasn't strong enough to hold Joey back. As the police car pulled away with her mother inside it, Joey wriggled out of the woman's sweaty grasp to chase after it in her bare feet, screaming for Ruby all the way down Willow Avenue until the car and the lights and her mother disappeared.

The newspapers would report the scene as heartbreaking. But for the residents who lived at 42 Willow Avenue, it wasn't exactly surprising. They'd known for a long time that something wasn't right. They'd seen the bruises and the hollowed-out look in the girl's eyes as she stood next to them in the elevator. They'd heard the shouting and the sounds of things crashing from inside Ruby's apartment at all times of the day.

"Well, it wasn't *every* day," Mr. Malinowski was overheard saying to the police the night of Ruby's arrest. He was the building superintendent who lived on the first floor. "I mean, was she skinny? Sure, but a lot of girls are at that age. Did I once see a bruise on her cheek? Sure, but she's a kid. Did I ask if she was all right? Of course I did, and her mother said she fell off her bike. What was I supposed to do, accuse her of lying?"

Except Joey didn't have a bike. Nor did she have a skateboard, or Rollerblades, or any of the other things that had supposedly caused the purple welts that occasionally popped up in different places on her face and body.

"She did have a bandage around her arm once," said Mrs. Finch, who lived down the hall from them with her unemployed adult son. She was eager to talk to the police since she was the one who had finally called them. "The girl looked embarrassed, said she tripped and fell, that she was a klutz. I always knew something wasn't right. But I never actually *saw* her mother do anything, so what could I do? And besides, it was none of my business. Okay, fine, I admit I never liked the woman much. She was a floozy, always wearing those short skirts and high heels, her tatas up to here, and every few months a different boyfriend. But the girl is what, twelve? Thirteen? If something was going on, she should have said so, or how else is anyone supposed to know?"

But they knew. Of course they knew.

The murder trial that followed was big news. Charles Baxter, the president of the large bank where Ruby worked, had died of exsanguination as the result of multiple stab wounds. Sixteen, to be exact, but it was the slice across the neck that ultimately killed him. Afraid to ask an adult what exsanguination meant, Joey looked it up in the dictionary. It turned out to be a very fancy and interesting-sounding word for something that just meant "blood loss."

Her mother's beauty only fueled the publicity. Ruby Reyes's long, glossy black hair and seductive smile were at the center of every article, every TV news report. They even gave her a nickname: The Ice Queen. She was thirty-five at the time of her arrest, but she could have passed for ten years younger.

"If I didn't have you," Ruby always said to her daughter, "I could tell people I'm twenty-five. I hate that you look like me."

Joey never doubted that she was the worst thing that ever happened to her mother. Just like her mother was the worst thing that ever happened to her.

After her mother's conviction, Joey was sent to live with her aunt and uncle in Maple Sound, a small town two hours north of Toronto. It was supposed to make things better. Flora and Miguel Escario had three small boys of their own, and they'd agreed to take in their niece when the social worker made it clear that it was either them, or foster care. Joey made the move a few days after her mother's arrest. Finally, she would have a real family. It was a chance at a fresh start.

Except it wasn't, because the kids at her high school knew exactly who Ruby Reyes was, which meant they knew exactly who Joey Reyes was. They knew because their parents read the newspapers and watched the news, as did their teachers. The new girl was the Ice Queen's daughter, and the Ice Queen was *fresh off the boat* and a *slut* and a *gold digger* who had *murdered* someone. The story was horrific and titillating and oh so much fun to talk about, and so they whispered and gossiped and speculated until the bits of truth twisted into more interesting rumors, which grew into outright lies. There was no getting away from it, from her mother, from the *story* of her mother.

After graduating from high school at the age of eighteen, Joey moved back to Toronto. Two years later, she died at home, alone, in a fire. It was a tragic end to a tragic life, and in all the years Drew has worked as a journalist, he promised himself he would never write about Ruby, because of Joey. He knew there was no chance he could ever be objective.

But he's not a journalist anymore. The newspaper he wrote for folded three years ago, forcing Drew to pivot hard if he wanted to continue paying his mortgage. He's a podcaster now, and *The Things We Do in the Dark* averages three million listeners every season. People tune in for his opinions. And when it comes to Ruby Reyes being presented as a victim of anything, he has a shitload of things to say. At the age of sixty, the Ice Queen is getting a second chance at life, while the daughter she abused for years died at the age of twenty?

Drew isn't just angry.

He's fucking furious.

CHAPTER ELEVEN

There's only one parking spot on the street in front of Junior's, and Drew snags it.

It never used to be this busy, but so much in the old neighborhood has changed since he last lived here twenty years ago. The video store where he and Joey used to work is gone. The Portuguese bakery is gone, too. But Junior's is still here, and so is the Golden Cherry, right beside it.

He locks his car and looks over at the iconic neon sign and blacked-out facade of the former strip club. Drew has been inside the Cherry exactly once, for a bachelor party he didn't want to attend, for a wedding that never happened. The Golden Cherry was popular back in the day, but when the strip club industry started to decline about ten years ago, the old "gentlemen's club" was turned into an upscale nightclub. The owner took on a partner, but kept the original name. Other than a fresh coat of paint, it doesn't look much different.

But Junior's does. The best Jamaican restaurant in this part of the city, famous for its jerk chicken, curry goat, and oxtail, is three times the size it used to be. There was a time when Drew would eat here at least twice a week, but he rarely comes back to this neighborhood anymore unless he has to. In fact, it would be fair to say he avoids it.

Everything here reminds him of Joey.

He pulls open the door, and the bells overhead announce his entry.

Gone are the days when the place was just a hole-in-the-wall with three tables and a busy takeout window. The restaurant, having taken over the bakery next door, is bigger and brighter, with fresh yellow paint, new green vinyl chairs, and glossy black tables. Samsung TVs are mounted in each corner of the dining room, and on the wall by the door is a giant framed photograph of a grinning Junior standing beside Usain Bolt. But while all these changes are good, Drew notices their prices have gone up. Their signature beef patties, which used to be 99 cents, are now a whopping $2.50 apiece.

He walks up to the counter and orders one anyway, then grabs a table while he waits for his lunch guest. As he savors the patty, which tastes exactly as he remembers, he watches the TV closest to him. Three pundits on CNN are arguing about something the US president just said, and while Drew doesn't find American politics that interesting, the news ticker scrolling across the bottom of the screen catches his eye.

PARIS PERALTA, CHARGED WITH FIRST-DEGREE MURDER, SET TO INHERIT $46 MILLION FROM LATE HUSBAND JIMMY PERALTA'S ESTATE

Forty-six million. *Damn.* So the wife probably did do it, then. Drew has never paid much attention to the trials and tribulations of celebrities, but the Jimmy Peralta murder is interesting. He just watched *Jimmy Peralta Lives* on Quan not that long ago, and is looking forward to the second special. Seriously funny shit, though the title of the first show is now ironic, and sad.

"As I live and breathe," a delighted voice says.

Drew turns away from the TV to find a woman standing a few feet away with a big smile on her face. It takes a few seconds to place her, but when it comes to him, his mouth drops open.

"*Charisse?*" He stands, trying to reconcile this lovely woman with his memory of the gangly middle schooler whose dad forced her to bus tables here. "That you?"

"Drew Malcolm," Charisse says, hip cocked. "What are you doing back in this neck of the woods?"

"Just meeting someone for lunch," Drew says. "Look at you. You're grown." And *fine*, he thinks, but that would be a hell of a weird thing to say, even though Charisse has to be in her thirties now. Gone are the skinny limbs and braces. This woman has curves and a twinkle in her eye.

"All right, give me the five-second summary," Charisse says. "Married? Kids? Home? Job?"

"Never married. One daughter, Sasha, nineteen, who just finished her second year at Western. I have a condo in Liberty Village, I was an investigative journalist for fifteen years for *Toronto After Dark*, and now I host a true crime podcast out of my den."

"*Toronto After Dark*?" She looks impressed. "I remember that newspaper. It came out every Saturday, right?"

"Until it shut down, yes."

"Ugh, sorry. Okay, my turn." Charisse clears her throat. "Married for ten years, now divorced, but we're still best friends. One amazing kid, Dante, eight. Just bought a house three blocks away, and I run this place now."

"Wow, Junior finally retired?"

Her smile fades. "No, Daddy died. Four years ago. Prostate cancer that spread to his bones."

"I'm sorry to hear that," Drew says, and he truly is. "Junior was a good man. Heart of gold and the best cook this side of Toronto."

"Amen," Charisse says. She raises an eyebrow and gives him the once-over. "So what, you waiting for your Tinder date?"

"You're funny. Work meeting, for the podcast."

She seems pleased by his answer. "In that case, both your lunches are on me."

He laughs. "Thanks, but that's not—"

"Already done." Charisse waggles her fingers. "Fitzroy is in the back cooking, and you'd better say hello before you go."

He grins as she walks away, then sits back down, marveling at how much things have changed. The neighborhood, the restaurant, Charisse. She might be an adult now, but in his head, Junior's daughter will always be twelve.

Just like Joey will always be twenty.

* * *

Drew recognizes the woman from her LinkedIn picture the second she rushes into the restaurant, though she looked a lot less harried in the photo. They trade introductions, and he waves off her apologies for being late, inviting her to sit down while he orders lunch for both of them at the counter. True to Charisse's word, the cashier refuses his money.

By the time he's back with their food, Dr. Deborah Jackson is calmer. Her coral blazer is draped over the back of her chair, her overstuffed tote bag sitting on the floor by her feet. She smiles at him warmly, and she reminds Drew of his mother before all the health issues started.

"You're handsome," she says, appraising him. "You could have mentioned that in your email. I would have been on time and worn something cuter."

He nearly drops the tray, and she laughs. It breaks the tension, and he appreciates her efforts to make things a little lighter for the both of them. They both know this won't be an easy conversation.

"I appreciate you meeting me, Dr. Jackson," he says, taking a seat across from her.

"Deborah, please." She picks up her fork. "I admit I had second thoughts on the way over. I quit doing social work a month after Joelle died. I realized when I couldn't get out of bed that being a caseworker probably wasn't the job for me. So I went back to school, and now I teach. Had you not told me about Ruby Reyes making parole, I'm not sure I could even bring myself to talk about Joelle. I think it's outrageous her mother is getting out, and that she used #MeToo to make it happen. It's offensive to the real victims. I'm glad you're doing the podcast."

Drew is relieved they're on the same page. "How long did you work with Joey?"

"From the night her mother was arrested to the day she turned eighteen. Just over four years. But we did keep in touch for a while after she aged out."

"Isn't it unusual to work with someone that long?"

"Very. Most foster kids have several caseworkers by the time they age out of the system, but since Joey was placed with family, I was able to stay with her. She was technically in kinship care, but there's not much difference."

She takes a bite of the dish she ordered, oxtail, and chews slowly. "This is good."

Drew also ordered them a side of fried plantains, and he pushes the plate toward her. "Joey and I used to come here all the time. Our house wasn't far from here."

"The one that burned?"

He nods.

"I've only been here once," Deborah says, glancing around. "Which was the last time I ever saw her. She told me she'd quit the video store, but she didn't mention she was dancing at the strip club right next door."

"She never told me, either," Drew says. "I found out the hard way."

They switch to small talk while they eat their lunch. Fifteen minutes later, a busboy clears their plates, and Fitzroy, Junior's nephew, pops out of the kitchen in a stained white apron to say hello. The two men shake hands vigorously, both agreeing that it's been too long and that the other still looks good for his age. Fitz has been cooking here ever since Drew can remember, and he promises to send over coffee and coconut cake, on the house, if Drew promises to come back more often. Deborah watches the whole exchange thoughtfully, a small smile on her face.

"I can see why Joelle liked you," she says when they're alone again. "She talked about you a lot the last time I saw her, and she told me that you and your girlfriend had just moved to Vancouver. She was sad about it. She said you were her best friend."

The words sting. "She was mine, too."

"But it was more than friendship for her," Deborah says. "She loved you, Drew. Like, *loved you* loved you. Would-have-married-you-and-had-your-babies-and-grown-old-with-you loved you. Not a crush. I don't think Joelle was capable of infatuation or anything shallow."

His heart lurches. "She never said anything to me."

"Well, you were in a serious relationship." Deborah takes a bite of the coconut cake. "She would never have interfered with that. All she ever wanted was to be nothing like her mother."

She couldn't be more right about that. "When did you find out she was dancing at the Cherry?"

"Not until after she died." Deborah wipes her mouth with a napkin. "I have a close friend who works for the police. He called me when the report came in, and I took it pretty hard. I hadn't meant to lose touch with her. I knew she still needed me; I felt it when we said goodbye that last time." She looks away. "I feel like I failed her."

"At least you didn't shame her for being a stripper less than two hours before she died," Drew says. "When I found out she was dancing, I didn't take it well. I said some really awful things."

"I'm sorry." Deborah touches his hand briefly. "So. What is it you need from me?"

"Joey's file," Drew says. "I know you're not a social worker anymore, but something tells me you might have kept notes. She told me some things, but I want to know more about her childhood."

"What will you do with it? Talk about it on the podcast?"

"Some of it, maybe?" Drew rubs his face. "The thought of Ruby getting out and restarting her life makes me sick. Even if people can forgive her because the man she murdered turned out to be a villain himself, Ruby was still a horrific mother. I want people to see that when they look at her."

Deborah is quiet for a moment. Then she reaches into her tote bag and pulls out a large manila envelope. His instincts were correct; she did keep a copy of Joey's file. She also removes six spiral-bound notebooks with colorful, pretty covers, and stacks them on top of the envelope.

"Her diaries?" Drew reaches for the notebook on top and stares at it in wonder. Joey's diaries led to Ruby Reyes being charged with murder in the first place. "How did you get these? They should still be filed away as evidence."

"They were," Deborah says, "but after Joelle died, it seemed wrong to leave them in there. I asked my friend to get them out of evidence."

"It's my fault she's dead," Drew blurts.

"If that's true, then it's my fault, too." Deborah touches the side of his face, and it's a motherly gesture, filled with compassion and understanding.

He can see his pain mirrored in her eyes. "There was nothing you could have done."

He appreciates her kindness, but she's wrong. There was a lot Drew could have done. He could have been nicer to Joey. He could have stayed with her. He can still remember every word of their last conversation, and had he known it was going to be the last, he would have just shut the fuck up and kissed her.

Because approximately ninety minutes later, Joey died.

CHAPTER TWELVE

Drew's first five seasons of *The Things We Do in the Dark* were all about strangers, people he had no emotional attachment to and would never meet. In contrast, the new season will be about someone he hates. Not dislikes, or disapproves of, but literally hates.

Not many people are aware that Ruby Reyes wasn't originally arrested for murder. She was arrested for child abuse. The hearing took place in closed family court just before the murder trial, the transcripts of which are sealed. Drew has put in a request to view them, and while normally a request like this would be denied, Joey is deceased now. His application is pending.

He's already sketched out a rough outline for season six, but he won't begin recording any episodes until he completes all his research and interviews. Even though the subject matter is intensely personal to him, true crime podcasting is still storytelling, requiring a strong narrative arc if you want to keep people listening. It made sense to start with Deborah Jackson, and he's glad he did, because it's hard to imagine that anything he reads in those sealed transcripts will be more painful than reading Joey's diaries. And he will read them, in order to prepare for his conversation with Ruby Reyes, which he's saving for last. In the meantime, he reads Joey's CPS file.

No child should have to live through what she lived through with her mother.

Ruby Reyes has already given several interviews to various publications, and it's safe to assume she's not going to shut up anytime soon. Among other things, the Ice Queen has always been an attention whore, and if she could have played herself in the made-for-TV movie about her, he's betting she would have. *The Banker's Mistress* was terrible in every way, but the crime it was based on captivated the public from the start.

Drew was in grade 10 when he first read about Charles Baxter's murder, and admittedly, he was hooked from the first article. At first, his mother was concerned about her fifteen-year-old son's obsession with a brutal crime, but when he told her he was thinking of studying journalism one day, she started saving the newspaper articles for him to read after school.

Unlike the family court proceedings, the murder trial was reported widely, the details of each day's testimony recounted in almost every Canadian media outlet. Only sketch artists were allowed inside the courtroom, but the newspapers were happy to publish full-color depictions of Ruby Reyes sitting at the defense table. In some of the sketches, she looked beautiful. In others, she looked vicious. She was both.

On the afternoon that Joey was scheduled to testify for the prosecution, the courtroom was closed entirely. Joey was a minor, so the media was prohibited from publishing her name or any identifying details about her. Still, things leaked, and any details that the Canadian media couldn't talk about, the American media was happy to provide. There was no publication ban in the US, so Drew's uncle in Buffalo was tasked with mailing every article about Ruby that he came across to his nephew.

The murder of Charles Baxter was, in a word, gruesome.

The picture the papers used showed a man who appeared to have it all. Still reasonably handsome and fit at the age of fifty-six, Baxter looked exactly how you'd expect a wealthy bank president to look. At the time of his death, he'd been married to his college sweetheart, Suzanne, for thirty years, and they had a son and daughter who were both away at university.

Pictures of Ruby and her lover were often shown side by side in order to highlight the stark contrast between them. Baxter was gray haired and older; Ruby was gorgeous and twenty-one years younger. He was white and privileged; she was an immigrant from the Philippines. He lived in a five-bedroom home in The Kingsway; she was raising her daughter in a shabby apartment in Willow Park. He was the company president; she was a customer service rep so many levels below him, it was amazing he even knew her name.

To make things even more titillating, the media also loved to show the picture of Suzanne Baxter standing right next to her husband's mistress at the bank's annual holiday party. Canadian Global threw a swanky black-tie dinner at the Royal York hotel each year, complete with champagne, filet mignon, and an eight-piece orchestra. A professional photographer was always on hand to capture memories of the event, and in all the photos Ruby was in, she was stunning. Tall for a Filipina at five eight, her long legs were on full display in her short, strapless gold dress. Her eyelashes were thick, her lips were red, and her long, shiny black hair spilled in perfect waves over her bare shoulders.

Suzanne Baxter, in comparison, was the same age as her husband and no more than five three, with teased blond hair. For the party, she wore a long red evening gown paired with a red sequined jacket. The wardrobe choice was unflattering. The jacket was too short and the dress too snug, highlighting the roundness of her stomach.

It had been so easy to villainize Ruby. This was long before #MeToo, and nobody seemed to blame Charles Baxter at all for the affair. Ruby was the other woman, a seductress, a home-wrecker who'd lured a happily married man away from his wife and family. She was obviously obsessed and clearly manipulative. She was Glenn Close in *Fatal Attraction*; she was Sharon Stone in *Basic Instinct*. There were no other narratives. After her conviction, Suzanne was quoted as saying, "I wish she had never come into our lives," as if her husband had been completely helpless, as if the affair—which lasted *two years*, by the way—had happened without his consent.

The story stayed with Drew long after high school, long after Ruby was convicted. Which is why, a few years later, he could not have been more shocked when Joey Reyes knocked on the door.

At the time, he and his girlfriend Simone were renting the basement apartment of a house owned by a man who spent half the year in India, leaving his twenty-year-old son to manage the property. The son never came around, more interested in his Camaro and the older Italian girlfriend his parents wouldn't approve of than the needs of his tenants. Calls went unanswered after the oven stopped working and the freezer wouldn't get cold enough to keep their ice cream from melting. When a family of raccoons made a home inside the chimney, Drew and Simone were forced to pay for a professional "raccoon removal" service themselves. The guy who showed up noticed the chimney was full of cracks and buildup, rendering the fireplace extremely dangerous. He told them that until it was cleaned and repaired, they should never light a fire in it, ever.

The place was a shithole, with peel-and-stick linoleum, no water pressure, and stained ceilings. But with student loans and credit card debt, it was what they could afford. Eventually, sick of being two months behind on every bill, Drew put an ad in the local paper that read "Roommate Wanted."

The last person he expected to answer the ad was Joey Reyes.

She was a shell of a person, drowning in baggy clothes and long hair that she wore like a security blanket. She had a hard time maintaining eye contact, and her soft voice didn't carry very far. But despite appearances, she was determined.

"I don't have a job yet," Joey said, standing across from Drew and Simone in the tiny kitchen with the black-and-white checkerboard floors. Beside him, Drew felt his girlfriend's shoulders slump. "I just moved back to Toronto this morning and came here straight from Union Station. But I've got cash, and I can pay six months' rent up front."

Simone perked up again. "Six months? Up front? That should be plenty of time for you to figure out the job situation. Right, Drew?"

He wasn't sure. Simone, who never read the newspaper and would've had zero interest in reading about criminals even if she did, did not recognize the shy person in their kitchen. Nobody would, as her name and picture were never published.

But Drew knew exactly who she was. It had been easy enough to figure out back when he was in high school. Willow Park Middle School was only a five-minute walk from Ruby's building. It hadn't been hard to dig up a copy of their yearbook, which included a photo of a pretty girl in grade 8 named Joelle Reyes, who, at the age of thirteen, already looked a lot like her mother.

At almost nineteen, she was a dead ringer for Ruby. It made Drew uneasy. It was one thing to meet the Ice Queen's daughter. It was a whole other thing to let the girl move in.

He felt Simone's elbow in his ribs. He knew they needed the money, and that it would take a person with extremely low standards to be willing to pay rent to live here. They weren't asking much, but six months up front would get them current on all their bills and credit card payments.

"Welcome home," Drew said to Joey. "By the way, we're not actually allowed to have a third person living here. So if anyone asks, you're just hanging out. Cool?"

"No problem," she said. "I'm used to pretending to not exist."

Joey moved in that afternoon. Or more accurately, she simply didn't leave. Everything she owned in the world was in the duffel bag and backpack she had with her. Her bedroom, which was technically a den, was the size of a postage stamp. She seemed genuinely thrilled.

"I haven't slept in a room by myself in years," she said.

The following week, still struggling to find a job, Drew recommended Joey to replace him at the video store down the street. He'd gotten a paid internship at the *Toronto Tribune*, and he started in two weeks.

"Gustav fired the last guy because a customer caught him watching porn on the store TV," Drew said. "So as long as you never do that, you're good. It's the easiest job. It's only busy on weekends, so during the week you can do homework, watch movies, whatever. Gustav is cool."

"I'll bring a book," Joey said.

He glanced at the paperback on her bed. "What are you reading?"

"*The Long Road Home* by Danielle Steel. It's about a girl whose mother abuses her."

Their eyes met. He waited to see if she might mention something about Ruby, but she looked away. It would be months before she felt comfortable enough to tell him anything, and even then, he would only learn about her life in fragments.

"I hated Maple Sound," Joey said to him a couple of months later at Junior's. "Worst town ever. My aunt and uncle never wanted me there, and the feeling was mutual. And my grandmother is an asshole."

Drew, who'd been both of his grandmothers' pets, couldn't even fathom that. "So you'll never go back and visit?"

"Trust me." She offered him a rare smile. "The way I left, they don't want to see me again."

Conversations about her mother wouldn't happen for another three months.

"You know who my mom is, right?" Joey asked him one night, out of the blue. Simone was working at The Keg by then, so it was just Drew and Joey, watching a movie she'd brought home from the video store. "I saw the way you looked at me when I first showed up."

He paused the movie. It was the first time she'd ever brought up Ruby. "You look like her."

"I hate that I do."

"She was beautiful."

Joey stared at the frame frozen on the TV for a few seconds. "She was something, all right."

"Did you ever visit her in prison?"

"Just once, right before the trial started."

She fingered her necklace, pulling the pendant up to her lips as if to kiss it. She did this a lot when she was thinking about the past. The pendant was a ruby surrounded by a halo of tiny diamonds, and it couldn't be a coincidence that the center gemstone was the same as her mother's name. He sensed an origin story there.

"You ever see that picture of her at the Christmas party?" Joey asked. "The one where she was standing next to Suzanne Baxter? It was in all the papers."

Drew remembered the picture exactly.

"My mother loved that picture," Joey said. "She actually taped it to the fridge. She found it so satisfying that Charles's wife looked like a hippo in a red dress—her words, not mine—and she was so sure he was going to leave her. But she felt that way about every man she slept with."

"How many were married?" Drew asked.

"All of them." She looked away. "My father, too."

He had a thousand more questions. But he had to tread carefully. He didn't want her to shut down.

"I asked her once if she loved Charles," Joey said. "And she laughed.

She said, 'No, baby. I don't love him. But I like him. And trust me, that's better.'"

She pulled her pendant up to her lips again. When it was clear she wasn't going to say anything more, he unpaused the movie.

A couple of months later, Drew asked her about the necklace. Joey said it was a birthday gift, and left it at that.

Now, as he finally opens her first diary to the first page, he understands immediately why she didn't elaborate. As he loses himself in her words—she might have become a writer one day, had she lived—he realizes that his instinct about the necklace having an origin story was correct.

Some people wear their hearts on their sleeve. Joey wore her trauma around her neck.

CHAPTER THIRTEEN

The night Joey was given the necklace, it was her twelfth birthday.

She sat at the small dining room table across from Charles and her mother, Joey and Ruby wearing matching red dresses with flared skirts. Joey was uncomfortable. She was too old to be dolled up like a mini version of Ruby, but the dresses had been a gift from Charles, and it would have been rude not to put hers on.

Charles had also paid for the pizza, the wine, the cake, and the unopened birthday gift that was sitting on the table in front of her. The small box was wrapped in thick silver paper and tied with a black velvet bow, and she knew that whatever was inside would be the nicest thing she would ever own. Joey looked at her mother, silently asking for permission.

Please let me have it. I don't even know what's in it, but I want it. Please, Mama.

Ruby took a drag on her Marlboro and exhaled a long stream of smoke from her red lips. "Go ahead, baby." She sounded magnanimous, even though the gift wasn't from her. "Open it."

Joey had already opened her mother's present, and it was a surprisingly thoughtful gift. When they were at the bookstore in the mall a month before, Joey had wandered around the stationery section, admiring the fancy pens, the scented papers, and the beautifully bound notebooks. The ones Ruby bought her for school were flimsy things with thin pages that ripped if your pencil was too sharp. These notebooks, in contrast, were luxurious, with gold spiral bindings. They came in a pack of six, and the covers all had different designs—butterflies, birds, rainbows, flowers, hearts, unicorns.

She knew better than to ask for them (*do you think I'm made of money*), but her mother must have gone back and bought them. Maybe Ruby had splurged to impress Charles, the current boyfriend, who was also her boss at the bank. Even if she had, who cared? Joey had squealed when she saw the notebooks, wrapping her mother in a tight hug. "Thank you, Mama," she said, which pleased Ruby, because Charles was watching.

Trying not to seem too excited now, she reached for the silver-wrapped present and untied the bow. Careful not to tear the paper (she would save it, of course), she unwrapped a blue velvet box. Inside, nestled atop a small cushion of satin, was a thin gold chain with a diamond-and-ruby pendant. Her mother had one just like it, and now Charles had bought one for her, too. Eyes wide, she gently detached it from the backing.

"Don't worry, sweetheart, you won't break it," Charles said with a laugh. "It's eighteen-karat gold. It's strong."

Joey held it up to catch the light, awed that something so pretty—and so expensive—was actually hers. A real ruby, surrounded by real diamonds, set in real gold.

"A lovely necklace for a lovely young lady." Charles's eyes were bright, his smile wide. "Come over here, sweetheart. I'll put it on you."

Another glance at her mother, but this time, Joey's heart sank. Ruby was smiling, but it was not a nice smile. Ruby was smiling *that* smile, the one that hid what she was truly feeling. Charles hadn't been around long enough to know that smile, and even if he had, he wouldn't have noticed, because he wasn't looking at Ruby. His attention was fully on Joey, and the one thing Ruby would not tolerate was anyone giving the attention that should be bestowed upon her to someone else. Including, and especially, her daughter.

Her mother's eyes flashed with jealousy. It was quick—blink and you'll miss it—but Joey caught it. The smoke from the Marlboro swirled around Ruby's face. The tip of the cigarette now had a centimeter of ash, and if she didn't tap it into the ashtray soon, it would fall into her lap. But her mother didn't move, the icy smile plastered on her face like a clown mask.

Charles was oblivious to all the unspoken communication. "Come on, honey. Let's see what it looks like."

Joey was damned if she did and damned if she didn't. Slowly, she walked around the table to the other side where Charles was sitting. He moved her hair off her shoulder, the gray fuzz on his forearm brushing along her jawline as he clasped the chain around her neck. She was close enough to breathe in his cologne. It smelled expensive.

Charles turned her around and stared at her, gazing at her throat, and then the pendant, and then her chest. He reached out again, arranging her hair so it fell around her shoulders once more.

"Gorgeous," he said. "You are a beautiful girl. You're going to give your mama a run for her money in the next few years." He winked. But not at Ruby, at her.

Her mother's smile flickered, but remained.

The next morning, Joey woke up to a quiet apartment. When she came out of her bedroom, her mother was sitting at the dining room table, still in her nightie, hair in disarray, looking out the window at the park across the street. She was smoking yet another cigarette. If Charles had spent the night, he was gone now; his shoes weren't by the door.

"So, you think you can flirt with my boyfriend, do you?" Ruby turned away from the window and stared at her daughter. "You little slut."

"What?" Joey said, still half awake.

It was just one word, and a benign word at that. But the minute it slipped out of her mouth, she knew it was a mistake. She had dared to *speak*, and that was all it took. Ruby was out of her chair, and before Joey could react, her mother's lit cigarette pressed into her neck just above her collarbone, a centimeter away from the chain of her new necklace. She cried out, the heat from the Marlboro searing and intense. Then Ruby spat in her face, her warm, tobacco-scented saliva spraying across Joey's eyes and cheeks.

"Mama, please—" Joey said, but before she could finish, her mother backhanded her across the face.

Then Ruby hit her again, and again, and again, until finally, blessedly, everything went black.

When Joey came to—one minute later? Ten minutes later?—she was lying near the sofa in the living room, the cigarette inches away from her face on the scratched parquet floor. Someone was rapping at the door, and judging from the volume and pace, they'd been knocking for a while.

Her eyesight cleared a little, and she watched as Ruby stomped toward the door to fling it open.

It was Mrs. Finch, their neighbor at the end of the hall. Her body was partially obscured by Ruby standing in the doorway, but her pale green housecoat and matching slippers were easily recognizable. She was on her way to the garbage chute; she had a stuffed white trash bag in one hand.

"What do you want?" Ruby snapped at the woman. "Has it ever occurred to you that if someone doesn't answer their door after five minutes, then maybe they don't want to?"

Ruby's tone was aggressive, and from her vantage point on the floor, Joey saw Mrs. Finch's slippered feet back up a step. "I . . . I heard . . ."

"You heard what?"

The neighbor took another step back, but not before she glanced past Ruby to see Joey lying on the floor. They locked eyes briefly, and while Joey could have tried to signal for help, she didn't.

It never worked. Nobody ever helped. It only made things worse.

Instead, Joey tried to smile, to reassure Mrs. Finch that she was fine, that it was just a silly accident, no big deal. If she could have actually said those words, she would have, but her brain was too fuzzy to form a coherent sentence. At least she didn't have the wind knocked out of her this time. While she knew now that a punch to the gut could trigger a spasm in her diaphragm that felt terrible but wouldn't kill her (*don't be ridiculous, you're always so fucking dramatic*), not being able to breathe for a few seconds always made her feel like she might die.

"Is she all right?" Mrs. Finch blurted. "Your daughter?"

Ruby's body turned rigid, and while Joey couldn't see her mother's face, she could imagine it. When Ruby answered, her voice was cool. "She's fine. She tripped."

The neighbor backed up another step, and now Joey couldn't see the woman at all. "She . . . she doesn't look well," she heard Mrs. Finch stammer from the hallway. "You should help her."

"Are you telling me how to parent my daughter, Mrs. Finch?" Ruby's voice dropped to a low growl.

Not a good sign. Mrs. Finch needed to leave. Right away.

"Just . . . keep it down, please," the neighbor said. It sounded like a weak imitation of someone trying to sound authoritative. But she did not sound authoritative. She sounded nervous, and scared. "I could hear screaming from the hallway."

"That was the TV," Ruby said. "And I would suggest you mind your own damn business. How many cats do you and your loser son have in your apartment now, Mrs. Finch? Is it three? Or four? From what I remember when I signed the lease, we're only allowed one pet. Be a shame if you got evicted."

No response.

"See?" Ruby sounded warmer now, almost cheerful, her voice back to its regular volume. "Isn't it annoying when people butt into what you're doing inside your own home?"

The door slammed shut. And then Ruby turned around, put her hands on her hips, and appraised her daughter.

Joey forced herself to sit up. Slowly, she leaned back against the sofa, clutching her stomach. It ached like she had just done a thousand sit-ups. Her head was pounding, and she could feel her lips swelling.

Ruby crouched down and cupped her chin so they were looking directly at each other. "Anything broken?"

Joey shook her head.

"Feel like you're going to throw up?"

"No." The word came out a squeak.

"That's my girl." Ruby patted her on the shoulder, one of the few places on Joey's body that didn't hurt. "Let's not fight anymore, okay? I'm exhausted. Charles was a beast last night."

Yes. He was.

"You must be hungry. I'll heat up last night's pizza."

Her mother pulled her up. She kissed the top of Joey's head, then wrinkled her nose.

"You smell like cologne. Go take a shower."

CHAPTER FOURTEEN

Drew has read five of the six diaries, and he's not sure how much of Joey's words will make it into the podcast. It's a fine line between talking about the horror of a mother Ruby was, and revealing Joey's personal pain for the world to see. It may not be possible to do one without the other, but ultimately, he owes it to her to tell the truth as best he can.

Back in the old neighborhood once again, he looks up at the black-painted exterior of the Golden Cherry, where the pink neon GIRLS GIRLS GIRLS sign used to be. All they've kept are the gold neon cherries above the same gaudy brass doors, but it's enough to hint at the nightclub's history. Drew could have stopped in after his lunch with Deborah Jackson the other day, but he wasn't ready then.

He's not sure he's ready now. But if he wants to learn about the last year of Joey's life, which was the year he was in Vancouver, then the former strip club is probably the best place to start. He called earlier, and whoever answered the phone had told him to stop in before the club opened.

He tugs on the door and it opens easily. It takes a moment for his eyes to adjust to the sudden dimness, but when they do, he can see quite well. There are light sconces on all the walls, and the pendant lights above the bar are turned on.

"Hello?" Drew calls out. "Anyone here?"

Without bodies to fill the space, his voice echoes. The room is cavernous. The main level, which used to be filled with tables and chairs, is now one large, empty dance floor. Still, there are reminders everywhere of the Cherry it used to be. The old sign from outside that read GENTLEMEN'S CLUB has been relocated above the bar, which spans the length of the side wall. The original stage has been converted into a raised VIP area with tables and loveseats, but the three stripper poles are where they've always been. Mounted on the wall behind the stage is a neon sign that reads CHAMPAGNE ROOM. And directly across the dance floor, just above the projection screen that's two stories high, is the original GIRLS GIRLS GIRLS sign. Everything is turned off, and the projection screen is blank, but he can imagine how cool it must all look when the nightclub is in full swing.

The memories come flooding back.

"Can I help you?" a woman's voice calls out.

Drew looks around, trying to determine the direction the voice is coming from, and spots a blond woman in a red pantsuit watching him from the second level.

"The deliveries come in through the back," she says. "You're supposed to ring the bell. My partner will be back soon."

He catches the tension in her voice. She probably didn't realize the front doors were unlocked.

"I'm not delivering anything," Drew calls up. "I phoned earlier, hoping to talk to someone who might have worked here back when this place was a strip club."

"And who are you?" she asks.

"I'm a journalist. I'm working on a story about a friend of mine who used to dance here back in 1998."

"Stay exactly where you are," she says, and disappears.

Ten seconds later, he sees her coming down the spiral staircase, one hand on the railing, the other carrying a pair of red high heels. When she reaches the bottom, she slips her shoes on, then heads straight to the bar and flicks a switch. The neon signs throughout the club light up in a burst of glowing color, and the giant screen projector turns on. An artsy slow-motion black-and-white video begins to play, and it's of strippers doing what they do best . . . stripping.

The effect is nothing short of astounding. Whoever transformed this place did an exceptional job of making the Cherry operate like a night-club, while still feeling like a strip club.

"This is incredible." Drew can't conceal his amazement. "Am I too old to party here?"

"You're asking the wrong girl," the woman in red says.

She remains behind the bar, her posture erect. It's obvious she's alone, and he can see he's making her nervous. *You're a man,* his mother used to constantly remind Drew when he was growing up. *Be mindful of how you appear to women, and keep your distance unless invited. Think of how your sisters would feel.*

Drew stays where he is, near the entrance.

"I remember every girl who worked for me," the woman says. "What was your friend's name?"

"Joelle Reyes," Drew says. "But everybody called her Joey."

"The name doesn't ring a bell." The woman frowns. "Back in ninety-eight, you said? Do you have a picture?"

"I don't." Drew realized the other day that he doesn't have a single photo of Joey. Somewhere in his storage locker at the condo is an ancient digital camera with a long-dead battery, and it's possible there's a picture of her on it from back in the day. But he doubts it. Joey hated having her picture taken. "She was half Filipino, about five five, with long black hair?"

The woman smiles. "I had two girls like that back then. One called herself Betty Savage. The other went by Ruby."

Drew isn't sure he heard her correctly. "Her stripper name was *Ruby?*"

The woman frowns again. "Her *stage* name was Ruby."

Jesus Christ. Joey had used her *mother's* name to dance here? Dr. Phil would have a field day with that one.

"She's the one who died in the fire, right?" the woman asks.

Drew nods. "I was her roommate. And her best friend."

"Come closer so I can see you better."

As he approaches the bar, he can see that she's not as young as he ini-tially thought. He had guessed maybe early fifties, but up close, she looks to be in her mid-sixties, platinum hair, slim but busty, with freckled skin that's seen a bit too much sun. He puts a business card on the counter and gives her a moment to read it.

She holds the card at arm's length, squinting at the small print. Her nails and lips are both painted the same vibrant red as her pantsuit. "Drew Malcolm of . . . *The Things We Do in the Dark* podcast. Sounds ominous."

Drew offers her his hand. "I'm sorry if I scared you, ma'am. The front door was unlocked."

"Two things." Her grip is firm to match her voice. "One, we've been having issues with the lock not catching, so that's not your fault. And two, never call me ma'am. It hurts my feelings."

"Then I apologize for that, too." Drew smiles. "What do I call you?"

"You can call me what everybody else does." She returns the smile. "Cherry."

"Cherry?" Drew is delighted. "As in, Cherry of the Golden Cherry?"

"The one and only," she says. "And if you're here to talk about Ruby, we're going to need a drink. Have a seat. I'll make you the best old-fashioned you've ever had."

Cherry places two cocktail glasses on the bar as Drew slides onto a stool. He watches as she drops a cube of sugar into each, then adds a dash of bitters and a tiny bit of water. She muddles the sugar until it dissolves, then adds ice cubes, a generous pour of rye, and two maraschino cherries per glass. It seems like a lot of work for one drink. But she's not done.

She plucks an orange out of the fridge behind her and deftly shaves off a thin section of peel. Using a lighter, she burns the rind for about five seconds while squeezing it, which creates a fairly decent flame. Then she rubs the burnt peel around the rim of the glass and drops that in, too. She slides his drink over. The aroma is out of this world, a citrusy, smoky caramel.

"Taste it," Cherry says. "And then tell me it's the best old-fashioned you've ever had."

Drew takes a sip. "It's the best *cocktail* I've ever had."

She lifts her glass. "To Ruby."

Fuck, no. "To Joey."

They clink, and they drink.

Somewhere nearby, a phone vibrates. Drew pats his pocket, but it's not his. He watches as Cherry reaches into her ample cleavage and pulls out a small gold iPhone.

"Yeah, I know what you're thinking," Cherry says, catching his expression. "I'm not supposed to keep my phone in my bra because it might cause cancer, blah blah blah. But trust me, honey, there's so much silicone in here, ain't no room for anything else to grow."

Drew laughs. That wasn't what he was thinking. At all.

"I'm having an issue with a delivery." She frowns at her screen. "This might take a few minutes. You okay to wait?"

Drew lifts his glass again. "I'm good."

But he isn't good. Not really.

Everything here at the Cherry reminds him of Joey. Because before today, the only time he'd ever been in here was the night Joey died. It was New Year's Eve, in the hours before 1998 turned into 1999.

It was also the night of his stupid bachelor party. Nearly two decades later, it remains the worst night of his life. Nothing before, or after, has even come close.

* * *

A New Year's Day wedding wouldn't have been Drew's choice, but there aren't a lot of options when it's a shotgun wedding. Drew was back in Toronto after a year in Vancouver, and though he had explicitly said he had no desire for a bachelor party, his friends surprised him with one anyway. They booked a VIP table at the Golden Cherry, which turned out to be a hell of a way to discover that Joey was a stripper.

Had it been any other female friend, it might have been comedy fodder, a funny bachelor party story that would be told and retold for years to come. But it was *Joey*. There she was, one of maybe fifty girls working at the Cherry on New Year's Eve, wearing high heels and her necklace and nothing else. There was nothing funny about it, and when Drew saw her, it was all he could do not to rip her out of his buddy's lap and carry her the hell out of there.

But he didn't. He'd pretended not to know her, and she had done the same. It wasn't entirely untrue. The Joey he knew was shy and modest, who shrank if people looked at her too long. This Joey was a confident, alluring stranger with false eyelashes, red lips, and a brand-new tattoo inked across her thigh.

It was a butterfly. A symbol of transformation. Was that what this was?

Maybe he'd know the answer if he and Simone hadn't lost touch with her not long after they moved to the west coast the year before. Or a more accurate way to put it would be that Drew had simply stopped returning Joey's calls. By the time he returned to Toronto for the holidays and the wedding, it seemed awkward to reach out. Too much had happened since he'd left for Vancouver.

Too much had happened since he left *her*.

After the countdown to 1999 was over, Drew cited the need for a good night's sleep and said goodbye to his friends, who were moving on to a nightclub downtown to finish out the night. It was a lie. There was no way he could sleep. Not until he talked to Joey. After they dropped him off at his mother's house, he borrowed his sister's car and drove back to the Cherry. He grabbed a roti at Junior's, then sat in the parking lot at the back and waited.

The dancers started coming out the back door after last call, around two a.m. Each one looked more tired than the last. He stepped out of the car, knowing Joey wouldn't recognize his sister's Sunfire, and stood shivering in the freezing air. He must have looked a little shady, because one of the bouncers eventually came out and asked him why he was hanging around so close to the staff entrance. Even now, Drew can still remember what the guy looked like. He used to watch professional wrestling back then, and the bouncer was a dead ringer for The Rock.

"I'm waiting for someone," Drew said, trying not to sound as cold as he felt. "It's a public parking lot, dude."

"Does she want to see you?" the bouncer asked.

"She's my friend. I already saw her inside."

"Does she want to see you?" the bouncer repeated.

"I guess we'll find out."

The Rock didn't like his answer, but that was fine, because Drew didn't like him.

A few minutes later, Joey came out the back door, all bundled up in her giant winter parka and snow boots. The fake eyelashes were gone, her face was wiped clean, and she looked absolutely exhausted. When she saw Drew, she froze.

Her eyes darted back and forth between Drew and the bouncer, and it was obvious she'd only been expecting to see The Rock. Was she planning to go home with him? Was she actually dating this dude? Drew felt a sudden pang of insecurity. He was six three, but the bouncer had two inches and probably fifty pounds of muscle on him, which made Drew feel . . . *small*. He didn't like it, he wasn't used to it, and so basically, it sucked.

"Hey," Joey said hesitantly.

Neither man responded, because neither was sure which one of them she was speaking to.

Joey's gaze finally settled on Drew. "You're still here."

"Can you tell this dude I'm your friend?" Drew said. It came out more hostile than he intended, and he saw the bouncer's jaw twitch. "He seems to think I'm stalking you."

"It's okay, Chaz," Joey said. "I do know him."

"So, you need a few minutes, or . . ." The bouncer's voice trailed off. He sounded annoyed, but Drew could detect something else underneath it. Dismay. *Hurt.*

"I can drive you home," Drew said to Joey, and when she didn't immediately respond, he added, "We used to live together, so I think I know the way." It was petty, but he couldn't resist the dig.

"You good with that, Joey?" the bouncer asked, and it was clear he wasn't going to leave until he heard it from her. She nodded, and the bigger man's face hardened. "Cool. Happy New Year."

"You too, Chaz." She looked like she wanted to say something more to him, maybe reassure him in some way—she hated to hurt people's feelings—but The Rock was already inside his car.

Alone under the bright lights of the parking lot, Drew and Joey stared at each other.

"What are you still doing here, Drew?" she asked again.

He walked over to the Sunfire and opened the passenger-side door. "Get in the car, Joey."

She bristled at his tone.

"Please." Drew's teeth were chattering. "I forgot how fucking cold it is here."

* * *

They didn't speak for the first half of the drive. Which wasn't long, as the house was only fifteen minutes away. But the radio wasn't on. It was too quiet. Neither of them seemed to know how to begin.

"How's Simone?" Joey finally asked.

"She's fine."

"When did you get back into town?"

"Christmas Eve," Drew said. "I'm staying at my mom's."

That hurt her. He could sense it. He'd been home for a week and hadn't called.

"So that was your bachelor party," Joey said.

"Yes."

"You're getting married tomorrow."

"Yes."

"My invitation must have gotten lost in the mail," she said. "Although that would be strange, since you and I used to *live* together."

He deserved that.

"Where's the wedding?" she asked.

"The Old Mill."

Joey slumped in her seat. He could imagine what she was thinking. The Old Mill was nice. The kind of place you'd choose if you wanted something traditional and a little bit fancy.

"There was a last-minute cancellation," Drew said, as if it would help anything. "Her parents are paying for it."

"And yet here you are." Joey glanced at the dashboard. "At . . . two thirty in the morning. Didn't your friends bail after midnight? What have you been doing for the past two hours?"

"Thinking."

"About . . . ?"

"You," he said tersely. "Tonight was . . . hard to watch."

A full minute passed before Joey spoke again. "I'm sorry if I ruined your night," she said. "I know you ruined mine."

"You give us both too much credit."

"Simone must be excited for tomorrow," Joey said quietly. "We haven't talked in a while, which I guess is the reason I'm not invited to the wedding."

"If it makes you feel better, Simone isn't invited, either. Apparently it's poor form to invite your ex-girlfriend to watch you get married."

Joey's mouth dropped open. He actually heard it, the sound of her lips parting, the small gasp. He hadn't meant to be so dramatic, but there was just no good way to tell her. He'd been avoiding this conversation for months.

"Simone and I haven't spoken in almost a year," he said. "We broke up not long after we got to Vancouver."

Joey twisted her entire body sideways to face him, not an easy maneuver considering the parka she was wearing probably weighed ten pounds. "Are. You. Serious."

"As a heart attack."

"I don't understand."

"She met another chef at the restaurant," Drew said, and even now, saying it out loud sounds weird. "She was seeing him for about a month before I figured it out."

"Simone *cheated* on you?"

"People change." He glanced at her. "Right?"

Joey turned to face straight ahead again, and Drew allowed her a moment to process. He understood it was a lot, and her reaction reminded him of the night he and Simone made the decision to move. She'd been offered a job at a five-star restaurant in Vancouver, and he'd been accepted at the University of British Columbia for graduate school. It was a good plan, the right decision, and a smart move toward their future. The only challenge—for him, anyway—was how to tell Joey. It was no secret she'd grown attached to them, and while Simone thought she'd be okay, Drew wasn't so sure.

They thought a good meal might soften the blow. Simone, who'd graduated with honors from culinary school, cooked a huge feast for the three of them, no small feat considering how crappy the kitchen was in their basement apartment. Roast chicken, garlic mashed potatoes, sautéed vegetables, sourdough bread baked from scratch. She even made apple tarts for dessert, Joey's favorite.

They had filled her up before they broke her heart.

"How'd you find out that she met someone else?" Joey asked.

"She started hanging out with the people from work after her shifts, and was coming home later and later. She was picking fights and never wanted to have sex—" Drew stopped, cleared his throat. "I felt it. I waited in the parking lot outside the restaurant one night. Watched from the car when she came out with some guy. I followed them back to his apartment. She didn't come out for three hours."

"You sat in the guy's parking lot the whole time?"

"We were in a four-year relationship. I had to be sure." He made a left turn onto Acorn Street. They were nearly home. "She saw me and froze. And that's when I realized I had nothing to say, because her face said it all. She turned around and went back into the building. When I got home, there was a message on the phone. All she said was, 'I'm sorry.'"

"Oh, Drew." Joey sounded genuinely distraught. "You know I loved Simone, but that was a shit move. Is that . . . is that why you both stopped calling me?"

"I can't speak for her," Drew said. "I didn't know how to tell you. I needed some time to grieve it, I guess. A couple months later, I met Kirsten. It was supposed to be a rebound, but . . ."

He didn't finish the sentence. They were home. And had he known how the night was going to end, he would have said and done everything differently.

CHAPTER FIFTEEN

Cherry is back, her red blazer unbuttoned. The lacey white camisole underneath is cut low. To think, somewhere in there is her phone. Drew tries not to stare, and she laughs.

"Oh honey, *look*," Cherry says. "I didn't buy 'em to hide 'em. Men looking at me was how I made my living for twenty years."

"You were a dancer?"

"I'm the OG here, as the kids would say. Married my best customer." She winks. "He then bought the club and renamed it after me. When he died, I took over. We had a good run until about ten years ago. I took on a partner, and we decided to change it into a nightclub."

"I was only here once," Drew says. "When my friend danced here."

"Ruby was a sweet girl," Cherry says. "Always on time, no whining or bitching. She was popular with the customers. She made a lot of money, more than most."

Drew needs a bit of liquid courage before he can ask the next question. He takes a long sip of his old-fashioned. "Was dancing the only thing the girls did for money?"

Cherry's eyes narrow.

"I'm trying to understand why she worked here," Drew says. "She was a really shy person. It seemed . . . out of character for her."

"There's no mystery to it." Cherry waves a manicured hand. "She was here for the same reason everybody else was. It was a job, one that paid very well if you were willing to put in the work. And it *was* work. You try dancing all night in five-inch heels."

He couldn't imagine dancing in *one*-inch heels.

"It was like any job, you know? There were nights you hated it, and nights that you had a really fucking good time." Cherry chuckles. "She wasn't the greatest dancer, mind you. We had to work on that. What made her special was the way she looked at you. She could look right into a man's eyes and make him feel like he was the only person in the room. She created a sense of real intimacy. Let me tell you, I can teach a girl to dance, but I can't teach a girl to do that."

Drew nods, but the person she just described doesn't fit the Joey he knew.

"I was so sorry to hear that she died," Cherry says. "That was a rough weekend. I only had two Asian dancers working here then, and I lost both of them around the same time. It's not politically correct to say this now, but there was a real demand for girls like Ruby. They weren't that common. I actually had a theory that—" She stops and finishes her drink. "Never mind, it's dumb."

"I love dumb theories." Drew sets his glass down. "Tell me."

The owner plucks a cherry out of her empty glass and pops it into her mouth. "Ruby and the other Filipino dancer, Betty Savage, became really close friends. When Ruby started working here, Betty kind of took her under her wing, helped her with her dancing, showed her how to work the room. But unlike Ruby, Betty was difficult. Always late for work, skipping out on shifts; I nearly fired her so many times, but the demand for Asian dancers was so high. Betty was trouble, though. I suspected she was selling drugs to the other girls. Her boyfriend was in one of those Vietnamese gangs."

"Which one?" Drew asks, his interest piqued even further. He had written a series on Asian street gangs for *Toronto After Dark*, had actually won an award for it. He knew them all.

"I can't remember now." Cherry shakes her head. "Anyway, the drug thing—I didn't like it, but what could I do about it? A lot of the girls couldn't work all night without being on something, and as long as they weren't snorting it in here . . . I had a business to run."

Her eyes search Drew's for any sign of judgment. She won't find any, not because he agrees, but because he needs her to keep talking.

"So, the night Ruby died, someone thought they saw Betty's boyfriend lurking around," Cherry says. "Betty hadn't shown up for work—again—and the lockers in the dressing room were ransacked that night. Nothing was taken, but everyone's stuff was all over the floor, as if whoever broke in was looking for something specific."

Drew waits.

"Betty's boyfriend had a terrible reputation." She hesitates. "I wondered if maybe he did something to both of them. Because of the fire, you know."

"Do you remember the boyfriend's name?"

She shakes her head. "I never even met him. But I heard about him. He made some of the girls nervous."

Drew's mind is working overtime to process what she just said. The fire that killed Joey started in the fireplace, and the fire inspector back then had confirmed it was an accident. Whoever this gangster boyfriend was, he wouldn't have had anything to do with it.

But Cherry had just said *both of them*. Implying something had happened to Betty, too.

"The same weekend Ruby died, Betty went missing," Cherry says. "And as far as I know, she was never seen again."

Drew's spine starts to tingle, something that hasn't happened in a long time. During his years writing for *Toronto After Dark*, he would feel that tingle any time he was onto something, any time a story he was investigating shifted in a direction he wasn't expecting.

"You want to see some old photos?" Cherry asks. "I used to take pictures of the girls when they were hanging out. I'm sure I have a couple of Ruby in one of the albums in my office upstairs."

Was she actually asking if he wanted to see pictures of Joey? Uh, *yeah*.

A bell rings, and then someone pounds on the back door. Cherry checks her watch. "That's my delivery," she says. "Go on upstairs. You've been here before, right?"

"Just once."

She smiles. "My office is in the old Champagne Room."

* * *

When Drew reaches the second floor, he sees that the strip club's original VIP area is now full of billiards tables and lounge chairs. The booths for lap dances that used to line the wall have been replaced with long sofas, and there's now a door where the velvet curtain leading to the Champagne Room used to be.

Drew can still remember how Joey looked that night, the way she'd turned to glance back at him one last time before disappearing behind the curtain with his friend Jake. She didn't look scared. She wasn't unwilling. She looked . . . resigned.

Later that night, as they sat in his sister's car in the driveway outside Joey's house, he wanted to ask her what happened with Jake in the Champagne Room. But he knew there'd be no good answer to his question. She'd either refuse to tell him, which would trigger his imagination to conjure up all kinds of scenarios, or she *would* tell him, and then he'd *know.*

They must have sat there for five minutes, neither of them speaking, but neither of them making a move to get out.

"How are Beavis and Butthead?" Drew had finally asked, because he had to say something to break the silence. Beavis and Butthead were their nicknames for the upstairs tenants, twin brothers who smoked pot all night long.

"They went to New Brunswick for the holidays to visit their folks," Joey said. "They stuck a joint under my door with a note asking if I'd take out their garbage."

"Smoke it yet?"

"You know I won't."

Drew appraised the run-down exterior of the old Tudor-style bungalow with the dirty bricks, broken eaves trough, and sagging front porch. He knew the inside was even worse, the main level only slightly less crappy than the basement apartment. "The house still looks like shit, I see."

"You expected different?"

"I didn't mean it as a dig. I miss living here." He stared straight ahead. "I miss living here with you."

He heard her sharp inhale.

Drew turned to face her. "Look, I'm sorry I didn't tell you about Simone. It's just that every time I thought about calling, I knew I'd have to tell you that we broke up, and I knew it would end up being a bigger conversation. Which I wasn't ready to have."

"Okay," she said, but it clearly wasn't. "So tell me about Kristen."

"*Kirsten*." He tapped the steering wheel, trying to think of the best way to explain. "We're in the same postgrad program. I think you'd like her. When we're finished with school, the plan is to move back here, and so maybe the three of us can get together . . ."

His voice trailed off. Because he knew what he was saying was stupid. There was no way Joey would want to meet Kirsten. Ever.

"I understand why Simone never called," Joey said. "She wouldn't want to tell me what she did. Friends choose sides after a breakup, right? She knew I'd choose you."

Drew let out a breath, feeling worse than ever.

"But what's the rush?" she asked softly. "With Kristen?"

This time, he didn't bother to correct her. He looked out the window. "She's pregnant."

There's a long silence. After a full minute, he chanced a glance in her direction, but she, too, is looking out the window. He reached for her hand, but she sensed him coming and moved her arm away.

"A couple of moments ago I didn't think I could be more shocked," she said. "But the hits just keep coming."

"Joey—"

She turned to him then, reaching a hand out to touch his cheek. Her eyes scanned over his face, as if she were trying to memorize the angles of his cheekbones, the line of his jaw, his eyes, his lips, his hair. He didn't like the way she was looking at him now, as if she knew this would be the last time they would see each other.

"You're getting married," Joey whispered. "You're having a baby. You're making a whole new life, and it doesn't include me."

"Joey—" he said again, but she dropped her hand.

"I'm happy for you, Drew. You'll be a great husband. And an even better father."

Her words sounded hollow, like she was only saying the things she was supposed to say, the things polite people would say.

"Do you love her?" she asked.

He couldn't lie to her. Not now.

"I love her enough," Drew said. "I grew up without a dad. I don't want that for my kid."

She nodded and pushed open the door. A sharp bite of cold nipped his face. Before she could move her leg out, he reached past her and pulled the door shut.

"There are still things to say," he said.

Joey sat back, and he saw that she was digging the fingernails of her left hand deep into the delicate skin on the inner wrist of her right. A spot of blood formed, and he grabbed her wrist to make her stop. She wrenched away.

"I already know what you're going to ask. Dancing pays the bills, okay?" She looked at him, her eyes flashing. "It's a job. It's legal. I even have a license to do it."

"But *why*?" Drew couldn't even pretend he understood. "For fuck's sake, Joey. You're only twenty. You're smart. You could be anything you want to be."

"You've always said that, but it's not true." There was a hitch in her voice, and her breath was coming faster. "I know your family didn't have a lot of money, and your dad died when you were little, but your mother and sisters gave you stability. They loved you, they protected you, they supported you. And for a long time, you also had Simone. And now you've got Kristen."

"Kirsten," he said.

"All I had was you and Simone. And then suddenly, you're both gone. After you guys moved out, I needed to find another job. I couldn't pay the rent by myself."

"Why didn't you talk to Gustav?" Drew asked. The owner of the video store was a good guy. "I'm sure he would have given you more hours—"

"You know Gustav. *The movie business is a weekend business, Joey*," she said, doing a passable intimation of Gustav's Austrian accent. "Well, as it turns out, so is dancing. I couldn't do both. And dancing pays a hell of a lot better."

"Except it's not always dancing, right?" The words were out before he could stop himself.

"Fuck you, Drew." Joey glared at him. "You guys *left* me. You knew I couldn't afford this shithole by myself. So don't you dare fucking judge me for doing what I had to do."

"Which is what, taking your clothes off for a bunch of skeezy assholes?" Drew's voice was a few decibels shy of a shout. "Rubbing yourself all over them until they get off? Get a fucking roommate, Joey. That makes a hell of a lot more sense than whoring yourself out."

She slapped him, and the instant her palm connected with his cheek, he knew he deserved it. The slap was surprisingly painful. She'd hit him hard.

"Some of those skeezy assholes tonight were your friends," she said. "And if you really think I'm a whore, then there's no point in talking anymore."

Drew rubbed his cheek, which was stinging like crazy. "So you'll get naked for anyone else except me?"

"Excuse me?"

"Don't you remember that night, about a week before we moved, when Simone was working—"

"Of course I remember that night," Joey snapped. "And you know damn well why I stopped. Do not make this about you, you selfish, self-righteous asshole. You might hate my job, but your opinion doesn't matter to me anymore. You left me. You *left*."

They were both breathing heavily, the windows fogging up all around them.

"I can't believe you slapped me," he finally said.

"Yeah, well," she said, opening the car door again. This time, Drew didn't try to stop her. "Like mother, like daughter. Have a nice life, asshole."

The door slammed. He watched as she let herself into the house, using the side door that led directly down to the basement. When the door shut behind her, and he knew she was safely inside, he reversed out of the driveway.

He didn't look back.

CHAPTER SIXTEEN

That conversation, which would turn out to be their last, did not go at all as Drew planned.

He'd spent an hour driving in circles after their argument, trying to clear his head. He knew he had been a total dick to Joey and that he owed her an apology, but he also knew it wouldn't sound sincere until he cooled off. He had a mother, two sisters, an ex-girlfriend, and now a fiancée, and he'd learned the hard way that women did not like it when "I'm sorry!" was shouted at them. All they heard was the tone, not the words.

He turned the car around at four a.m. By the time he got back to Acorn Street, there were two fire trucks, an ambulance, and two police cars blocking the road. It seemed that, in the hour and a half or so since he'd left, there had been a fire. He slowed the car and rolled down his window to get a better look. There were no flames anywhere. He wasn't even sure which house was the problem.

But the smell of smoke was unmistakable.

Many of the neighbors were outside, boots and parkas thrown on over their pajamas, a few still wearing their New Year's party outfits. They stood on their lawns, speaking quietly to each other, shaking their heads in disbelief. Half the street was blocked off, so Drew parked the car as close as he could to the action and got out, scanning all the faces, looking for any sign of Joey. She was nowhere to be seen.

The first knot of fear formed in his stomach.

He made his way closer to the house, his old house, *Joey's* house. The side door leading to the basement apartment was open, and a firefighter in full gear stood just inside the doorway.

A second knot of fear tied itself around his heart.

"Drew," someone said, and he whirled around. "Hey man, I didn't know you were back in town."

"Rick." Drew was relieved to see someone he knew. His former neighbor was a few years older, with a wife and small kid, and lived three houses down. "What the hell happened? I can smell the smoke, but the house looks okay?"

"The fire was contained to the basement," Rick said. "The alarm must have been going off for a while before any of the neighbors heard it, because the upstairs tenants are out of town. The trucks got here quick, but . . ."

The fire was in the basement.

A third knot of fear tightened around his throat.

"But what?" Drew forced out the words, his voice strangled.

Rick blinked and then looked around, as if he couldn't believe he was the one who had to tell him and was hoping someone else would magically appear to take over the conversation.

"I'm so sorry, man," Rick finally said. "Joey . . . they said Joey didn't make it."

His former neighbor had spoken actual words, and Drew had heard them. But strung together in that order, those words didn't make any sense. "What do you mean, Joey didn't make it?"

Rick shifted his weight from right to left, clearly uncomfortable. "I overheard one of the firefighters saying it was the fireplace. I don't know exactly how it happened, but they think it started there. I didn't realize that house still had a wood-burning fireplace in the basement. We had ours filled in when we renovated last year, because the contractor told us it wasn't up to code. They . . . they couldn't get Joey out in time."

Drew stared at him, waiting for the punch line. It didn't come.

"But I was just here," he said, and his voice sounded strange to his own ears, almost like it wasn't him speaking. "I was just *here*, and she was fine, she was . . . she . . ."

He saw the firefighter step out of the basement entrance, and a few seconds later, a paramedic appeared. He was holding one end of a stretcher, slowly shuffling backward as he maneuvered his way out the side door. Drew could see a lump the shape of a body emerge. It was covered in a yellow plastic tarp.

He bolted toward it.

"Hey," a police officer said, getting in his way. "Sir, this is a—"

"I live here," he said instinctively, unable to take his eyes off the yellow tarp.

"You have ID?"

Drew pulled his wallet out and held up his driver's license. He'd never bothered to update it when he moved to Vancouver, so it still showed this address.

"She's my . . . she's my girlfriend," Drew said. "I need to see her."

The officer let him through.

Drew kept walking until he reached the paramedics, who were preparing to lift the stretcher into the back of the ambulance. Without thinking, he reached for the edge of the tarp, but a paramedic stopped him.

"She's badly burned," the EMT said. "I really don't think—"

Drew lifted the tarp a few inches, not realizing he had pulled it from the top. He caught a glimpse of burned hair and a face that . . . wasn't a face. The skin looked both raw and charred, a horrific mix of pink and white and black, and the odor that wafted out was unlike anything he'd ever smelled. Before he dropped the tarp and sprang back, he caught a glimpse of the necklace. Joey's necklace, the one she'd had since she was a kid, the birthday gift from Charles Baxter. It was still around her neck, intact, and though the gold chain was blackened, the ruby in the pendant was still red.

His stomach turned, and he managed to step back a few more feet before he vomited all over a snowbank.

Another police officer approached him then, a tall woman with curly brown hair. The other officers seemed to defer to her, so he assumed she must be the one in charge of the scene. She gave Drew a moment for his stomach to settle down, holding a finger up to the two paramedics so they wouldn't yet load the body into the ambulance. When Drew finally straightened up, she introduced herself.

"I'm Constable McKinley. You live here, you said?" She had a British accent and spoke kindly, though there was no mistaking the authority in her voice.

"I did live here," he said. "With Joey. I need to know if that's her. Joelle Reyes." Just saying her name made Drew want to throw up again. "Please."

The police officer looked at him closely. "Her body is badly—"

"Please," he repeated. He was usually more articulate than this, but it was all he could think to say.

"I can show you a part of the body that isn't so damaged." The officer spoke gently. "But first, can you tell me if she has any tattoos?"

"No, none," Drew said automatically.

And then he remembered. Joey did have a tattoo, because he'd just seen it at the Golden Cherry. Jesus, had that only been a few hours ago?

"Wait," he said. "She does have one tattoo. A butterfly. On her thigh."

"Let's look," the officer said, and walked him back to the ambulance. She pulled out her flashlight and then lifted the tarp, from the middle this time. He braced himself.

And there it was, in a spot where the skin wasn't as badly burned. A butterfly, midflight, the colors still vibrant though the surrounding skin was bright red.

"It's her," he gasped. "It's Joey."

He sank to his knees on the ice-cold sidewalk, his breath coming out in shallow bursts of white steam in the freezing, smoke-scented air.

Joey was dead. And it would forever be Drew's fault. Because he'd left her.

Again.

* * *

If Cherry notices that Drew looks emotional when she gets up to her office, she doesn't say anything.

She has an entire row of photo albums lined up neatly on the bookcase behind her desk, and she runs a long red fingernail along the spines until she gets to a faded pink album labeled *1998*. She pulls it off the shelf and reaches for her reading glasses. Flipping through the pages, she smiles at some of the memories until she finds what she's looking for. She turns the album around to face Drew.

"There's your girl."

Drew examines the photo behind the protective plastic sheet. It's surreal looking at Joey's face after all this time. But this is not the girl he remembers, the one who wore jeans and baggy T-shirts every day. This is Joey dressed as *Ruby*, her mother, with the eyelashes and red lipstick and a skimpy gold dress that shows off the tattoo on her thigh. She's relaxing in the dressing room with her feet up on the vanity table, stilettos discarded on the floor beside her chair, reading a book.

Drew's heart pangs. Despite looking like Ruby, the photo captured the essence of who Joey was perfectly. She always had her nose in a book wherever she went.

"There might be another picture of her in there somewhere," Cherry says. "You're welcome to look."

He turns the pages slowly, scanning through photo after photo of women in various stages of undress. Finally, on the last page, he sees a picture of Joey with two other dancers, the three of them posing like Charlie's Angels. Joey is wearing her gold dress, and the young Black woman in the middle is wearing a silver dress—if it can even be considered clothing—that appears to be made entirely of strings. The woman on the right must be the other Filipino dancer, Betty Savage. She's wearing a traditional green Chinese *qipao*, and while the skirt ends at midcalf, the dress is extremely tight, with a high slit on one side only.

"Betty never had a problem catering to the customers' Asian fetishes. For Halloween, she dressed as a geisha." Cherry is looking at the photo upside down. "You can't do that kind of thing now, but back in the nineties, in a strip club? It made her a lot of money."

Drew stares at the picture. "Did Joey do that, too?"

"I would say so, but it was less obvious," Cherry says. "Ruby knew what she had that made her different from the other girls, and she worked it well. Those two looked so much alike, don't you think?"

Normally Drew would be annoyed by a comment like this. Just because they were the only two Asian dancers in the club—and both Filipino—didn't mean they looked alike. But looking closer, he has to admit Cherry has a point. Joey was slightly taller and Betty had a smaller frame, but their noses and face shapes had a similar roundness, and their hair was the same color and length. They could have passed for sisters.

In the dark, they could even be twins.

Drew feels another tingle in his spine. "What was Betty's real name?" he asks, his throat dry.

"I can't remember."

"What else can you tell me about her boyfriend?"

Cherry shakes her head. "All I know is that his gang was all over the news back then for shooting up a nightclub in Chinatown—"

"The Blood Brothers." Drew exhales.

He remembers the story well. The nightclub shooting was thought to be part of an ongoing turf war between the Blood Brothers, a Vietnamese gang, and the Big Circle Boys, a rival Chinese gang. Three people died that night. He has dozens of old files on his computer at home from the series he wrote on Asian street gangs, and he might be able to dig up Betty's boyfriend's name from the research he's already done.

Drew lifts up the corner of the protective sheet. "Mind if I take a picture of this with my phone? And the other one, too?"

"You can take them," Cherry says. "I can see she meant a lot to you."

There's a crackling sound in the quiet office as Drew peels off the plastic, carefully detaching the photos from their sticky backing. The tingling hasn't stopped. Joey and Betty, so similar in appearance. One dead, the other missing, in the same damn weekend. Betty's boyfriend, involved with the Blood Brothers at a time when the gang was at its most violent, most power hungry, seen hanging around the club on New Year's Eve. And then a few hours later, Joey is dead, in a fire that was ruled an accident . . . but might not have been. After all, fires are a great way to destroy evidence.

What if Joey's death wasn't accidental? What if it was murder?

Betty Savage might know. But he can't talk to her, because she's missing. Or is she?

Drew gives his head a little shake. *Now* who's the one with the dumb theory?

"What is it?" Cherry asks, catching it.

"Nothing." He forces a smile and returns the album to her. "While I'm here, any chance you have old personnel files lying around? I wouldn't mind tracking down this Betty. Since you mentioned she and Joey were good friends, I'm wondering if she can give me some insight into the last year of Joey's life."

"I used to keep files on all the girls with their performers' licenses photocopied so I'd have them on hand during random inspections," Cherry says. "But they were shredded years ago. You could try contacting the city. Dancers can't legally work without a license, but without Betty's real name, that would be a lot of licenses to sift through. There were a lot more dancers back in 1998."

"Thanks for the tip, and I appreciate your time. Just wondering, though—" Drew hesitates. Cherry's been helpful, and he doesn't want to offend her. "Why didn't you float your theory past the police back then? About Betty's boyfriend maybe doing something to both her and Joey?"

Cherry lets out a bitter laugh. "What police? Nobody came around to ask me anything about either of them. And what was I going to do, march down to the nearest police station and volunteer my suspicions that a Vietnamese gang member killed one of them, or both? Last thing I needed was a target on my back."

Drew nods. Of course that makes sense. The club owner is a shrewd lady, full of street smarts.

"My advice?" Cherry files the photo album back on the shelf. "Don't go looking for Betty. She was bad news."

CHAPTER SEVENTEEN

Of *course* he's going to look for Betty.

It's been a long time since Drew investigated something, and holy hell, he forgot how good it feels to chase down a story. The more he thinks about it, the more it feels like a real possibility that the basement fire was no accident. After all, Joey knew the chimney was in rough shape, because he and Simone had warned her about it after she moved in. The three of them never lit a fire, not once.

But did *Betty* know about the chimney? If the girls were good friends, and she spent time with Joey in the apartment, she might have. It never did sit well with Drew that Joey made a fire that night. But what if she wasn't the one who lit it? What if it was someone she was close to? Someone with a boyfriend who supplied her with drugs that she sold to the other girls at the club?

Murdering someone is a great reason to go "missing."

Back at his condo, Drew puts in a call to the licensing office at the City of Toronto and explains his situation. He's transferred to the records department, where he explains it all again, only to be put on hold for twenty minutes before the call simply disconnects. He then sends an email. Thirty minutes later, he receives a reply from an administrator at the licensing office, who tells him she can't give out information about licenses unless they're requested by the person themselves, or by an officer of the court. He scrolls through his contacts and puts in calls to three police officers he personally knows. Nobody picks up, so he leaves voice mails.

Investigative journalism is not nearly as sexy as it appears on TV.

Racking his brain, he googles *house fire Toronto Acorn Street January 1 1999* and gets hits for two articles mentioning the fire at his old place.

In the first article, the fire inspector explained that the blaze was caused by the fireplace in the basement, the chimney of which had not been cleaned or maintained in over a decade. It contained a buildup of creosote, a tar-like material that is highly combustible. The fire in the hearth caused the creosote to ignite in the chimney, which was full of cracks, allowing the fire to spread to the wall. It consumed the rest of the small basement apartment within minutes, leaving no time for the occupant, who was likely asleep at that time of night, to escape.

"The importance of regular chimney maintenance cannot be overstated," the fire inspector is quoted as saying. "Unfortunately, I've seen this scenario too many times."

The second article said more or less the same, only its headline was more dramatic: DAUGHTER OF RUBY REYES PERISHES IN NEW YEAR'S EVE HOUSE FIRE. The article was clearly written to titillate. Not only did it make a point to mention that Joelle Reyes, age 20, had been working as an exotic dancer at the Golden Cherry Gentlemen's Club, it also spent a paragraph summarizing her mother's crime, which means the reporter had managed to make the connection between Joey and Ruby. The article finishes with a brief quote from Police Constable Hannah McKinley, who confirmed that no foul play was suspected.

Drew remembers McKinley. She was kind to him that night. He googles her name and learns that she's a detective now, a sergeant, in homicide. A couple more clicks and he has the email address for her department. He types quickly, explaining who he is and reminding her how they met. An hour later, McKinley phones. He'd forgotten she had a British accent until he hears her voice.

"This was a long time ago, so I'll have to refresh my memory. Give me a second," Sergeant McKinley says. Drew can hear her typing, and can only assume she's at her desk at the station. "Right, I remember now. House fire on New Year's Eve, one deceased, Joelle Reyes, daughter of Ruby Reyes. Victim ID provided by . . . Drew Malcolm. Oh, right, that's you."

"That's me," he says. "Can you tell me if there were photos taken at the scene?"

"I'm sure there would have been, by the insurance company, at least," she says. "Would have happened the next day."

"What about photos of the deceased?" An image of Joey's burned face flashes through Drew's mind. "Would there be pictures of that?"

"At the scene? Definitely not. The fire department would have prioritized removing her at the soonest possibility."

Drew tries again. "What about the morgue? They'd have photos, right?"

"Possibly, but you're not going to want to see those, assuming any were taken, and assuming they were filed properly and can even be located after all these years. But from what I recall, she was DOA when they pulled her out." McKinley pauses. "Why would you want to see photos? From what I remember, your friend's body was very badly burned."

"Not everywhere." Drew clears his throat. "There was a part of her leg where her tattoo was still visible."

"Ah yes. Which is how you were able to ID her. That, and . . ." A pause. She must be reading. "The necklace. I noted she was wearing a gold necklace with a diamond-and-ruby pendant."

Drew nods, even though she can't see it. "Did they ever confirm her actual cause of death?"

"It's usually smoke inhalation, but it seems like this fire tore through the basement pretty fast," McKinley says. Another pause. "Why do you ask? Are you saying that after nineteen years, you've now got questions about how she died?"

Her accent is messing up his ability to interpret her tone. He can't tell if she's interested or annoyed, and already he's starting to feel a bit stupid asking a seasoned cop these questions after so much time has passed. Still, what has he got to lose, other than a little bit of dignity?

"I'm saying I'm not sure now," Drew says. "I know it sounds nuts after all this time, but what if she was already dead, and the fire was just a cover-up?"

"What brought this up?"

"Ruby Reyes, Joey's mother, made parole. I'm doing a podcast series about her and her relationship with her daughter, and I'm trying to fill in some of the gaps in Joey's life. I just learned that Joey was involved with some shady people back then, which I didn't know at the time."

Silence from McKinley. He can only imagine what must be going through her head. She probably thinks it's crazy, because it really kind of is. Also, it's a long shot, based on no evidence, just a hunch. Fine, not even a hunch. A *tingle*.

"Hello?" Drew is holding his breath. "You still there?"

"I'm looking to see if there was an autopsy done on the body. There wasn't. But I figured it was worth checking."

He's relieved she didn't hang up. "Does it say why they didn't do one?"

"Because the death wasn't ruled suspicious. Joelle was found lying on the sofa in front of the fireplace, which is where the fire started. It's the only point of origin. The theory is she fell asleep, and sometime later, the fire sparked in the chimney. Seems fairly cut-and-dried how it all happened, as long as we're sticking with the presumption that nobody wanted her dead." The sergeant pauses again. "Do you now think someone wanted her dead?"

"Earlier today, I went back to the strip club where she worked, and the owner told me that Joey was close friends with another dancer, who went by the name Betty Savage. Betty was selling drugs at the club, which were supplied by her boyfriend, who was in a gang. The night Joey died, he was seen hanging around the club, even though Betty wasn't there that night."

A thought occurs to Drew then, and if there's a limit to how big a dumb theory can get, this might just test it.

"Joey and Betty looked a lot alike," he says. "They were both Filipino. I know it's a stretch, but . . ."

"Go on," McKinley says. "You've come this far."

"What if the boyfriend killed Joey by mistake? And set the fire to cover it up?"

"Well, where's Betty now?"

"She's missing. She disappeared the weekend Joey died."

"Okay, that *is* interesting." A pause. "Then I suppose you need to find Betty, and ask her what she knows about that night."

Drew exhales. So the sergeant doesn't think it's stupid. That's something, at least. "The problem is, I don't know her real name. She went by Betty Savage at the club. I put a request in to the city to check for a performer's license, but the woman who replied to my email won't give me any information unless I'm an officer of the court."

"Bloody hell, you're all over this thing," McKinley says. "Who's the person you emailed? And any chance you can send me a photo of Joelle and this Betty?"

He puts her on speaker and uses his phone to snap photos of the pictures Cherry let him keep, then sends the sergeant everything. Five seconds later, he hears her computer ping.

"They really do look alike, don't they?" McKinley says. "Bollocks, now you've got me intrigued. I'll check missing persons reports around that time. Anything you can tell me about the boyfriend?"

"He was part of a Vietnamese gang called the Blood Brothers. I don't know his name." *But I might be able to find out.*

"Okay, I'll get back to you. It's not like I don't have ten other things I could be doing, but now you've put a bug up my arse." McKinley sighs. "I'll text when I know something."

"I get that this is absolutely bonkers," Drew says. "And I'm not sure it even changes anything, because I'm ninety-nine percent certain the fire was probably an accident."

"But you were a hundred percent certain before," McKinley says. "That one percent can eat you alive. Trust me, I know that feeling."

He appreciates her understanding, because he does need to know. However, finding out the truth might not make him feel any better. He's been telling himself he's doing this podcast for Joey, to tell her story and expose Ruby for who she is. But deep down, in the cracks of his soul where he stuffs all the painful thoughts he can't bear to deal with, he knows he's doing it to try to alleviate his own guilt. For abandoning her.

Joey had her own share of guilt, too. Incredibly, she blamed herself for her mother being charged with Charles's murder. After their neighbor called the police, and Ruby was finally arrested for child abuse, Joey had allowed the social worker to read her diaries, where she'd written about the night Charles was killed.

"You wanted your social worker to know, though, right?" Drew had asked her. They were sitting at the table by the window at Junior's. "Was giving her your diaries your way of telling her, without actually having to tell her?"

"I don't know that I was thinking about it that way," Joey said. "As stupid as it sounds, I never wanted Ruby to go to prison. I just wanted to not live with her anymore. But in the end, she got the last laugh. Living with my aunt and uncle didn't make my life better. All it did was make it a different kind of shitty. And there were many times when I wished I had just stayed with the devil I knew."

Joey almost never talked about her years in Maple Sound.

Drew reaches for the last diary, and starts reading.

CHAPTER EIGHTEEN

After her mother's arrest, Joey spent two nights in an emergency shelter with a dozen other kids. She slept on a bottom bunk, underneath a girl who talked (*cried*) in her sleep. When the social worker finally came back for her, Joey was relieved. All she wanted was to see her mother and make sure she was okay (*not mad at her*).

But they weren't going to see Ruby. They were going back to the apartment in Willow Park so Joey could pack her things.

The social worker (*you can call me Deb*) explained on the drive over that due to the child abuse charge, Joey would have to stay separated from her mother for a while. In the meantime, her aunt Flora and uncle Miguel in Maple Sound had agreed to take her in. Joey was surprised. She couldn't imagine what sales pitch (*witchcraft*) the social worker had used on Tita Flora and Tito Micky, but it must have been some serious hocus pocus for her mother's sister—and greatest enemy—to take in Ruby's only child.

The apartment somehow seemed smaller and shabbier than it had been only two days before. Or perhaps Joey was just seeing it through the social worker's eyes, which were full of compassion as she looked around, taking in the broken dishes, the cracked photo frames, and the busted lamp on the floor.

"Take your time," Deborah said. "I know this must be difficult."

Joey pulled Ruby's old suitcase from the closet and began to fill it with what few clothes she owned. She took a few of her mother's things as well. The hair dryer. The Mason Pearson hairbrush Ruby had splurged on after she got her first job in Canada. Her signature lipstick, MAC "Russian Red."

Deborah lent her a second suitcase, which Joey filled with as many of her mother's books as would fit. Danielle Steel, Judith Krantz, and Sidney Sheldon were Ruby's favorite authors, as they all wrote dishy, sweeping sagas filled with drama, broken hearts, and angst. Joey read all the novels, too, and discussing them with her mother was always when she was happiest. It was the one thing they could do together that never resulted in a negative outcome.

Everything else in the apartment, Deborah told her, could remain until the end of the following month, when the unit would be put back on the rental market.

"But where will my mom go?" Joey asked. "After the trial?"

Deborah touched her shoulder. "It may be a long while before she comes home, honey."

In every place she and Ruby had lived, Joey learned to find a secret hiding spot, a place where she could store things her mother wouldn't find. One of those things was the necklace from Charles. Ruby had sold hers in a rage when Charles dumped her (for the third time), and Joey, becoming familiar with the pattern, told her mother that she had lost her own necklace at the park. Except she hadn't. She hid it, so Ruby wouldn't sell hers, too.

"What are those?" Deborah asked when Joey pulled the necklace out of a loose floorboard near the radiator. She didn't seem surprised that Joey had a secret hiding spot. She also wasn't referring to the necklace. She was looking at the stack of small, pretty notebooks that were also in the floor.

"They're my diaries," Joey said. "I think I'm just going to leave them here."

"That would be a shame. What do you write about?"

Joey shrugged. "Everything, I guess." She picked them up. "Why, did you want to read them?"

"Would you like me to read them?"

Joey shrugged again.

The social worker made no move to take them, remaining perched on the edge of the bed. In that position, Joey couldn't help but notice that Deborah's body was shaped like a potato. Ruby, who always had strong opinions about other women's bodies, would have said she was fat. But when Deborah had hugged her two nights ago after the arrest, the woman had felt so soft, so safe, her rolls and squishiness warm and comforting. She was a pillow in human form, the exact opposite of Ruby.

"I would like to read them," Deborah said. "It might help me know you better, so I can support you the best I can. But it has to be okay with you, Joelle."

"Whatever. I don't care."

The diaries were now in the back seat.

A strawberry-shaped air freshener dangled from the rearview mirror of Deborah's Honda Accord. It was fuzzy like an oversize scratch 'n' sniff sticker, and though it didn't smell anything like strawberries, it did make the car smell nice. Ruby's car always smelled like smoke.

"You doing okay, Joelle?" Deborah glanced over, the sunlight reflecting off her smooth, poreless dark skin. "I'll need to stop for gas soon, if you need to go to the bathroom."

If Deborah meant *okay* as in not currently injured and not physically ill, then sure, Joey was okay. She stared straight ahead, aware of Deborah's black curls bobbing to the mixtape in the cassette deck. The social worker seemed too old for Young MC, but she knew all the words to "Bust a Move." *She's dressed in yellow, she says hello* . . .

Deborah glanced over again, still waiting for an answer. Finally Joey shrugged. She knew adults hated when kids did that, but not Deborah, who seemed to understand that sometimes there were no words. Sometimes the answer was a shrug.

"When will they let me see my mom?" Joey looked out the passenger-side window, where she could see her reflection. She appeared translucent, like a ghost (*I wish I was a ghost*).

It took Deborah a few seconds to answer. "I wish I knew, honey. But I bet your aunt and uncle are excited to see you."

The social worker said it so kindly that even though she knew the opposite to be true, Joey couldn't bring herself to disagree. She'd only been to Maple Sound once before, a few years earlier. The visit had been a disaster. It was the day she met her grandmother (*lola*) for the first time.

It was also the day she realized that her bad mother also had a bad mother.

* * *

At the gas station, Joey waited in the car while the social worker went inside to pay. They were an hour into the two-hour drive up to Maple Sound, and it was going by at warp speed. With every kilometer, her heart grew heavier. It felt like this car ride was the dividing line between the *before* and the *after*. Once she arrived at her aunt and uncle's house, she would cross into the after, and there would be no going back.

Deborah plopped back into the driver's seat and handed Joey a plastic bag. Inside were several packs of Skittles.

"I know your aunt has three boys, but that candy is yours, Joelle, and you don't have to share it with anyone." Deborah's tone was serious as she started the car. "Whenever you're feeling lonely, have a couple of Skittles. Think of them as me giving you a hug. By the time you've finished the candy, I'll be back for a visit. And I'll bring you some more."

Joey stared at the bag. An adult had just given her a present, and it wasn't even her birthday. True, it was just Skittles, but it was the best gift she'd ever received. Because it was in exchange for . . . absolutely nothing.

"Thank you." She willed herself not to cry.

An hour later, they arrived in Maple Sound. The entire family was outside on the porch when they pulled up. The two-story house was at the top of a hill, and while it had pretty views of Lake Huron, it was much smaller and more isolated than Joey remembered.

"It's really pretty here." Deborah sounded surprised as she cut the engine. She rolled down the window. "Smell that? Fresh air. And is that a pond I see over there? It's so cute. Listen . . . you can hear the frogs—"

At first Joey didn't understand why Deborah stopped speaking so abruptly, but then she realized it was because of her. She was *crying*, dammit, and she didn't even know she was doing it until she saw the look on

Deborah's face. She swiped at her cheeks, embarrassed to be caught *feeling* something—and furious at herself for allowing it to show.

Tita Flora appeared near the driver's-side door with a big smile. She did not look how Joey remembered, either. Her hair was cut short and lightened to an unnatural shade of auburn. Her three boys—Jason, Tyson, and Carson—remained on the porch, wrestling with each other behind Tito Micky, who seemed oblivious to the chaotic energy of his sons. Her uncle had changed, too. He had almost no hair left on his head, and he was skinnier, the sinewy muscles in his arms and legs all but gone from years of inactivity. His belly, in contrast, protruded firmly over his saggy green basketball shorts. An unlit cigarette dangled from his mouth, and he had a lighter in his hand.

Her grandmother was the only one who had not changed. Lola Celia's hair was dyed the same blue-black as before, and like the last time, she was dressed in sweatpants and a sweatshirt, even though it was summer. She lifted a bony hand in their direction. Joey knew her frail appearance was just an illusion. Within that small, aging body was a woman whose eyes missed nothing and whose tongue was as sharp as a straight razor.

After all, Ruby had gotten it from somewhere.

Introductions were made, and Tita Flora planted a perfunctory kiss on Joey's forehead before greeting Deborah with a too-wide smile that showed all her teeth. Her *lola* said hello in English, her beetle eyes crawling up and down her granddaughter's body as she stretched her hand out, palm facing down. Joey took it and bowed, pressing the back of Lola Celia's hand lightly to her forehead.

When she'd first met her *lola* a few years before, Joey had not known what the *mano* was. Her grandmother had ripped into Ruby in furious Cebuano, presumably for not teaching her young daughter how to greet her elders with respect. The only word Joey had understood from that verbal lashing was *puta*, which meant "whore." Lola Celia had screamed it at Ruby, not once, but twice. Later, on the drive back to Toronto, Ruby had been uncharacteristically quiet. *You have a bad mother,* she said to Joey in a resigned voice before turning on the radio, *because I had a bad mother.*

Tita Flora nudged her husband. Tito Micky stuck his unsmoked cigarette in his pocket and grabbed the suitcases. They all went inside.

"Mick, show Joey where her room is," her aunt said. To Joey, she said, "Your *lola* made adobo for dinner. I know that's your favorite."

Favorite sounded like *pay-bor-it*. Her aunt's Filipino accent had not softened much over the years. In contrast, Ruby's accent was nearly gone, because her mother had been determined to lose it. Occasionally it came back when she was talking (*yelling*) at Joey, but around other people (*boyfriends*) she almost sounded Canadian (which, for Ruby, meant *white*).

"Wow, so heavy," Tito Micky said as he dragged both suitcases toward the staircase. Heavy sounded like *hebbee*. "What you got in here, a dead body?"

The joke was in poor taste, and Deborah blinked. Tita Flora spoke sharply to her husband in their Filipino dialect, and his shoulders slumped. Joey only caught one word. *Buang.* It meant "stupid."

She followed her uncle up the stairs to the bedroom at the end of the hall. Joey looked around in dismay. While the window had a view of the pond, the room was no better than the sleeping situation at the foster home. Bunk beds were pushed up against one wall, and there was a thin twin mattress lying on the floor closest to the door. It was covered in a plain pink cotton sheet so new, it still had creases from the packaging.

"You'll be sharing the older boys' room." Tito Micky was wheezing slightly, the years of cigarettes and booze preparing him not at all for any sort of heavy lifting. Interestingly, his back injury—the reason he was able to collect disability—seemed fine. "Everything happened so fast we didn't get a chance yet to buy a bed."

"That's okay," Joey said.

Tita Flora appeared in the bedroom doorway with Deborah, who frowned.

"This is just temporary," her aunt explained. "Our youngest boy sleeps with my mother because he still needs help using the bathroom. But in a few months, Carson can sleep with his brothers in here, and we can move Joey's bed into her *lola's* room."

"What bed?" Deborah's tone was blunt. "All I see is a mattress, and Joelle *will* need a proper bed so she's not sleeping four inches from the floor. When we spoke on the phone, you assured me her room would be ready."

"It's ordered." Tita Flora looked at her husband. "From Sears. Right, Mick?"

It took Tito Micky a second to catch on. "Yes, it's coming soon." He was a terrible liar. "They're, ah, they're late with the delivery." *Dee-lib-or-ee.*

"So, Deborah." Tita Flora's smile was all teeth again. "When might we expect the first payment?"

The social worker had explained to Joey that her aunt and uncle were eligible for monthly kinship-care payments from the government, similar to foster-care payments. How much they'd receive, Joey didn't ask, but she knew the money was the only reason Tita Flora had agreed to this arrangement.

"About three weeks." Deborah's voice took on a flat note Joey hadn't heard before. "Which is around the time I'll be back here to check and see how things are going."

The warning was obvious, but her aunt merely nodded and directed Deborah back out to the hallway to check out the rest of the second floor.

Joey moved toward the window in the room she'd be sharing with her cousins, who were eight and six. Deborah was right. It was pretty here. Maybe everything would be fine. It had to be, because there was simply no option for it not to be. It was either here or foster care, especially if (*when*) her mother was convicted.

She felt a hand graze her lower back, and jolted.

Tito Micky had joined her at the window, his palm pressing lightly into the indent just above her tailbone. He smelled like tobacco and whiskey. She moved over a few inches, just enough for his hand to fall away, and he looked over at her with an innocent smile.

"I can't believe how big you are now, Joelle," he said. Believe sounded like *bee-leeb.* Maybe one day she'd stop hearing his accent, but for now, it sounded foreign, and obvious. "'*Sus.* You look so pretty."

Joey cringed at her uncle's use of her formal first name. When Deborah called her Joelle, it sounded grown-up, respectful. But when Tito Micky said it, giving equal weight to each syllable of her name as if they were two separate names (*Jo-Elle*), it made her skin crawl.

"You know your Tita Flora didn't want you here, because your mom has done something very bad." Tito Micky spoke softly, conspiratorially, as if they had a delightful secret just between the two of them. "But I told her, you're family. This is your home, okay? If you need anything, you just ask your Tito Micky."

Her uncle moved closer until their shoulders touched. His hand was back on the base of her spine, and she could feel his finger moving in slow, lazy circles. Tito Micky was no longer looking out the window, he was looking at her. He sighed, and his whiskey-tinged breath caressed Joey's cheek.

"*Sus*," he sighed. The word—which wasn't really a word, more like a syllable—was Filipino slang for "Jesus." "So pretty, Joelle."

He leaned closer and whispered into her ear.

"You look just like your mother."

CHAPTER NINETEEN

Deep in his overstuffed storage locker, somewhere between the artificial Christmas tree and his daughter's neglected ukulele, Drew finally finds the box he's looking for. It's filled with notebooks, scrapbooks, newspaper clippings, photos, hard drives, and memory sticks. Basically all the work he did during his fifteen years as an investigative journalist for *Toronto After Dark*.

Drew chased all kinds of stories for that Saturday weekly. He discovered that the homeless woman who earned thirty thousand a year in spare change was actually a grandmother with a car and a house in the suburbs. He exposed an eighteen-year-old pimp who insisted he never intended to get into the business of sex, he just happened to know a few girls at school who were willing to sleep with his friends for extra money, and so he took a fee for arranging the dates ("Like the Baby-Sitters Club," he told Drew earnestly. "Only without the babysitting.").

And at the height of his career, Drew published an award-winning series on the Asian street gangs that had ruled Chinatown back in the nineties, some of which are still in operation today. Which means that everything there was to know about them back then will be somewhere on one of these old hard drives. Drew takes his best guess, plugs one of them in, and begins searching. If he doesn't find what he's looking for here, he's got seven more.

Had it been up to him, he'd have stayed with *Toronto After Dark* until he retired. But like all the smaller newspapers, it had gone the way of the dinosaurs in the last few years. It shut down right as Sasha was sending out university applications, and while some of her tuition would be covered by the fund he and Kirsten had set up when she was born, the rest would have to come from Kirsten's parents, who'd already done so much. Drew took every freelance gig he could find, but it wasn't until the online piece he wrote about murdered billionaire couple Barry and Honey Sherman went viral that things took a turn for the better. He was invited to appear on CBC public radio to discuss it, and the interview was so popular, he was invited back several times to discuss other criminal cases.

And that's how *The Things We Do in the Dark* was born. At a time when it seemed like everybody and their dog had a podcast, nobody was more shocked than Drew when his show took off.

Bingo. He clicks on a folder and finds what he's looking for. Drew's notes, interviews, and rough drafts are all here, basically everything he worked on when he wrote his series about the Chinatown gangs. Within ten minutes, he has the name of someone who was thought to be a high-ranking member of the Blood Brothers. The guy, now solidly in middle age, lives in Oakville, a wealthy suburb west of Toronto. Google Maps shows his address as a large waterfront house on Lakeshore Road, a far cry from the dilapidated Chinatown apartment he used to share with his parents and younger brother back when they first came to Canada from Vietnam.

It takes a few phone calls, but the meeting is arranged. After a quick shower and shave, Drew is on his way to meet the man rumored to be responsible for importing half a billion dollars' worth of illegal narcotics into Canada in the nineties.

And that's just the stuff they know about.

* * *

The deeper Drew gets into Oakville, the bigger the houses get. Eventually he finds himself driving past properties ranging well into the millions. Out of curiosity, he asks Siri to look up the listing price of a house for sale that resembles a small château in the South of France. Siri tells him the asking price is $12,999,999. For fuck's sake, who are these real estate agents kidding? Just round it up to thirteen million.

The house next to it isn't on the market, but it is the one he's looking for. He pulls into the U-shaped driveway. Parking behind a Lamborghini and a Maserati, he stares up at the mansion in awe. Three stories high, stucco facade, four-stall garage, pristine views of the lake. Officially, Tuan Tranh—who goes by Tony—is a furniture manufacturer with a large factory in Vietnam. But sofas and bed frames might not be the only things moving in those shipping containers. Clearly, being in the illegal drug business pays.

Out of habit, Drew locks his car, although he can't imagine anyone will try to steal his eleven-year-old Audi when they could have a Lambo. He walks up to the front doors of the mansion and rings the bell, looking up into the camera mounted above. A moment later, the huge mahogany door opens. A small, wrinkled face peers out, dark eyes narrowing when she sees the tall Black man standing there.

"Yes?" she asks. The woman can't be more than four ten. She's wearing khaki pants and a loose green T-shirt, with well-worn shearling slippers on her feet.

"Hello, ma'am," Drew says. "I'm here to see Tony Tranh."

"He know you coming?" Soft Vietnamese accent, suspicious tone.

"We have a meeting, yes." He pulls out a business card and offers it to her. "Drew Malcolm."

"You wait here." She plucks the card from his fingers and closes the door. Drew hears it lock.

While he waits, he looks at the houses across the street on the other side of Lakeshore Road. They're not waterfront, which decreases their value significantly, but some of them are just as big. Somewhere on the other end of Oakville, farther away from the lake, Simone's parents live in a small townhouse. Mr. and Mrs. Bailey always did like him. Maybe he should drop by for a visit, catch up, find out whether Simone married the dude she cheated on him with, since she doesn't have any social media accounts.

Yeah, hard pass.

The door opens again. "Come inside," the tiny woman says, and Drew steps through the door.

His entire two-bedroom-plus-den condo could fit in this entryway alone. The ceilings are probably eighteen feet high, and there's a clear view from the foyer straight through to the back of the house, which is completely walled in glass. The view of Lake Ontario should have been unobstructed, except that right in the center of the foyer is a nine-foot marble statue of a voluptuous, naked woman with long, wavy hair and nipples the size of grapes. The statue is awesome, gaudy, and completely distracting.

The small woman waits patiently as he takes it all in, as if it's normal for everybody to gawk at the house, the lake, and the statue when they first get here. Which they probably do, in that order.

"No shoes." She looks down at Drew's feet, which are encased in clean white Nikes. Using her pinky finger, she points to a large wicker basket by the door. It's filled with slippers. All styles, all colors, all in various states of wear. "You want wear slippers?"

"I'm sure he doesn't," a tall blond woman says as she comes around the corner. She's wearing slippers, too, but hers are furry and bright blue. "And if he did, I'm sure we don't have anything in his size. *Cảm ơn.*"

The older woman nods and leaves.

"Lauren Tranh." The blonde stretches a languid hand out toward Drew. "Tony's wife. You must be Drew. He's just finishing up a call in his office."

Mrs. Tranh is white, at least five ten, and stunning. She looks vaguely familiar. Former actress or model? Reality star? If there ever comes a day when Bravo decides to introduce a *Real Housewives of Oakville* to their franchise, Lauren Tranh will be a shoo-in.

He shakes her hand. "Should I remove my shoes?"

"Yes, please."

He takes them off and places them neatly by the door. When he stands and turns around again, she has a small smile on her face.

"What is it?" He returns the smile.

"It's just nice to have someone in the house taller than me," she says, amused. "Doesn't happen often."

She's standing right beside the marble statue, and it hits him where he's seen her. Same hair, same lips, same—

He swallows. The naked statue is of her. *Damn.*

It's exactly what she wanted him to see, and, satisfied, she leads him down the hallway.

* * *

Tranh's office is at the back corner of the house, and like everything else, it's enormous. He's still on the phone when Drew is led in, but he smiles and gestures for his guest to sit. Drew points to the bookcases covering the entire side wall, and Tranh nods again, mouthing *go ahead* in English before continuing his conversation in Vietnamese.

The built-in bookshelves are so tall, they require their own ladder. Tranh's collection is impressive. Drew finds everything from a first edition of *Little Women* to a signed hardcover of *The Shining*. While he doesn't really envy Tranh his house, his lake view, his cars, or even his wife, he does feel a stab of jealousy over these bookcases.

If only he were the head of a violent gang that killed people and got kids hooked on drugs, he'd be rich, too.

"See any you like?"

Tony Tranh is off the phone and standing right beside him. They shake hands, and though Tranh is nearly a foot shorter than Drew, he doesn't seem the least bit intimidated. A trim man in his early fifties, he's wearing a perfectly tailored black button-down, pressed chinos, and leather Gucci slides. Drew feels a bit lame in his cheap white athletic socks from Costco. Twelve bucks for a pack of eight.

"All of them," Drew replies with a smile. "Your collection is impressive, as is your home."

The answer pleases Tranh. He gestures to the chairs facing the windows and the lake, and they both sit.

"So you mentioned to my assistant that you host a true crime podcast." Though he was born in Saigon and didn't immigrate to Canada until he was sixteen, Tranh speaks with no accent at all. "I listened to your inaugural episode about the billionaire murders. So fascinating. How many listeners do you have?"

"About three million per episode."

"And what does that pay?"

Very direct. "Not as much as I'd like." Drew keeps his tone light. "But enough to eat and pay my mortgage."

"Hmmm," Tranh says. "So it's more like a monetized hobby, then?"

Drew stiffens but doesn't reply. It's not the first time he's heard it.

"You have a master's in journalism, right? And then you worked at *Toronto After Dark* for fifteen years, until it folded?"

Uh-oh. "Yes, I did."

Tranh nods. "You did a series on all the Chinatown gangs. It was an interesting read. I knew some of those boys when I still lived in that area. You seemed to have a lot of inside information. Who gave it to you?"

Drew smiles. "I never reveal my sources."

"What if I paid you a hundred grand? Cash? Right now?"

Surprised, Drew laughs. That was a first. "Tempting. But still, I can't."

"That's too bad." Tranh's eyes fix on Drew's. "I would have liked to know who talked to you."

"So is this your way of confirming that you're part of the Blood Brothers, one of the gangs I wrote about?"

It's Tranh's turn to smile. When he does, he looks like a teenager. "The BB weren't a gang. More like, you know . . . a monetized hobby."

Drew can't help but laugh.

There's a knock on the office door, and the same tiny woman from earlier brings in a tray. She sets down a pot of green tea, two teacups, and a plate of brown cookies.

"This is my mother," Tranh says. "She makes the best cinnamon-sugar cookies, an old family recipe. Try one."

Drew is not a cookie person and has never had much of a sweet tooth. But both the old woman and Tranh are looking at him expectantly, so he takes a cookie and bites into it.

"Delicious," he says, and means it.

"*Cảm ơn,*" she says with a smile, then leaves.

Tranh pours them both tea and settles back into his chair. "So. If I understand correctly, you're here to talk to me about someone *I* might know, who dated a woman that was friends with someone *you* used to know. Do I have that right?"

"I know that's vague—"

"Exceptionally."

"A good friend of mine died in a house fire a long time ago," Drew says. "Her name was Joey. The fire was supposedly accidental, but there are a few things I've learned recently that suggest it might not have been an accident at all. But the woman who might know more about it has been missing for nearly twenty years. And this missing woman might have dated someone you know."

"What's her name?"

"That, I don't know. She was a dancer at a strip club called the Golden Cherry. Her stage name was Betty Savage, and her boyfriend was someone in the Blood Brothers."

If any of this is ringing a bell for Tranh, he's not letting on. "And you need me to do what, exactly?"

"I'm hoping you'll tell me who *he* is, so I can figure out who Betty Savage is, so I can find out where she is, and talk to her."

A small smile. "Do you have a photo of this Betty Savage?"

Drew pulls out his phone. He taps on the photo he sent to Sergeant McKinley earlier, and enlarges it so only Betty is showing on the screen. He hands Tranh his phone.

Tranh examines it closely. "Oh yes. I remember her. That's Mae. I don't recall if I ever knew her last name, but I did meet her a few times."

Jackpot. "So she was dating someone in the Blood Brothers?"

Tranh hands the phone back. "She was my brother's girlfriend."

Oh. *Shit.*

This is not what Drew expected to hear. Of course he was familiar with Tranh's younger brother, Vinh—who went by Vinny—as he was thought to have been involved in the nightclub shooting in Chinatown. A year after that, he was shot and killed, supposedly over a drug deal gone bad.

Which, thinking back to his research notes now, wasn't very long after Betty—*Mae*—went missing. It might have been less than a week after the fire. And though it was never proven, the bullet was rumored to have come from a member of his own gang. Someone had ordered a hit on Vinny. And only someone high up could do that.

Someone like his brother, Tony Tranh. Who's now watching Drew with eyes that seem to know exactly where Drew's mind just went.

"I'm sorry," Drew says. "I understand Vinny died years ago. If I had thought he might be Betty's—Mae's—boyfriend, I would never have come here. I apologize if I've brought up a painful memory."

"Thank you," Tranh says. "It was a shame to lose him so young. He was only twenty-three. It was very hard on our mother."

Drew hesitates, unsure if he should ask his next question.

"Go ahead," Tranh says, sipping his tea. "Say what's on your mind."

"Betty—Mae—went missing around New Year's Eve 1998. I realize it was a long time ago, but do you have any idea where she might have gone?"

Tranh frowns again. "Why would I know anything? She was Vinny's girlfriend, not mine."

"Apparently, she just stopped showing up for work. And her boyfriend—which I now know is your brother—was concerned enough to go to her club looking for her. Vinny never mentioned anything to you about this back then? About his girlfriend disappearing? I mean, that's kind of a . . . big thing."

"Oh, he mentioned it. He was actually quite distraught about it. As was I." Tranh uncrosses his legs, then recrosses them the other way. "But then he was murdered on January fifth, 1999. If he did tell me anything about his missing girlfriend, it likely slipped my mind as I was comforting our mother and planning his funeral."

"I'm sorry," Drew says again.

Tranh sips his tea. Outwardly, he seems relaxed, but Drew's gut is telling him that the other man is far from it. "You're probably well aware that Vinny had a reputation for violence. We had a rough childhood, but we turned out very differently, much to our mother's dismay."

Drew doesn't buy it. The only difference between Tony Tranh and Vinny Tranh was that the older brother was smarter and possessed more self-control. Which, in the end, made him much more dangerous than Vinny ever was.

"As tragic as it is, my brother got himself killed because he was stupid." Tranh seems more annoyed than sad. "He was very impulsive. As was Mae. I wasn't surprised she disappeared. She had no family, and Vinny told me she grew up in the system. He wasn't always kind to her, but then again, Mae was bad news."

It's exactly how Cherry described her.

"In what way?" Drew asks.

"She was a thief." Tranh's eyes are cold. "I didn't like her from the beginning. I sensed she was trouble, and that's exactly what she turned out to be. She and Vinny had a very passionate relationship—and not always in a good way. It was causing him to become unreliable, which wasn't good for business."

"What did Mae steal?"

"Does it matter?" Tranh offers him a cold smile. "It wasn't hers to take."

It's not much of an answer. There are some people Drew can push, but Tony Tranh is not one of them.

"Thank you, Mr. Tranh." Drew places his teacup on the table and stands up. "I appreciate your time."

"That's it?"

"That's it."

Tranh escorts him back to the front door and they shake hands again. As Drew is putting on his shoes, Tranh's mother rushes toward him with a plastic container. It's full of cinnamon cookies.

"You take home," she says. "For your family."

"She likes you," Tranh says with a grin. "And you should know my mother doesn't like anyone. She hated Mae."

Tony Tranh lowers his voice. He speaks so quietly that Drew has to lean down slightly to hear him.

"And if you ever find her, let her know I'd like back what she took from me."

CHAPTER TWENTY

Drew opts to take Lakeshore Road all the way back to Toronto from Oakville, as traffic at this time of day has the highway jammed. It's a slow but easy drive, giving him time to sort through his thoughts.

Occam's razor: The simplest explanation is usually the right one.

Okay, fine, so he only knows this because of the movie *Contact*, starring Jodie Foster. It was one of his and Joey's favorites, and they would find any excuse to work the line into a conversation. It drove Simone nuts.

Drew: I can't find my wallet, I think someone stole it.
Joey: Did you check the jeans you were wearing yesterday?
Drew: Found it!
Joey: The simplest explanation is usually the right one.
Simone: Oh my God, would the two of you shut the fuck up?

A good chunk of people who are considered "missing" are either dead or don't want to be found. If Mae is still alive, then whatever she stole from Vinny and the Blood Brothers—Drew is guessing drugs—is the reason she can never come back.

The thing is, though, it's not that easy to disappear. You can't just go someplace new and get a job and rent a house and start over. First, you'd need a new name, which requires new ID, which takes time to procure.

You'd have to keep your story straight for anybody new that you meet. And you'd need start-up money. In cash. A lot of it. To assume a whole new identity and build a whole new life takes time, commitment, and an exceptional talent for telling lies.

Occam's razor. The simplest explanation, the one that makes the most sense, is that Mae is dead. Vinny killed her, and then Vinny got killed, because that's what gangs like his do. Live by the sword, die by the sword, and all that.

But did Vinny murder Joey, too? If Drew is being logical about it, the answer is probably no. The fire in the basement apartment was ruled an accident all those years ago, and there was never anything back then— nor is there now—to suggest otherwise.

Drew needs to accept that maybe he wants the fire to *not* have been an accident so there's someone to blame for Joey's death, other than himself.

He sighs into the silence of the car. It would have been nice to have a conversation with Betty Savage, one of the few people Joey let herself get close to during the last year of her life, the year Drew wasn't a part of. There are probably a thousand things Mae could have told him about Joey, like how she decided to become a stripper, and why, out of all the names in the world, she would choose to call herself *Ruby*.

Joey used to call her mother Ruby. Literally. She hardly ever referred to her as "Mom" or "Mother." Drew can still remember asking her about it, because the conversation it led to was the last one they ever had while they were still living together. Simone was taking the job in Vancouver whether Drew was coming or not, and he had not yet decided.

"Why do you call your mother by her first name?" he'd asked Joey.

It was just the two of them in their usual spots on the sofa, eating junk food in front of the TV while Simone worked a dinner shift at The Keg. They were watching *Showgirls*, which was arguably the worst movie in the history of cinema, but he and Joey loved it precisely because it was terrible. The two of them would compete to see who could remember the best worst lines.

Zack: Nice dress.
Nomi: It's a Ver-SAYSE.

Al: You're a fucking stripper, don't you get it?
Nomi: I'm a DANCER!

"Do I call her Ruby?" Joey seemed surprised, and then she grew thoughtful. "Yeah, you're right, I guess I do. That's weird, right? You don't think of your mother as Brenda, do you?"

"No, because my mom's name is Belinda," Drew said, and they shared a laugh. "I don't know if it's weird. After everything she put you through, thinking of her as Ruby instead of 'Mom' probably gives you some emotional distance."

"The night she was arrested, I was worried about her," Joey said. "She was on a rampage, ripping photos off the wall, breaking plates, threatening to jump off the balcony. She'd been a paranoid mess ever since Charles's body was discovered, and I was scared she'd actually hurt herself. But when the cops showed up, they took one look at me and arrested her on the spot. Which was ironic, because she'd only hit me a few times that night."

Only. That night. "You looked that bad?"

She shrugged. "Bloody lip, black eye, the usual. But later, at the hospital, they did a more thorough examination. I guess they didn't like what they found."

From her file, Drew knows now that the hospital discovered bruises on Joey's buttocks, back, and inner thighs. X-rays showed that her ribs had been broken twice in the past, along with her wrist. There were old cigarette burns on her upper arms and one just above her collarbone. Some of the injuries were recent. Some had been there a very long time.

And the hospital discovered other things, too.

"If I hadn't given the social worker my diaries, the police would never have known what Ruby did to Charles," Joey said. "She might have gotten away with it."

When the cops came to question Ruby about Charles Baxter's murder the first time, Ruby had given them an alibi. She was with her daughter, she said. They'd gone out to a movie that Saturday night, and she could prove it because Joey still had the ticket stubs in the pocket of the shorts she had worn.

But Joey's diary told a different story. They never made it to the movie. They went to Charles's house, where, at some point in the night, Ruby and Charles had argued, and Ruby stabbed him. Her bloody dress was found in a trash bag in the large bin behind their apartment building, along with the murder weapon. Sorry, murder *weapons*. Both of them. Ruby had tasked her thirteen-year-old daughter with disposing of the evidence, and Joey didn't know where else to put it.

During opening statements, the crown attorney told the jury that Charles Baxter was stabbed multiple times with a kitchen knife. Based on the haphazard entry points all over his torso—sixteen of them in total— the crown argued it was done in a rage by a woman the same height as Ruby. Miraculously, no major arteries were hit. Later, the medical examiner testified that if Ruby had stopped there, and if Baxter had received emergency treatment, he likely would have lived. The charge could have been aggravated assault. Maybe even self-defense, if her lawyer was savvy.

But it had not stopped there. While Charles lay bleeding on his bedroom floor, Ruby walked down the hall to his daughter's room. She removed one of Lexi Baxter's ice skates from the closet and brought it back with her into the master bedroom, where she took a seat on the chair in the corner. Ruby put the skate on, *laced it up*, and then stomped on her lover's neck.

Boom. First-degree murder.

Charles Baxter was nearly decapitated. And that's why Ruby Reyes was called the Ice Queen.

"People always assumed Ruby was cold," Joey said. "But she was the opposite. She was hot-tempered. She could scald you." She fingered her pendant absently. "But sometimes, she could be warm. On her good days, she was sunshine, and there was nowhere else I ever wanted to be."

"Do you still love her?" Drew asked. "After everything?"

"She's my mother," Joey said simply. "Everything I feel for her is intense, and I feel it all at once. Intense love, intense fear, intense hate. They all swirl together, like . . . I don't know, like melted Neapolitan ice cream. The flavors are impossible to separate."

"It's okay to feel different things at once."

She smiled. "You should be a psychologist."

"Thought about it," Drew said. "What about you? What did you want to be when you grew up?"

"I never expected to grow up."

Drew kissed her then. He didn't think about it, he just leaned over and kissed her. Her lips were salty from the potato chips they were eating, her breath sweet from the orange Fanta they were drinking. She kissed him back, and it felt right, and good, and he couldn't remember the last time he kissed someone he cared about so much. He loved Simone, but with Joey, it felt like his feelings were on an entirely different level. It was terrifying, and wrong, and amazing, and right.

He cupped her face, his tongue finding hers, and she pressed herself against him, pulling him closer. His lips moved to her cheek, and then her throat, and then back to her lips again as his hand slipped under her T-shirt, his fingers caressing her bare skin. She made a little sound when his hand found her breast, somewhere between a soft moan and a gasp, and his other hand slipped into the waistband of her sweatpants. He had never wanted anyone so much in his life. He lifted her onto his lap, and she straddled him as he lifted up the hem of her shirt.

And then suddenly, Joey pulled away.

"I can't," she gasped. She sprang off his lap and fell onto the sofa cushion beside him. When he tried to move closer to her again, she stuck her arm out, blocking him. "I can't. You only want me because you think you can fix me, Drew. But you can't. I can't be fixed."

"That's not true—"

"I'm broken," Joey said. "I'm no good to you. I'm no good to anyone."

Being the stupid, selfish tool he was back then, all Drew could hear was that he was being rejected. The next day, when Simone asked him if he'd made his decision, he told her he would go with her to Vancouver.

It was the wrong decision even before Simone cheated on him.

* * *

Drew's phone rings, snapping him out of the memories. It's Sergeant McKinley. He hits accept, and the call connects through the car's Bluetooth.

"Hallo, Drew Malcolm," McKinley says. "Is this a good time?"

"It's the perfect time," he says. "I was just going to call you—"

"Hang on, let me go first." She sounds excited, buoyant, and he can hear her shuffling papers. "You'll be pleased to know that I finally figured out the full name of Joelle's friend. The licensing office emailed me a list of the four hundred entertainer's licenses that were issued in 1998. Let me tell you, that was a lot to sort through, but by approximating her age and restricting her home address to a twenty-kilometer radius around the Golden Cherry, it turns out there were only thirteen licenses issued that year to women performers."

"Actually, I—"

"Not finished yet. So then I looked them all up in our database and found one that looks just like our Betty Savage. Her name is Mae Ocampo, and it turns out she has a record. The earlier arrests are for shoplifting and public intoxication at a concert—that one actually sounds grossly unfair—and she had one minor drug arrest. But two of the arrests were for assault. The first was dismissed because apparently the other girl started it, but the last one, she broke the girl's nose *and* arm. She did three months in jail, which means it wasn't just her boyfriend who was violent. Mae was, too."

"I'm glad you—"

"Still not done. Her last known address was an apartment near Humber College, which she shared with two roommates. I tracked them down, and both confirmed that the last time they saw Mae was a couple of days before New Year's Eve. They didn't file a missing persons report because Mae often disappeared for chunks at a time without telling them; the word they used was 'flaky.' So now all that's left to do is track her down. She's out there somewhere, I can feel it."

McKinley is so revved up, Drew doesn't have the heart to tell her that he's a step ahead of her. But Mae serving time for assault is something new, and neither Cherry nor Tony Tranh had mentioned it. Cherry likely didn't know. Tranh likely didn't care.

He feels that damned tingle again. What if it was *Mae* who killed Joey? He mentally slaps himself. *Stop it.* No more dumb theories.

"I appreciate all this," Drew says. "But after having a bit of time to think it over, I think we should let it go. I don't think we should look for her."

"Wait. What?" McKinley sounds dumbfounded. "Why not?"

Drew chooses his words carefully. He can't tell the sergeant his theory that Vinny killed Mae and that Tony Tranh killed his own brother. McKinley is a homicide detective, after all, and he can't be sure what she'll do with that information. And like Cherry said the other day, the last thing he needs is a target on his back.

"Whatever happened back then, Mae probably had no choice but to run," Drew says. "She was involved with a dangerous guy, who was involved with dangerous people. Wherever she is now, I think it's best to leave her there. For her own safety."

"I worked on this for almost two hours." McKinley doesn't sound happy.

"I'm sorry," Drew says, and he means it. "I didn't mean to drag you down the rabbit hole with me. Ruby Reyes's parole is messing with my head. It feels like . . ." He pauses, searching for the words. "I feel like I'm grieving Joey all over again. I'm having a hard time letting her go. Maybe once this podcast is finished, I'll finally be able to . . ." *Forgive myself*, he says in his head, but he can't say it out loud, because it's too hard. "To move on," he says instead.

"I'm sorry, mate." The detective's voice is full of compassion. "I can imagine that Ruby Reyes being released would trigger all kinds of feelings. One of the things I learned early on is that if we want something to be true badly enough, we'll find all the proof in the world that it is. Same if we don't want something to be true. From everything I've read, Ruby Reyes is a monster, and it's absolute shit that she's getting out. You can spend the rest of your life trying to make sense of why she gets a second chance at life while her daughter—your friend—is dead, but it may never make sense. Learning to live with it doesn't mean you're betraying Joelle."

Even though he's alone in his car, Drew nods.

"So this is my unsolicited advice," McKinley says. "Do your podcast. Give a voice to Joelle, and rip the Ice Queen to shreds so people will never forget who she is. But be kind to yourself, too. Whatever guilt you're holding on to, it's okay to forgive yourself and let it go. I'm sure Joelle would want you to move on."

Drew doesn't know if he can do that. "Great advice. Thank you, ma'am."

"'Ma'am'?" McKinley says, sounding indignant. "I looked you up, and I'm only six years older than you, you tosser."

He swears he can hear the smile in her voice before the line disconnects.

The sergeant is right, Drew knows that. On some level, he understands that he's trying to make it up to Joey somehow, as if righting a wrong today will somehow make up for the mother she had, and the life she lived.

Joey's diaries stopped once her mother's trial began. But in the last few entries, which Joey wrote in vivid detail, was the voice of a girl who had learned to accept that her life would always be shitty, because nobody ever told her she deserved better.

CHAPTER TWENTY-ONE

Joey was still sleeping on a mattress on the floor when Deborah Jackson came for her second visit. The social worker was not happy, and she spoke sternly to Joey's aunt and uncle in the kitchen while Joey lingered (*eavesdropped*) in the living room.

"I'll make it easy for you," she heard Deborah say. "I'll order the bed, and we'll deduct the amount from your next payment. I passed a very nice furniture store in town that does next-day delivery."

Tita Flora and Tito Micky talked to each other in Cebuano in hushed voices, and then Joey heard her aunt say, "There's a sale at Sears. Mick will go now and buy something."

"Great," Deborah said. "I'll stick around and see what he brings back. In the meantime, I'd like to take Joelle out for lunch."

Twenty minutes later, Joey was plucking the pickles out of her Quarter Pounder as they sat in the only McDonald's in Maple Sound.

"I'd like to talk to you about the upcoming hearing in family court next week," Deborah said. "Most of what the judge needs to know will be presented through your medical exam, and testimony from other witnesses. You don't have to be there, but I would like to ask your permission to read out passages from your diaries. Would that be all right?"

Joey shrugged.

"I understand you love your mother very much, Joelle." Deborah's voice was soft. "And I know this is painful, and confusing. I'm honored that you trusted me with your diaries, because I know trust doesn't come easy for you. But once I read them, I was obligated to keep you safe. I have a feeling that's why you let me take them."

Joey could feel her face about to crumple, so she stuffed her mouth with french fries.

"Now, as you know, your mother's murder trial is separate from the child abuse hearing." Deborah speaks gently. "Your mother has requested a speedy trial, so the judge has set a date for the fall."

"Will I have to testify?"

"Yes."

"Will my mom be there when I do?"

"Yes. And so will I. But you'll be well prepared. In the next few weeks, you'll have to come back to Toronto to meet with the crown attorney—the prosecutor who's trying your mother's case—so she can go over all the questions you'll be asked."

"How will I know what to say?"

"All you have to say is the truth," Deborah said. "*Your* truth. She'll just help you practice the best way to say it."

They sat in silence for a moment as Joey sipped her chocolate milkshake and pondered the difference between *truth* and *your truth*. The truth was that Ruby had stabbed Charles repeatedly. Joey had heard them arguing, because she'd been staying in his daughter's bedroom down the hall.

But Joey's truth was that she was glad Charles was dead.

"Also, Joelle . . . your mother would like to see you." Deborah looked at her closely. "You can say no. It's totally up to you."

"I'll see her." As soon as she said the words, she felt her heart swell with happiness, and then shrink with fear. "I need to talk to her." *I have to tell her I'm sorry.*

"I'll arrange it," Deborah said. "Hey, I saw a cute little bookstore on Main Street. When we're finished here, let's check it out before we head back."

The trip to the bookstore was exactly what Joey needed, and for the first time since she arrived in Maple Sound, she felt a spark of joy. The store was having a two-for-ten-bucks sale on mass market paperbacks, and Deborah told her to pick anything she wanted. Joey selected *IT* by Stephen

King and *A Time to Kill* by John Grisham. She had never read either author before, but they were the fattest books on the rack, which meant hours of reading time and escape.

When they got back to the house, Joey's new bed was upstairs, already assembled. It wasn't really an improvement, as the headboard and frame made the room feel smaller than it already was, but Deborah seemed pleased.

It was time for the social worker to head back to the city, and just like the last time, there was a knot in Joey's stomach at the thought of saying goodbye. As she walked Deborah back out to her car, she wondered, and not for the first time, what her life would be like if Deborah were her mother. The social worker probably lived in a cozy house, maybe with her husband, whose name was . . . Ben. And maybe Joey would have a little sister and little brother to play with, whose names were . . . Stephanie and Michael. Maybe there was even a family dog, one of those roly-poly ones with a snuffly nose whose name was . . . Gracie. There would be laughter. Warmth. Affection. She would feel safe. She would belong.

I wish I was your kid.

"Where did you go just now?" Deborah asked gently, as they stood beside her Honda.

Home with you.

"Nowhere," Joey said. She desperately wanted a hug, but didn't know how to ask.

The social worker made the decision for her, wrapping her arms around Joey tightly. "Hide these," Deborah whispered, placing a plastic bag in Joey's hand. Inside were four packs of Starburst candies. "Put them in your special place."

Joey did have a special place, in the back corner of the closet she shared with the boys. Using a mini hacksaw she found in Tito Micky's toolshed, she pried up the carpet and cut open the floorboard. So far, there wasn't much inside. Her candy stash. Her necklace. And a box cutter, which she'd also pilfered from her uncle's shed. During the day, the box cutter stayed in her hiding spot. But before bed each night, she'd take it out from under the floorboard and slide it between the wall and the mattress.

Now she could hide the box cutter between the mattress and the new bed frame, where she could reach for it quickly, should Tito Micky ever decide to come into the bedroom in the middle of the night.

So far, all he did was stand in the doorway and watch her sleep.

* * *

In the late summer days leading up to both the trial and the start of school, Joey was beginning to realize that her opinion of Maple Sound had largely been crafted by her *mother's* opinion of Maple Sound. While her aunt and grandmother never went out of their way to be nice to her, at least they fed her.

For the first time in Joey's life, she wasn't hungry.

There was always food. Nobody ever forgot to buy groceries. Someone was home every single day to cook. More often than not, Joey awoke to the smells of Lola Celia making breakfast in the kitchen. *Longanisa* had become her favorite, and her grandmother fried the small, fat Filipino sausages at least twice a week. Joey had gained ten pounds since she arrived in Maple Sound.

"*Mangaon na ta,*" Lola Celia would say to everyone when the food was ready. *Let's eat.* She said this three times a day.

But what Joey gained in food, she lost in sleep.

Because her bed was right by the door, she could tell who was coming down the hallway by the sound of their footsteps. A light shuffle was Lola Celia, who was always up by six. A quick, even gait was Tita Flora, who was either leaving early or coming home late. Staccato steps were Carson going to the bathroom.

And the slow, careful walk was Tito Micky. The footsteps would always stop at the bedroom doorway, and there'd be a soft *swoosh* as the door rubbed against the carpet when he opened it, just a few inches.

After a minute or two, the door would close and the footsteps would retreat. And then it would take Joey a long time to fall asleep.

During the day, there were accidental grazes. His thigh resting against Joey's when he sat down on the couch next to her. His shoulder rubbing hers as they passed in the hallway. It was never anything concrete, nothing she could *accuse* him of, but she tried to avoid him as much as possible.

Since Tito Micky preferred to stay indoors most of the day, the best place to be was outside. And if she needed a break from the boys, too, then her only option was to hang by the pond, since her cousins were forbidden to go near it. Any time they did, Tita Flora would shriek, *Get away from there it's slippery and the water is deep in the middle!*

A week before the trial was to begin, Joey was sitting in a folding chair by the pond's edge, immersed in her new Stephen King book, when she heard a small splash. The sound yanked her out of Derry, the book's fictional town, and she looked up to see the two older boys pulling the youngest one out of the water. Alarmed, Joey stood up so fast that she knocked her chair over. But then she saw Carson was already out of the water, and fine. He was soaked from the neck down and laughing, while Tyson tried to keep him quiet. Jason, the oldest, caught Joey looking over. He put a finger to his mouth. *Shhhh.*

Joey nodded. They would all be in trouble if anyone had seen this, but Tita Flora was at the hospital, Tito Micky had gone into town, and Lola Celia had fallen asleep watching her soaps in front of the TV.

Except their grandmother wasn't asleep. The front door banged open, and the old woman came outside. She bellowed at the boys in Cebuano, her voice a blend of anger and fear. Joey heard Jason say, "We told him not to, but he was trying to catch a frog."

"*Ha-in ma's Joey?*" she heard her grandmother snap.

All three boys pointed across the pond, and Lola Celia gestured for her to come over. Joey braced herself for the verbal beating she was sure to get. But then again, how bad could it be if she couldn't understand most of what her *lola* was saying?

But Lola Celia didn't yell at her. As soon as Joey got close enough, her grandmother stepped forward and smacked her across the face so hard and so fast, she saw stars.

"*Tanga,*" the old woman spat.

The boys gasped at the sight of the slap and the sound that it made. The two younger ones cringed into their older brother, whose eight-year-old mouth dropped open in stunned horror. It was obvious they'd never been slapped before, or even witnessed someone being slapped. As Joey put her hand to her face, feeling the heat blossom on her cheek from Lola

Celia's small, steel hand, she actually felt a little sorry for her cousins, that they had to see it, and that they were scared.

"*Wa'y kapuslanan.*" Lola Celia's tone was calmer now, as if she was stating an indisputable fact.

Joey had picked up more Cebuano words since she'd been here, but these ones, she knew from living with her mother. *Tanga* meant "idiot." *Wa'y kapuslanan* meant "useless."

I had a bad mother, too, Ruby's voice whispered in her ear.

Yes, Mama. You did.

* * *

Two days before her mother's trial was to begin, Tito Micky and Tita Flora drove Joey down to Toronto, while the boys stayed home with Lola Celia. Her aunt and uncle had planned for the trip like it was a mini vacation. They made lunch and shopping plans, and let friends know they'd be back in the city. The drive went quickly, because they were in a great mood.

Joey was a nervous wreck.

After checking into the hotel, her aunt and uncle took her to meet Deborah, who would then bring Joey to visit her mother. Joey was anxious. She had not seen Ruby since the night of the arrest two months earlier. Tita Flora had zero desire to see her sister. When Joey asked if she wanted to come, her aunt said, "Next time," as if there would actually be a next time, as if it was a dinner invitation, and not a jail visit.

Joey chose McDonald's again, but there was no burger for Deborah today. She was trying to lose a few pounds, she said, so she ordered a salad instead, which she ate like it was a chore.

"I got a funny feeling when I talked to you last," Deborah said, swallowing a mouthful of iceberg lettuce. "Is everything going okay at your aunt and uncle's house?"

Tito Micky's midnight shadow flickered through Joey's mind, followed by the sting of Lola Celia's slap. "Everything's fine."

"All right, I'm just going to ask." Deborah stuck her fork into her salad and set her hands in her lap. She looked right into Joey's eyes. "Joelle, has your uncle ever made you uncomfortable?"

Joey looked down at her burger, trying to think of what she could say to make Deborah believe everything was okay, even though it wasn't. *Go ahead, tell her. You think you'd be better off in foster care? Nobody takes in other people's kids unless they're perverts.*

"I mean, it's a little weird living with a man," Joey said. "My mom's boyfriends never lived with us."

"I understand." Deborah nodded, seeming relieved by her answer. "Give it time."

Joey took a deep breath. What she was about to ask, she had rehearsed the night before, shifting the words around in her head until they sounded just right. "Deborah, can a kid choose who they want to live with?"

"Well, that depends. If you had other family—"

"I don't have any other family," Joey said. "I just . . . I wondered if you'd ever taken a kid like me in. I mean, because you'd get paid to do it, right? I wouldn't be annoying or in the way, I promise."

"Oh, honey." Deborah reached forward and grasped Joey's fingers. "I wish it were that simple. I'm a social worker, not a foster parent, and those are two very different things. But I'm always here to help you, okay? If at any time you think you would be safer in a different place, I want you to tell me."

"It's fine." Joey forced a smile. "It was a dumb idea anyway."

"It was not a dumb idea. I'm flattered. Anyone would be lucky to have a kid like you around." Deborah resumed eating her salad. "By the way, you look wonderful. Healthy. You've grown since I saw you last."

What Deborah didn't say was that Joey was getting boobs. There was no way the social worker didn't notice. It felt like everyone was noticing. Especially Tito Micky.

Joey always thought it would be great when she finally got boobs; her mother certainly seemed to be in love with hers, treating them like an asset meant to be showcased and displayed at all times. But Joey's were growing, so they hurt. And she was self-conscious. She'd tried to ask Tita Flora to buy her a bra, but her aunt just laughed.

"For those mosquito bites?" Tita Flora had said. "Enjoy them while they're small. When you're older, you're going to hate wearing a bra."

"Um, Deborah?" Joey said in a small voice. "Do you think maybe next time, when I come back for the trial, we could go shopping for a . . . a bra?" She knew her face was red; she could feel it.

The social worker didn't laugh. Instead, she checked her watch. "If you can finish that burger in five minutes, we can go now. And I know just the right bra, because I bought one for my daughter last week. But for you, we'll buy two. One to wear, one to wash."

It was the first time she'd ever mentioned having children, and it felt like a gut punch. Deborah had a *daughter*.

As Joey finished her burger, she could only think of one other time she'd felt this kind of jealousy. She was in grade 2, and Nicole Bowie had brought her Garfield to school. The stuffed cat had perfect orange and black fur, and large plastic eyes that looked bored and unimpressed, just like Garfield did in the comics. Nicole let Joey play with it for five minutes at recess, and by the time she asked for it back, Joey was in love.

She had never wanted anything as badly as she wanted that Garfield. She finally asked her mother for one for Christmas, but Ruby said there might not be any Christmas presents that year.

"Toys cost money," her mother said. "Wrapping paper costs money. Tape costs money. Christmas is expensive, Joey."

So she did the only other thing she could do. She wrote a letter to Santa Claus.

Three weeks later, Joey woke up on Christmas morning to find a cat-size box under the tree. There were a few other presents, too, but the tag on this one said TO JOEY, LOVE SANTA. Squealing with excitement, she tore the paper off while Ruby smiled the entire time. Under the paper was a box with a clear plastic window, and the name across the top said CHESTERFIELD.

Chesterfield?

Joey pulled it out of the box. It was definitely a stuffed cat, but its fur wasn't orange and black, it was gray and brown. The plastic eyes weren't white with huge black pupils, they were green. And in the middle of its tummy, there was a button that said PRESS ME. When she pressed, a cheerful voice said, "*Hi, I'm Chesterfield. What's your name?*"

This wasn't Garfield. This was some cheap imitation cat. It wasn't even from Santa, because the clearance sticker from Zellers was still on the box. This dumb cat was so unpopular, the store had to reduce the price *twice* just to get rid of it.

"It's not Garfield!" Joey cried, unable to help herself. "And it's stupid!"

Her mother's face changed. Joey shrank, certain she was going to get a punch—or three. But Ruby simply stood and headed down the hallway to her bedroom, where she shut the door. A minute later, Joey heard her mother sobbing.

Her mother *never* cried, and the sound scared her more than thinking Ruby was going to hit her.

Twenty long minutes later, her mother came out of the bedroom. The wrapping paper was still on the floor, and there were a few presents under the tree that had yet to be opened, including the small gift that Joey had made for Ruby at school. Joey was sitting in the same spot near the tree with Chesterfield in her lap, which she hoped would let her mother know that she was sorry, so very sorry, for her outburst.

Ruby calmly strode past her and into the kitchen, appearing a few seconds later with a garbage bag. She put the unopened presents into it and then cleaned up the wrapping paper. Then she plucked the stuffed cat out of Joey's lap and left the apartment. A few seconds later, Joey heard the *clang* of the metal door as her mother threw everything down the garbage chute.

"Better?" Ruby asked when she came back into the apartment, empty-handed. "By the way, we're three months behind on rent, so we're out of here on New Year's Eve. I don't know where we're going, but anything that doesn't fit in my suitcase can be thrown away."

Joey couldn't speak. She was only seven. What was there to say?

And now, sitting across from Deborah, the kindest person she knew, she felt the same as she did with Nicole Bowie. Jealous. Resentful. Desperate for a better life, a different life, though she knew it wasn't possible, because she didn't deserve anything that was good. Deborah was only here because it was her job. Her aunt and uncle only took her in because they were being paid.

There was nobody in Joey's life who was here simply because they wanted to be.

Deborah's daughter was the luckiest person in the world. And if Joey could have killed that girl to trade places with her, she would have strongly weighed her options on the best way to do it.

CHAPTER TWENTY-TWO

Drew finished reading the last of Joey's diaries the night before, and he's spent half of the five-hour drive to Sainte-Élisabeth wondering what her life was like after she moved to Maple Sound. If she kept any diaries during her five years there, they're long gone now. And the only people who would know anything about Joey's life in the small town aren't talking. Her Tita Flora declined his request for an interview. Of her three cousins, only the youngest replied to Drew's email, and all Carson said was that he was too young back then to remember much.

And her Tito Micky? Dead. Five years ago. Emphysema.

Check-in happens fast once Drew reaches the prison. He's interviewed inmates at a few different correctional facilities over the years, and he knows the drill. The corrections officer passes him a bin for his phone, belt, wallet, and keys, and then he stands with his arms out as the CO pats him down quickly.

"You're the sixth visitor she's had this week," the officer says as she buzzes him through. "She loves making people wait, so be sure to grab a magazine to pass the time."

"I appreciate the heads-up," Drew says. "*Merci.*"

"*De rien.*"

It's Drew's first visit to the Sainte-Élisabeth Institution for Women, and it's unfair how nice it is. Like all correctional facilities, it offers GED classes, psychological counseling, and parenting workshops, but inmates here can also sign up for yoga, tai chi, and meditation. There are organized sports, game nights, movie nights, even a book club. It houses 115 women, only five of whom are in maximum security. Ruby Reyes is not one of them. Joey's mother is apparently a model inmate, and is therefore allowed to roam as freely as medium security allows.

This isn't a prison. This is a fucking wellness retreat.

The visiting area is annoyingly cheerful, and barely a third full. Drew chooses a table close to the vending machines, where he purchases an assortment of overpriced snacks. The magazine rack turns out to be a disappointment, mostly filled with tabloids and celebrity fluff, but he picks up the newest issue of *People* with the late Jimmy Peralta on the cover. He also snags an older issue of *Maclean's*.

He's nearly finished skimming the Canadian news journal when the door to the visitors' room buzzes open. A tall woman with shoulder-length black hair enters, strolling in as if she has no cares in the world. She's slim, almost drowning in her lavender-colored prison scrubs, but she walks as if she's wearing the same gold dress she wore to the holiday party twenty-five years ago.

He stands as the Ice Queen approaches.

"Drew Malcolm," he says, and they shake hands briefly. "Thanks for meeting with me, Ms. Reyes."

"It's Ruby, please." She scans him from face to feet before taking a seat, then appraises the assortment of snacks. "These for me?"

"Help yourself."

"I hardly get any visitors." Ruby twists open the bottle of Dasani. "Then suddenly, after my parole is approved, I've now had six. None were as good-looking as you, though. Where were you twenty-five years ago?"

"In high school," Drew says. *Reading about you in the paper.* "Thank you, ma'am."

"Are you trying to insult me? I said call me Ruby." She smiles. "I'm amazed anyone is still interested in all my ancient history, but I suppose I have Lexi Baxter to thank for that."

She only has a trace of a Filipino accent, and you'd have to be listening for it to hear it. Seated, she looks so unassuming, which doesn't fit with what Drew's always imagined. In his mind, Ruby Reyes is a formidable presence, someone dangerous, someone to be feared. The woman across from him now seems like none of these things. She's disappointingly . . . regular.

It bothers him that she looks like Joey.

She leans forward, picking through the small pile of snacks, and finally settles on the bag of Lay's potato chips. "I do love my salt. So. You're a journalist. For which newspaper? The guy I met with yesterday wrote for some online thing. I didn't like him."

"I'm an investigative journalist," Drew says. "And they're all online things now. I have a podcast."

She munches on a chip. "I'm not even sure I know what that is."

He briefly explains it. "I focus on one story at a time and usually break it down over six to eight episodes."

"And people actually listen to this?"

"Three million of them do, yes."

Ruby seems impressed by the number. "So you're here to make me the focus of your next one?"

"Not exactly, though I admit the #MeToo twist is interesting."

She smiles again. "Of all the people I thought would vilify me at my parole hearing, I assumed it would be Charles's children. His son certainly had some vicious things to say to the parole board, but it turned out that Lexi was on my side."

"And what side is that?" Drew knows the answer already, but he wants to hear it from her.

"The victim side, of course. Charles was the president of the bank. I was a lowly customer service rep. He shouldn't have even noticed me, except he was a predator. I saw him a few times at the coffee shop when I was with my daughter. It's probably why he targeted me."

Wrong. You targeted him. You made sure you were at the Second Cup whenever he was. That came up at the trial.

Ruby sighs. "At the time, he was wonderfully charming."

"It didn't bother you that he was married?"

"Not even a little bit. His life, his wife, his choices." She eats another potato chip. "Anyway, about a year ago, Lexi wrote about her father on her lifestyle blog. I still can't believe that's a real job—writing about your own life on the internet." She rolls her eyes. "She sent me a print copy here in prison. I found it very eye-opening. It turns out her father molested her, like he did Joey."

You placed Joey right in his path.

"In her letter, Lexi said she forgave me, and that a part of her was glad he was dead. She's now estranged from her mother, you know. When Lexi went public with the story last year, Suzanne cut her off."

That part, Drew did not know.

"And then, of course, once that blog went everywhere—and oh, there's a word for that—"

"Viral."

"When her blog went viral, a whole bunch of women who'd worked for Charles came forward. They all had terrible stories. One even said Charles raped her, in his office, after everyone went home for the night. And just like that, Charles goes from victim to villain."

Ruby hides her smile behind a sip of water.

"It's funny how quickly the narrative can change," she says. "No longer is he the good man who was stalked by an obsessed home-wrecker. Now he's the pedophile who molested his own daughter, the powerful man who assaulted the women who worked for him."

"You realize that both those things can be true," Drew says. "He can be a sexual predator, *and* you can be the psychopath who murdered him when he tried to end your affair."

Ruby pauses, then shrugs. "Whatever. There's nothing to be done about it now. Charles is dead."

"Because you killed him."

She eats another chip.

"How did you convince the parole board to let you out?" Drew asks.

"I didn't," Ruby says. "Lexi did. She came to my parole hearing and spoke out in support of me. She told the board that while her father's murder was not okay, she understood the rage behind it. She said as far as she was concerned, her father was a criminal himself, and were he alive today, he would most certainly be in prison. She said I deserved compassion, and that twenty-five years behind bars was long enough. She was very compelling."

She gives Drew a wide smile. "The whole thing was very dramatic. Suzanne Baxter stood up and called her daughter a liar. Lexi then accused her mother of being complicit. And then, as Lexi was walking out, Suzanne *spit* on her. Imagine that? Horrible mother."

Takes one to know one.

"Is all this going into your podcast?" Ruby asks. "Because I'd be happy to say it again, if you ever want to record it."

"Maybe some of it," Drew says. "But let's be honest. Enough has been said about you."

She frowns. "Then why are you here?"

"I want to talk about your daughter, Joey."

"Wait a minute." Ruby puts down the potato chip bag and cocks her head. "I know who you are now. My sister told me that after Joey left Maple Sound—and stole *all* their money, by the way—that she moved back to our old neighborhood. That she was living with some Black guy and his girlfriend."

Drew raises a hand. "Some Black guy."

"So were you two fucking?"

Ah. There you are. The first real glimpse of the Ice Queen. It's strangely satisfying, and Drew can't resist a smile.

"My girlfriend? Yes."

"What about you and Joey?"

"We were just very good friends."

"Friends who fucked."

"Never happened."

"But you wanted it to."

"Why wouldn't I? She was beautiful."

Ruby stiffens. "So you must have been really sad when she died."

"Devastated." Drew holds her gaze. "Weren't you?"

"Of course I was." She looks away briefly. "No mother wants to outlive her child."

Please. You'd have thrown Joey overboard if the two of you were in a leaky canoe and only one of you could make it to shore.

"No matter what you think about me, I loved my daughter," Ruby says.

"You had an interesting way of showing it."

"I wasn't perfect," she snaps. "But neither was she."

"She was a kid. She didn't need to be."

She appraises him. "It doesn't matter what I say, does it? I'm always going to be the villain in her story."

"You're the villain in everyone's story. *Ma'am*."

A pause. "You know how I found out she died? My sister sent me a condolence card, with a clipped newspaper article folded inside, about the fire. Flora was always such a cold bitch, even when we were kids." Ruby reaches for the chips and resumes eating. "Is it true that Joey was working as a stripper?"

"For about a year."

"Was she any good?"

"She was incredible," Drew says, because he knows it will bug her.

It does, and her face darkens. "So you're going to sit here and tell me that you weren't fucking the stripper who lived in your apartment?"

"We weren't living together by then." Drew leans forward. "And you seem awfully interested in your dead daughter's sex life, ma'am. Why is that?"

Ruby doesn't respond.

"You abused Joey her whole childhood." He speaks evenly, trying to keep his emotions in check. "You should not be getting out of prison."

Ruby's lips flatten into a thin line. "I spanked her, so what. Nothing that happened to her was anything different from what happened to me. The police and the courts made a big deal over nothing. When I was growing up, it was normal to discipline your children. My mother used to do it with a belt. You know what they say. Spare the rod, spoil the child."

"What about punching them? Kicking them? Breaking their arms? Their ribs? Burning them with cigarettes?" Drew is fighting to stay calm, but he's not managing it very well. "What about allowing pedophile boyfriends access to a child? *Your* child? Is that normal?"

Ruby's eyes flash, and she pushes the now empty Lay's bag aside. "You think you knew her, but you didn't. I was so easy to hate back then, and she was so easy to feel sorry for. Well, what about me? Do you have any idea how hard it was to raise a kid in Toronto as a single mother on a customer service rep's income? Do you know how hard it was when I first moved to Canada? This was the seventies. I would walk down the street and people would call me chink, slant-eyes, yellow girl . . . I had to blow someone to get my first job. You have no idea what it's like to be a single mother, so don't you dare judge me."

"Ma'am, my mother was a single parent after my father passed away, and Black to boot. And she raised her three Black kids on a teacher's salary, and somehow managed to never hit us. Not once." Drew is breathing hard. "Added bonus? We're all still alive."

"Eat shit."

"You first."

"Look at you. Such a handsome, angry man." Ruby's voice drops to a purr. "So committed to your self-righteousness. I can't pretend I understand why. You knew Joey for what, a couple of years? You weren't even fucking her, and yet this bothers you so much. You poor thing, you have so much guilt. It must keep you up at night."

"You really are a monstrous human being." Drew can't hide his disgust. "You beat her. Your boyfriends molested her. I looked up your dating history from the murder trial transcripts. You had two boyfriends before Charles Baxter who are now on the sex offender registry. You pimped your daughter out, and now she's dead. You don't think that's *all* your fault?"

"She was more like me than you think."

They stare at each other. Drew has run out of things to say. Actually, that's not true. He's just sick of hearing her lie. As if sensing he's growing tired of her, Ruby smiles.

"Aren't you going to ask me what my plans are when I get out?" She sips her water. "Everyone else has."

Drew is about to snap that he doesn't give a shit what she does once she's out. But he actually does care, because the idea of her living any kind of normal life is just offensive to him. "What are your plans when you get out in two days?"

"I'll be spending some time in Maple Sound with my sister," Ruby says breezily, and it's clear this is her prepared answer. "Her boys are grown, and she's been alone ever since her husband died. I'm told Maple Sound has turned into somewhat of a tourist destination, with lots of cute stores and cafés. My mother lives there, too. It'll be so nice to spend time with family."

Drew can't help but snort. "Bullshit."

At this, Ruby throws her head back and laughs. "I knew you wouldn't buy that. Everyone else did, though. I'm sure Joey told you what a nightmare our family is. Especially my mother."

"Well, you had to get it from somewhere."

Ruby ignores that. "The real answer—and I feel like I can be honest with you, considering our personal connection—is I'm hoping not to be in Maple Sound too long. Me, in that bumfuck town, living with two of the worst bitches I can think of?" She shudders. "Anyway, my plan is to move back to Toronto and buy myself a little house. Somewhere right in the heart of things, so I can enjoy the pulse of the city. Maybe I'll get one of those electric cars. I can't wait."

"With what money?" Despite himself, Drew's curiosity is piqued. "You think you can get paid for interviews? Or some publisher will pay you to write a book? As a convicted murderer, you can't profit off your crime."

"No, but I can profit off someone *else's* crime." Ruby's smile lights her face, and she wiggles in her chair, giddy. "I'm being paid to keep a secret. I'm actually dying to tell someone about it, but that's all I can say for now. It's funny, though, how things are working out in my favor. For once."

Drew doesn't believe her. Ruby is a liar. It's in her DNA. "What secret could you possibly know that anyone would pay you money to keep?"

She doesn't answer, and his mind sorts through all the possibilities. Secrets plus money can only mean one thing.

"Are you blackmailing someone?" he asks.

Ruby clasps her hands together and rests them on the table. "I prefer to think of it as receiving compensation for withholding information that someone does not want to be made public."

"Are you going to tell me or not?" Drew waits five seconds, and when she doesn't answer, he stands. He has no idea what game she's playing, but they're finished here. He selects the pack of Twizzlers from the snack pile for the long drive home. "I'd thank you for your time, but all you've had is time."

She nods toward the issue of *People* he never got to read. "So sad about Jimmy Peralta, isn't it? We used to watch *The Prince of Poughkeepsie* in here all the time. Fascinating case. Murdered by his fifth wife, who was almost thirty years younger than he was. Did you know she's a Filipina?"

Drew did not know that, because he doesn't pay attention to celebrity marriages. "A Filipino woman murders an older white rich guy? Sounds familiar."

"You should do your next podcast about it." Ruby settles back into the chair, looking pleased with herself. "When you're done with me, of course."

Drew sticks the Twizzlers in his back pocket. "Ma'am, I am so done with you, there isn't even a word for it."

CHAPTER TWENTY-THREE

Though Drew is exhausted when he gets back to Toronto—an hour with Ruby Reyes would do anyone in, not to mention the ten hours of driving—he heads for his mother's place. Since Junior's is on the way, he impulsively stops for takeout, and makes small talk with Charisse while waiting for his food.

Fifteen minutes later, he arrives at Red Oak Senior Living, where Belinda Malcolm has lived for the past two years. He gets to her apartment just as one of the staff nurses is leaving.

"Hey, Maya," Drew says with a smile. "She good today?"

"Blood pressure's a little low, but we're keeping an eye on it. I'd like her to eat more." The nurse glances at Drew's takeout bag. "Ooh, Junior's. That should help. Enjoy your dinner, you two."

"Well, aren't you a sight," his mother says warmly, when Drew closes the door behind him. She's seated in her wheelchair, and he bends down to give her a kiss on the cheek. "Is that curry goat I smell?"

"Yes, ma'am, and I got plantains, too. I hope you're hungry."

He sets the takeout bag down on the table and tidies the half dozen magazines his sisters have left here. Same as the prison, it's mostly celebrity crap and a couple of fashion magazines. He begins unpacking the food.

"Maya likes you." His mother wheels herself over. She says this every time Drew visits. "You know she's single, right?"

He takes a seat across from her. "You've mentioned it."

"She's cute. Those big brown eyes. And I saw you looking at her booty."

"I only look at women above the neck."

"She just bought her own condo."

"She's also twenty-eight. Way too young for me."

His mother gives him a sideways glance. "How do you know how old she is?"

"I looked her up," Drew says, and they both burst out laughing.

His mother opens the bag of takeout and starts eating. Her second bite goes down with more enthusiasm than the first, and he notices she's lost more weight. She was hit by a drunk driver four years ago, and two surgeries and several complications later, she's permanently in a wheelchair. It was her suggestion to move into assisted living. As a retired teacher, she has an excellent pension, so at least there's no financial burden. She seems to like it here. The staff is friendly, and there are plenty of activities. She even has a gentleman friend his sisters have seen her giggling with a few times, which Belinda refuses to acknowledge.

"I did have a nice chat with my granddaughter today," his mother says.

"Sasha calls you more than she calls me."

"I don't grill her about her love life."

"She's too young to have a love life."

"You were living with Simone when you were her age," Belinda says pointedly.

"Yeah, and look how that turned out."

The TV is playing an episode of *Real Housewives*. Drew can't tell which city it is, but all the women are blond and drunk. He reaches for the remote to switch the channel, but his mother stops him.

"Don't," Belinda says. "I'm getting into it. These ladies are crazy. All this money, and they still fight about the pettiest things."

Drew opts not to share his opinion of the reality show. At least she's not watching *The Bachelor*.

"What's going on with you?" Belinda asks. "You seem distracted."

"No, ma'am. I'm right here with you."

"Me and the girls finally finished listening to season five of your podcast," his mother says. "I was surprised to hear you say that your next series is going to be about Ruby Reyes. You always said you'd never go there."

"That was before they decided to let her out."

"I've been reading all the controversy about her parole." Belinda shakes her head. "The way it's being written, Ruby is coming across like another one of Charles Baxter's victims. Which is a damn insult to his actual victims."

"I fully agree."

"But at the same time, who really knows what went on?" his mother muses. "He was the bank president. The power balance was completely off. If Ruby had wanted to say no, would she have been able to?"

"She didn't want to say no, because she was the one who pursued him."

Belinda looks at him with knowing eyes. "Is that the objective journalist in you talking, or the very biased friend of Joey's?"

"Just stating the facts." Drew swallows what he has in his mouth. "Don't get me wrong, I feel bad for all of Baxter's victims, including his own daughter. But I will never agree that Ruby Reyes was one of them."

"Joey was such a sweet girl. Remember that time you and Simone brought her to Thanksgiving? She took a huge helping of Monica's cranberry sauce, when your sister forgot to put sugar in it. Poor thing didn't know it wasn't supposed to taste like that."

"She ate the whole thing, too." The memory makes Drew smile. "She didn't want to be rude."

"You still have all those articles from the Buffalo papers Uncle Nate used to mail you?"

"I kept everything. Been reading them all again to prepare for the podcast. It's been a real mindfu—" Drew clears his throat. His mother abhors bad language. "It's been a trip, reading back how different the conversation was about Ruby back then, compared to now."

"You know, if your daddy and I were living in the time of #MeToo, he probably never would have asked me out," Belinda says. "And you and your sisters might never have existed."

They fall into a comfortable silence as she turns her attention back to the TV.

Drew ponders what his mother just said. His parents met at Belinda's first job, where she was the social studies teacher and he was the principal. She was twenty-five, Carl Malcolm thirty-nine. They were married six years, long enough to have three children, until his dad died of a heart attack at the age of forty-five. Drew, the baby of the family, was only two.

His mother cackles as she eats, thoroughly entertained by the two blond women arguing on TV. Drew picks through his sisters' abysmal magazine selection before settling on the Jimmy Peralta issue of *People* he didn't get to read earlier. A much younger version of the actor's face takes up the whole cover, and the headline reads:

Jimmy Peralta, 1950–2018
His Life,
His Loves,
His Legacy.

"Shame about him, huh?" Belinda's show has ended, and she glances over before turning the channel to CNN. "I loved *The Prince of Pough-keepsie.*"

Drew, who was more of a *Fresh Prince of Bel-Air* fan, can only remember watching a handful of episodes of Jimmy Peralta's sitcom, which was about a family-owned bakery in—where else?—Poughkeepsie, New York. The premise was funny, if extremely far-fetched: on the day his divorce is final, a single dad has a one-night stand with a mysterious European woman he meets at the bar his friends drag him to. Six months later, she shows up at the bakery, pregnant. It turns out she's an actual princess from a tiny country (never specified), who's been disowned by her entire family for being pregnant out of wedlock (gasp), and by an American to boot (yikes). With nowhere else to go, she marries Jimmy (whose name is Jimmy on the show, too) to stay in the US, and starts working at the bakery with his intrusive, meddling family (because what else would they be). Hilarity ensues.

He skims through the generous six-page feature. Jimmy Peralta was accomplished, there's no doubt about that, and Drew is reminded of all the movies the stand-up comic turned actor had been in. He'd won Emmys and a Golden Globe, and he even snagged an Academy Award nomination. But he had his demons, too. Four divorces, three trips to rehab, and two overdoses; the last one nearly killed him.

But then, in his sixties, a new leaf. Sobriety. Retirement. A permanent move back to his hometown of Seattle. A new marriage. And then, after a viral joke during the election put him back on people's radars, he signed a thirty-million-dollar deal with Quan, a new streaming service comparable to Netflix and Hulu.

"Jacqui watched his comedy special, and she said it was really funny," Belinda says, and Drew nods. "And there's a second one coming out soon. Did you know his wife is going to inherit something like forty-six million dollars? Oh, and did you know she's Filipino?"

Ruby Reyes did mention that.

"Look," Belinda says, pointing to the TV screen, where a woman wearing a bloodstained tank top, sweatpants, and pink slippers is being led out in handcuffs. "She sure looks guilty. And she's so young. Compared to Jimmy Peralta anyway."

Drew looks up at the screen. His heart stops. He blinks. Then blinks again.

Holy shit. There she is. Betty Savage. On TV.

It's *Mae.*

He grabs the remote and attempts to pause the TV, only to remember that his mother's television doesn't have that function.

"What is it?" Belinda asks, concerned.

"Hang on," Drew says, reaching for his phone instead. "I just need to look up something."

If his spine has been tingling the past few days, it's vibrating now as his mind flies back to his earlier conversation with Ruby. Somehow, the Ice Queen must have figured out that Mae Ocampo is alive and married to a rich celebrity. Only someone like that would have the money to pay Ruby enough to buy a house. Here in Toronto, even a little one that needs work would cost well over a million dollars. Ruby must believe that Mae had something to do with the fire that killed Joey. And if she's blackmailing Mae, she must know she can prove it.

Any normal mother with a dead daughter would want justice. But it's the Ice Queen. What she wants is to get paid.

He's googling *jimmy peralta wife* when his screen suddenly goes black. He has an incoming call. *Shit.* Letting out a grunt of frustration, he's about to decline it so he can get back to his google search, and then he realizes it's Hannah McKinley calling. He jabs the green accept button.

"Hey, Sergeant. Can I call you—"

"This won't take long, mate," McKinley says, barging right in, as usual. "I missed something about Mae that I wanted to tell you about. I know you said you no longer wanted to search for her—"

I think I've found her.

"—but there was something noted on her last arrest report that I didn't catch. I know I might be sending you right back down the rabbit hole you so painstakingly climbed out of, but remember how Mae had a minor drug arrest? Well, it was during her time as a dancer at the Golden Cherry, though it didn't happen at the club. The charge didn't stick—"

Hurry up. Drew keeps his gaze focused on the TV, where they're still talking about Jimmy Peralta's murder.

"—but on the arrest report, it notes she has a tattoo on her thigh. I checked all the previous reports, and it's not mentioned anywhere, so the tattoo must have been new." McKinley clears her throat. "It's of a butterfly, and it was photographed when she was booked. I'm going to text it to you now. Can you pull up the picture that shows Joelle's tattoo? I think they look quite similar."

The TV has gone to commercial. His mother is watching him questioningly.

"Hold on," Drew says. "I still have a photo of it in my phone."

He puts McKinley on speaker, and pulls up his photo app to take another look at the pictures he snapped of the photos Cherry gave him. He selects the picture of Joey dressed as Ruby reading a book in the dressing room, her legs up, and zooms in on her thigh.

"The butterfly is maybe four inches by three inches, and it's blue, purple, and pink," he says. "It's like a side profile, as if the butterfly is in flight."

McKinley exhales. "Check the photo I just sent you."

Three seconds later, his Messages app receives a photo. Drew enlarges it. McKinley has sent him a close-up of Mae's tattoo. It is, indeed, a butterfly. Blue, purple, and pink, side profile, midflight.

It's not just similar to Joey's. It's *identical.*

"Holy shit, they had matching tattoos," Drew says, more to himself than to McKinley. In his peripheral vision, he can see his mother's frown at his use of a curse word.

How did he not catch this earlier? He swipes to the next photo, where Joey is standing with Mae and another dancer. While Joey's dress is so short it shows both her thighs, Mae's dress is longer, with a slit on only one side. Joey's tattoo was on her right thigh. Mae's would have been on her left.

"When you ID'd Joey, do you remember which thigh her tattoo was on?" McKinley asks. "I don't have it here in my notes from the night of the fire . . ."

The police detective is still speaking, but Drew can't hear her anymore. The buzzing in his head is too loud. His mother has flipped to the final page of the Jimmy Peralta tribute article. There, in a box at the bottom, is a wedding photo of the comedian and his fifth wife. Drew slides the magazine toward himself and turns it around.

Jimmy Peralta is in a tux, his bride in a simple white dress. They're on the beach, holding hands, and the caption at the bottom reads, *Paris Peralta is wearing an off-the-rack wedding gown from Vera Wang, purchased from Nordstrom.*

He stares at Paris Peralta. Her black hair is in a simple updo, a few stray strands blowing around her face, a pink flower pinned over one ear. A younger Ruby Reyes stares back, but it's a version of Ruby without the sharp angles and hard edges, without the arrogance and cynicism and self-entitlement. This version of Ruby is fuller, softer, with a sweeter smile, her eyes alight with genuine love and affection for the man at her side.

It looks like Ruby, but it's not Ruby at all.

And it's not Mae, either. Mae is not the one who disappeared nineteen years ago and somehow ended up married to Jimmy Peralta.

It's *Joey.*

What. The. Actual. Fuck.

PART THREE

That night in Toronto with its checkerboard floors

—THE TRAGICALLY HIP

CHAPTER TWENTY-FOUR

Some mothers send birthday cards with sweet greetings. Paris's mother sends blackmail letters with threats.

Ruby Reyes is the only person in the world who knows her daughter did not die in that house fire in Toronto nineteen years ago, and if Paris doesn't pay her the money, the rest of the world will know it, too. It won't matter what her explanation is. She faked her death and assumed a new identity, and the ashes in the urn with Joey Reyes's name on it aren't hers. And now here she is, just like Ruby, about to be on trial for the murder of a wealthy older white man.

The irony isn't lost on her.

She's certain another letter will arrive any day now, especially since the latest issue of *People* is featuring Jimmy. Since she can't exactly pop out to the CVS down the street to buy a copy without being followed and photographed, she asked the concierge at the Emerald Hotel to do it for her. She wouldn't even have known the magazine had done a tribute if Henry hadn't told her.

The magazine chose a headshot of Jimmy from the nineties to grace the cover. Crinkled blue eyes, LA tan, still-dark hair, trademark smart-ass grin. It was taken at the height of his fame during the last season of *The Prince of Poughkeepsie*, which was also when he was the biggest asshole. At least according to Jimmy himself.

"There's no magic secret to reinventing yourself," Jimmy said to her once, shortly after they met. "You pick who you want to be, and then you start acting like it. It just takes time. A shitload of money doesn't hurt, either."

She understood the concept of reinvention better than he realized.

The *People* article doesn't mention Paris until the very end, and the short paragraph only gives three details: she and Jimmy met in a yoga class; they were married a year later in Hawaii; she's been charged with his murder.

Only two of these three things are accurate. Paris and Jimmy didn't meet in a yoga class; that's just the story they'd agreed to tell everyone. While it wasn't quite a lie, it wasn't exactly the truth.

Ocean Breath had just moved into its new location, and Paris didn't recognize Jimmy Peralta when he first walked in. Nobody did. In the dim lights of the hot yoga room, he looked like any other student arriving for class, dressed in a pair of loose shorts and tank top, a rolled-up mat tucked under his arm, Mariners ball cap pulled low.

Midway through the class, she noticed that her new student was struggling. The hot room is kept at 108 degrees, and the key to getting through the hour-long class is hydration. Jimmy's water bottle was empty. Concerned he might pass out, she approached him to see if he was okay.

Up close and face-to-face in the darkened room, her heart stopped when she realized who he was. And it wasn't because he was famous. It was because they'd met *before*. Back in a different life, when she was twenty, and a dancer at the Golden Cherry. He was in Toronto shooting a movie. They'd spent a couple of hours together, and then she never saw him again.

If Jimmy remembered her, he didn't let on. He accepted the fresh bottle of water she offered him, and she helped him with his postures while managing to avoid eye contact. After class, he thanked her at the reception desk where she was standing next to Henry, who finally recognized him and started fanboying.

After a month of classes, Jimmy asked Paris if they could grab a coffee. Normally she would decline a male studio member's invitation, but she agreed. They walked a block over to the Green Bean, where they sat at a corner table. He kept his ball cap on and his back to the room.

"I've spent the last month trying to place where I've seen you before,"

Jimmy said in a low voice. "But I remember now. Toronto, right? The strip club? I believe we spent some time together in the Champagne Room."

Paris felt the heat bloom in her cheeks, a dead giveaway. She couldn't have lied in that moment if she wanted to. "I'm not that person anymore."

"When people say that, they always mean it metaphorically. But I can tell you mean it literally. And believe me, I understand. I'm not that person anymore, either." Jimmy's eyes were intense. For a comedian, he could be very serious. "I've reinvented myself, too."

Not like I have.

"I was using a lot back then," Jimmy said. "There are entire chunks of my life I can barely remember. I don't know why, but I remember you. And if I ever did anything back then that made you uncomfortable . . . if I ever, you know, forced you to do something that you didn't want to do—"

"You didn't force me." Paris didn't want him to finish the sentence, because she didn't want him to actually say it out loud. "You were respectful. And I was an adult."

"Barely."

"I was twenty," Paris said. "A year over the legal drinking age in Ontario. And for what it's worth, I was sober the whole time, even if you weren't." She picked up her coffee, realized her hands were shaking, and set it back down. "I left that life behind when I left Toronto. I'm not proud of it. Quite the opposite, in fact."

His vivid blue eyes remained fixed on hers. "I've upset you."

"I'll be fine."

"I understand more than you think," Jimmy said. "You might have one previous version of yourself you don't like. I have several. But this version of me, sitting here with you, is a version of myself I actually do like. And I don't want to fuck it up by getting kicked out of the studio. You're the best yoga instructor I've ever had."

"How many have you had?" Paris asked, curious despite herself.

"Kid, I'm from Los Angeles. I've had at least two dozen. But the worst instructor ever was this guy named Rafael. The guy was always sweaty. He had zero body hair, and he always wore these little red *Baywatch* shorts. Anyway, one day he was helping me raise my leg, and I fell on him. We were like two wet, salty seals sliding over each other . . ."

Paris laughed. And continued to laugh for the next hour, until it was time to head back to the studio.

Over the next few months, coffees led to lunches, which led to dinners. He took her to a couple of outdoor concerts at the Chateau Ste. Michelle winery, where they saw Barenaked Ladies (one of her favorite bands growing up) and Frankie Valli and the Four Seasons (Jimmy knew Frankie personally). After the second concert, she kissed him. It felt like the most natural thing in the world, despite the twenty-nine-year age gap.

"Do you think he's too old for me?" Paris asked Henry the next morning. "Be honest. Does it look bad?"

"Honey, he's *Jimmy Peralta*." Henry rolled his eyes. "The fact that he makes you laugh makes him a keeper, and retired or not, he's still got it."

"Got what?"

"*It*. That thing that makes him special." Henry saw the confusion on Paris's face and laughed. "You've been happier than I've ever seen you, P. Don't self-sabotage by overthinking it. You deserve good things. You deserve *him*."

It was easier said than done. She wasn't used to good things, to things being easy, to people being kind. When she was thirteen, Deborah had told her that some people were just born into hard lives, and their job was to claw their way out.

Or, Paris has since learned, you could simply become someone else.

She tosses the magazine into the recycling bin. She doesn't need it—she lived with the man. And the photo *People* used is framed on their mantel at home, anyway.

* * *

In the five days she's been at the Emerald, she hasn't heard a peep from her lawyer. Assuming Elsie still *is* her lawyer. It's Hazel who calls to tell Paris that the police have finished with her house and that she can finally go back home.

The smug hotel manager is happy to see her go. He even calls her a car service, and there's a black Lincoln Town Car waiting at the same back entrance where she was dropped off. The driver takes a good look at her ankle monitor, but politely says nothing about it until they turn down her street, where they see a huge swarm of people with cameras milling around.

Thankfully, the Town Car's windows are tinted dark. If anything, the crowd is even bigger than it was the morning of her arrest. At least the yellow crime scene tape she saw on the news is gone. From the outside of the house, you'd never know anything happened. She has no idea what the inside is going to look like.

"Someone needs to tell them that the view is the other way," the driver says, looking at her in the rearview mirror. "So. How would you like to do this? I'm assuming you don't want them to get a shot of you with that ankle monitor on. If you want, I can pull straight into your garage, assuming you have a door that connects to the inside of the house."

It's clear he knows exactly who she is, but if it bothers him, it doesn't show.

"That would be great," Paris says. "I can open the doors from my phone."

He pulls into the driveway and idles while Paris taps on her new iPhone, connecting to the home Wi-Fi. She spent the last two days at the hotel trying to set up her new phone like her old one, which the police still have. But the app doesn't seem to be working. She's logged in, but the actual hardware inside the house appears to be off-line. The police must have disabled the system.

"I can't get the app to work," Paris says, frustrated. "I'm sorry, but would you mind getting out and entering the code directly into the keypad? I promise I'll give you a massive tip."

"What's the code?" he asks, turning around. She tells him the four digit number, and he gives her a wink. "I'd have done it for you anyway, but I got kids, so I won't say no to the tip."

As soon as he gets out of the car, cameras flash. She can hear her name being shouted. *Paris! Paris! How does it feel to be home? Did you kill Jimmy for the money?* The driver punches the code in quickly, and when he gets back in the car, he seems freaked out.

"Wow. Now I know how those Kardashians feel."

It's the second reference someone's made to the Kardashians, and while Paris doesn't appreciate the comparison, she's pretty sure the Kardashians wouldn't, either.

He pulls into the garage, parking between Jimmy's Cadillac and her Tesla, then shuts the engine off. Without prompting, he gets out and presses the button on the wall. Slowly, the garage door closes, shutting out the noise along with the daylight. Paris exhales. The driver helps her bring everything inside the house. Since the hotel paid for the car service, she Venmos him a hundred bucks.

He grins and hands her his business card. "Call me if you ever need a personal driver. The way things are going, I'm thinking you will."

She enters the house through the connecting door. Sticking only her hand out, she presses the button again to open the garage to let him out. When the garage door closes again, she lets out a long sigh of relief.

She's home.

Nothing appears any different, although the house smells like bleach and citrus. Paris sits in her usual spot at the kitchen table. She can almost pretend things are normal. When she looks out the window into the backyard, she half expects to see Jimmy there, fiddling with his tomato plants, fishing leaves out of the pool with his net, barbecuing chicken on the grill.

But Jimmy isn't here. Jimmy will never be here again.

His ancient Sony boombox is still in its usual place on the counter, and she picks through the neat stack of cassette tapes beside it. Her husband owned three portable stereos of the same vintage—one here, one in his office, and one in his bathroom upstairs. Not long after they got married, one of them had stopped working, so Paris bought Jimmy a brandnew stereo with a CD player instead of a cassette deck, Bluetooth, and an auxiliary plug for MP3s.

She discovered it on one of the garage shelves a few weeks later, still in the box. His old portable stereo was working again, because he'd made Zoe find a place that would repair it.

"Don't be offended," Jimmy said to Paris. "I've had these stereos since the eighties, and I'm attached to them." He kissed her on the forehead. "Besides, technology sucks, kid. Always best to go old school."

She wasn't offended at all. Jimmy liked what he liked, and she didn't marry him to change him.

She chooses a cassette at random and inserts it. The buttons are so loose it takes no effort to press play. She turns the volume up loud. As the opening bars to "Free Bird" by Lynyrd Skynyrd waft out of the speakers, it's like Jimmy is here again, dancing with her in the kitchen. *If I leave here tomorrow, would you still remember me . . .*

A sob of grief wells up in her throat, so thick she can't swallow it back down. For once, she doesn't try. The sobs come so fast and hard, they physically hurt her stomach, racking her entire body until it feels like she can't breathe.

The last time she cried like this, she was a child. She had reached for her mother for comfort, but Ruby had remained where she was, smoking a cigarette, observing her daughter with disgust, as if she were a cockroach Ruby had just stepped on. *You're going to cry now? Really? Are you trying to make me mad?*

Paris feels a hand on her shoulder, and jumps. She looks up to see Jimmy's assistant—*former* assistant—standing over her.

"It's okay," Zoe says. "It's okay, Paris. Let it out. I'm here. It's okay."

CHAPTER TWENTY-FIVE

Zoe offers her a box of tissues, and Paris yanks out a bunch so she can dry her eyes and blow her nose. The woman has some fucking nerve showing up here. One, she called Paris a murderer. Two, she was fired.

"Why are you even here?" Paris finally asks when she can speak properly. "Did you forget that you don't work here anymore? How'd you even get in?"

"I rang the doorbell but nobody answered, and my code still works. I just came to pick up some things I left." Zoe hesitates. "Can we talk?"

"No."

Zoe takes a seat perpendicular to her at the kitchen table. "I am so, so sorry—"

"No."

"Paris, *please.*" Zoe's face is filled with anguish. "I know I should have talked to you first, but try to look at it from my perspective. I saw Jimmy in the tub and you on the floor, and then I saw the razor, and there was blood *everywhere* . . . it looked so bad, and I was scared, so I called 911. If I'd given myself a chance to at least think about it, I would have known that you couldn't have hurt him. I know you loved him. I know you didn't marry him for the money."

"Oh look, you're still here," Paris says.

"I worked for Jimmy for fifteen years." Zoe rubs her head, her brown hair bouncing around. "I actually knew his last two wives, and right from the get-go, it was obvious why they were with him, and it had nothing to do with love. The last one, I don't even think she *liked* him. When I met you, I assumed you'd be the same. But you weren't. You aren't. You're younger than he is, yes, but you're independent. You have a job. You have your own business. And I could see the way you two looked at each other. You loved each other, but you also really, really *liked* each other."

A tear escapes down Paris's cheek, and she swipes at it. "So then why have we never gotten along?"

"Because you don't like me," Zoe says simply. "You've never liked me."

Paris stares at her. "That's not true."

"You thought I was using him, just like I thought you were. I could tell you couldn't understand why I followed Jimmy here from LA, why I stuck around to work for someone who'd retired. But Jimmy . . . he treated me like family. I moved to LA at eighteen to be a singer-songwriter. I was so naive. Within three months, I was broke."

Zoe looks down and smiles. "But then Jimmy hired me. At first it was just a way to pay the bills, but the work was okay. He let me have time off for gigs. He helped me pay for my studio time when I recorded my first demo. You didn't know Jimmy back then, but he was basically an asshole ninety percent of the time. But the other ten percent, he was generous, and supportive."

Paris has heard lots of stories about Jimmy's ugly side. She'd never seen it herself until recently.

"Seven years ago, when he hit rock bottom, I didn't think he'd make it out of that." Zoe's voice is soft. "He was in such a dark place, lashing out at anybody who tried to help him. It was like he was determined to burn every bridge he had, and he almost succeeded. Everybody bailed. His manager quit, his agency dropped him, even Elsie stopped taking his calls for a chunk of time. Nobody could do it anymore, and I didn't blame them. But I stuck around. I was scared to leave him alone. He finally got clean, announced his retirement, and I helped him move back here to Seattle. And then I just . . . stayed."

It occurs to Paris then that this is the first time she's heard Zoe's backstory. She was so busy judging the other woman that she'd never bothered to try to know her. Just like people used to do to her. The thought makes Paris feel ashamed.

"When Jimmy met you, he came back to life." Zoe offers her a small smile. "And when he started telling jokes again, it was like he had finally become the version of himself he always wanted to be—sober *and* funny. When Quan called, I admit, I wanted him to do it. His material was so good, so relevant, it deserved to be out there. I should have known, though, that the pressure of it all would make him start using again. It's all my fault."

"So you knew?" Paris says, incredulous.

Zoe nods, and slumps.

"You know how *I* found out he was using again?" Paris's voice is hot. "When Elsie told me what was on the toxicology report. Why the hell didn't you say anything?"

Zoe's face crumples. "I only saw him do it once, in the dressing room, right before his last performance of the second special. He promised me it was a one-time thing, just a bump to get him through the next hour. He asked me not to tell you. And then he went out onstage and absolutely killed it. I don't think he's ever been funnier. I never saw him use again." She looks away. "But that doesn't mean he didn't."

Paris was there that night, in the audience. Under the spotlights of the Austin City Limits stage, he was transformed, his comic genius on full display. There is nothing more exhilarating than watching a person do what they do best, better than anyone else.

But the demons were lurking beneath the surface. Paris knew that, and she was getting more and more worried. His memory lapses were becoming more frequent, and no matter what she said, Jimmy refused to go to the doctor. Any time she brought it up, they would argue.

"I haven't had a chance to talk to you about this, but when you were at the yoga conference, Jimmy had that charity gig," Zoe says. "He went into it sober, I made sure of it. His jokes were funny, but he was off with the delivery, and at the very end, he blew the punch line. Afterward, he was so upset, and all he wanted to do was go home and practice. I probably should have stuck around, but he was so angry, yelling at me about little things, like why didn't I order more cassette tapes, why can't I just do my fucking job . . ."

Zoe completely falls apart, her shoulders shaking as she sobs. Paris pushes over the Kleenex box.

She understands what it's like to be on the receiving end of Jimmy's anger, the kind that comes from someone who's having a hard time accepting that he might have a disease for which there's no cure, the same disease that killed his mother slowly, bit by agonizing bit, until there was nothing left but a shell of the woman she used to be. Early in their marriage, he had told Paris about his mother's Alzheimer's, and she had seen the horror and grief in his eyes.

"I wouldn't wish it on my worst enemy," Jimmy had said. "It's absolutely fucking brutal."

It's time to tell Zoe.

"Listen to me," Paris says. "Jimmy was having trouble with his memory. There was no official diagnosis because he wouldn't go to the doctor, but I noticed early signs of dementia. He didn't want to blow the Quan deal, so he made me promise not to tell anyone. But even if he wasn't sick, Zoe, you are not responsible for his drug use. It was not your job to save his life."

Zoe's eyes well with tears again.

"I'm sorry I fired you the way I did," Paris says quietly. "Truthfully, I'm not even sure I *can* fire you. You worked for him, not me."

"I worked for Peralta Productions. Which I'm pretty sure belongs to you now." Zoe takes a breath. "Paris . . . I swear I didn't know anything about the inheritance. I never thought Jimmy would leave me anything. He had already paid me a bonus when he signed with Quan, and honestly, I felt guilty for taking it. *They* came to *him*, and I helped facilitate the discussions and find an entertainment lawyer in LA to help with the contracts. But other than that, everything else I did was just regular assistant stuff—scheduling, travel bookings, emails. I was shocked when I heard how much he'd left me."

"I believe you," Paris says, and she does.

"Have you heard from Elsie?" Zoe asks.

Paris shakes her head. "Not since she dropped me off at the hotel. Right now, I'm not even sure I have a lawyer."

"The last time I heard from her was when she asked me to get you some stuff for your hotel stay. I did reach out after that, but she never got back to me. She doesn't like me, either." Zoe lets out a small laugh. "But I can help you find a new lawyer, if you want. I can make some calls."

"Would you?" Paris says, relieved. "I'm happy to put you back on the payroll."

Zoe waves a hand. "No. I think it's time for me to move on. But I'll help. As a friend."

They exchange tentative smiles.

"Hey," Paris says. "Before you go, can you fix the smart home thing? It's not working on my new phone. I think it might be disconnected."

"It wasn't working on mine, either." Zoe stands up and frowns. "I can call the company and ask them to reset it, but technically Jimmy is the administrator, so they might not talk to me." She looks around the kitchen. "Are you all right for now? I stocked the fridge, so there's stuff to cook if you want to."

"I'm okay," Paris says. "I just . . . I don't know where I'll sleep tonight. I'm not sure I can bring myself to go upstairs."

An image of Jimmy in a tub full of his own blood flickers through her mind.

"I called a cleaning service that specializes in crime scenes," Zoe says. "They cleaned the whole house first thing this morning, including Jimmy's room. I didn't want you to come home to . . ." She stops. "I didn't want you to be uncomfortable in your own home."

Paris impulsively reaches forward to give the other woman a hug. How could she have so misjudged this person? After all, she knows exactly how it feels to have people assume you're something you're not. For Paris, the only way to get away from it was to become someone new. That was not an option now.

Unlike nineteen years ago, she can't just set a fire and run.

CHAPTER TWENTY-SIX

It was never her plan to become Paris. It's just the way it worked out.

The night she faked her death started off like any other, only she was actually looking forward to going to work. The Golden Cherry had been advertising their New Year's Eve party for weeks, and the fifty-dollar cover charge included a free drink and a champagne toast at midnight. It was sure to be a big money night for all the girls.

The first time Joey ever danced at the Cherry, she nearly threw up. She had spent her entire life up until then doing everything she could to be clothed and covered from the gazes of strange men, and suddenly, there she was, working the main floor in a dress so skimpy, she might as well have been naked. Luckily, she was a quick learner. Eventually, it all became normal—enjoyable, even. In the club, she was in total control. Nobody was allowed to touch her without her consent, and it was surprisingly empowering.

The trick, she discovered, was to not be Joey. The trick was to be *Ruby*.

A year later, she'd become one of the club's highest earners. Though she expected her time as an exotic dancer to be short, she found she was in no hurry to move on. The money was too addicting.

There was already a lineup outside the Cherry when Joey stepped off the bus for her shift. A man in a sequined top hat with *1999* emblazoned across it spotted her and hollered, "Happy fucking New Year!" She ignored him and headed straight for Junior's.

"Well, if it isn't my favorite Filipino fantasy," Fitzroy said with a grin when the bells above the door chimed her entrance. "They got you working New Year's Eve, Joey?"

"Working till last call, and I won't make it on an empty stomach." She knew the menu by heart and ordered, handing Fitzroy a ten. He gave her back four loonies, and she dropped one in the tip jar. Before she started dancing, it wouldn't have occurred to her to tip for a takeout order. Now that her income relied solely on the generosity of customers, she tipped everybody.

All three tables in the tiny restaurant were full, so she went back outside to wait for her food. The lineup outside the Cherry had grown longer, and she saw that Chaz was working the door. Even from this distance, he looked huge. For his size—six five, with biceps like wrecking balls—Chaz was surprisingly tender in bed. It helped that he loved her. She knew this because he'd said it once, but when she didn't say it back, he never said it again. They were only sleeping together casually, of course; he wasn't her boyfriend, though she knew he wanted to be.

Chaz was taking his time checking the IDs of a large group of nervous-looking young men, peering at each driver's license with a mini flashlight. There was almost always someone under nineteen with a fake ID, but they all passed. The next group in line stepped forward, and she caught a glimpse of someone familiar. Her heart skipped a beat. Tall, same twists, same goatee. But then he turned, and she got a better look at his face. It wasn't Drew.

Of course it wasn't. He was in Vancouver, with Simone.

It had only been a year since her roommates left for the west coast, but it felt like a lifetime had passed. Strip club life was like that. One year could feel like ten, and it aged you. And if you didn't take care of yourself, you'd be an old woman by the time you hit thirty. Sugar, a dancer Joey thought was in her forties, turned out to be twenty-eight. *Twenty-eight.* If Joey was still dancing at the Cherry in eight years, she'd jump into the lake and drown herself.

The takeout window slid open. "So tell me, Joey," Fitzroy said, handing her a white plastic bag knotted at the top. "What's your New Year's resolution?"

She considered for a moment. "To marry an old rich man with one foot in the grave and the other on a banana peel."

Fitzroy let out a hearty laugh. "Well, I hope you meet him tonight. Be safe, okay? Happy New Year, sweet girl."

"Happy New Year, Fitz."

"Hey, geisha girl!" a man in the lineup called out to her as she headed toward the alleyway that led to the back entrance of the Cherry. This one was wearing a gold plastic crown. "What you got under that coat, China doll? I want you to love me long time."

It was one thing for customers to proposition the girls inside the club, but out here on the sidewalk, before her shift, it breeched some kind of unspoken etiquette. And three Asian stereotypes in ten seconds? Had to be a record. Whatever. As long as they were paying, she would be whatever Asian they wanted her to be. *Inside* the club.

Mae had taught her that.

"Who gives a shit if they think you're Chinese, or Korean, or whatever," Mae had told her the night they first met. As the only two Asian dancers in the club—and both Filipino to boot—they'd bonded immediately over their shitty childhoods. Mae had lived in several different foster homes before running away at fifteen. "Most of the guys who come in here don't know the difference, and even if they do, they don't care. Your job isn't to teach them, it's to make money. So go get your money, bitch."

It was going to be a big money night, and the night was young.

As she approached the staff entrance of the club, she could hear the music pulsing from inside. There was always supposed to be a bouncer stationed at the back door to prevent customers from sneaking in, but at the moment, it was unguarded. Joey pulled on the handle, and stepped into a whole different world.

* * *

"Hey, girls," Joey said, placing her takeout bag at an open spot at the long vanity table that ran down the center of the dressing room. She dropped her knapsack on the floor and shrugged out of her parka. "Where is everyone?"

"Already on the floor." Dallas, a platinum blonde of indeterminate age who was dressed as a Cowboys cheerleader, was carefully applying her strip eyelashes two spots over. "A lot of big groups coming in tonight. Money, money, money."

"Not if they're snaking," Candie said from the other side of the vanity. This was the new Candie, with an *-ie*. The previous Candy, with a *-y*, had gotten a boob job and left to work at the Brass Rail downtown. Richer clientele, better tips. "And let's hope they're not all rocks. Last Thursday I barely made enough after the house fee to cover my babysitter."

It had taken Joey a while to learn the lingo of the club. A customer who watched the lap dance someone else was getting was "snaking." "Rocks" nursed their drinks all night and didn't pay for lap dances at all. The "house fee" was what the dancers paid to the club just to work there.

Joey had done the math. In order to earn a comfortable living after the house fee and the nightly tip out to the DJ, bouncers, and other staff, she had to earn at least six hundred dollars a week. It was expensive to be a stripper.

Fortunately, Joey made much more than this. On a regular night, she earned about five times what she used to make working for minimum wage at the video store. On a good night? Double that. It was also lucrative to be a stripper.

"Bump?" Dallas said under her breath, offering her a small vial of cocaine. "Just stocked up."

"Nah, I'm good." Joey opened her Styrofoam takeout container, and the heavenly aroma of jerk chicken wafted out. "And hide that shit until everyone's gone. Cherry will kill you."

"Ewww, what is that smell?" a voice said, and she looked up to see a dancer named Savannah staring at her food as she spritzed perfume all over her body. "You shouldn't eat that in here. It stinks."

"No, you stink." The quick response was from Destiny, who was rubbing homemade glitter lotion onto her brown skin. Joey had the same mixture in her bag, which was just unscented Jergens mixed with gold glitter from the dollar store. Under the stage lights, it made your skin shimmer. Destiny's eyes, which were bright blue tonight, flashed. "You smell like a five dollar hooker with that cheap perfume."

"It's Liz Claiborne," Savannah said, offended. She spritzed herself one more time before putting the cap back on her perfume bottle.

Obviously the Cherry didn't have a human resources department, so the dancers had created their own zero tolerance policy for ignorant comments. But Joey was in a good mood, so she let it slide. Savannah had only started a week ago, and the newbie would learn soon enough what would happen if she said the wrong thing to the wrong girl.

"These new girls are so stupid," Destiny said after Savannah left. "She might be fresh as a daisy with nineteen-year-old tits now, but in a year, she'll be a cokehead trying to save up for a boob job." She touched Dallas's shoulder as she headed out. "No offense, girl."

Here at the Cherry, they were all referred to as "girls." Even Dallas, who could've been anywhere from thirty-five to fifty, was a girl. And Destiny wasn't wrong. The job changed you. It had to, or you wouldn't last. Nobody working here had listed "stripper" as their career goal when they filled out their guidance counselor's questionnaire in high school. Though they all came from different backgrounds, it was a universal truth that no one here had expected to end up a dancer at the Golden Cherry.

The Cherry was where you landed when life didn't go as planned. It didn't have to be a bad thing. But it wasn't really a great thing.

One of the bouncers poked his head into the dressing room. "Hey, Betty."

"Fuck off, Rory," Dallas said. "No men allowed."

"I just need Betty for a second," the bouncer said. "Hey, Betty. *Betty.*"

Joey swiveled to face him, her mouth full of chicken. "Sorry, wrong Asian stripper."

"Shit." Rory deflated when he saw her face. "You know if Betty's coming in tonight?"

"Don't know. My Filipino telepathy isn't working at the moment."

Beside her, Dallas snorted. After Rory left, Joey turned to her with a grin, but saw that the other dancer wasn't laughing. It was just a line of coke going up her nose.

"Okay, where'd you score that?" Joey glanced back over her shoulder to make sure no one else was around. "You know you can't do that shit inside the club. Cherry will fire you."

"Betty hooked me up." The dancer adjusted her breasts inside her blue crop top. Because she was so thin, her breast implants made her boobs look like bolt-ons (even Dallas called them that), but it worked for her. Onstage, when she untied her top, they'd burst out, and it always got a loud cheer. "This batch is cut with too much shit, though. Two hits and I can barely feel it. Usually she gets the good stuff."

Joey sighed and finished her dinner. She'd tried so many times to talk Mae out of selling, but the money was even better than dancing. The two of them had opposite personalities—Joey was the calm, while Mae was the storm—and it was impossible to tell Mae what to do. Still, they balanced each other out, and their friendship had become meaningful. A few months earlier, on a whim, they'd gotten matching butterfly tattoos, which made the people at the club mix them up even more. Everybody already thought they looked alike, though Mae and Joey couldn't see it.

Lately, though, being mistaken for Mae had become a problem. Her boyfriend was part of the Blood Brothers, and Mae was now the club's main dealer of illegal narcotics. She could get anything anyone asked for. Cocaine was most requested, as it kept the dancers going all night.

The first time Joey met Vinh—who went by Vinny—he was picking Mae up after work one night. She was surprised at how tiny he was, five four at most, his skinny body drowning in jeans and a sweatshirt three sizes too big for him. He looked like a teenager who played Nintendo all day, nothing like the gangster he was reputed to be. Mae's voice fluctuated between pride and fear whenever she told Joey about the violent, crazy things Vinny had done to the people who crossed him and the gang. And apparently his older brother, a high-ranking member of the BB, was even worse.

More than a few times, Mae had come into work with bruises, and once, even a sprained wrist. When Joey expressed concern, her friend shrugged it off. "I hit him, too," Mae said. "This is why body makeup was invented." It didn't matter how many times Joey encouraged Mae to break up with Vinny, her friend had to get there herself. And Joey was worried that if she didn't get there quickly enough, he would kill her.

Yet Vinny was always polite. "Nice to see you, Joey," he would say, and he and Mae would offer her a ride home in his souped-up Civic any night she wasn't going home with Chaz.

"Girls," a commanding voice said from the dressing room doorway.

Beside her, Dallas jumped, the coke vial disappearing into the palm of her hand. Joey didn't have to look up to know that it was Cherry.

"Hey, Cherry." Joey was applying a thin line of glue to her false eyelashes. "I'll be ready on time."

"After the stage, head up to VIP, okay?" Cherry was speaking to Joey, but her eyes were focused on Dallas. "Eight-person bachelor party requested the hot Asian chick they saw outside. Since Betty hasn't shown up, that must be you."

Joey looked up, waving the strip lash in her hand so the glue would turn tacky, which made it easier to stick on. "A bachelor party? On New Year's Eve?"

"New Year's Day wedding, tomorrow afternoon." Cherry shrugged. "They don't look like high rollers, but they're trying to be. They asked about the Champagne Room."

Champagne Room? Joey exchanged a look with Dallas. Two hours in the Champagne Room could earn a girl a thousand bucks, minimum.

"Do they need a blond cheerleader, too?" Dallas piped up, hopeful.

"No." Cherry turned her attention to Joey fully. "Hey. You been in touch with Betty? This is the second shift in a row she's blown off. I don't want to fire her ass until I know she's okay."

"Aw, Cherry, don't fire her," Dallas said. "I know she's a flake, but the customers love her."

"Was I talking to you?" the owner snapped.

"I haven't talked to her in a couple days," Joey said. "But she has roommates who'd look after her if she was sick. I can check in on her tomorrow."

Cherry's gaze shifted back to the older dancer. "Dallas, that better be face powder on your nose. Finish getting ready, and get your ass out there."

"It's not just my ass they're here to see," Dallas replied smartly, but she wiped her nose and got up to stow her things in her locker. Before leaving the dressing room, she said, "For real, girl, I don't know how you do this job without being on *something*."

It's easy, Joey thought. Makeup finished, she shimmied into her gold dress and strapped on her stilettos. She stared at herself in the full-length mirror. Ruby stared back.

I just pretend I'm my mother.

CHAPTER TWENTY-SEVEN

Paris doesn't realize she's fallen asleep on the sofa until the doorbell wakes her up. It takes her a few seconds to remind herself where she is—home? Jail? Toronto?—but then she hears the photographers shouting on the street, and remembers. Seattle. Jimmy is dead. Murder charge. No lawyer.

The doorbell rings again, followed by what sounds like a kick. Whoever it is, they're persistent. Paris tries the smart home app on her phone again, but the door cam, along with the rest of it, is still not working. She pads over to the front door and looks through the peephole the old-fashioned way, bracing herself for a ballsy reporter or paparazzo waiting to surprise her with a camera in her face.

It's Elsie.

She opens the door and steps aside quickly as the woman pushes her way in. Behind her, cameras flash and questions are shouted. Elsie is carrying a cardboard box, on top of which is her briefcase, on top of which is a takeout bag from Taco Time. A bottle of wine sticks out from a tote bag over her shoulder.

"Vultures," the other woman says, shutting the door with her foot. "Lock it, quick."

Paris locks the door, then grabs the takeout bag and briefcase before they can slide off.

Elsie sets the cardboard box down on the floor. "This was on your doorstep. Jimmy's mail. The post office must have forwarded it here."

Paris stares at her. "Hello to you, too."

"Talk later, eat first." Elsie plucks the bag of food and her briefcase from Paris's hands and heads straight for the kitchen. "I brought wine."

Paris looks down at the box of Jimmy's fan mail, which seems so unremarkable sitting on the floor of the foyer. There's no doubt in her mind that it will contain another blackmail letter from Ruby. Her mother will know by now that Jimmy is dead, which means she'll know about the inheritance, and that her daughter has been charged with first-degree murder.

The apple doesn't fall far from the tree, does it, Mama?

* * *

She and Elsie sit in the kitchen and eat. The other woman pours herself a second glass of wine before Paris is even halfway through her first. It's not until they finish the tacos that she notices Elsie is crying, though it's not a full-body thunderstorm like Paris had when she first got home. Elsie's cry is like a steady rain that will last a little while.

But grief is grief, however it's expressed.

"Did Jimmy ever tell you about our senior prom?" Elsie's voice is thick.

"All he said was you were boyfriend and girlfriend in high school." Paris hands her an extra napkin. "I assumed you went to prom together."

"Actually, we didn't." Elsie dabs her eyes. "The week before, we got into a huge fight and broke up. Someone told me he was seen flirting with Maggie Ryerson. She was a cheerleader, big boobs, perky, you know the type. He denied it, but I didn't believe him. So he dumped me. I was devastated."

Paris sits back in her chair and listens.

"There was no way I was missing my senior prom," Elsie continues. "So I asked a boy named Fred, who I knew had a crush on me, to take me. When we get to the gymnasium, who do I see? Jimmy, with Maggie Ryerson."

Paris shakes her head. "Well, that's a dick move."

"I managed to ignore him, tried to have a good time. But later, I found him skulking in the hallway. Maggie had ditched him, and he'd found her in the parking lot making out with Angelo DeLuca, a boy her parents hated. Maggie had used Jimmy as a cover so she could be with Angelo at the prom without her parents finding out. He deserved it, but I couldn't help but feel sorry for him. We left prom together, and ended up grabbing burgers and milkshakes at Dick's. Then we came here to Kerry Park and sat on the benches to look at the city lights."

"What about Fred?"

"Guess that makes me a dick, too." Elsie looks away. "Kerry Park was always our favorite place. We'd come here to talk, make plans, dream. It was chilly that night, and Jimmy put his tuxedo jacket around my shoulders. Powder blue, to match my dress, but we never got a prom photo." She smiles, her eyes distant. "He asked if I would take him back. Of course I said yes."

Paris feels a small stab of jealousy. Not because Elsie was Jimmy's old girlfriend, which she already knew, but because she had something with him that Paris never did: *history*. She'd only known her husband for three years. Elsie had known Jimmy for five *decades*. They had fifty years of friendship and laughter and stories and inside jokes that only two people who've shared that kind of time together can have. Elsie had seen Jimmy in all his incarnations, had stood by him through all his ups and downs. Paris had been Jimmy's wife, but Elsie may well have been his soul mate.

The loss . . . it must be unbearable. Paris has been so busy thinking about herself that she had never stopped to think how this must be affecting *Elsie*, who had loved her best friend Jimmy so much that she'd stepped up to defend his wife when she had every goddamned right to throw Paris to the wolves.

"It's not the end of the story," Elsie says with a sad smile. "The day after graduation, Jimmy calls, says he's going to come by. He wanted to 'talk.'" She crooks her fingers into air quotes. "I thought to myself, 'This is it. He's going to propose.' In those days, it was pretty common to get married right after high school. So I wait for him on the porch, and I'm wearing a nice dress and my hair is curled and I'm ready. I was accepted to Brown in the fall, and I thought if we got married, Jimmy could come with me to Rhode Island, since he wasn't planning to go to college.

"He pulls up in his father's old pickup truck, and I see that the back is filled with all his belongings. He gets out of the car, walks over to me, and says, 'Babe, I'm heading to Los Angeles.' Just like that. At first, I misunderstood, and I asked him when he was coming back. He said he wasn't. He had come to say goodbye. 'The next time you see me,' he said, 'I'll be on the *Tonight Show.*' The bastard broke my heart."

"Oh, Elsie," Paris says.

"And wouldn't you know, ten years later, there he was, riffing with Johnny Carson, just like he said he would be. The sonofabitch." A small laugh. "Yeah, Jimmy could be a real asshole. He had this tunnel vision for what he wanted his life to be, and if anything ever got in the way of that, he could be so cruel. He was incredibly self-centered, which is why none of his marriages ever lasted, and why all of his ex-wives hated him. It's why I sometimes hated him. But I can't blame him for all of it. I willingly fixed his problems. I flew wherever he needed me to be so I could clean up his messes, made apologies on his behalf. I knew there were times he was just using me, like a gap filler, something to do while working toward the next great thing that wouldn't include me."

Elsie looks out the window again. "But then something shifted. He hit rock bottom. He got clean. Announced he was retiring and moved back here. And things *were* different this time. *He* was different. Calmer. Remorseful. Sensitive. He was going to therapy, and really doing the work. We started to get close again . . . really close. I thought maybe, finally . . ." She looks directly at Paris, who catches her meaning, loud and clear. "But then he met you."

Paris doesn't know what to say. Obviously she hadn't known any of this, because Jimmy had never told her. From the day they'd had coffee after yoga class three years ago, Jimmy had been so single-minded in his pursuit of her that she'd never even considered there was someone else getting run over in the process. Tunnel vision, as Elsie just said. It explained a lot about how Elsie treated her when they first met.

It explained everything, actually, and Paris sags into her chair.

"I'm glad his last years were happy ones. Up until the end, at least. He really loved you." Elsie pats Paris's hand. "Anyway, that was my long-winded lead-up to telling you that I can't be your lawyer anymore."

Paris's head snaps up. "Wait. What?"

"Don't panic, I've made a few calls." Elsie finishes her wine. "A lawyer named Sonny Everly will be coming by tomorrow at eleven. He's an excellent criminal defense attorney with twenty years of trial experience."

"Okay," Paris says slowly. "I understand. You were being loyal to Jimmy by helping me, but obviously if you think there's even the tiniest possibility that I might have done it—"

"That's not why." Elsie sets her glass down and looks Paris straight in the eyes. "The reason I asked Sonny to step in is because I'm too rusty. I didn't handle your arraignment as well as I should have. I was caught off guard by the new will, and that happened because I'm too close to the situation. Any other lawyer, that's the first thing they would have checked, but it didn't even occur to me that Jimmy would find another lawyer to draft up a whole new will. I missed it, which means I have no business diving back into criminal work. You'll be in excellent hands with Sonny."

"Would Sonny have gotten me a lower bail?"

"Probably not, but—"

"Then you did your job, Elsie," Paris says. "And I'm grateful. But I'm not sure I can afford him. I've already leveraged almost everything to pay the bond, which I'll never get back." She looks down at the circle of pink diamonds on her left hand. "I guess I could sell my wedding ring. And the Tesla, too, since I can borrow Jimmy's car."

"I'm paying Sonny," Elsie says. "When you're acquitted, you can pay me back. Fair warning, though: the man is an absolute prick. But that's what you need. You want someone who's not afraid to get in the mud and slug it out, and it seems I've forgotten how to do that outside of litigation."

"Thank you," Paris says. "If you trust him, I'll trust him."

"I also called the attorney who drafted Jimmy's last will and requested a copy. His firm's reputation is impeccable. The will is valid."

"That's bad news for me." Paris slumps farther into her chair. "All that money makes me look guilty as hell. And what's the point of being rich if I'm spending the rest of my life in a four-by-nine cell?"

"Tell me something," Elsie says. "You remember in court, how Salazar implied Jimmy's drug use might have been a one-time thing? I have to ask you, was Jimmy using again?"

Paris sighs. "Zoe just told me that she caught him doing it once at a taping for the second special. He promised her it would be the only time, to help him get through the last performance. She never told me because he asked her not to, and obviously she was loyal to Jimmy." She looks down. "I'm ashamed to say I never noticed."

"Don't be. Jimmy had decades of practice hiding his addiction." Elsie frowns. "When did you talk to Zoe?"

"Yesterday. She came over, apologized for not giving me the benefit of the doubt. Surprisingly, she's a really sweet person, when she's not being annoying."

"I don't buy it." Elsie's voice is flat. "She was too attached to Jimmy. What employer leaves an assistant five million dollars in his will? I'm starting to wonder if she's the reason he changed it. Think about it—Zoe spent more time with Jimmy than either of us. How is it possible she didn't notice his memory lapses? I personally think she knew something was off, and she covered it up."

Paris considers this for a minute. It *was* a little intense, Zoe and Jimmy's relationship. His assistant had known better than most how much he'd struggled with his addiction and mental health issues. Even using one time was dangerous, and if she really did care about her boss, the best thing she could have done was speak up.

A sense of unease washes over Paris. Had Zoe duped her yesterday?

Elsie reaches into her briefcase and pulls out a printed document with at least two dozen pages. She flips through it, then stops at a highlighted paragraph. She pokes the page with a coral-painted fingernail. "Read this."

It's Jimmy's will. Paris reads the paragraph carefully, which states that Zoe Moffatt will inherit five million dollars.

"Okay," she says to Elsie. "We knew that already."

Elsie flips the pages again until she gets to another highlighted paragraph. "Now read this."

It appears to be the section of the will where Jimmy's corporate holdings are detailed, and a lot of it is worded in legalese that goes over Paris's head. She has to read it three times before she understands it, and when she finally does, her mouth drops open.

Zoe Moffatt will inherit *20 percent* of all Jimmy's earnings from the Quan deal.

"The prosecutor made such a big show of telling the courtroom how much money you'd be getting as Jimmy's wife," Elsie says. "But he never mentioned anything about what Zoe would be receiving on top of her five million. Salazar knew it would muddy the waters, and he didn't want to say anything that would take away the focus from you, the prime suspect."

The lawyer leans forward. "Everyone knows that the Quan deal was worth thirty million. Twenty percent of that is—"

"Six million." Paris continues to scrutinize the paragraph. "And Zoe would have received another twenty percent for the third special, had there been one. But even without it, she's getting eleven million dollars."

That was a hell of a lot of money for somebody who, in her own words, didn't even do much because Quan came to Jimmy, and so most of what she helped with was just "regular assistant stuff."

"What did Jimmy leave her in the original will?" Paris's voice is faint as she works to process it all.

"Not a dime." Elsie's face is grim. "Look, I'm not saying she killed him, because I don't think anybody did. I truly believe Jimmy died by suicide, as do you. But Zoe is the one who made sure you were arrested. Making you look guilty of murder is an effective way to distract people from suspecting that maybe she was the one who got Jimmy to change his will."

"But she apologized," Paris says in wonder. "She really seemed sorry."

She sits with it for a moment, second-guessing every second of her conversation with Zoe from the day before.

"So what now?" she finally asks.

"You get some rest, that's what now," Elsie says briskly. "I'll be back in the morning for your meeting with Sonny."

"I thought you weren't my lawyer anymore."

"I'm not." The older woman stands, and Paris follows her to the front door. "I'll be here to consult. As a friend. And as your friend, I'm going to remind you to be completely honest with Sonny about everything. Be as transparent as possible."

There's another round of camera flashes as Elsie steps out. Paris shuts the door and then leans against it.

Transparent? When has she ever been transparent in her life?

* * *

The newest letter from Ruby is not on lavender-colored stationery, nor was it mailed from Sainte-Élisabeth, Quebec. This one arrives in a plain white envelope, and the return address is in Maple Sound, Ontario. Which means one thing.

Ruby Reyes is officially a free woman.

Dear Paris,

My deepest condolences on your recent loss, and my most heartfelt congratulations on your newfound wealth. In light of recent circumstances, I believe ten million would now be the appropriate amount. My banking information is included below.

You'll be glad to know I finally found your urn. I assumed your Tita Flora would have set it in a place of honor, but it seems she doesn't have the fondest memories of you. In any case, once I receive the money, I will lovingly scatter your ashes in the lake, so that you may rest in peace forever.

By the way, did you kill your husband? You can tell me. I'll keep your secret. I'm happy to keep all your secrets, so long as I'm properly rewarded.

Warmest regards,
Ruby

P.S. Every night when those pond frogs croak, I imagine setting the whole place on fire. You're an expert. What's the best way to do it?

Ruby got one thing right. Paris *is* good at making fires.

This time, she takes the letter into the kitchen and turns on the gas stove. She touches the corner of the paper to the blue flame and watches it ignite, the fire eating through her mother's words in seconds.

Her first demand was one million. Then it was three million. Now it's ten million. *Ten million dollars.* It was ridiculous, except it wasn't. Ruby has nothing to lose by asking. And Paris has everything to lose if she doesn't figure out what to do about this, and soon.

Just before the letter can singe her fingers, she drops it into the sink, where it burns until all that's left are a few tiny bits of charred paper.

If she'd given herself more time to think about it nineteen years ago, she might have handled Mae differently, come up with a different plan, chosen a different path.

But sometimes the only way to start over is to burn it all down.

CHAPTER TWENTY-EIGHT

"Joey."

Nobody at the Cherry called Joey by her real name, and the music was so loud, she assumed she'd misheard. Other than Cherry, Chaz, and Mae, most people here didn't even know what her real name was.

"Joey," the voice said again, floating in the darkness of the hallway. "Joey, over here."

She definitely heard it that time, and turned to find Mae's boyfriend leaning against the wall near the dressing room. She'd just finished her stage routine and needed to pee again before heading up to VIP for her bachelor party request. Champagne Room possibilities, big money night.

"Vinny," Joey said in surprise. "You're not allowed to be back here. Staff only."

"Shhhh. I snuck in, don't tell anyone." Vinny gave her a boyish smile.

Joey walked closer to him so she could hear him better, marveling once again at how difficult it was to equate him with the gangster she knew him to be. He was just so *little*, and in her five-inch heels, she towered over him.

"I'm looking for my girl," Vinny said. "I peeked in the dressing room, but I didn't see her. Any idea where she might be?"

"She didn't show up for work tonight," Joey said. "Cherry's not too happy. You don't know where she is, either?"

"I've been calling and leaving messages, but she hasn't called me back.

I'm starting to wonder if maybe she dumped me and forgot to tell me." Vinny smiled again, which seemed out of place, considering what he just said. "You don't know if she's seeing anyone else, do you?"

"Of course not," Joey said immediately. His smile was making her nervous. "She loves you, Vinny. But now you got me worried. Should we call someone?"

"Who would we call?" Vinny asked. "You know she's got no family."

His hand brushed her arm, and it was all Joey could do not to jerk away. His smile wasn't just making her uncomfortable—it was starting to scare her. She was familiar with that smile; she'd seen it too many times.

It was the smile monsters wore when they were pretending they weren't monsters.

"Maybe you can help me, Joey," Vinny said. "I gave Mae something of mine to hold on to a few days ago, and I really need it back. Like, tonight. Can you think of any place she might have stashed it?"

"I'm sorry, I have no idea." Joey glanced around, hoping someone she knew was nearby, but they were alone in the dark hallway. "Um, I should really get back to work, or Cherry will be pissed."

"Of course. Sorry to bother you on such a busy night." Vinny turned away, but before she could exhale, he spun back around, as if something had just occurred to him. "Oh, hey. I know you said she's not seeing anyone else, but you wouldn't be lying to me, would you, Joey? I don't really like it when people lie to me. I know you girls talk." That smile again.

She did her best to smile back. "Vinny, I promise. Mae would never cheat on you. I know how much she loves you."

But the truth was, Joey knew no such thing. Like most girls their age, Mae was either gushing about her boyfriend, or bitching about him. The difference was, Vinny was capable of extreme violence. Joey had not fully understood that until right this moment. Every part of her body was on high alert. This conversation needed to end, and fast.

"You know what, maybe we should call someone," Joey said. "The police, maybe. We could file one of those missing persons reports?"

At the word *police*, Vinny took a step back. "Nah, I don't think we need to go that far. Just tell her to call me, okay? I really need back what I gave her. She'll know what that means." His smile didn't waver. "Happy

New Year, Joey. You ever want to make some real money, let me know, I'll hook you up."

A cold gust of air swept into the hallway as Vinny left through the back door, which was still unguarded. Joey leaned against the wall to steady herself. Her whole body was vibrating. There was a pay phone in the dressing room; she needed to call Mae and let her know that her boyfriend was looking for her. Whatever Mae had that belonged to him, she needed to give it back. Immediately.

Joey entered the dressing room and stopped in her tracks.

Every locker door was open. Everyone's stuff was all over the floor. Every single lock had been cut.

Joey's instincts were correct. She learned a long time ago that if your Spidey senses are tingling, villains abound.

* * *

After leaving Mae a message on her home answering service and cell phone, Joey headed upstairs, trying to get into a better headspace. A VIP request was a big deal.

There were three sections at the Golden Cherry, which essentially meant there were three levels of pay. The majority of the Cherry's patrons would spend their evenings on the main floor, watching the stage shows and enjoying the attention from the girls working the room. This is where most of the dancers were stationed on any given night, and their goal was to entice the customers into buying a lap dance. Full nudity on the main floor was not allowed, so if you wanted a dance at your table, the dancer would stop short of removing her G-string. If you wanted to see what was under the G-string, you'd have to move to a designated area at the back of the room. Lap dances were a flat ten bucks per song, but tips were encouraged. Nothing at the Cherry was free, and the rules were posted everywhere:

No photos or videos
No touching
Two drink minimum per hour

The rules were different in VIP, which was on the second level of the club. The fifty-dollar cover charge went straight to your bar tab, and the drinks and service were generally better. Lap dances took place in semi-private booths lining the side wall, and touching was allowed, but only by the dancer, only over the clothes, and only if she offered. Tips were expected. The more you paid, the longer she stayed, and the more you got to see.

And at the very back of the VIP area was a velvet curtain with a purple neon sign that read CHAMPAGNE ROOM. It was guarded by a bouncer at all times, and $250 would get you past the curtain and into the oval-shaped room, which had its own stage and pole right in the center. A dozen private booths lined the perimeter, each with a loveseat and a curtain that closed completely. There were no rules in the Champagne Room, and anything that happened in a Champagne *booth* was a negotiation between the dancer and her customer. It was not unheard of for a girl to earn two to five thousand a night in there. But to earn that much, you had to be willing to do . . . extras.

At first, Joey was appalled when she heard about the things that happened behind the velvet curtains. But the longer she worked at the Cherry, the less of a big deal it all seemed. You didn't have to do anything you didn't want to, and if you were ever uncomfortable—or if you changed your mind—a red button in each booth would summon the bouncer right outside.

It helped if you drank with your customers first. Some girls, like Dallas and Mae, got high. Joey didn't need alcohol, and she never did drugs.

All she needed to do was be Ruby.

Her first time in a Champagne booth was with an older gentleman who said, "I'll pay you a hundred if you let me touch you wherever I want."

"Okay," she said.

Three songs later, he said, "I'll give you two hundred if you touch *me* wherever I want."

"I'm sorry, no."

"Three hundred."

She shook her head.

"Five hundred."

Five hundred dollars. Joey had rent to pay. Groceries. Cable. Phone. Her bus pass. Clothes. And a hiding spot full of cash that she added to as soon as she got home from work each night. This would not be her life forever. This was only her life for now. And the more she earned, the faster she could get to wherever it was that she was meant to be.

She said yes, and then closed her eyes, allowing Ruby to take over. Ruby always knew what to do. Joey's mind was someplace else by the time the customer moved her hand where he wanted it. She was at the top of Mount Everest. She was on a grassy hill, looking up at the stars. She was at the beach, on a hot day, with the sand between her toes and the sun on her face, somewhere she was loved, somewhere she was safe, somewhere she was free.

She earned a thousand dollars from that one customer that night. She was surprised at how easy it was. Because in the dark, it didn't matter.

In the dark, it didn't happen.

* * *

Joey saw the guy in the stupid gold crown a second before he saw her, and when their eyes met, he waved. Yep, same idiot from outside. Plastering a smile on her face, she sauntered over to the table. She counted seven of them, not much older than she was, maybe mid-twenties at most. She was told there'd be eight, so one wasn't here yet.

The gold crown guy had to be the one getting married, so Joey focused her attention on him.

"All hail the king," she said, and the table of guys laughed.

"I knew you were gorgeous under that big coat, China doll." Gold Crown's loud voice carried easily over the music as his eyes feasted on her body. He patted his thighs. "Come and sit on my lap."

"Bro, she won't just *sit* on you," the friend next to him said, rolling his eyes. "You have to pay her first."

Joey poked his crown. "So I hear tomorrow's the big day?"

"Fuck, no," he said with a grin. "The guest of honor went to make a phone call. What's your name, China doll?"

"My name is Ruby," Joey said. "And for the right price, I'll let you polish my gem."

A roar of laughter followed. It was such a stupid line, but it was always a hit.

"I'm Jake," he said, and then proceeded to go around the table introducing everybody. It was completely unnecessary because she didn't care, and there was no way she'd remember. By the time he was back where he started, she'd already forgotten his name.

Fleur, one of the VIP cocktail waitresses, brought over a tray of shots.

"You ordered ten?" one of the guys said. His expression was glazed as he watched Fleur place them on the table, his words heavy and slurred. "But there's only eight of us." *Thersh only eight of ush.*

"That's because these two are for the ladies." Jack—or was it Jake?—handed Joey and Fleur their own shots, and then he looked around the table with a grin. "Bottoms up, motherfuckers."

Joey exchanged a look with Fleur, who shrugged and slammed hers back like it was nothing. Joey followed suit, the liquid searing its way down the back of her throat. She found whiskey revolting. The taste and smell reminded her of Tito Micky.

But those were Joey's memories, and Joey wasn't here tonight.

She leaned over Jack-or-Jake, her barely covered breasts right in his face. "How about a private dance while we're waiting for your friend?" she said into his ear.

"Not so fast, baby," he said with a grin. "I want to see what I'm getting first."

He pulled out his wallet and made a big show of extracting a twenty. Every group had a guy who wanted to show off to his buddies. She picked up the twenty and cocked an eyebrow.

"Sweetie, this won't even get my dress off."

All the guys at the table laughed as Joey held his gaze. It was an unspoken challenge, and they all knew it.

He replaced the twenty with a fifty. "What does this buy me?"

She smiled at him just as the song changed. Prince's "Kiss" started playing, which was perfect, because not only was the song the exact right tempo, it was only three and a half minutes long.

Showtime.

Keeping her eyes on Jack-or-Jake, she began moving her body. She knew she wasn't the best dancer—Cherry had said as much during her audition—but she'd worked hard to improve over the past year. In any case, it didn't matter all that much. There were naked women all over the club, and any of them could move just fine. The thing that made it special—the thing that made the customer want more—was how you made him *feel.*

And that was Ruby's specialty.

The hoots and cheers of the guys at the table were loud at first, but they got further away as Ruby took over. Joey's mind began to drift. She reminded herself to try Mae again on her break, assuming she even got a break tonight. Cherry had been made aware of the locker break-in but had declined to call the cops, not wanting to scare off the customers on a big money night. She felt Jack-or-Jake's hand on her thigh and absently moved it away. *Nice try, asshole. Not for fifty bucks.*

She peeled off her dress, placing the gold fabric around his neck like a scarf while his buddies cheered. Her bikini top came off next, and she tossed it onto the table, where three of the guys immediately grabbed for it. Then she picked up the last whiskey shot, the one that was meant for the guy who was getting married tomorrow who wasn't even here. She poured it over her breasts, rubbing the liquid into her bare nipples.

"Oh my God," she heard someone say. "That's so fucking hot."

She looked into Jack-or-Jake's eyes, allowing her tongue to trace the contours of her top lip. His pupils were fully dilated, and they looked like raisins, which reminded her that she needed to go grocery shopping. She stepped out of her G-string and was now fully nude except for her necklace and heels. She could see Jack-or-Jake's erection straining against the crotch of his jeans, and she turned around so she didn't have to look at it. Slowly—because everything had to be done slowly—she bent all the way forward until her hair touched the floor and she could grab her ankles. She sighed with pleasure as the pendant from her necklace hit her chin; this was such a good hamstring stretch. At Cherry's suggestion, she'd taken up yoga to improve her strength and flexibility, and it was amazing how many stripper moves were actually yoga moves. Right now she was practicing *prasarita padottanasana*, or wide-legged forward fold—except she was naked, with her ass in someone's face.

Behind her, she could feel Jack-or-Jake's hands lightly touching her butt, but this time she decided to allow it, since the Prince song was about to end. The more turned on he was, the more he'd want to go private. She began to roll herself back up again, engaging both her legs and core to keep the movements sensual. This was a hard enough move on a mat in yoga class, let alone on a hard floor, with a whiskey shot in her, wearing stilettos.

As soon as she straightened up fully, she saw him.

He was coming out of the hallway where the bathrooms were, as tall and lean as ever, same familiar gait, blue Nokia cell phone in one hand. Even in the dim light, she could tell he looked different. The twists were gone, the goatee was gone; he was clean-shaven now, with a simple fade. The shorter hair made his face look more chiseled. The glasses were new as well, rectangular-framed and stylish.

But it was unmistakably, undeniably *Drew*.

Her first instinct was to run, duck, or throw herself under the table, basically anything so he wouldn't see her. But her feet wouldn't step forward, her head wouldn't turn away, her hands wouldn't cover her face. All she could do was stand there, naked, her breasts still moist from the whiskey, utterly frozen.

And then he saw her.

Recognition bloomed on his face as his gaze darted from her eyes to her breasts to her crotch to the new tattoo on her thigh he was seeing for the first time, and then back up again. Recognition turned into shock, and shocked morphed into confusion. If a hole were to suddenly open up in the floor, she would have gladly dropped into it. Because anything was better than the way Drew was looking at her right now.

He was *seeing* her, and there was nowhere to go, and no way to rewind.

The music was too loud for her to hear him actually say her name, but his lips formed the word *Joey*, and that was enough to bring her all the way back into herself. Just like that, Ruby was gone, and now she was herself again, buck naked in a strip club, and painfully, excruciatingly ashamed. It felt like one of those anxiety dreams where you thought you were clothed, only to realize that you were naked in front of a roomful of people.

Except it was actually fucking happening, and there was no way to wake up. Joey was in a nightmare of her own making.

A couple of Drew's friends spoke to him, gesturing for him to sit down. Someone poured him a beer from one of the many pitchers on the table. He finally took a seat, but pushed the beer away. Someone else smacked him on the shoulder, waving a twenty and pointing to Joey. Drew shook his head decisively. No, he did not want a lap dance. Or, perhaps more accurately, he did not want a lap dance from *her*.

Jack-or-Jake had his arms wrapped around her waist from behind in a too-snug embrace. Normally she would never have tolerated this, but staring across the table at the person she loved most in the world, she wasn't sure her knees wouldn't buckle. She felt dizzy. Nauseated. There was a ringing in her ears. Her stomach hurt.

"Baby, let's do the Champagne Room," Jack-or-Jake said into her ear. She could feel him pressing against her. "I have to be alone with you."

She opened her mouth to say no—because surely she couldn't do that, she couldn't go with one of Drew's friends into the goddamned Champagne Room while Drew was *looking right the fuck at her*—but no words came out.

Instead, she nodded dumbly as Jack-or-Jake pulled her away from the group and toward the room with the curtains and the velvet booths, where two hundred fifty was just the starting price for a bottle of champagne and a whole lot more. As Jack-or-Jake fumbled through his wallet to pay the bouncer, Joey chanced one last look back. She made brief eye contact with Drew before he took off his glasses and turned away.

He understood what was happening. He just didn't want to see.

CHAPTER TWENTY-NINE

In hindsight, Paris doesn't believe that Drew meant to shame her when he drove her home later that night. He was shocked, embarrassed, and upset, and while he didn't express any of those feelings very well, they were understandable.

Unlike what was happening now.

Paris's new lawyer is in his late forties, with a shaved head, a bulldog neck, and biceps the size of footballs bursting out of the sleeves of his fitted Lacoste golf shirt. Paris had found herself a little starry-eyed when Elsie first introduced them; she had not expected Sonny Everly to be such a hunk.

And then he spoke.

The three of them are sitting at the kitchen table, drinking the coffee Paris brewed and eating the doughnuts Elsie brought.

"Come on, Paris. Why'd you really marry him?" Sonny asks. He isn't happy with her first two answers. "No jury is going to believe you genuinely loved the guy. He was almost thirty years older, with a history of addiction, who was basically a dick to everyone. He was officially a has-been when you met. The jury needs to understand your relationship so they'll sympathize that you lost him."

"He was *retired* when we met, and I don't know that version of Jimmy you just described." Paris's arms are folded across her chest. She's aware that it makes her look defensive, but at the moment, she doesn't care.

"Bullshit. You saw a meal ticket and grabbed it. Or you have daddy issues. Maybe you sensed his mind was starting to go and figured you wouldn't have to wait too long to talk him into killing the prenup."

"Fuck you," Paris says, her voice hot. She looks over at Elsie. The woman doesn't exactly have a warm personality herself, but compared to Sonny, she's a cruise ship director. She gives Paris a tiny shrug. *I told you.*

"None of the above," Paris says. "We started as friends and we got closer. We liked and respected each other—"

"Did you guys have sex?"

Paris's cheeks are burning. She glances at Elsie again, who's now picking at an invisible speck of lint on her blouse. It's one thing to answer this question for, say, Henry, who was forever interested in other people's bedroom activities and wanted all the details. But she can't imagine discussing it with a man she's just met and a woman who's probably slept with Jimmy more times than she has.

"Our sex life was normal," she says.

"Did he require any pharmaceutical assistance to perform?"

"Why is this relevant?" Paris snaps. "What does this have to do with him being dead?"

"It has everything to do with it." Sonny leans forward, looking right into her eyes. "Everything about your very abnormal, short-lived marriage is relevant. The prosecutor is going to pick your life apart, find all the ways your relationship wasn't perfect, and paint you as an unhappy, selfish, gold-digging bitch who murdered her elderly husband for the money. The more you tell me now, the more I can prepare for that."

"Jimmy wasn't elderly. And I didn't kill him. Next. Fucking. Question."

Sonny sighs and looks over at Elsie. "You didn't talk to her about this?"

Elsie shakes her head. "We never got that far."

Sonny leans back in his chair, stretches his arms up, and laces his fingers behind his head. Paris once read that this was a power move, something that people—men, usually—subconsciously did to demonstrate their dominance over the people around them.

"Paris, it doesn't matter whether you killed him," Sonny says, and for the first time since he arrived, he doesn't sound completely abrasive. "For the purposes of your trial, I don't give a shit whether you did it or not.

That's between you and your God. What matters is what story we can sell to a jury in order to plant reasonable doubt that you *didn't* do it. In court, what matters is what the prosecutor can prove, and the burden of proof is on them. Nico Salazar is going to craft the most plausible narrative he can to paint a picture for the jury of why and how you murdered your husband."

"And Sonny's job is to refute that story," Elsie says. "He'll poke holes, he'll discredit witnesses, he'll take every scrap of evidence the prosecution has and demonstrate how it can be interpreted three different ways. But if he also has his own narrative that he can sell to the jury about what happened, even better."

"So then why don't you both tell me what you think the story should be." Paris speaks through gritted teeth. "Better yet, just tell me what the hell you want me to say, and I'll say it. Because clearly me telling you the truth isn't enough."

"*Now* you're getting it." Sonny grins, exposing a row of very white teeth. It's a shark smile if there ever was one. "Which doesn't mean we don't tell the truth. But we need to *package* it in a way that makes it easiest for the jury to actually believe."

"I understand," Paris says. "You want to reinterpret the information so it tells a whole different story of what happened."

"Bingo," Sonny says. "I knew you were smarter than you looked."

Gee, thanks, you mansplaining, roid-raging prick.

Sonny pulls several folders out of his briefcase and slides them toward Paris. "I need you to look carefully at all of these."

"What are they?"

"Police reports, medical findings, forensic analyses, autopsy photos, and crime scene photos," Sonny says. "Everything the prosecutor is using to build his case against you."

"I don't want to look at photos," Paris says.

"Too bad." Sonny cracks his knuckles. "This is your life we're trying to save, and if you want to help yourself, then you need to see everything Nico Salazar sees. You need to be prepared." He taps the top folder. "Start with this one."

Paris looks at Elsie. "Do I have to?"

The other woman nods. "It's going to be okay. You've already seen the real thing. These photos will look a lot more . . . clinical. I've looked through them already."

In this moment, Paris resents them both. Bracing herself, she opens the folder.

It's one thing to get a look at Jimmy in the bathtub for a moment or two before hitting her head and passing out. It's a whole other thing to see a brightly lit photograph of her husband's dead body lying in a tub full of blood and water, in high definition, from multiple angles, some of them close-up.

Although, as Elsie said, it's not quite as shocking as she was expecting. She never did see the wound where the straight razor cut him. The laceration on Jimmy's thigh is small, straight, and neat. It's crazy to think that his entire life's essence drained out of that one small spot. And even with the vacant stare, his face looks peaceful in the photo, which is not how she remembers it. It does help her to know that he died peacefully.

Unlike Charles.

Unlike Mae.

She works her way through all the photos. The crime scene unit photographed absolutely everything in the bathroom—the tile, the towels, even the contents of the vanity.

"Stop," Sonny says, when she comes to a photo of the inside of one of the vanity drawers. "Explain this to me."

Paris looks down at the photo, not sure what he's asking. It's obvious what they are. Jimmy kept his small collection of straight razors in the drawer, and the photo shows three of them lined up neatly in their cases, on top of a microfiber cloth. Across the table, Elsie looks uneasy, as if she knows exactly where Sonny is going with this.

"Why are his straight razors in the bathroom?" Sonny asks. "According to his medical records, Jimmy had a benign tremor in his right hand. And according to you, he was presenting symptoms of early dementia. So why, exactly, were these very sharp—and obviously deadly—straight razors in his drawer?"

"I . . . I never thought about it." Paris looks at Elsie, and then back at Sonny. "I mean, we still have knives in the kitchen, an ax in the shed, a saw in the garage, a weed whacker . . ."

"But none of those things are meant to go over your throat," Sonny says. "Weren't you concerned that he might forget that he wasn't supposed to shave with a straight razor anymore?"

Paris begins to understand the point her lawyer is making, and she slumps in her chair. That's actually exactly what happened the morning she left for Vancouver, and a huge argument ensued. She'd assumed Jimmy was being reckless and stubborn, and that he'd gone back on his promise to switch to the electric shaver she'd bought him. Jimmy had lashed out, furious, saying he didn't want to be told what he could and could not do. He'd accused her of treating him like a child.

But looking back now, that wasn't why he was angry at all. Jimmy had been using his electric shaver without protest for a year. That morning, though, he had *forgotten* how he was supposed to shave. And anger was always his reaction whenever he realized he had forgotten something. Anger was his way of hiding his fear that he was losing his memory.

She had misread the situation entirely. Because she had been distracted.

"The prosecutor will want to know why you left those straight razors within easy reach if you really thought Jimmy's memory loss was becoming a problem." Sonny stares at her. "It makes you look . . . indifferent. Which fits the image of you Salazar is trying to create, that you didn't really care about Jimmy at all."

"Of course I did." Paris looks over at Elsie, feeling helpless, and then back at Sonny. "But I can't argue with what you're saying. I have no excuse. I missed it." *I had other things on my mind.*

"We all missed it," Elsie says firmly, squeezing her arm. "But what does that matter if she has an alibi? Let's not forget, if we can find proof that Paris was nowhere near the house at the time Jimmy died, this all goes away."

Sonny stares at Paris a little longer, and then finally shifts his gaze to Elsie. "Where is US Border Patrol at with sending us the time-stamped footage of when she crossed back into the country?"

"They had technical issues that night," Elsie says. "The system crashed, and they lost an hour's worth of border crossing information. At this point, there's no way to know if they'll be able to recover it. The person I spoke to suggested it's happened before. It never matters until . . . it does."

"And the officer at the booth doesn't remember her?"

"There were two of them when I pulled up," Paris says. "They were talking to each other, trying to sort out the system."

"So all we have is your word that you crossed at about . . ." Sonny consults the police report in front of him. "Midnight. Which means you got home at around two."

"There was a lineup at the border when I got there," Paris says. "It took about a half hour to cross."

"Okay, so then you're home at two thirty. Jimmy had a charity gig that night at the Grand Hyatt, which he left around nine, and got home at, say, nine thirty. The medical examiner estimates that Jimmy died somewhere between then and midnight, but Salazar will make sure the jury knows that's an approximation." Sonny looks up. "You have smart wiring for the house, right? An app that can open and close the garage door, set the security alarm, adjust the heat and air-conditioning, see who's at the front door?"

"Yes, it does all of that," Paris says. "But it hasn't been working the last few days. I think it needs to be reset. Zoe was supposed to take care of that."

"Was it working over the weekend?"

"I don't know for sure. I do know that the alarm wasn't set when I got home, but Jimmy often didn't bother. That, or he forgot. Both are equally likely."

"I have the same system at home," Elsie says. "It's not hard to deactivate. Jimmy might have done it by mistake."

"Let me see your phone," Sonny says to Paris.

She unlocks it and hands it over. It looks like a toy in Sonny's huge hands. Tapping on her screen, he frowns.

"What happened to all the usage reports?"

"I have no idea," Paris says. "Maybe they got deleted when the system disconnected."

"Where does the data save?"

"What do you mean by 'save'?"

Sonny sighs. "The app tracks usage, right? The reports are then stored—archived—somewhere else, like iCloud or Dropbox, so it doesn't take up space in your phone. Where does the app archive its data?"

"I don't know," Paris says. "Like I said, Zoe was the one who originally set it all up."

"You've said that name twice now. Zoe Moffatt is Jimmy's assistant, right?" Sonny holds up her phone. "Whose email address is this?"

"That's Jimmy's," Paris says. "But Zoe has access to it because she set up his email, too."

"Were you aware that you're not an administrator of the account?" Sonny asks. "Only Jimmy was. Which really means Zoe. Which means she has the ability to delete anything she wants. You're just a user. You couldn't deactivate your own system if you wanted to."

Paris looks at Elsie, and then back at Sonny. "So Zoe deleted the reports and the archived data using Jimmy's login?"

"Bingo."

It's the second time he's said that word. She restrains herself from rolling her eyes.

"But why would Zoe do that?" Elsie asks with a frown. "To set Paris up?"

"Well, that's the forty-six-million-dollar question. You were supposed to be in Vancouver the whole weekend, right?" Sonny asks Paris, and she nods. "Jimmy died Saturday night. No matter what caused his death, you were not expected by anybody to be back in the country until Sunday afternoon. The only reason Zoe would have to wipe the data is to hide something pertaining to *herself*. Nothing else makes sense."

"Zoe drove Jimmy home after the charity event," Paris says. "And then said she went right home afterward. She would have left around nine thirty, maybe nine forty-five."

"That's within the window," Sonny says. "The police have CCTV pictures of her car on the next street over around that time, but she could have driven him home, stabbed him, and left."

"Are we actually going to suggest to the jury that *Zoe* killed Jimmy?" Paris looks back and forth between the lawyers. "Even though we're pretty sure she didn't?"

"It's either her, or you," Sonny says with a shrug. "If Zoe *could* have done it, then there's *your* reasonable doubt. After that, it would be up to Salazar to build a case against her."

He leans back and appraises the two women. "But let me ask you this.

Why are you both so sure it's suicide? Why aren't either of you willing to consider that maybe someone *did* murder him?"

It's a fair question. The best Paris can answer is that it *feels* like Jimmy took his own life. He had a lot going on. The pressure of performing. The memory loss. The slip back into drugs. And a wife who missed every single one of the signs because she was completely focused on her own goddamned problems.

"Because we knew him," Elsie says quietly, answering for them both. "It just . . . fits."

All Paris can do is nod.

"Moving on," Sonny says. "Let's talk about Vancouver. There are some holes during your time there that need to be filled."

Paris's heartbeat quickens. "What holes? I kept all the receipts, and I've already provided those to Detective Mini Wheats."

Elsie snorts. Sonny looks confused, but neither woman offers to explain.

"Walk me through it." He closes the folder with the crime scene photos and opens a different one. "I can see your registration for the . . . International Yoga Convention and Expo? That's seriously a thing? What do you do, go to panels that discuss different variations of child's pose?"

She doesn't bother to respond to that.

"Okay, I can see a copy of your check-in at the hotel with your signature on Thursday. And here's a copy of your valet card, which confirms you parked in the hotel garage for three days and never left. I can see you signed into the event, received your attendee badge, had dinner at the hotel that night, and again on Saturday, because you signed those two meals to your room."

"So what's the problem?"

"The problem is, nobody saw you at all on *Friday*," Sonny says. "None of the convention organizers can remember seeing you at any point that day. You didn't provide any other meal receipts—"

"I ate outside the hotel and paid cash," Paris says. "It's better than using my credit cards, because the exchange fees are always high."

"And one of the hotel employees thinks he saw you catch a taxi early Friday morning. He recognized you as Jimmy Peralta's wife because apparently word had gotten out that you were attending the convention. The cab company confirmed there was a fare from the Pan Pacific hotel at the time the employee says he saw you. The requested destination was the airport. At the time, the cabdriver didn't recognize you as a famous comedian's wife, but when asked to describe his passenger after the fact, he described you. So why did you go to the airport, Paris?"

"I didn't go to the airport, Sonny." Paris speaks evenly, not too fast, not too slow, not too emotional, and she doesn't add anything more. When lying, volunteering too much information is a dead giveaway. "Whoever that was, it wasn't me."

"This is easily disputed," Elsie says to Sonny. "Is there hotel security footage from that specific entrance? Was there a camera in the taxi with a time stamp? There were apparently eighteen hundred registered attendees that weekend. Paris not being *seen* is not the same thing as her not being *remembered*."

"You seem to think I flew somewhere," Paris says to her lawyer. "You can check with the airport for that information, can't you?"

"That part is challenging." Sonny seems to enjoy the sparring, and Paris is beginning to realize that maybe it helps him by sharpening his focus. "The hotel staff was cooperative, but the general manager won't authorize the release of any security footage without a warrant. Same with the airport. And to get a warrant, we need the cooperation of the Vancouver police. And since you're not a terrorist, a fugitive, or a serial killer on a killing spree, that's not likely to happen anytime soon. You're not a priority in Canada."

Inwardly, Paris collapses with relief, silently cheering her birth country's utter lack of interest in helping. Outwardly, she says, "I'm curious. Where is it you think I went?"

Sonny shrugs. "Don't know. But I have a feeling you're the kind of woman with a lot of secrets."

Bingo.

CHAPTER THIRTY

The truth is, Paris did go to Vancouver. She just didn't stay there. Whichever hotel employee saw her hop into a taxi Friday morning was correct.

The day Zoe released their wedding photo, Paris began to panic. It felt like it was just a matter of time before someone from her old life started asking questions about why Jimmy Peralta's new wife looked an awful lot like a dead stripper from Toronto. Paris didn't have a plan for how she'd handle this, other than to deny it. There was no proof, and people had doppelgängers all the time. Looking like someone else isn't a crime. If anyone asked, she would simply deny, deny, deny.

Until Ruby's first letter arrived, Paris had no idea that the ashes supposedly belonging to Joey Reyes were in an urn somewhere in her aunt's house in Maple Sound. It never occurred to her that the body would be cremated and sent to her next of kin—she hadn't given much thought to the body at all after she'd burned it. And it wasn't until she googled it that she learned ashes could be tested for DNA.

The best defense was a good offense, so Paris got to work. She started by creating a new email account under a fake name, which allowed her to create a fake Facebook account that said she was a retired nurse who used to work at Toronto General, the hospital where Tita Flora worked before the family moved to Maple Sound. She sent out friend requests to as many nurses as she could find who'd worked there, and then sent a request to her aunt. Tita Flora accepted immediately, likely because they had so many mutual friends.

Boom. Now Paris had a way to track what the family was up to. And the first thing she saw on her aunt's page was that Tito Micky was dead. There was a photo of Tita Flora laying flowers at his grave on the fifth anniversary of his death, in the cemetery behind St. Agnes Catholic Church in Maple Sound. It looked like a pretty, peaceful spot.

Paris didn't know how to feel about that.

It would be another two months before a window of opportunity presented itself, and when it happened, it was because of Carson. Her youngest cousin, the little boy who used to follow her around, was almost thirty now, and he was getting married. The whole family—minus her late uncle, of course—would be attending the wedding in Niagara-on-the-Lake, three hours away from Maple Sound. They'd be gone the whole weekend—Lola Celia, too, who was still alive at the age of eighty-eight. Why was it always the meanest ones who lived the longest?

This meant the house in Maple Sound would be empty.

The plan was straightforward: all Paris had to do was break into the house, locate the urn, switch out the ashes, and get the hell out. When the family returned from the wedding, they'd never know anyone had even been there.

Next: her alibi. This one was easy. The yoga convention in Vancouver was the same weekend in June, giving her the perfect reason to cross the border. Paris registered online and booked a last-minute cancellation at the convention hotel from Thursday to Sunday.

While stalking Tita Flora on Facebook, Paris also spent a lot of time on anonymous message boards searching for someone with a specific type of expertise. Eventually she was given an email address for a guy named Stuart. Using another fake email, she contacted him. He quoted her ten grand, and said it would take two weeks. Paris withdrew half the amount in cash from her savings account, and drove down to Tacoma later that day.

Stuart turned out to be a nineteen-year-old college dropout covered in Cheetos dust. He lived at home with his parents, who both worked during the day. He ushered Paris upstairs to his bedroom, where she stood in front of a plain white wall as he snapped a few headshots of her with his iPhone. She paid him five thousand dollars, and he told her to wait for his email.

"I know you," he said, as she was leaving. "You're married to that old guy. The comedian. What do you need a fake Canadian ID for?"

"You don't know me," Paris said. "And if I tell you, I'll have to kill you."

Thirteen days later, an email from Stuart said her new Canadian driver's license, credit card, and burner phone were ready. She was in Tacoma ninety minutes later, where she paid him the rest of the money.

"The limit on that Visa is only a thousand." Stuart handed over her ID. "So don't go crazy. It's activated and good to go. The birthday on the driver's license is the PIN for the card. Makes it easy to remember."

She looked at the ID. It was her picture, but the name on it was Victoria Bautista, which was fine by her.

"Thanks," Paris said. "And if anyone ever asks . . ."

"You were never here." Stuart rolled his eyes. "Lady, this is my business. If I tell on you, you'll just tell on me, and that benefits nobody."

"You're smart," Paris said. "But you're too young for this kind of work. Be careful, okay?"

"You ever need a passport, it's fifty large," he said with a grin. "It takes three months, so plan ahead. You got my email."

"I'll keep that in mind," she said, and she would.

The following weekend, she left her iPhone at home on the nightstand and made the three-hour drive north to Vancouver. At the border, she held her breath as a Canada Border Services official checked her Paris Peralta passport, but it was fine, like always.

She arrived at the Pan Pacific hotel in the late afternoon and valet parked. At the registration desk during check-in, the hotel exchanged her US cash for Canadian. From there, she headed straight down to the conference level to sign in for the convention, where she put on her attendee badge. She ate dinner at one of the on-site restaurants, and signed the meal to her room.

Before she went to bed, she put the DO NOT DISTURB sign on the door, called the front desk to request complete privacy for the weekend—no housekeeping or turndown service needed—and then tossed and turned the rest of the night.

Early the next morning, she locked her Paris Peralta passport and driver's license in the hotel room safe, and caught a taxi to the airport. She didn't want to use the credit card she bought from Stuart until she had to, so she paid the fare in cash. Two hours later, at Vancouver International, "Victoria Bautista" boarded a domestic flight to Toronto using only her driver's license. She landed at Pearson International at eight Friday evening, where she used her brand-new Visa to rent an economy car from Enterprise.

She reached her aunt's house in Maple Sound just before midnight. She drove halfway up the long hill, cut the lights, and then drove the rest of the way in the dark. Before she reached the top, she stopped and did a three-point turn, so the car was facing downward in case she needed to make a quick getaway. She left the key in the ignition and the driver's-side door slightly ajar, then grabbed the small knapsack she brought with her.

She was eighteen when she left Maple Sound, and she hadn't bothered to say goodbye. The day after her high school graduation—which she didn't attend—she cleaned out the empty coffee canister above the fridge where Tita Flora hid her grocery money from Tito Micky. Then she swiped the gambling winnings Tito Micky hid from Tita Flora from the bottom of his fishing box in the toolshed. Last, she plucked out the roll of bills Lola Celia kept stuffed in a sock at the back of her underwear drawer, money the old woman was saving to pay for her yearly flight back to the Philippines. All that, combined with five years' worth of cash that she'd pilfered little by little and stashed in her hiding spot, came out to twelve thousand dollars. Severance pay for five years of babysitting, cooking, cleaning, doing laundry . . . and Tito Micky.

The only thing she didn't touch were the kids' piggy banks.

She stood in the dark and stared up at the two-story house, backlit by the moon over Lake Huron. All the lights inside were off. From somewhere nearby, an owl hooted, and she could hear the sounds of small animals rustling in the bushes.

She never thought she'd see this place again.

An older Nissan Altima was parked at the side of the house where Tito Micky's wood-paneled station wagon used to be, but her aunt and grandmother would have only needed one car to get to the wedding. The pond looked the same, as did the tree swing and the toolshed. But the brown porch was now white, and there were hydrangea bushes all along the front of the house. Whatever. Tita Flora could pretty this place up all she wanted, but it would never fully cover the ugly that lived inside it.

Paris felt for the old house key in her pocket, and clutched it as she made her way toward the front door. After all these years, she'd never bothered to throw it away. Perhaps she'd kept it as a reminder of what she'd lived through. Or maybe she'd sensed that she might need it again someday.

Someday had finally come.

Right as she stepped up onto the porch, a bright light turned on. She froze, heart pounding, ears cocked for the sounds of footsteps coming from inside. When she heard nothing, she realized that the floodlight above the door was motion-activated, and it turned off after ten seconds. It made sense that they'd finally installed one, and now that she was prepared for it, she moved quickly toward the door as it turned on once again. Thankfully, the old key slid into the lock easily. She entered the house as quickly and quietly as she could, then remained still. When it was dark again, she exhaled and reached into her knapsack for her flashlight.

She probably didn't need to be so stealthy. Nobody was here. The property was four acres total, and you couldn't see the house from the main road. But it was better to be safe than sorry.

The floors had been upgraded, and there was a new beige sectional where the old floral sofa used to be, but Lola Celia's old rocking chair was still in its usual spot near the window. A 60-inch Samsung had replaced the old tube TV, but otherwise, everything looked the same. It even smelled the same, a combination of stale cigarettes, Filipino food, and the slight swampy odor of the pond that always made its way inside.

And then, as they always had, the frogs by the pond started croaking in unison, the perfect soundtrack to the life she'd lived here, and the things that had happened in the dark.

She needed to find the urn and get the hell home.

* * *

It wasn't on the fireplace mantel next to the framed family photos, nor was it sitting on any of the curio shelves, or stored inside any of the kitchen or dining room cabinets. She even checked the bathroom and the coat closet. Wherever the urn was, it was nowhere on the main floor, which left her two choices: go up or go out.

It was hard to imagine that an urn filled with human remains would be stored in one of the bedrooms. It was likelier to be in Tito Micky's shed. But it was equally possible that the family had spread the ashes nineteen years ago, and that Ruby had lied to her, pretending she had leverage on her daughter that she didn't.

The motion-activated light flicked back on as Paris went out again, but it was off by the time she reached the toolshed. It was never locked, and Tito Micky, for all his faults, had always kept the small space pretty organized. She scanned her flashlight beam over the tools, old cans of paint, musty blankets, cheap folding chairs, and the newer lawn mower. She even looked inside her uncle's old fishing box.

No ashes, no urn. *Dammit.* It had to be somewhere on the second level of the house. Assuming it even existed at all. She exited the shed and then stopped.

Something felt off. She paused, wondering what was different. It hit her a moment later.

It was too quiet. The frogs had all stopped croaking.

Paris switched off the flashlight. Instinctively, she looked up at the second floor of the house, at the window of her old bedroom. Was there someone in there? She blinked. No, there couldn't be. Everybody was at the wedding, three hours away.

Weren't they?

Something moved in the window, and she froze. At first she thought she was seeing things, but then a person-like shape moved closer to the glass. A face appeared, blurry from this distance, but unmistakable none-theless. They locked eyes.

Tito Micky.

She was back in the rental car in two minutes, her armpits sweating and her heart pounding so hard, she could hear it in her ears. She started the car, keeping the lights off until she made it back onto the road, her eyes darting to the rearview mirror every other second for any sign of someone following. She stepped on the gas, watching the needle on the odometer climb from sixty, to seventy, and then a hundred kilometers an hour, a good twenty over the speed limit.

It wasn't until she was all the way out of Maple Sound that she remembered Tito Micky was dead.

She had seen a ghost, and that ghost was with her in the car now, whispering in her ear, his hot, sour breath on her neck. The skin on her entire body was crawling, as if a tub of tiny spiders had been poured over her head and were now inside her clothes, looking for crevices to explore. The memories were taking over, and they were vivid, and terrible.

'Sus. You look just like your mother.

CHAPTER THIRTY-ONE

While Joey had never liked looking like Ruby, her mother had hated it even more. The best part of Joey's night was when she finally got to wipe Ruby's face off hers. When Cherry gave her the go-ahead to leave, the first thing Joey did was peel off her eyelashes and cold cream her skin.

The other girls in the dressing room looked just as tired as she did, and they all exchanged hugs and "Happy New Year" wishes as they left for home one by one. Joey had four thousand dollars in her knapsack that she didn't have when she first came in, which officially made it her best night ever at the Cherry. All she wanted to do was get into Chaz's car and go home. Hopefully he'd understand when she didn't invite him in, and with any luck, she'd wake up on the first morning of 1999 thinking the whole thing had been a bad dream.

But apparently, the nightmare wasn't over yet. When she finally stepped out of the back entrance and into the cold night air, the first person she saw was Drew. Standing next to Chaz.

Neither man looked happy.

After an awkward exchange, she said goodbye to Chaz and allowed Drew to drive her home. It should have been an opportunity for her and Drew to really talk, but the conversation didn't go well. In the driveway, still reeling from the news that Drew had a baby on the way and was getting married, Joey had slapped him. Her hand stung once it made contact with his cheek, a sure indication that if it hurt her, it must have really hurt him. She'd only slapped one other person in her entire life, and she was ashamed to admit that it had felt just as good now as it had then.

And, like the first time, she regretted it immediately.

She waited inside her apartment door until she heard him drive away, then sat down on the stairs and sobbed. The only thing worse than Drew marrying Simone was Drew marrying someone else. And the only thing worse than *that* was the two of them having a baby.

Kirsten. Any girl with a name like that had to be tall. Athletic. Outgoing. She was probably bubbly as hell, with a hundred friends who all looked like her. Since they had met in graduate school, she was obviously smart and going places, a girl exactly on Drew's level.

Joey had never hated someone she'd never met so much.

Wiping away her tears, she headed all the way down the stairs, peeling her clothes off as she went. She didn't bother to turn on any lights as she walked straight through the pitch-black apartment to the bathroom. She wasn't afraid of the dark anymore. There was nothing the dark could do to her that it hadn't already done.

By the time she reached the bathroom, she was naked. She turned on the tub faucet and avoided her reflection in the mirror as she lit the three vanilla candles she kept around the sink, all in various stages of melt. The flicker was soothing, and when the tub was full, she sank into the warm water.

Joey was certain she would have felt okay if Drew was marrying Simone, but this other person, this *Kirsten*, was an . . . interloper. Someone who was trespassing on something that didn't belong to her. Joey didn't know a thing about Kirsten, but already she resented everything about her.

Even the baby. Which made her a horrible person, but she couldn't help it. Drew and Kirsten's baby would tie them together forever.

I'll always be here for you, Drew had whispered in her ear as they hugged goodbye in the driveway the day he and Simone moved out. A year later, it turned out to be a lie. Because that's what men do. They lie to get what they want. And once they get it, you're discarded, like a shirt with a stain that won't come out, even though the shirt is new, and they are the stain.

Clutching her knees to her chest, Joey found her wrist with her fingernail and started digging. And digging. And digging. She felt so dirty. Everything she hated about herself was written all over Drew's face. She was disgusting. Unworthy. Stupid.

All the things Ruby always said she was.

* * *

When the bathwater cooled, Joey pulled the plug and reached for her bathrobe. She padded back through the dark apartment to her bedroom, and only then did she turn on a light.

She froze, taking in the scene.

Every drawer was open. Closet doors, too. The small desk in the corner had been ransacked. The floor was covered in her clothes, makeup, books. Just like the dressing room in the club, someone had been here, looking for something.

Vinny.

Of course it made sense that he would look for Mae here. Joey hadn't been able to get a hold of her friend, and after she saw Drew at the club, she'd forgotten all about it. Mae did hang out here, not all the time, but enough that she knew what snacks were in which cupboard, and which drawer Joey kept her pajamas in. Occasionally, if they were watching a movie and it was too late to go home, Mae would borrow something to sleep in and crash on the sofa.

Vinny would know that. Which was why he'd come here.

But how had he gotten in? The door was locked when she got home. *Shit.* The spare key. Mae knew where she hid it, inside the base of the light sconce mounted on the brick above the side door. She must have told Vinny about it at some point.

Was he still here?

No, he couldn't be. If he was still in the apartment, waiting for her, he would have shown himself while she was in the bathtub, naked and vulnerable.

A thought occurred to Joey then. Vinny might not have found whatever he was looking for, but did he find her cash?

She rushed to her nightstand drawer, which was open, its contents rifled through. She didn't keep anything interesting in here—bottles of nail polish, two half-read paperbacks she'd lost interest in, an open box of condoms Chaz had brought, an issue of *Cosmopolitan*—but it was what she hid *under* the drawer that she cared about.

Kneeling on the floor, she emptied the nightstand quickly, tossing everything onto the bed. Then she pulled the drawer out as far as it would go. Placing her palms flat against the bottom of the drawer, she slid her hands to the back of the nightstand and pressed down hard on each corner. The false bottom popped up. Holding her breath, she removed it and looked inside.

It took a few seconds to process what she was seeing.

Her small fireproof box was still there. She removed it from the drawer and opened it, sighing with relief when she saw that her cash savings—a little over forty grand that she'd saved from her tips over the past year—was still intact. But that wasn't what she was having trouble with.

It was the five thick stacks of cash that were also inside the drawer, each one secured with a rubber band. They all appeared to be in hundred-dollar bills. She couldn't imagine how much money it was, but she sure as shit wasn't about to count it. Beside the cash was a plastic-wrapped brick of what looked like cocaine. Or maybe it was heroin. How the hell would she know?

What she did know was that none of this was hers. It had to be what Vinny was looking for. He had given his girlfriend drugs and cash to hold for him, and for reasons Joey couldn't begin to fathom, Mae had decided to hide it here. Joey had never revealed her hiding spot to anyone, but at some point, on one of her visits, Mae must have spied Joey stashing away her tips for the night.

And if her boyfriend didn't get back what he was looking for, he was going to kill her. She needed to get a hold of Mae and talk her into giving it back.

Joey picked up her cordless handset and punched in her friend's phone number. In her ear, the line started ringing. Three seconds later, she heard a sound coming from somewhere outside the bedroom, and her head snapped up.

Had the TV turned itself on? No, that wasn't it. A radio? The only stereo she had was here, in the bedroom, and it was off. She walked to her bedroom door, ear cocked, and finally realized what it was she was hearing.

It was a *ringtone*. The tinny opening notes of "Für Elise" were playing from somewhere in the dark apartment. She was calling Mae's cell phone, and somehow, Mae's cell phone was *here*.

Carrying the handset with her, Joey followed the sound through the kitchen, flicking on the lights as she went, her eyes peeled for any sign of Mae's red Nokia. Right as she reached the living room, the ringtone stopped. In her hand, she could hear Mae's voice coming through the receiver, distant and small. *It's Mae. You know what to do after the beep.* She switched on the living room lights. And then she dropped the cordless, jumping so far back that her ass hit the bookcase behind her.

Blood, everywhere.

Dead girl, on the sofa.

Joey squeezed her eyes shut. Counted to three. Opened them again. The scene hadn't changed. There, lying on the sofa, head resting on a throw pillow, right leg dangling off the edge, left arm splayed above her head, was a girl wearing torn sweatpants, torso exposed.

Mae.

At least . . . Joey thought it was Mae. Her T-shirt was sliced open vertically from collar to hem, and it fell open like an unbuttoned blouse to expose the cuts and slashes all over her stomach and across her breasts, some long, some short, some shallow, some deep.

And her face . . . oh God, oh Jesus, her *face*. It was cut so badly that even from eight feet away, Joey could see bone. Whoever had done this to her hadn't just wanted to kill her. He wanted to desecrate her. This was the work of a sociopath, someone in a deep rage, with no impulse control, and a propensity for violence.

Like Vinny.

Like Ruby.

Joey blinked and saw Charles Baxter. Then she blinked again and saw Mae. A scream welled up in her throat, but before it could materialize, Mae moaned.

Joey gasped so hard, the air scraped her throat. *Holy shit*. Mae was alive. Snapping out of her shock, Joey rushed toward the sofa.

"Mae," she said, leaning over her friend. "Mae, I'm here. Can you hear me? It's Joey."

Mae breathed out a sound. It was wet and gurgly.

"Mae, I'm going to call 911, okay? We're going to get you to a hospital." Joey looked around wildly for the phone she had dropped. She spotted it near the bookcase, but it was split in half from hitting the hard linoleum-covered cement of the basement floor. She picked it up anyway and pressed the buttons, but there was no dial tone. *Fuck*.

The other handset was on the opposite side of the room, sitting on the end table closer to Mae's head. She strode toward it, but as she picked it up, she saw immediately that it hadn't been placed correctly on the charger. That phone was dead, too. *Fuck*. This could not be happening.

Mae moaned again.

"Hang on, Mae," Joey said, desperately looking around for her friend's cell phone. She'd heard it ring; it was here somewhere.

She spotted Mae's purse on the floor behind the end table, its contents scattered all over the floor. In the midst of the mess, she saw the red Nokia and grabbed it, pressing the button to make a call. Nothing happened. She checked the screen. There was no cell reception.

"Fuck this fucking basement!" Joey shrieked, resisting the urge to hurl the phone across the room. It had a signal before, because it *rang*, goddammit. She waved the cell phone around, trying to see if she could catch a signal in a different part of the room. Then she tried dialing 911 anyway, but after she hit send, there was only silence. She checked the screen again. The cell phone had gone dead.

"This cannot be fucking happening," Joey said with a sob.

On the sofa, Mae moaned again.

The upstairs tenants had a phone, of course . . . but then she remembered they were gone for the holidays, and she did not have a key to their part of the house. This was absolute bullshit. She'd have to leave Mae here and go get help. It was three a.m. She'd have to bang on the neighbors' doors until someone woke up.

"Mae, hang on, okay?" Joey said, wrapping her bathrobe tighter around herself. "I have to go find a phone. I'll be right back."

Mae said something indecipherable. And then, with great difficulty, she said, "No. Joey . . . no. *No.*"

Joey walked back to her friend and kneeled, feeling the blood on the floor squish into her bare knees. It was horrific to be this close, to see the damage Vinny had done to Mae's face and chest. If he had been determined to destroy something beautiful, he had succeeded. If not for her eyes, Mae would be unrecognizable. Joey took her friend's hand and squeezed it. It was limp and alarmingly cold.

"Mae, I have to get you help."

Mae's eyes were glassy, but they were focused on Joey's face. "No," she said again. "Don't . . . don't leave . . ."

"Mae, I have to find a phone," Joey said, trying not to cry so she could talk. "I'll only be gone a minute. I promise I'll come right back. You just have to hang on."

"No," Mae said. "Stay . . . with me. Please, Joey. *Please.*"

Joey watched as her friend inhaled, then exhaled. And then, her eyes still open, Mae died.

CHAPTER THIRTY-TWO

The decision to burn Mae's body took three seconds.

It took one second to close Mae's eyes.

Another second to remember all the phones in the basement apartment were dead.

And a final second to realize it was time to leave.

For the past year, Joey had been telling herself that she'd know when it was time to start over somewhere new. She was certain there'd be a moment when it would be crystal clear to her, and here it was. This wasn't how she'd imagined it, but that didn't matter now, did it? Vinny had murdered his girlfriend in Joey's apartment looking for something he hadn't yet found, and to do something that horrific, and that fucking *reckless*, meant he wasn't being smart, or logical. There was no doubt in her mind he would come back. Maybe to dispose of Mae's body. Maybe to kill Joey, too. Either way, she didn't want to be here when he did.

There was no option to call the police. And then what? They arrest Vinny? Even if he went to prison, she would be the girl who testified against the Blood Brothers, and from everything she'd heard about them, she'd be as good as dead.

If that was her fate, she'd rather take her chances and run.

It was crazy to think how fast a life-changing decision could be made when you were forced to make it. She had done it once before, with her

mother. She'd felt the same then as she did now. Devastated, terrified . . .
and furious.

Joey dressed quickly, changing out of her bloody robe into jeans and
a sweatshirt. Grabbing her duffel bag, she packed quickly, only taking
things that nobody would notice were gone. Everything else, including
her purse and all her identification, would stay behind. This wouldn't
work otherwise.

She emptied her lockbox and stuffed her cash, the drugs, and the
bricks of hundred dollar bills into her knapsack. Heading to the kitchen,
she grabbed a garbage bag, then went back to the living room to pick up
Mae's purse. Everything Mae had brought with her—all the stuff on the
floor, including her phone—went into the garbage bag, which Joey would
dispose of somewhere far away from here. She took a look around, making
sure she hadn't missed anything, and then placed everything at the top of
the stairs. Then she put on her parka and boots.

Once she lit the fire, there would be no time to put her winter gear on.

Drew had always said the fireplace wasn't up to code, that it was filled
with cracks and dangerous gunk. Before he and Simone left for Vancouver, he'd warned Joey again.

"Never, ever make a fire in there unless you want to burn the house
down," he said.

She was going to burn the house down.

There was no firewood, but that was okay. She knew from her time in
Maple Sound that her books would burn just fine. One by one, she emptied her bookshelves, tossing paperback after paperback into the hearth
until she'd made a stack that approximated the size of a few logs. She
didn't need the fire inside the fireplace to last, she only needed it to *start*.
Then she scattered more books on the floor until they were dotted around
the living room like lily pads. She reminded herself that it was just paper.
She could replace them. She had done it before.

In the bathroom, she opened the medicine cabinet and took out a
bottle of nail polish remover she'd bought at the beauty supply shop a
couple of months back. It was 100 percent acetone, and near full. Acetone
is flammable; it said so right on the bottle. Reading the fine print on the

back, it also said that nail polish remover should never be used anywhere near an open flame, such as a pilot light or any object that sparks, because the vapors could ignite.

It wasn't so much the liquid. It was the *fumes*.

She took the matches she used for her candles and stuck them in her pocket, then extracted one of her hand towels from the small rack beside the sink before leaving the bathroom. She opened the nail polish remover and placed it on the floor close to Mae. The odor of the acetone was distinctive, but it was nowhere near enough to cover the smell of blood.

There was only one more thing to do.

Gently, Joey removed Mae's belly button ring. She also removed Mae's earrings, watch, and bracelet. Then, reaching behind her own neck, Joey unclasped her necklace.

She looked at the ruby-and-diamond pendant one last time. Maybe this was the reason she'd kept it all these years. Maybe this was why she was compelled to wear it, when she could have easily sold it or thrown it away. Maybe on some level she knew that the thing that had broken her would also be the thing that saved her, allowing her to escape from this life, one that had only ever been filled with violence and trauma and death.

Bending down, she clasped the chain around Mae's neck. It wasn't easy. Her fingers were slippery from the blood. After the necklace was fastened, she wiped her hands on the towel and tossed it into the hearth.

"I believe you would tell me that this is okay," Joey said quietly. "Thank you for being my friend, Mae."

She heard a small noise and jerked. It was nothing, a creak of the house, but every random sound she heard was Vinny coming back.

It was time to go.

Standing at the fireplace, she took a deep breath, struck a match, and tossed it on top of the books. She did it again, and again, until the fire in the hearth slowly began to grow. Then she moved away, and waited.

There was no way to know if this would work. But if it did, and the whole basement apartment caught fire, then everyone would believe that this was how Joey died. Vinny sure as shit wasn't going to dispute it. Why would he? The fire would destroy all the evidence that he'd murdered Mae, that he'd ever been here. As sick as it was, she was doing him a favor.

Mae would be presumed missing. There would be nobody to look for her.

And if, for some reason, they figured out it really *was* Mae's body in the fire, then they'd know it was Joey who was missing. Other than the Blood Brothers, there would be nobody to look for her, either. That was the chance she'd have to take.

The fire began to gain momentum. And when she saw the bottle of acetone suddenly ignite, the flames shooting up and catching the sofa, and then catching Mae, Joey bolted.

* * *

At three thirty a.m., the streetcar was half full, which would have been unusual on any other night of the year.

"Happy New Year," a drunk guy sitting across from her said. He was drinking something out of a brown paper bag and looking at her with bleary, bloodshot eyes.

"Happy New Year." Joey's hand went to her throat, her fingers searching for her pendant, but it was no longer there.

Ten minutes later, she pulled on the cord above her head. The driver stopped to let her out, and she heaved her duffel bag and knapsack full of cash and drugs off the streetcar and into the freezing cold. Probably the only good thing that could be said about winters in Toronto was that the lake didn't stink. It was crazy to think that when she was small, she'd swim at the beach not far from here, she and Ruby in matching swimsuits, Joey wishing for all the curves her mother had that made the dads stare longingly and the mothers glare resentfully.

She was now in the area known as the Motel Strip, and she started walking. Because it was a holiday, every motel she passed had its NO VACANCY sign lit, until finally, she reached one that might have a room available.

RAINBOW MOTEL
SATELLITE / JACUZZI / BREAKFAST INCL

The lobby was warm when she entered, and the entire space smelled like pot. The stoned clerk barely said a word to her as he slid a form across the desk for her to fill out. The Tragically Hip was playing on his CD player, and years later, the song "Bobcaygeon" would always remind her of the night Mae died. Because it wasn't just Mae.

Joelle Reyes had died, too.

"I lost my ID," Joey said, sliding the form back to the clerk, blank, along with four worn fifty-dollar bills. "Lost my credit card, too."

"No problem." The clerk was unfazed as he slipped the money into his pocket. "But you'll have to prepay. How many nights?"

"Let's do a week."

He gave her the total, and she paid him in cash. He handed her a room key. As was the case in most of these old motels, it was an actual brass key on a keychain. The plastic-shaped rainbow was so worn that the colors had faded.

"There's no housekeeping included," the clerk said, which told her that this entire transaction was off the books.

She was okay with that. "Is it clean?" she asked.

He shrugged. "Depends on your definition of clean."

* * *

The room had a rainbow bedspread with matching rainbow curtains, and was gaudy as hell. But the sheets smelled like detergent, the bathroom smelled like bleach, and the TV worked just fine.

Joey made a phone call, figuring there was a fifty-fifty chance he was still awake at four a.m. He was, and while he was surprised to hear from her, he agreed to come to the motel. She was just coming out of the shower when she heard a soft knock. She checked the peephole, then opened the door.

The room felt smaller the instant the big man stepped inside.

"Why are you here?" Chaz asked, looking around. "Is that guy sleeping at your house or something?"

He meant Drew, of course.

"No," Joey said. "He's gone. I won't ever see him again."

As soon as she spoke the words, she felt an imaginary hand wrap around her heart, and squeeze.

She took a seat on the bed. Chaz sat beside her, and leaned in to kiss her. She put a hand on his chest. "I'm sorry, I can't."

"I thought I was here to—"

"I'm leaving Toronto," she said. "And I need your help. I need a new ID, and I need your help unloading this."

She reached for her knapsack, opened it, and showed him what was inside.

"Jesus Christ," Chaz said. "Where the fuck did you get that?"

"It's better you don't know." She pulled out the brick of white powder and placed it on the bed between them. "I don't know what this is worth, but I'm sure it's a lot. And I'll give it to you, in exchange for a driver's license, a birth certificate, and, if possible, a passport."

Chaz looked down at the drugs, and then at her. "Joey, what did you do?" he asked softly.

"You'll find out soon enough," she said. "But you're the only person I can trust. I can't stay here, Chaz. I know you have that cousin who's into some. . . . off-the-grid stuff. If you can get him to unload this, then you guys can split the money. All I need is an ID. I need to leave the country."

"Are you for real?" Chaz was looking at her like she'd lost her damn mind. "You want me to call Reggie?"

"You're right, I'm asking you to do too much. This was stupid. I'll just flush it down the toilet."

She took the brick and stood up, but before she could get to the bathroom, Chaz said, "Wait. Give it to me. I'll see what I can do."

Then he sighed and rubbed his face.

"Fuck, Joey. I would only ever do this for you."

* * *

Three days later, Chaz was back at the motel, having procured what she asked for. He didn't look happy.

"Everybody at the Cherry is mourning you. They're having a little memorial service this weekend."

"I'm sorry," she said. "I really am." She hesitated. "Aren't you going to ask me who it was? In the fire?"

He shook his head and sat on the bed. The mattress sank under his weight. "The less I know, the better."

"You're not going to ask if I killed her?"

"If you did, you had your reasons, and it wouldn't change how I feel about you," he said quietly. "But I know you didn't."

She sat beside him and took his hand.

"I could go with you, you know," Chaz said. "You don't have to do this alone."

"You can't come where I'm going." Joey leaned her head against his arm. "But I can't tell you how glad I am that we met."

He wouldn't look at her as he handed over her new ID. The name on both the driver's license and birth certificate was Paris Aquino.

Joey frowned. *Paris?* Aquino was fine, but she'd been hoping for a more mundane first name. "She doesn't look anything like me."

"She looks like you enough." Chaz shrugged. "You'll have to work with it. You know how hard it was to find a license *and* birth certificate for a Filipino girl close to your age and height?"

She scanned the stats on the license. The age was close enough; their birthdays were the same year and only two months apart. "Nobody will believe this is me. You can tell from her face that she's heavier than I am."

"That's why it will work," Chaz said. "Look at the date—the driver's license expired a month ago. When you go to renew it, bring your birth certificate. If they question you, just tell them you lost weight. You can get a new photo taken. And then, after you get the new license, you can apply for a passport."

Joey remembered when Tita Flora had to get a new passport. Her aunt needed to have two pictures taken, and have the backs of both photos signed by her family doctor to confirm her identity. "But won't I need someone to verify that it's me? And how do I know that this Paris didn't already have a passport?"

"This isn't without risk, Joey." Chaz put a piece of paper in her hand with a name and phone number on it. "This guy is a friend of Reggie's, and he works in the passport office. He's expecting a call from you, but he knows your name is Paris. Let him know what day and time you're coming in, and he'll make sure he's the one who helps you."

She stared at her new ID. *Paris.* It didn't suit her at all. But like Chaz said, she'd have to make it work.

"Thank you," she said.

"Don't thank me," he said. "You paid way too much for this. The street value of that coke is around a hundred grand. A fake ID would have cost you a couple thousand at most."

They both stood up. She reached for him and pressed her face into his chest, allowing herself the comfort of his arms around her one last time. His heart was pounding. You wouldn't know it from the outside.

He kissed the top of her head. "I almost said I'll see you around sometime, but I won't, will I?"

"No." Her voice was muffled.

"Take care of yourself, Joey." Chaz held her a moment longer, and then he was gone.

An hour later, she stopped by the front desk to drop off the key. The same clerk was there, and just like he'd never asked her to sign anything when she checked in, there was nothing to do now that she was leaving. "Bobcaygeon" by the Hip was playing once again.

"Good luck," he said.

"For what?" she asked.

"For whatever it is you're running from."

Not running from, she thought, as she caught a taxi outside the motel. *Running to.*

She was Paris now.

PART FOUR

Don't think I haven't been through the same predicament

—LAURYN HILL

CHAPTER THIRTY-THREE

Paris is slowly getting used to her lawyer's attack-style way of speaking, but Sonny Everly's best quality is that he never tells her anything other than the truth. Elsie was right that the man is an absolute prick, but at least he's Paris's prick.

They still don't have a trial date, and according to Sonny, it could be a year or more.

"A case this high profile, the prosecutor is in no rush," Sonny says, packing up his briefcase. "They can't afford to be sloppy."

"Can't we ask for a speedy trial?" she asks as she walks him to the door. "I don't want be in limbo for a year."

"So you want to get to prison faster?" Sonny says. "You don't want a speedy trial, not with your situation. Anything can happen, and we can't afford to be sloppy, either. In the meantime, go back to work. Have your friends over. Meditate. Get your nails done. Do whatever it is women like you do."

"Women like me?" Paris sighs. "Every time I think I might actually like you, Sonny, you remind me why I don't."

He grins. "You'll love me when you're free. Trust me, okay? This ain't my first rodeo."

It ain't Paris's, either.

As soon as he opens the door, one of the photographers hanging around the house shouts out a question. "Hey Sonny! How does it feel to represent the woman who murdered the Prince of Poughkeepsie?"

"Don't you cockroaches have anything better to do?" she hears her lawyer snap as he gets into his BMW. "Fuck off."

In fairness, the photographers actually might not have anything better to do. Paris can relate. She didn't realize how few friends she had until all this happened. Most of her social circle—if it could even be called that—had been Jimmy's social circle, and other than Elsie, none of them have checked in.

Even Henry is keeping his distance now that he's running the studio solo. She tried to go back to Ocean Breath to teach her six a.m. Sunrise Hatha class, but a crowd of gawkers had waited outside the front doors all morning. It had scared off the members and upset the other instructors.

Everywhere she went, photographers followed.

"Honey, I'm sorry," Henry told her. "But as your partner, I have to tell you that you're bad for business."

Paris has never not worked, not since she finished high school, and she isn't used to sitting around all day. At the moment, books and TV are her only companions. Interestingly, she isn't overly concerned about Ruby at the moment. Paris being charged with Jimmy's murder is actually helpful when it comes to her mother, because if she's convicted, she'll have no money to pay the blackmail. It's in Ruby's best interest that Paris is acquitted. As much as her mother might genuinely enjoy ruining Paris's life by exposing the truth about Mae, ultimately, Ruby cares about herself more. And if there's any hope of getting her money, Ruby will wait.

It feels like she's watched everything on Netflix, Hulu, and Prime, so Paris switches to Quan, looking for anything different to take her mind off things. Under the category "TV Shows We Picked For You," she sees *The Prince of Poughkeepsie*, and smiles. They have all ten seasons, which was part of the deal Jimmy made with them. She keeps scrolling, and then stops when she sees they've added a new show.

Except it's not new. Just like its counterparts *Dateline* and *20/20*, *Murderers* has been around a long time. It used to air back when she was in high school, and there's obviously no shortage of killers, because they're still making new episodes today. Each hour-long installment is a dramatic reenactment of a real-life murder case, and eight seasons of the thirty-year-old show are now streaming on Quan.

Paris has watched *Murderers* exactly once. Surely they won't have the Ruby Reyes episode.

The night it first aired, the boys were already in bed. Tita Flora had switched shifts at the hospital so she'd be home to watch it. Tito Micky made popcorn. Even Lola Celia, who was normally in her room by nine, had stayed up and was settled in her rocking chair when the show's cheesy opening theme song began to play.

Joey sat on the floor of the living room, her back against the wall. When the narrator announced the episode in his ominous voice with its slow, dramatic cadence, it was nothing short of surreal. "Tonight . . . *Murderers* presents . . . 'Ruby Reyes . . . The Ice Queen Cometh.'"

Right off the bat, her aunt and grandmother did not approve of the actress who was selected to play the Ice Queen.

"She's too pretty to be Ruby," Tita Flora griped, at least three times. "It's not realistic."

"*Ni Filipina siya*," Lola Celia grumbled, at least four times. *She's not even Filipina.*

Joey was so consumed with the show, she only half listened to their ongoing snark. She agreed with her grandmother that *Murderers* could have at least used a Filipino actress. But her aunt was just plain wrong. While the woman playing Ruby was very pretty, she lacked the natural charisma and sensuality that the real Ruby had been gifted. At best, she was a cartoon version of the Ice Queen, and in Joey's opinion, her mother was much more beautiful.

Tito Micky enjoyed the episode thoroughly. He passed the popcorn around as if *Murderers* was entertainment, as if Ruby wasn't family and her daughter wasn't sitting in the same living room, mortified to see her mother portrayed on TV for the whole world to see. The kids at her high school had finally started to forget who Joey's mother was, and now this stupid TV show would remind them all over again.

As they watched, she was surprised that despite the dramatic overacting and the almost comically foreboding voice of the narrator, *Murderers* actually got a lot of the details about Ruby and Charles Baxter right. They did first meet at the Second Cup coffee shop near the bank, a "chance encounter" that wasn't by chance at all. Ruby did make the first move.

Charles did promise he was going to leave his wife for her. And Ruby did stop by his house unannounced the night of the murder, after Charles had ended their affair for the third or fourth time.

Where *Murderers* got it wrong was the relationship between Ruby and her child. For the purposes of keeping Ruby's daughter's identity a secret, the show had changed Joey's name to Jessie. In the scene where Jessie meets with Ruby in prison just before the trial, the exchange is portrayed as loving.

In reality, it had been anything but.

* * *

It had been almost two months since Joey had seen her mother, and she was shocked to see that Ruby looked older.

She and Deborah were sitting at a table in the visitors' room when Ruby was brought in by a prison guard (*corrections officer*). The orange jumpsuit hung on her. Her hair was greasy, tied up in a bun. There were creases in her forehead that weren't there before. She looked like she had aged ten years.

Joey wanted to cry. She had done this; she was the reason her mother was in here, looking like a criminal. This was all her fault.

"It's okay," Deborah whispered, as if sensing her anguish. "You got this."

When Ruby reached the table, she saw the look on Joey's face and snorted. "It looks like all the fat I lost, you gained. At least I finally reached my goal weight."

"You look good, Mama," Joey said, her voice timid, but her mother had already lost interest.

"Who's this?" Ruby looked at Deborah with a raised eyebrow, scrutinizing the social worker from head to toe.

Deborah introduced herself, but did not offer her hand. They were told at check-in that no physical contact was allowed, other than a brief hug at the beginning and end of the visit.

"So you're the one taking care of my girl," Ruby said.

"I'm doing my best, but Joelle is pretty good at taking care of herself."

Deborah pointed to a table a few feet away. "Joelle, I'll be sitting right over there, okay? Take your time."

"Well?" Ruby said to Joey when the social worker walked away. "Hug me already, *Joelle*."

Joey wrapped her arms around her mother tightly. She could feel all the bones in her mother's back.

Ruby pulled away to examine her. "Look at you. You're a little piggly wiggly now."

They took seats across from each other. The visitors' room was half full, and there were boyfriends and husbands and a couple of noisy babies. It hurt Joey to think that her mother had been here for over seven weeks, and nobody other than her lawyer had come to visit her until now.

"How's school?" Ruby asked.

The kids don't speak to me. "Fine."

"How's Tita Flora?"

"Fine."

"Speak up, I can't hear you."

"She's fine," Joey said, louder. "I don't see her all that much. She works all the time."

"Has she been saying smug, nasty things about me?" Ruby's gaze was fixed on Joey's face. "I bet she can't shut up. Self-righteous bitch."

"She hasn't said anything about you." It was a necessary lie. Her mother would not want to know the things her sister had said. "Not a word."

"Oh." Ruby's shoulders relaxed. It was hard to tell whether she was relieved or disappointed. "What about Maple Sound? You like it there?"

"No."

"What about your Tito Micky?" Her mother's voice lowered a notch. "He bothering you?"

Joey met her mother's gaze. "Not really."

They fell into silence for a moment. Joey glanced over at Deborah, who had a magazine she wasn't reading spread open on the table in front of her. She gave the social worker a smile to let her know everything was okay. Deborah smiled back.

"I don't like that woman," her mother said, her eyes narrowing as she followed Joey's gaze. "I don't like the way she looks at me. Judging me. What have you been telling her?"

"Nothing." *And you shut up, Deborah is perfect.*

"Move your chair closer," Ruby said, and Joey shuffled her chair forward a few inches. Her mother leaned in. "Listen, I want to talk to you about the trial. You know you have to testify, right? The crown attorney considers you a witness."

She nods.

"I need you to be smart, Joey," Ruby said. "There's nothing I can do about the things you wrote in your diaries, because they're evidence now, and everyone has already read them. I was mad for a while, but I understand you were upset when you wrote those things. I'm not mad anymore, okay?"

Of course you're not mad. You're enraged.

"You really fucked things up for us, but you can still fix this, okay? You need to fix this. For me, and for us. You understand that, right, baby?"

"How do I fix it?" Joey asked.

Ruby reached for her hands, then stopped when the nearby corrections officer shook her head. Joey looked down at the table. Her mother's nails, usually long and painted red, were bare and bitten down to the quick.

"When you testify," Ruby said, "I need you to make it very clear that Charles was . . . hurting you. You said a lot of things in your diaries, but the one thing you didn't write about was what Charles was doing to you."

Because I couldn't write about it. Writing about it makes me relive it. Writing about it in my diary means it really happened.

Joey stared at her mother. "You knew, Mama?" she asked softly. "You knew what Charles was doing?"

"Oh, stop." Ruby waved a hand. "I didn't really know, okay? I don't remember you saying anything to me about it. How could I know anything if you don't tell me?"

Because you'd blame it on me if I did.

"I didn't know anything for a fact until that night." Ruby spoke earnestly, as if she were saying this to someone who didn't know her. "I was shocked."

"I don't know if I can talk about it," Joey said. "Out loud, I mean. In court."

"But he was hurting you." Her mother cocked her head. "Why wouldn't you want to tell everyone that he was hurting you?"

Because he wasn't just hurting me, he was raping me. And I can't say that out loud without feeling like I'm being raped all over again.

"Baby, if you tell the jury about Charles when you testify, it helps me, do you understand?" Her mother's face is inches from her own, her voice the volume of a stage whisper. "Because then the jury will understand why I did what I did. I'm your mother, and I did it to protect you. This is extremely important for my defense. If you don't tell them about Charles, I will go to prison forever. And then where will you be? Stuck in Maple Sound, that's where. I might only do six months on the child abuse charge with good behavior and the completion of some bullshit program. Six months, Joey, and then we'd be together again. Don't you want me to get out?"

I don't know.

"Baby, please," Ruby said. "You need to do this, okay? You need to say all of the bad things that Charles was doing to you. Don't hold back. Tell them everything."

So now you want everyone to hear it, now that it helps you.

In a soft voice, Joey said, "You know he wasn't the only one, Mama."

Ruby exhaled. "You're mad at me. That's fine. I'm sorry, okay? I'm sorry I had some bad boyfriends. But we can talk about that after I get out. For now, we have to stay focused. Just Charles, okay? You need to tell them specifically about Charles. Promise me, Joey, or else I will die in prison. And I guarantee, you will never be able to live with that."

That part was probably true.

Joey did love her mother. She really did. She had come to understand that her mother had done her best, considering who her own mother was. Joey's mother had a bad mother, too.

"Joey." Ruby looked at her. "If you love me, you will do this for me. It's really the least you can do."

Joey made her decision.

"Okay, Mama," she said. "I'll tell them."

Her mother let out a long breath. "That's my good girl," she said, her face breaking into a triumphant smile. "I know you'll be great up there. A few tears won't hurt, either. Really sell it, okay?"

"Okay," Joey said. "I love you."

Say it back. Please. Just say it back once.

Ruby sat back in her chair and folded her arms across her chest. "I'll believe that when you do this for me."

Conditional love, the only kind her mother knew.

* * *

Paris finally finds Ruby's episode of *Murderers*. It's in season 7, episode 12. Despite common sense telling her that watching this will not provide the distraction she's looking for, she hits play and settles into the sofa.

Ruby has certainly never seen this episode, nor has she seen the terrible made-for-TV movie about her called *The Banker's Mistress* that aired a year later. But she has to be aware of them both, and there's no doubt she would hate them. In the gospel according to Ruby Reyes, the most grievous sin isn't murder. It's the airing of her dirty laundry.

The first time Joey learned this lesson, she was six years old. She and Ruby had just left a meeting with Joey's first-grade teacher, who was concerned that she was falling asleep in class. When Mrs. Stirling asked Joey why she was so tired, Joey said her mother's boyfriend had slept over, and the two of them had made noise all night long.

After the meeting, Ruby slammed the car door and peeled out of the school driveway. When they stopped at a red light, she reached over and pinched Joey's arm. The pain was sudden and sharp, and Joey squealed.

"You *never, ever* talk about our lives," her mother hissed. "What happens at home is between you and me, do you understand?"

"But Mrs. Stirling asked me," Joey said. "And we're supposed to tell the truth."

Ruby pinched her again, and again, until Joey cried.

"The truth is whatever I tell you it is," her mother said. "You embarrassed me. Don't you ever do that again."

From a young age, the notion of truth had always been a fluid concept to Joey. You could take a completely true story, omit a few key details here and there, diminish certain facts while highlighting others, and end up with a completely different narrative. Was the story still true? Yes. It was just a different expression of the truth, designed to tell the story in a specific way to garner a specific reaction.

It wasn't just the bad guys who did this. It was the good guys, too.

The morning after she met with her mother in jail, Deborah took Joey to meet with the crown attorney to prepare for her testimony. Madeline Duffy (*my friends call me Duffy*) was a nice lady like Deborah said, but a bit relentless. She had Joey walk her through the events of the night of Charles's murder a dozen times, making her go over it and over it, adjusting her questions to best prompt the answer she wanted. Then she fine-tuned Joey's responses until everything was worded exactly as she needed it to be for maximum impact.

"Okay, last one," Duffy said. Normally Joey wouldn't feel comfortable thinking of an adult by just their last name, but she was so tired, she'd stopped worrying about it. "I know it's been a long day, and I'm sure Deb is ready to get going."

"Joelle's aunt and uncle will be here soon to pick her up," Deborah said. "They'd like to get on the road before traffic gets bad."

"No problem." Duffy gave Joey a smile. "We're almost done."

Deborah patted Joey's shoulder. "I have to step out to make a phone call, honey. And then I'll be outside to meet your aunt and uncle when they get here."

Please don't leave without saying goodbye.

Deborah leaned over and spoke into her ear. "Don't worry, I would never leave without saying goodbye. You're one of my most favorite people."

I love you, Deborah.

When they were alone, Duffy kicked off her heels and leaned against her desk. "Okay, Joelle. When I ask you this next question, I want you to think about all the married men your mother was involved with and how each of those relationships ended."

"They all ended badly."

"That's right," Duffy said. "And at least two of your mother's boyfriends that we know of were pedophiles."

It wasn't a question, so Joey didn't answer.

"The jury will want to know what your mother's state of mind was the night she killed Charles Baxter. So when I ask you 'Why do you think your mother did it?' you'll have to give an answer. This will be framed as an opinion, so this is your opportunity to say exactly what you think, okay? So tell me. Why do you think she did it?"

Joey had given it a lot of thought, and the answer was difficult to articulate. Her mother had stabbed Charles because she was angry and couldn't control her behavior. She wasn't being a protective mother that night. When had she ever?

The truth was that the night she stabbed Charles, Ruby had been *jealous*. And Joey asked herself, if their situations were reversed, what would Ruby say?

And then she told Duffy exactly that.

CHAPTER THIRTY-FOUR

When Ruby's trial began in Toronto, Tito Micky started keeping a scrapbook in Maple Sound of all the newspaper articles about it. He subscribed to all three of the major Toronto papers, and the scrapbook sat on the kitchen counter at all times. Joey never looked at it. Instead, she spent most of her time in the bedroom, reading.

Both Deborah and the crown attorney assured her that her name would never appear anywhere because she was a minor, but that was of little comfort. Anyone who knew Ruby knew she had a daughter. Ruby had always worn Joey like an accessory, showing her off when she wanted sympathy or admiration for being a single parent, and discarding her if she determined that Joey was a barrier to something she wanted.

Two days before her testimony, she was a bundle of nerves. She had spoken to Madeline Duffy on the phone twice after their initial meeting, and while she felt prepared, it scared her to imagine the jurors' faces. Duffy explained that the courtroom would be closed to spectators and journalists, but that still left twelve pairs of ears in the jury box listening to every word she said and how she said it. Twelve pairs of eyes would be observing her body language, her facial expressions, her tears.

And her mother would be there. Watching.

"Remember that it's all right to cry," Duffy said during their last phone call. "Everyone in that room is on your side. It's important to express what you feel."

It was the exact same thing her mother had said, but what Duffy didn't know was that Joey had been trained not to cry. There was little chance she'd be able to summon tears tomorrow, as much as the crown attorney was not so subtly asking her to.

"Joelle," a soft voice said, and she looked up to find Tito Micky standing in the doorway of her bedroom.

She'd been so immersed in her novel that she hadn't heard her uncle's footsteps coming down the hallway. It was her third reread of Sidney Sheldon's *If Tomorrow Comes*, her absolute favorite book, which was about a woman who's framed for a crime she didn't commit. When she finally gets out of prison, she becomes a professional thief who travels the world pulling off daring heists, changing her name and appearance whenever she needs to. And of course she gets revenge on the people who wronged her, and also falls in love along the way.

"You want to come with us into town?" Tito Micky asked. "Summer activities at the YMCA. I have to drive the boys." *Dribe da boys.* "Afterward, you can help with the groceries. Now that you're helping your *lola* with the cooking, she wants you to help with the shopping."

In the daytime, her uncle was just a skinny man with a potbelly, not a monster lurking in the dark. Still, Joey couldn't think of anything she'd rather do less. Alone in the car with Tito Micky? No thanks.

"After we do the shopping, I can drop you at the bookstore. And I'll give you ten dollars to spend there. Good distraction, huh?" Her uncle attempted a charming smile, exposing a row of tobacco-stained teeth.

Wait. Ten dollars? That was a new release paperback with change to spare.

"Okay," she said tentatively, sitting up.

"And while you're at the bookstore, I can go to the sports pub across the street. There's a baseball game on, and I've made a little bet about who will win." Tito Micky winked. "Just don't tell your *tita.*"

A few minutes later, Joey was sitting in the front seat of her uncle's station wagon, excited. Only the two older boys were going to the YMCA that afternoon, as Carson had an upset tummy. After the boys were dropped off, she and Tito Micky headed to the supermarket. They finished the shopping quickly, and Tito Micky placed the meats and cheeses in the cooler he kept in the trunk. Then they headed over to Main Street.

"At Christmastime, they put up a big tree in the square." Tito Micky pulled into a parking spot right in front of the bookstore. "It's thirty feet tall, and they light it all at once. There's Christmas carolers and a Santa Claus parade." *Santa Clowse parade.* "We always take the boys and get hot chocolate. You'll enjoy it."

Joey felt a pang. Her first Christmas without her mother. She hadn't even thought about that.

Her uncle opened his wallet and plucked out a ten-dollar bill, his fingertips brushing hers unnecessarily as he handed it to her. He pointed across the street to a sports bar called the Loose Goose. "I'll meet you back here at three forty-five, okay? We have to pick the boys up at four."

She had two whole hours to herself in a bookstore, with ten whole dollars to spend. She was so giddy, she was practically bouncing. They both got out of the car, and Tito Micky leaned against the driver's-side door and lit a cigarette.

Standing on the sidewalk, Maple Sound was so different from what Joey was used to. Unlike Toronto, which was filled with people of all races and religions, and who spoke many different languages, Maple Sound was so . . . *homogeneous.* Her mother never did understand why her sister and brother-in-law had opted to move to a small town two hours north, away from the diversity of city life.

"You'll be dog piss on white snow," Ruby had said to Tita Flora back then. "You're going to hate it there, and they're going to hate you."

Joey suspected that her aunt and uncle actually did hate it here, and would bet that Tito Micky would move back to the city in a heartbeat if he could. But Tita Flora seemed determined to stick it out, if only to prove her sister wrong.

At the moment, though, none of that mattered. When Joey stepped inside the bookstore, she took a long, deep inhale, and felt a genuine burst of joy. Every bookstore, everywhere, smelled the same.

It smelled like home.

* * *

Jason and Tyson were starving when they got home, and they headed straight to the kitchen to eat whatever snack their grandmother had prepared for them. Joey put the groceries away while Tito Micky headed straight back outside. The moment they walked in the door, Tita Flora had barked her displeasure at the giant pile of leaves her husband had left on the pond side of the house. He'd raked them that morning, and the leaves were supposed to be burned by the time she got home from work.

Joey skipped up the stairs with her two new paperbacks. The bookstore still had their two-for-ten sale, and the owner—whose name was Ginny—remembered Joey from her first visit with Deborah.

"Any luck?" Ginny had asked.

"I can't decide," Joey said, feeling shy. She had found two she wanted—another Stephen King book called *Needful Things*, and a book by Scott Turow, an author she hadn't read yet, called *Presumed Innocent*—but with the sales tax, she wouldn't have enough money for both. "Which one would you recommend?"

"Tough choice," Ginny said with a smile. "So how about you get both, and I won't charge you the tax."

Today was Joey's best day in Maple Sound by far. Oddly, she had Tito Micky to thank for that. All the upstairs windows were open, and she could smell the leaves burning outside. It smelled like a campfire, and it added to her happy mood. She pushed open her bedroom door.

Carson, the youngest boy who'd been left at home that afternoon because he was sick, was sitting in the middle of the bedroom floor. Clearly he was feeling better, because he had a pair of safety scissors in his small hand and was studiously cutting the cover off *If Tomorrow Comes*. And if that wasn't horrific enough, in front of him was a large sheet of bristol board, on top of which lay six more snipped covers, all in a row.

No, not just laying on the board. There was a fat yellow stick on the carpet beside the bristol board that said ELMER's. Her four-year-old cousin was *gluing* them down, and strewn all around were the books themselves, stripped of their covers, naked and exposed on the carpet like dead animal carcasses.

A white-hot rage unlike anything she'd ever felt before filled Joey's stomach. This little asshole, who probably had a hundred toys to play with all throughout the house, who had never wanted for anything, who had never felt unsafe, who had never been forced to have margarine and stale crackers for dinner because there was nothing else to eat, was destroying her most precious possessions. Her paperbacks. The only things that had any value to her, other than her necklace.

She would have rather he destroyed the necklace. The necklace might have been forgivable.

"What are you doing?" Joey asked. To her ears, she sounded like someone else, someone who was about to explode.

Carson didn't pick up on her tone. "I'm making a poster for you, Joey." He looked up and grinned. "Do you like it?"

No, she did not like it. She did not like it one bit.

Without thinking, Joey snatched the book out of her cousin's little hands and smacked him, as hard as she could, across the face.

The slap made a sound very similar to the one Lola Celia had given her out by the pond, and God help her, it was extremely satisfying. Joey had never hit anyone before, and oh wow, did it ever feel good to hurl that anger at someone.

But three seconds later, regret replaced her rage as she watched Carson's little face transform from shock into pain, and then, finally, fear. He was only four years old, maybe half her size, and totally unable to fight back. As Joey looked at him, so small and helpless, and so utterly terrified of her, she saw herself. In this moment, he was Joey, cowering on the floor.

And she was Ruby.

"I'm sorry," she whispered, as the horror of what she'd done sank in. "Carson, I'm so sorry."

She took a step toward him. He scuttled away from her. Then he opened his mouth, and howled.

The sound was awful, and he wouldn't stop. Every time she took a step closer, he wailed louder, the tears coming faster, his face growing redder. The cheek where she smacked him was almost maroon. Joey heard Tita Flora call out Carson's name from somewhere in the house. A few seconds later, she heard footsteps pounding on the stairs as not one, but *two* sets of feet rushed up to the second floor.

By the time Tita Flora and Lola Celia arrived at the bedroom, Joey's little cousin had worked himself into hysterics, sobbing as he scampered straight for his grandmother, burying his head in her robe.

"What did you do?" Tita Flora asked Joey, though it was pretty fucking obvious what she had done. The shape of Joey's palm was now an angry purple blotch on the little boy's cheek. "What the fuck did you do to him, you stupid bitch?"

Joey attempted to explain, sputtering and gesturing to the stripped paperbacks. She understood the scene looked bad. Had she thought it through for even one second, she would never have hit him. Carson was a sweet kid, and he adored her. And he was so *little*. Joey knew exactly what it felt like to be that small and be hurt by someone you loved, someone bigger than you, and more powerful, who always won, no matter how wrong she might be.

Unsatisfied with her niece's attempts to answer, Tita Flora's shrieking grew louder. "Do you think we wanted you here? Look at you, you're just like your mother, *wa'y kapuslanan.* You're going to grow up to be a *puta*, just like her. If they weren't paying me to do it, we would never have taken you in, you useless, ungrateful little bitch."

Despite her aunt being shorter and wider than her mother and with a less pretty face, Tita Flora's wrath made her look and sound exactly like her sister. And just like with Ruby, the words were bullets, peppering Joey's ears and heart with wounds that would never fully heal. The louder Tita Flora shouted at her, in a combination of Cebuano and English, the harder Carson cried. The little boy seemed to understand the gravity of the situation, and that what was happening now to his older cousin might actually be worse than what had just happened to him. He tried twice to go over to Joey, but both times, his grandmother held him back.

Lola Celia was quietly observing the scene with her small, black eyes, her gnarled fingers stroking her grandson's hair. So far she'd said nothing. Only when Tita Flora finally paused, red-faced and heaving, did her *lola* finally speak. Carson had calmed down a little by then, and her grandmother's tone was soft, almost gentle.

"*Sunoga ang iyang mga libro. Ang tanan.*"

Joey couldn't put together what the old woman just said. She knew *libro* meant book. Maybe she was trying to remind Tita Flora that Carson should not have cut the covers off Joey's paperbacks, and was trying to defuse the situation. Things with Lola Celia had been going much better since Joey started helping with the cooking. Maybe her grandmother was actually on her side.

But then she saw a look of understanding pass over her aunt's face, which then morphed into smugness. No. Whatever Lola Celia had just said, the old woman was definitely *not* on her side.

A rope of fear knotted in Joey's stomach. They were going to kick her out. They were going to call Deborah and tell her what Joey had done, and oh God, Deborah would know, and would turn away from her, because she'd realize Joey was just like her mother.

And then where would she go? She'd be passed over to another social worker, someone who didn't like her and didn't care, who'd throw Joey into a foster family who also didn't care. Or maybe she'd be sent to one of those facilities she'd heard about at school, like a prison for girls, the place where bad seed kids were sent.

Because of course Joey was a bad seed. She'd come from a rotten mother.

"I'm so sorry," she said desperately. "Carson, I love you, I'm so, so sorry."

"Joey," the little boy said, reaching for her, but Lola Celia held him firm.

Her aunt went to the closet and grabbed the tall plastic hamper filled with the kids' dirty clothes. She dumped them out onto the carpet. Marching back toward Joey's bookcase, she swept all the books off the shelf and into the basket, tossing in both the stripped paperbacks *and* the two brand-new novels Joey had just bought. When all the books were in the hamper, she dragged it out of the bedroom and into the hallway. A few seconds later, Joey heard thumping as her aunt pulled it down the staircase.

Panic set in, and Joey ran after her.

"Tita Flora, please, I'm so sorry. Please."

Tito Micky looked up in surprise when the two of them came bursting out the back door. He was about to light a cigarette, and it nearly fell out of his mouth as his wife bumped past him to get to the steel trash can where he'd just finished burning the leaves. It was still smoking.

Tita Flora was small, but she was a nurse, and she was strong. Joey watched as her aunt, bending at the knees, picked up the heavy hamper and tipped the books straight into the metal trash can. Tossing the hamper aside, she grabbed the can of lighter fluid at Tito Micky's feet. She generously doused the books with it and then snatched her husband's matchbook right out of his hand. She lit it and tossed it in, stepping back as the flames flared up, renewed.

Burning leaves smell one way. Burning paper smells a little different, and the scent gutted Joey from the inside out. She sank to her knees as the orange flames roared. In that moment, it might as well have been Joey on fire. Her books were the only things that weren't attached to painful memories. Nearly all those books had belonged to her mother. They were the only good things Joey had.

A sound beating would have hurt less.

Joey looked up at the bedroom window, where her little cousin stood watching the whole thing, his small face crumpled with tears and regret. Behind him was Lola Celia, her hands still on his shoulders, smiling a smile that really wasn't a smile at all.

Joey knew that smile. Her mother had the same one, and it came to Joey then, what the old woman had said.

Burn her books. All of them.

* * *

Joey woke up the next morning after a fitful sleep. It was the day she would be heading into Toronto to testify, and she had been plagued all night with bad dreams she now couldn't remember.

She rolled over to find a large envelope beside her on the bed. A floppy heart was drawn on the outside in red crayon, and inside there was a bunch of coins. Pennies, nickels, dimes, quarters. A few loonies. And at the very bottom, a two-dollar bill.

Carson was sitting on the floor in the same spot where he'd cut up her books the day before, still in his pajamas. It was clear he'd been there awhile, waiting for her to wake up. Behind him, his older brothers were still asleep in their bunks.

"What's this?" Joey whispered.

"My piggy bank money," Carson said, struggling not to cry. "You can buy more books. I'm sorry, Joey."

She put the money back in the envelope and carried it with her as she sat on the floor beside him.

"You don't have anything to be sorry about," she said, her voice catching when she saw the bruise on his cheek. She looked him right in the eyes. "I did something very bad. Hitting is bad, and I promise I will never, ever hit you again. I'm so sorry, Carson. You are such a good boy, and I am so sorry. Nobody ever should be hit."

"But Lola hit you," he said. "At the pond."

There was nothing she could say to that.

He scooched over to her and climbed into her lap. She hugged him tight and rubbed her cheek on his soft, baby-shampoo-scented hair. They stayed like that for a full minute.

I am not my mother. I will never be my mother.

I would rather die.

CHAPTER THIRTY-FIVE

When the bailiff opened the doors, the first thing Joey saw was that all the spectator seats were empty, just as Deborah said they would be.

The second thing she saw was the judge seated at the very end of the aisle, up high on the bench, wearing a black robe, just like on TV.

The third thing she saw were the faces of the jurors in the box to the right, all turned in her direction.

And finally, she saw her mother, seated at the table on the left. Her lawyer had turned around, but Ruby had not, which made her the only person in the room not currently looking at Joey. Her mother remained facing front, her long, glossy black hair smooth and shiny once again, the posture of her shoulders and back perfect.

Deborah held her hand as they proceeded down the aisle. Madeline Duffy smiled encouragingly at her from her seat at the table closer to the jury box. Ruby had still not turned around, but she did adjust her posture a little, sensing her daughter's approach.

There were six men and six women on the jury. Some of them—women, mostly—made eye contact with Joey. One offered a smile. Duffy had told her earlier that morning that many of the jurors were parents, some with children close to Joey's age.

As they were about to pass the defense table, her mother finally turned. Their gazes locked, and Ruby smiled. Her lawyer smiled, too, but Joey could only see one person.

She knew every line of her mother's face; she knew what every millimeter of every facial expression meant. Joey had spent her entire existence trying to predict the weather of her mother's emotions, always on high alert for a brewing storm and that split-second shift from clear skies to a Category 5 hurricane. Ruby had many smiles, but today, right now, *this* smile was sunshine.

Joey broke free from Deborah's hand. Squeezing past the lawyer, she threw herself into her mother's arms.

Ruby hugged her back just as tightly, her fingers stroking the back of Joey's hair. "Remember what we talked about," she murmured.

Neither of them let go until the bailiff came over to separate them.

Joey took a seat on the witness stand. Deborah sat two rows behind the crown attorney's table, right by the aisle, so she and Joey could see each other clearly. She gave Joey a soft smile and a head tilt, as if to say, *You got this.*

Duffy began to ask her questions. They had been over this, they had practiced, and Joey knew exactly what to say. During prep she had found herself detaching whenever the questions got too hard and the memories were too much. Each time, Duffy would force her to come back. *You have to stay present, Joelle. The jury needs to understand what you've been through, and to understand it, they need to feel it. And for them to feel it, you need to feel it. If just for this one time. I know you can do this, Joelle.*

Joey answered questions about her upbringing, the various apartments they'd lived in, the bare cupboards, the closets she sometimes slept in when she didn't feel safe in her bed. She told the jury about the physical abuse, her mother's revolving door of boyfriends, the sounds of sex happening in the next room that she wasn't supposed to hear. The jurors' facial expressions changed constantly. One moment, they were sad for her. The next, they were angry at Ruby. And in between, there was pity. So much pity.

"I know this is hard, Joelle," Duffy said. "And I want to reiterate how wonderfully you're doing, and what a brave young lady you are. But now I want to talk about Charles Baxter. I want you to walk us through the night he was killed. Can you tell us what you saw?"

For this, Joey could not look at her mother. And she could not look at Deborah, either. Instead, she focused on Duffy's face. She had no emotional connection to the crown attorney, who once again was just another person who said she wanted to help because she was being paid to do it. She would pretend that the jurors were just blank pages, waiting to be filled with the truth.

It didn't necessarily have to be *the* truth. Just *her* truth.

Joey took a deep breath, and began.

* * *

A few days before Charles Baxter was killed, he had ended his affair with her mother for the fourth time in two years. Ruby was, to put it mildly, very upset.

"The asshole won't answer his phone." Her mother was on her third cigarette in twenty minutes as she paced around the living room. "He thinks he can just drop me? Oh no. No no no."

Joey was curled into the corner of the sofa. She had seen this before. Her mother was like this after every breakup, bouncing from anger to self-pity and back again, like she was playing Ping-Pong with herself. This was the anger, and there was nothing to be done about it. The only thing Joey could do was listen and nod and agree. Anything else would only make things worse.

Ruby pressed the redial button on their cordless phone, which was, ironically, a gift from Charles. Joey could hear it ringing on the other end. After six rings, it went to voice mail. Again. She whipped the phone at the couch, where it missed Joey's foot by a few inches.

"I should just call the fucker at home. I'll talk to his wife. Want to bet how quick he calls back then?"

Very bad idea. "I don't want him to be angry at you, Mama."

Her mother stopped. "You're right. He would be. And then he'll never pick up the phone." She finished her cigarette, walked over to the sliding door that opened to the balcony, and flicked the butt over the edge. Walking back toward Joey, she said, "I need a distraction. Let's get out of here. Let's go see a movie. Anything you want."

Joey perked up. Going to the movies was a rarity, and it was even rarer for her mother to suggest it. "I'll check the listings."

Her mother didn't respond, so Joey picked up the phone and dialed 777-FILM. The call was answered almost immediately. *Hell-O! And welcome to Moviefone . . .*

She listened to that weekend's movie listings and memorized them, then turned to her mother. "The only PG movie is *Batman Returns*," she said, holding her breath. *Please please please . . .*

Ruby shrugged. "Fine."

"It's opening day, so we might have to pick the tickets up early. There's a nine o'clock show."

"Okay."

"Maybe if we leave soon, I could get the tickets, and then we could have dinner at the diner while we wait?" Joey knew she was pushing her luck.

"Sure."

Yay. "I can go find your glasses while you take a shower."

Her mother had not showered in three days.

"All right."

Impulsively, Joey gave her mother a kiss on the cheek. Ruby reeked of unwashed hair, body odor, and smoke. "Thank you, Mama. You're the best."

She was rewarded with a tiny smile.

Forty-five minutes later, Ruby waited in the car in front of the box office while Joey bought two tickets for the nine o'clock show. She skipped back to the car, excited to get to the Jupiter Diner, her favorite restaurant. It had a separate menu just for ice cream, and each of the old-fashioned booths had its own mini jukebox full of 1950s hits. A quarter bought five songs. She already knew what the first one would be: "Rockin' Robin." *Tweet, tweet . . . tweedily-dee.*

But as they drove away from the theater, she sensed her mother growing agitated once again. When they reached the next intersection, instead of making a left to get to the diner, Ruby suddenly made a right. Joey's heart sank.

"Mama?"

"I just want to drive by Charles's house quickly," her mother said. "He told me he couldn't meet in person to talk things over because he would be at the cottage with *her* this weekend. I want to make sure he isn't lying to me."

Her always meant Suzanne, Charles's wife. Joey wasn't sure why it mattered where Charles was. He'd already dumped her. But there was no point reminding her mother of that. She slumped in her seat. Maybe they wouldn't have time for the diner, but there was a good chance they could still make the movie.

They headed toward The Kingsway, a neighborhood that was very expensive. Even if Ruby hadn't told her how much the houses cost, it was obvious that the people who lived here were wealthy. Ruby drove through the lush tree-lined streets while Joey looked out the window at all the big, beautiful homes. What would it take to own a house like that, in a neighborhood like this?

They stopped in front of a gigantic house that, aside from the roof, was made entirely of cream-colored stone. The driveway could fit six cars, but there was only one parked there now. Ruby did not pull in behind it. Instead, she kept her old Mercury Monarch idling at the curb on the opposite side of the street.

"Wow," Joey breathed, leaning forward to look past her mother. "Charles is really rich."

"You should see the inside." Her mother did not look happy. She was fixated on the shiny black Jaguar in the driveway. "He's home, the motherfucker. I knew he lied to me. I can see him in his office."

It doesn't matter. He broke up with you.

Ruby pulled down the sun visor and examined her face in the mirror. "I need more makeup," she said, passing Joey her purse. "Find my lipstick and eyeliner. See if there's blush in there, too." She reached into the glove box and pulled out the travel-size hairbrush she always kept in the car.

Joey rifled through her mother's handbag and found an old CoverGirl eye pencil and blush, and an old tube of Maybelline Great Lash mascara. Then she dug out a tube of MAC lipstick in "Russian Red," Ruby's signature shade. She watched as her mother fixed her face.

"Wait here," Ruby said. "Don't worry, we won't miss the movie, okay? I'm going to shut the car off. Roll down the windows so you don't get too hot."

She was out of the car before Joey could answer, smoothing the skirt of her summer dress before crossing the street quickly. She marched right up to the front door and rang the doorbell. Joey watched through the open car window as Charles answered. She was too far away to hear what Charles was saying, but Ruby's voice was getting loud. Charles pulled her inside and shut the door.

Ten minutes passed. Then twenty. Then thirty. Joey's stomach was rumbling. She found a half-finished pack of Juicy Fruit gum in the glove compartment, unwrapped two pieces, and folded both of them into her mouth.

After another ten minutes, she was starting to get sleepy when the driver's-side door opened. Her mother plopped into the seat beside her. Ruby looked lit up, and Joey noticed her mother's red lipstick was completely gone.

"I need to move the car to the playground down the street, so his neighbors don't see it," she said, her eyes sparkling. "Charles and I made up, so we're staying for dinner. He wasn't lying to me—he had to stay behind at the last minute for work. But *she* won't be back from the cottage until Tuesday."

He's still lying to you, Mama. "But we'll miss the movie. We already bought the tickets." Joey reached into the pocket of her shorts and held them up.

"For fuck's sake," Ruby said, starting the engine. "This relationship is more important than a stupid movie, okay? Look at his house. If I play my cards right, it could be us living here. He admitted he made a mistake breaking up with me. He only did it because he doesn't want his wife to have half of everything if they get divorced. But he's decided it's worth it if it means he and I can be together."

Joey was skeptical. She had heard this story before; Charles wasn't the first man to promise Ruby he was leaving his wife, only to not do it.

"I can take the bus home," Joey said.

"You are staying with me." Ruby's tone left no room for argument.

"Charles is looking forward to seeing you, and we're spending the night. He's got a giant TV in the basement and about a hundred movies. That's better than sitting in a cold theater with everyone kicking the back of your seat."

No, it isn't. "But I don't have pajamas or a toothbrush."

"Charles has everything," her mother said. "Literally everything. Go on inside. I'll be right back after I move the car."

Joey put her hand on the door, then hesitated.

"Stop being a brat." Ruby's voice hardened. "Charles is waiting for you."

CHAPTER THIRTY-SIX

The court was eerily silent, both the judge and the jury hanging on Joey's every word. Her throat dry, she turned her face away from the microphone and coughed, then reached for the small bottle of water beside her.

"What happened when you and your mother went back to Charles Baxter's house?" Duffy asked.

"Charles showed me around," Joey said, her voice echoing through the speakers above her. "He said it was nice to have a little girl in the house again. His daughter was away at school, and she rarely came home anymore. And then we all went down to the basement."

* * *

Joey hadn't realized that houses could have basements like this, with furniture and carpet and different rooms. It was a kids' paradise.

The Baxters had a billiards table, a Ping-Pong table, two pinball machines, and an original *Galaga* arcade cabinet, a game that Joey had only ever played at the supermarket when her mother remembered to go grocery shopping. Charles seemed genuinely delighted to see her, and he explained that she didn't need quarters to play any of the games.

"All you have to do is press this red button, and the game will start," he said. "And you can play as many times as you want. Let's see if you can beat my scores."

On the *Galaga* screen, Joey could see the names of the other players. Someone named Brian had the top score; that must be Charles's son. The second highest belonged to Lexi, who must be Charles's daughter. What a nice name, *Lexi*. Upstairs on the fireplace mantel, Joey had seen a portrait of the whole family, which looked like it was taken by a professional photographer. The Baxters seemed like a completely normal family, except that Charles had a mistress named Ruby.

The video games kept Joey occupied for a while, as did *Father of the Bride*, the movie she selected from the extensive VHS collection. She was tired when the movie finally ended, so she wandered upstairs to see where she was supposed to sleep.

There was laughter coming from the second floor, and she found her mom and Charles propped up in his bed, feeding each other fruit and cheese, with some black-and-white movie playing on the TV. The master bedroom was almost as large as their apartment, with double doors and huge closets and an enormous bathroom. Charles was cutting the cheese into cubes with a long, thin knife, and feeding them to Ruby like it was a barbecue skewer.

"Hey, baby," her mother said. Her face was flushed, her hair mussed. Her dress was hiked up, her long legs bare and exposed. Charles's free hand was caressing her thigh. "Going to bed?"

"I'm not sure where I should sleep."

Charles popped a piece of cheese into his mouth and grinned. "At the very end of the hall is a guest bedroom, the one with the white bedspread. You'll find toothpaste and toothbrushes in the bathroom, along with soap and shampoo and all that good stuff."

"I, um, don't have any pajamas."

"I'll lend you one of my T-shirts." Charles pointed to the dresser, which was beside the entrance to the bathroom. "Second drawer from the top. Choose anything you want. You're so small, it'll be a nightgown for you." He laughed, and Ruby laughed too as she played with his hair.

Joey headed for the dresser and pulled open the second drawer to find a row of neatly folded shirts. She took the first one she saw, which turned out to be a T-shirt from the University of Toronto.

"That's my alma mater," Charles said. "Be careful with it, okay? I've had that shirt longer than your mother's been alive, and it's not in nearly as good shape as she is."

Ruby laughed again. "You're so silly, my darling."

Joey said good night to both of them and trudged down the hallway. She passed a bedroom filled with sports paraphernalia—signed basketballs, footballs, hockey sticks, two framed jerseys. Brian's room.

She kept going, then stopped at a bedroom where the walls were painted pink. It had to be Lexi's room. Curious, she stepped inside, and instantly, she was awestruck. There were posters on the walls of Jason Priestley, Luke Perry, and Brian Austin Green; Charles's daughter was clearly a *90210* fan. There were also posters of Madonna, Mariah Carey, and Marky Mark and the Funky Bunch. Her mother had once mentioned that Lexi was a student at Dalhousie University in Halifax, and that she almost never came home to visit.

"She doesn't get along with her father," Ruby told her. "That's what happens when you spoil kids rotten."

Being spoiled didn't sound so bad to Joey. Lexi Baxter had more stuff than Joey could have ever imagined one girl having. There was a stereo, a CD collection, a small TV. She had an entire wall of bookshelves that didn't contain a single book, and were instead filled with trophies, plaques, ribbons, and medals. 1990 Skate Canada International, second place. 1986 Autumn Classic International, third place. 1987 US International Figure Skating Classic, seventh place. Lexi Baxter had been a competitive figure skater, and if these trophies were any indication, a pretty good one.

Joey trailed her fingers along the bed as she headed toward Lexi's closet, which was so big it needed its own lighting. Picking through the clothes, she saw that everything was brand name. Benetton. Polo. Tommy Hilfiger. Ralph Lauren. Clean-cut preppy designer clothing, for the girl who had everything.

And on display, right in the middle, hung Lexi's ice skates. Charles's daughter owned three pairs, two white and one beige, in various states of wear. Joey picked up one of the white ones and slid off the skate guard. The blade was extremely thin at the edge, sharpened almost to a V. Joey recalled what one of the commentators had said during the Albertville Winter Olympics, when the women's free skate event was on.

The better a skater you were, the sharper the blade would be.

She put the skate back as she found it and went to check out the photos. All around the room—on the pin board, on the headboard, taped to the dresser mirror—were pictures of Lexi, blond and trim, at all different stages of her life. Half the photos showed her skating, and the other half showed her with family and friends. Lexi was popular. And she was close to her mom and brother, it seemed. There were lots of pictures of the three of them, smiling, laughing, doing things together. She looked like her mother, but she had her father's eyes.

What would it be like to be Lexi Baxter? Lexi had a mother who loved her, and a father who provided for her. She had a brother to play with or fight with, depending on the day. She had friends. Skating. University. No worries about money. Lexi had been born into a dream life. She had won the family lottery.

It was so unfair.

Joey left Lexi's room and made her way down the hall to the guest bedroom, which was beautifully decorated and completely impersonal. She found a toothbrush in the ensuite bathroom like Charles said she would—even the Baxters' guests had a better life than she and Ruby did. She could understand why her mother would want to live here and be Charles's wife. Under any other circumstances, Joey might have wanted to be Charles's stepdaughter.

Except there was already one monster in the family.

She left Charles's T-shirt in the bathroom, climbed into bed, and, still wearing all her own clothes, fell asleep.

* * *

The courtroom was so quiet that Joey could hear the rumbling of the bailiff's stomach from six feet away.

"Did you stay asleep the entire night?" Duffy asked.

"No. I woke up when I heard a noise."

"What time was that?"

"A little after one, maybe."

"Walk us through what you did then."

"I sat up," Joey said. "The room was dark, so I turned a lamp on because I was a bit freaked out. And then I realized my mom and Charles were arguing. It went on for a little while, maybe ten minutes. And then my mom came into the guest room. She was upset."

Joey paused, as Duffy had coached her to do. She had specific instructions to not rush this part. She counted to two, and then continued.

"She was holding a knife, the same one I saw Charles use to cut up the cheese from before. It was covered in blood. And so was she."

She took a breath and held it. It felt like everyone in the courtroom was doing the same.

"What did your mother say to you?" Duffy prompted, just as they'd rehearsed.

"She said, 'You have to help me. I killed him. Charles is dead.'"

There was a rustling in the courtroom. It came from the jury box, and Joey glanced over to see that most of the jurors were looking at Ruby. But there was one member who was still looking at Joey, and it was the same woman who'd smiled at her when she was first brought in. The woman wasn't smiling now. Her face was full of sympathy, her eyes sad and moist.

"What happened then?" Duffy asked.

"She was hysterical and panicking. She wanted to leave. I told her we should stay and call the police, say it was accident, that she didn't mean to hurt him. She said she didn't want anyone to know what she had done. She said if we left right away, they might think someone broke in, like a robber or something. She kept pulling my arm, but I told her that if she didn't want to call 911, then we had to make sure she wasn't leaving anything behind. I mean, I know the police can check for fingerprints and all that, but I also knew my mom had been to his house at least a few times before. We just had to make sure nobody knew she had been there that night."

Joey took another breath.

"I found a garbage bag under the bathroom sink. I told her to drop the knife in and said she should take off her dress and put that in the bag, too. She put on Charles's old T-shirt, and I found a pair of sweatpants in one of Lexi's drawers. And then I told her to go out the back entrance and get the car."

"*You* told her to go?" Duffy already knew all this, but she said it in a tone of disbelief. "You, her thirteen-year-old daughter, told your *mother* to go?"

"I was scared she would make things worse. She wasn't thinking straight. She was stumbling around and crying and saying things."

"What did she say?"

"Things like, 'Oh God, what did I do, what did I do?' I just felt like it would be easier to try and clean up without her there. She finally left."

"And then what did you do?"

"I brought the garbage bag into Charles's bedroom. The door was wide-open and the lights were all on . . ." Joey's voice trails off.

Duffy gives her the tiniest nod of approval. "Tell us what you saw, Joelle," she said softly.

"I saw Charles lying on the floor on his side. There was blood everywhere, but most of it was on the carpet where he was. His eyes were closed, and he wasn't moving. He looked dead. I . . . I almost threw up . . ."

"That's understandable. Go on."

"I started picking up everything my mom left behind. Her purse was on the bedside table, and I found her lipstick in the bathroom by the sink. I didn't know what to take, so I just took everything: the napkins, the forks, the wine bottle, her glass, which had her lipstick on it . . ."

Another breath.

"And then I heard him moan. I think I jumped, the sound scared me. I turned around to look at him, and his eyes were open. I thought he was going to get up, but he just lay there and said, 'Joey, call 911. Please. She stabbed me.'"

"Did you call 911?"

"No."

"Why not?" Duffy asks.

"Because my mother came back. She was paranoid that he wasn't dead, and she needed to make sure. She saw that his eyes were open and that he was trying to speak, and then something . . . changed."

"What changed?"

"*She* changed. She told me to finish cleaning up, to check everywhere, especially in the bathroom. She'd used Charles's wife's hairbrush and deodorant, and she wanted me to get them and put them in the bag. While I was in the bathroom, she must have left and gone into Lexi's room. When I came out, she was sitting on the chair in the corner, and she had one of Lexi's ice skates. She was putting it on and lacing it up. I couldn't understand what she was doing. And . . ."

"Go on." An imperceptible nod of encouragement. The crown attorney's eyes were gleaming. She was going in for the kill.

Joey hesitated, as they'd practiced. She took a breath, as they'd practiced. And then she lifted her chin, looked Duffy square in the eyes, and spoke clearly, just as she'd been asked to do.

"My mother stomped on his neck."

A couple of the jurors gasped.

Duffy waited a few seconds, and then she said softly, "Tell us the rest, Joelle."

"She took off the skate and dropped it into the garbage bag with everything else." Joey looked down at her hands. "And then we went home."

CHAPTER THIRTY-SEVEN

The judge, fully immersed in the testimony, almost forgot to acknowledge that the crown attorney was finished. Madeline Duffy had been seated for a good five seconds before he finally remembered to say, "Mr. Mitchell, your witness."

Joey watched as her mother's lawyer stood up. He was a shorter man wearing a shiny gray suit, and he only had hair on the sides and back of his head.

"Joelle, I'm Don Mitchell," he said. "I want to thank you for being here today. I know this is hard. I'll try and keep it brief, okay?"

"Okay," Joey said.

He walked reluctantly toward her, acting as if he was sad to have to put her through this. But Duffy had explained that just as they had practiced Joey's testimony, Ruby's lawyer would have done the same with her mother. Everything in court was a stage act. Everything was rehearsed.

"You said you woke up in the guest bedroom to the sounds of your mother and Charles arguing. Did you hear what the argument was about?"

"I only heard bits and pieces."

"Can you tell us about those bits and pieces?"

"My mother was mad that Charles wanted to break up again. She was yelling that he was just using her, and he was yelling at her to leave."

"What else did they say?"

"That's all I could hear."

"So they weren't fighting about you?"

Joey looked over at Duffy. "No. Not that I heard."

Don Mitchell paced slowly. "So you didn't hear your mother and Charles arguing about you at all?"

"Objection," Duffy said. "Asked and answered."

"Sustained," the judge said.

Mitchell looked at the jury, then back at Joey. "We heard earlier testimony that two of your mother's previous boyfriends are on the sex offender registry. Joey, have you ever been abused by any of your mother's boyfriends?"

"Objection," Duffy said. "How is this relevant?"

"It's relevant, Your Honor," Mitchell said. "I'm getting there."

"Get there faster," the judge said.

Mitchell cleared his throat. "At the family court hearing when your diaries were read out loud, you implied that one of your mother's boyfriends—"

"Objection," Duffy said loudly, standing up. "Permission to approach, Your Honor."

Both lawyers moved toward the judge, who covered his microphone with his hand. They spoke in whispers for about a minute, and even though the courtroom was quiet and Joey was straining to hear them, she couldn't make out what anyone was saying. But Duffy had told her this would probably happen.

Joey stared straight ahead. In her peripheral vision, she could sense her mother's eyes on her. Deborah's, too. She couldn't bring herself to make eye contact with either of them.

The judge removed his hand from the microphone.

"The jury will disregard the last question," he said, looking over at the jury box. "The details of the family court hearing are sealed for the protection of the child." He looked down at the court reporter. "Strike it."

The court reporter nodded.

"Okay, Mr. Mitchell," the judge said. "You need to tread lightly here. Remember that your witness is a minor."

"I apologize, Your Honor," Mitchell said. He looked over at the jury, a rueful expression on his face, as if to communicate that he was being prevented from revealing something very important that they needed to hear. "One last question, Joelle, and then we're finished."

Joey nodded, and Mitchell turned away from the jurors to face her directly, his hands in his pockets.

"On the night that Charles died," Mitchell said, "your mother testified that she woke up around one a.m. to discover that Charles was not in bed beside her. She went looking for him and found him in the guest bedroom. He was in bed with you."

Ruby's lawyer now had the same gleam in his eye that Duffy had earlier.

"Was Charles sexually abusing you, Joelle? Please remember, you're under oath."

Joey took a deep breath, and when she exhaled, she looked over at her mother. To anyone but her, Ruby's face was neutral, almost expressionless. But to Joey, her eyes were commanding her daughter to say everything they'd agreed she would say.

For once, her mother was expecting her to tell the truth, the whole truth, and nothing but the truth. *If you don't tell them about Charles, I will die in prison.*

I love you, Mama. I'm sorry.

"No." Joey spoke clearly into the microphone. "Charles was a really nice man. I liked him. He never touched me. Not once. Not ever."

* * *

Joey stepped down from the witness box. She had to pass her mother on the way out of the courtroom, but she would not make eye contact, she would not say goodbye. As far as she was concerned, they had already said their goodbyes, in the visitors' area of the jail where Ruby asked for her help.

All the years Joey had told her mother what was happening to her, what was being done *to* her, Ruby did nothing. Half the time, she accused Joey of lying. The other half, she blamed Joey for inviting it. Either way, it

CHAPTER THIRTY-EIGHT

It took the jury ninety-three minutes to declare Ruby Reyes guilty of first-degree murder in the death of Charles Anthony Baxter.

Joey wasn't present for the sentencing. She heard about it from Deborah first, and then an hour later, it was all over the news. Ruby had received a life sentence, with the possibility of parole after twenty-five years. Though Joey had been expecting it, it felt like her mother had died. And all there was to do now was grieve.

The next chapter had officially begun.

That night, Joey fell asleep a few minutes after her head hit the pillow, drifting off to the sound of the frogs at the pond. They were croaking in unison as they always did, their loud, throaty harmony providing an amphibious white noise she found peaceful. Just before sleep found her, she imagined a little frog conductor standing up on his hind legs, his skinny arms directing the choir. How else would they all know to start and stop at the same time . . .

She jerked awake to find Tito Micky perched on the edge of her bed.

He had never come in this far before. But tonight, he was sitting at the bottom of her mattress, the side of his face illuminated by the slice of moon beaming in through the windows, a silhouette with half a face. The curtains were never fully closed. The boys didn't like to sleep in total darkness, and though Joey would never admit it to them, she felt the same.

Bad things happened in the dark.

never stopped. Her mother had never, and would never, protect her. Ruby was only out for Ruby.

The only way for Joey to save herself . . . was to save herself.

She walked with her head up, her eyes staring straight ahead. But before she could pass her mother, Ruby reached into the aisle and gripped Joey's arm.

"You lying little bitch."

Her uncle stared at her with whiskey-glazed eyes. Joey blinked, then blinked again. Maybe this was a dream. Maybe her testimony at the trial had brought up some terrible memories.

She felt his hand on her thigh.

"Joelle," he breathed. The smell of whiskey on his breath was pungent.

Across the room, she could hear the boys snoring in their bunks. She could hear the frogs and smell the swampy damp of the pond below. She could hear the rustle of the wind in the trees outside. She could hear Tito Micky's slight wheeze.

This was not a dream. This was real, and she could feel her body stiffening from the fear that was beginning to suffocate her. In her mind, she screamed at herself, *Don't freeze! Say something! Turn the light on!* Light vaporized monsters the way water dissolved the Wicked Witch of the West.

But the lamp was too far away, and when she tried to reach for it, her body wouldn't comply. She no longer had the instincts other people had. Her fight-or-flight response had been stolen from her a long time ago. She was frozen.

The only thing she could do was not be *here*.

"Joelle," Tito Micky said again, and she felt his hand move an inch higher.

She closed her eyes and listened to the frogs, willing herself to drift away. She pictured the little green choir director, and imagined she was down at the pond for the live performance. Finally, blessedly, she began to float out of her body and out the window, where she hovered on the other side of the glass, peeking in at the girl on the bed with the monster looming over her.

It's okay. It will be over soon. Just don't look. Just don't feel.

The frog conductor morphed into a *Looney Tunes* cartoon she used to love. A man happened to discover a frog that could sing and dance, and because the frog had a lovely, showtune voice, the man stole him and tried to get him to perform at a concert in front of a huge audience for money. But when the curtain opened, the frog just sat there onstage, and croaked. It always made her laugh.

She imagined herself as the man.

"Sing," she said, and for her, the frog finally complied.

Hello, my baby, hello, my honey, hello, my ragtime gaaaal
Send me a kiss by wire
Baby, my heart's on fire
If you refuse me, honey, you'll lose me
Then you'll be left alone
Oh baby, telephone, and tell me I'm your owwwwwn

"Joelle," Tito Micky breathed again.

The sound of her name thrust her back to the present, and she was angry, because it was hard to transport herself somewhere else if someone was *speaking* to her. She mentally shut her ears; she could not listen, because listening made it real. She squeezed her eyelids tighter; she could not see, because seeing it made it real.

She willed herself back down to the pond. The frogs would sing her through this. The only thing she needed to do was breathe—inhale, exhale—but it was hard because her stomach was clenched like she was doing sit-ups.

Five more, Joey, she could hear Ruby say, and she flew to her mother, relieved to see her, if only for this one time. Ruby was lying on an exercise mat and a calisthenics tape was playing in the VCR. She was doing sit-ups, and so Joey was doing sit-ups, too, because she liked to do everything her mother did. Joey was seven. *Boys like flat stomachs,* Ruby said. *I blame you for every single one of these stretch marks.*

Someone coughed, and she was back in the bedroom again with the monster. She wanted to thrash, scream, and wake the house up, anything to make him stop.

But she couldn't. Tita Flora would never believe her, and even if she did, it wouldn't be Tito Micky leaving the house. He was her husband, the boys' father, and they were a family, and Tita Flora would not break up her own family. Joey, on the other hand, was an inherited nuisance, the daughter of her murderer sister, the unwanted niece she was paid to care for.

And where would she go anyway? To a foster home full of strangers where there was another Tito Micky?

Because there was always another Tito Micky.

She heard another sound, a bad sound, and this time, she opened her eyes. She didn't mean to, but now she was looking at Tito Micky, and he was looking at her. It occurred to her then that he was interpreting her stillness as *permission*.

But not saying no was not the same thing as saying yes.

NO! she screamed, and while it was only in her head, it was enough to unfreeze her.

She slid her hand out beside her, feeling her way to the little crack between the mattress and the bed. The box cutter was perfectly placed, right where it always was, right where she'd put it as soon as her bed frame had arrived. She grasped it, pushing her thumb onto the slider to extend the blade. She pushed out the sharp metal a quarter of an inch, and then another quarter of an inch, and then just a tiny bit more.

Down by the pond, the frogs went silent.

She brought her arm up and stabbed the box cutter right into Tito Micky's thigh as hard as she could, until the blade met resistance from the plastic sheath. Then she pulled the blade down, slicing an inch of him open vertically, which was more difficult than she thought, because flesh was more unyielding than she thought.

But it was enough.

Her uncle yelped and sprang back, and oh, it felt so good to feel his blood, it felt so good to cause him pain, it felt so good to hurt the monster who was hurting her, if only for tonight. She kicked him hard, and he rolled off the bed, landing with a *thud* on the carpet. He climbed awkwardly to his feet, his whiskey-glazed eyes clearing as his face morphed into panic.

She never knew that blood looked black in the dark.

"*Pasayloa ko*," he gasped, looking over frantically at the opposite wall where his two young sons were beginning to stir in their beds from the noise. "I'm sorry. I'm sorry."

Then he stumbled away, his shoulder bumping the doorway, and he was gone.

A sleepy voice from the other side of the room said, "Are you okay, Joey?"

She wiped the box cutter on her fitted sheet, then slid the blade back inside the plastic. She would wash her bedding tomorrow morning, and if anyone asked about the blood, she would say she got her period. Lies were more easily believed than the truth.

"Go back to sleep," she whispered.

The frogs began to croak again.

She was not okay. Not even a little bit. She should have told Deborah the truth when she asked, but really, what would it change? Her mother was in prison, and there was nowhere to go, and so this was her life, because it had always been her life, and it would either kill her, or she would survive it.

Tonight, both sounded equally terrible. She was being punished. For the lie she had told.

And in the end, it wasn't even worth it. There were monsters everywhere. It was like playing that old carnival game, Whac-A-Mole. As soon as she pounded one monster down, another one popped up.

Unable to sleep, Joey lay with her eyes open all night long, watching as the moonlight changed to morning. Only when the sun came up and the room was bright did her eyelids finally grow heavy, and she slipped the box cutter back between the mattress and the bed frame, back into the crack where nobody looked, because nobody cared.

PART FIVE

We're just two lost souls swimming in a fish bowl

—Pink Floyd

PART FIVE

CHAPTER THIRTY-NINE

Paris stares at her lawyers from across the kitchen table. Well, one of them is her lawyer. The other is *a* lawyer. But both their faces are somber, and the way they're looking at her now is scaring the shit out of her. They look like they're on the verge of dropping some incredibly bad news.

"Okay, who died?" Paris asks. She winces the second she hears what she just said, and curses her mouth for being faster than her manners. "I'm sorry, bad choice of words. Let me try it again. Why are you both here, and how worried should I be?"

"It's not bad," Elsie says. "It's quite the opposite."

"It's an early Christmas present," Sonny says, his shark grin finally appearing. "Unless you're Jewish, in which case it's all eight days of Hanukkah rolled into one."

Elsie jabs him with her elbow. "You can't say things like that. You'll offend someone."

"Counselors," Paris says, her gaze shifting back and forth between the two of them. "I have no idea what you're talking about."

Sonny slides the folder he brought with him across the table. "Happy fucking holidays."

Paris opens the folder. Inside are three black-and-white photographs of herself, enlarged to 8x10s. She's in her car, and it's nighttime. The first picture shows her full face; she's looking straight ahead through the windshield. The second picture is a 45-degree angle of her looking up as she hands over her passport. And the third photo is of her profile as she waits for the gate to lift. All three are time and date stamped.

US Border Patrol has finally come through, and Paris is looking at proof that she crossed back into the country at the exact time she said she did.

"Got these about an hour ago. The DA's office emailed them to me." Sonny reaches over and taps a thick finger over the time and date stamp. "You crossed at 12:22 a.m., which means the soonest you could have gotten home is two thirty, just like you said."

Paris is afraid to breathe.

"But wait," Sonny says. "There's more."

"What are you going to do, sell her a Thigh Master now?" Elsie shakes her head, but she's smiling.

Her lawyer pushes another folder toward her. "The medical examiner's final report. As we thought, it confirms Jimmy's time of death as between nine thirty and midnight."

Paris is confused. "I thought you said that was too close for your liking."

"Not anymore," Sonny says. "Take a closer look at that report. What does it say right there?" He taps a box in the middle of the page.

Paris follows his finger. "It says cause of death is exsanguination due to a severed femoral artery."

"Not that," Sonny says. "Below it."

Paris looks closer. Under the box for *Underlying Cause of Death*, the box for *Homicide* has been left unchecked. So too have the boxes for *Natural Causes* and *Suicide*. However, there is an X in the box beside *Undetermined*.

"Undetermined? What does that mean?" Paris looks up. "Are they saying they're not actually sure how Jimmy died?"

"Bingo," Sonny says. "The ME is saying that there's no direct evidence confirming that Jimmy's death was the result of a homicide. And you can't be charged *with* a homicide if there wasn't one."

Paris holds her breath, unable to react until she hears him say it. One of them needs to say it.

"The DA has withdrawn the murder charge," Elsie says. "It's over."

Paris waits three seconds. "Okay," she says slowly. She refuses to relax until she understands it fully. "But they can still press charges in the future, right?"

"Against you? No." Sonny cracks his knuckles. "The border crossing photos provide more than enough reasonable doubt. Against someone else? Maybe, if the cause of death changes, which it won't, or if new evidence comes to light. But if they haven't found it by now, I doubt they will."

"All that's left to do is return your ankle monitor. And I'm happy to take care of that for you." Elsie reaches across the table and squeezes Paris's hand. "It's really over."

Paris exhales so hard, she collapses in her chair. The tears follow a moment later, which turn into sobs that rack her whole body. She's only vaguely aware of each lawyer's hand touching her shoulder as they leave quietly.

Life has a way of balancing everything out. And the only reason this moment feels so good is that what happened to Jimmy was so bad. She knows the feeling won't last. When Paris is finished crying, all she'll be left with is the guilt that her husband was so unhappy and in such a dark place that he felt the only way out was to end his own life. And she'll spend the rest of her life trying to understand how he got there, how she could have missed it, how she might have saved him.

When the sobs subside, she heads upstairs to her room to wash her face and change into something comfortable. She needs to call Henry, and then she needs to finish making plans for Jimmy's funeral. Per his wishes, he'll be cremated, and his urn will rest next to his mother's in the family mausoleum.

A little way down the hall, she sees that the door to Jimmy's bedroom is open. She can still smell the bleach coming out of it, reminding her that it's been cleaned and that it's safe to go inside. She takes a step toward it, then stops. The last time she was in Jimmy's bedroom was the night he died.

She's not ready.

Jimmy, I love you. And I'm sorry. I'm so, so, so sorry.

* * *

All that's left to do now is grieve. And the way Paris grieves is: she cooks.

For the past couple of hours, she's been listening to Jimmy's cassettes on his old boombox in the kitchen. It's nice. Every song on his "Hits of '70s" compilation cassette has a memory of her husband attached to it. Right now, The Hollies are playing, and she can picture Jimmy sitting at the table with his reading glasses on, drinking his coffee as a light rain comes down on the window. *Sometimes, all I need is the air that I breathe . . .*

She lifts the lid off her Le Creuset and gives the lightly simmering pork adobo a stir. Every cook has their own recipe for the traditional Filipino stew. Some like it saucy. Some like it dry. But the basic ingredients in any Filipino adobo are soy sauce, vinegar, bay leaves, and patience. She's also making *lumpia* (spring rolls) and a huge batch of *pancit* (noodles), and when she's finished, she'll have enough leftovers for a week. The only good thing that ever came out of her time in Maple Sound was that Lola Celia taught her to cook.

The doorbell rings. Paris checks the clock on the stove and frowns. She can't imagine who could be at the front door at nine o'clock at night, other than a photographer hoping for a picture or a journalist hoping for a comment. But the crowd that was camped outside for the past week is finally gone now, and the neighborhood is back to normal, with its usual amount of city gazers taking photos at Kerry Park.

The doorbell rings again, and this time, it's followed by a knock. Whoever it is, they know she's home, because all the lights are on inside the house. She looks around for her phone to see if she's missed a text. Maybe Henry was planning to stop by. But she left her phone upstairs on the charger.

A thought occurs to her. What if it's *Ruby?* She's out on parole now, and although she's forbidden to leave Canada, her mother has always been crafty. And she can be very motivated when someone else has something she wants. Like husbands. And money.

The knocking stops. Paris keeps her ears perked, waiting for the doorbell to ring again. It doesn't. Padding down the hallway to the front door, she finally looks out the peephole to see if she can at least catch a glimpse of who it might have been. But there's no one there.

Feeling a little rattled, Paris heads back into the kitchen. She'd started cooking around six o'clock when her stomach began to rumble, and then got carried away—she's knee-deep in it now. The song has changed to "Midnight Train to Georgia," and she sings along softly with Gladys Knight. *I'd rather live in his world than live without him in mine* . . .

Something crashes outside, and she jumps. *What the* hell *is going on?* Is someone in the backyard? Are they trying to break in now?

In a panic, she reaches for the closest sharp object she can find: the cleaver she used to chop all the vegetables for the *pancit*. There's a glare on the kitchen windows and patio doors from the overhead lights, preventing her from seeing anything in the backyard, so she flicks them all off before approaching the glass to see if there's anyone outside.

A man appears at the patio door, and she screams, nearly dropping the cleaver. Whoever he is, he must have hopped the fence. He's dressed in dark clothing, wearing a black ball cap with some kind of red insignia on it. She fumbles for the switch to the backyard lights, but it's dark, and all she ends up doing is flicking the kitchen lights back on again. The face vanishes behind a reflection of white.

The man pounds on the patio door.

"Go away," she says, as authoritatively as she can muster. "You are trespassing, and I'm going to call the police."

But how can she call? Her fucking phone is all the way upstairs.

He pounds on the glass again, and her fingers finally find the lights for the backyard. She switches them on, and sees a tall Black man staring in at her.

"Come on, Joey," Drew says, his voice muffled behind the glass. "Let me in."

CHAPTER FORTY

Paris hasn't had the wind physically knocked out of her since she was a child, but this feels almost the same. An emotional gut punch, right to the diaphragm, and now she can't breathe.

There was a sci-fi action movie she and Drew had rented a long time ago called *Timecop*, starring Jean-Claude Van Damme. It's set in the future, where a cop is sent back to the past via time travel to prevent something bad from happening. She can't remember the specific details of the plot now, but she does remember that the younger version of Jean-Claude cannot in any way touch the older version of Jean-Claude, or they'll both explode into nothing, like a supernova. There was a line that was quoted throughout: *The same matter cannot occupy the same space.*

Joey Reyes and Paris Peralta cannot both be here. And yet, looking at Drew through the glass of her back patio doors, this is exactly what's happening. Her mind flies through the possibilities of what she should do next.

Option one: She can pretend she's not Joey and insist she doesn't know this man. As stupid as it was, this was always her plan if she ever found herself confronted with her past. If you deny something over and over again, and for long enough, people might eventually believe you. It works for politicians. Bonus: You might even convince yourself it's the truth.

Option two: She can call the police, say she has a stalker, and have him arrested for trespassing.

Option three: She can kill him.

But it's too late for any of those. Drew is looking right at her, and she at him, and she knows that the mindfuck of the situation has got to be written all over her face. Maybe if she'd known he was coming, she would have had time to prepare, to practice her reaction. But that's exactly why he didn't call first, or text, or send an email. He needed her reaction to prove she was Joey. He needed to make sure she wouldn't run.

The past is melding with the present. The truth is mixing with the lies. This is a supernova.

"Joey, I didn't come all this way to fuck up your life," Drew says through the glass. "If I was going to do that, I would have just called the cops. Come on, open the door."

She stares at him, unable to move, feeling her mind trying to disconnect, trying to not be *here*.

"Joey, please," he says again. "I came all this way. I just want to talk to you." He glances up at the dark sky. "And it's starting to rain."

Even now, nineteen years since she last heard his voice, Drew sounds maddeningly, infuriatingly *reasonable*.

She reaches forward and turns the deadbolt, and then reaches up to flip the security latch. She steps back as Drew pulls open the door and steps into the kitchen. He takes off his ball cap, shakes off the moisture, and then puts it back on.

He looks around. He takes in the kitchen, the food simmering on the stove, the kitchen table where she was wrapping *lumpia*, and then his gaze is back on her. She realizes then that the red insignia on his hat is a dinosaur claw shaped like a basketball. A Toronto Raptors hat. Because it's Drew Malcolm. From Toronto.

"Do you think you could put down the cleaver?" he asks.

Paris opens her mouth to speak, but nothing comes out. She's imagined this moment a thousand times, of course, in various scenarios, this one included, but now that it's actually happening, it feels nothing like she expected.

"You're scaring me right now," Drew says. "You have this look on your face, and I can't tell whether you're going to kill me or ask me if I'm hungry."

"*I'm* scaring *you?*" she says, incredulous.

"Joey." Drew's voice softens into a gentler tone. "It's *me*. I came here straight from the airport. I didn't come all this way to hurt you, I promise. I just needed to see for myself that you're really alive. And here you are. Alive. And you should know that despite everything, I'm really glad that you are."

"What do you want, Drew?" she asks.

She hates the way her voice sounds, small and timid. It's like she's nineteen again, hoping to find a place to stay, armed only with a duffel bag and the cash she stole from Maple Sound, facing Drew in that shitty little basement apartment kitchen with the checkerboard floors, crossing her fingers that he'll see past his preconceived notions since it's clear he knew who she was. Only now, it's Drew standing in her decidedly not-shitty kitchen, and she's still hoping he'll see past everything he thinks he knows and allow her to explain.

Drew steps forward slowly, his hands up. When he's a couple of steps away from her, he reaches forward and carefully takes the cleaver out of her hands, and places it in the sink. He then lets out a sigh of relief. As if he actually thinks she might have whacked him with it.

In fairness, she did consider it for a split second. But that's because he surprised her, and she was panicking.

"You faked your death?" Drew says. "Are you fucking serious?"

"I'm sorry."

"You're *sorry?*"

She looks up at him. He looks down at her. She forgot how tall he is. There are specks of rain on his glasses. She doesn't know what to say, other than to apologize. If their positions were reversed, she would be angry as hell, too. And in this moment, standing in front of him, his body less than two feet away from hers, she suddenly can't remember why she did it, why she ran, why she ran away from Toronto, why she ran away from him.

Drew is waiting for her to say something. She needs to say something. Anything. *Goddammit, speak.*

She bursts into tears.

He steps forward and wraps his arms around her, squeezing her tight, and he feels different but the same, and he smells different but the same, and as terrified as she is that he's found her, he's *here*, and she's glad. She feels his lips brush her hair. He breathes into her ear as he speaks slowly and evenly, enunciating every word.

"I am so fucking mad at you."

* * *

"Are you hungry?" Paris asks.

He chuckles, as if he knew she would ask that, and nods. "Starving. Last thing I ate was seven hours ago."

"I'll fix you a plate," she says. "There's beer in the fridge. Help yourself."

She sticks a few rolls of *lumpia* in the air fryer, then putters around the kitchen. She fills a plate for him, and then a plate for herself, scooping freshly made rice out of the cooker before spooning a generous amount of adobo on top. *Pancit*, too. It feels good to have a task that allows her to be busy so she doesn't have to look at him while she compiles her thoughts. She can feel him watching her, and is suddenly aware that she's wearing the oldest, baggiest sweats she owns, her hair in a loose, messy ponytail. She pulls two beers out of the fridge.

She can't decide whether to tell him the truth, or some of it, or none of it. She sets his plate down. He takes a bite, chews slowly, then nods. "It tastes just like I remember."

They eat in silence, the two of them darting looks at each other between bites. It feels awkward and familiar at the same time. He hasn't changed all that much, though there's a softer thickness to his body now, the kind that comes with age. There are a few lines around his eyes and mouth that weren't there before. His hair, cut short, is still mostly black, with only a hint of gray at the temples. She wonders what he's thinking about her. His face has always been hard to read.

She reaches for the ball cap sitting on the table beside him and examines it, running her finger along the embroidered Raptors logo.

"Think they'll ever win a championship?" she finally asks, breaking the silence.

"Yes," he says. "You ever think to call and say, 'Hey, Drew, guess what, I'm not dead'?"

She puts the hat down. "I couldn't."

"Why not?"

"Because I couldn't ask you to keep that secret."

The air fryer dings, and she gets up to retrieve the *lumpia*. She serves them with a store-bought sweet chili dipping sauce.

"I cook when I'm sad," she says. "You know that."

"I'm sorry about your husband," Drew says. "I heard on the way over here that the murder charge against you was dropped. Still, do you mind if I ask—"

"I didn't kill Jimmy," Paris says. "The official cause of death is undetermined, but we believe he died by suicide."

"'We'?"

"The people who knew him best," Paris says, and leaves it at that.

"I'm sorry," Drew says again. "I understand you're grieving, but I grieved *you*. Do you understand that? For nineteen years, I blamed myself for your death."

"Why?" Of all the things she imagined him saying, him thinking her death was his fault had never crossed her mind. "The fire had nothing to do with you."

"It would have been nice if you told me that," he says. "I was the one who ID'd your body that night."

She nearly chokes. "What? How?"

"I came back," Drew says. "After we talked. You went inside, I drove away. And then I came back. There were fire trucks, police. They were loading your dead body onto an ambulance, and I looked under the tarp."

"Oh God." Paris stares at him. "Oh, Drew."

"And so before we get into anything, and we *are* going to get into it," he says, raising an eyebrow, "I want to start with an apology."

"I'm sorry," she says.

"Not you. Me." Drew's plate is empty, and he pushes it to the side. "I owe you an apology for the things I said to you that night. There hasn't been a day I haven't thought about it. All I ever wanted was to rewind and go back to those last moments in the car with you and take back everything I said. I'm sorry. For judging you when it wasn't my place. For making you feel like shit. Do you forgive me?"

Paris can see from his face that he means every word. She swallows, and then nods. "How . . . how was the wedding?"

"I never got married," Drew says. "And don't try and change the subject. A girl died, Joey. You have some explaining to do."

CHAPTER FORTY-ONE

She tells him about Mae, and Drew doesn't say a word the entire time she's speaking. He'd always been a good listener. The only time he shows any kind of reaction is when she tells him that Chaz, the bouncer from the Cherry he met that night, was the one who got her the Paris Aquino ID. Drew's face does a thing, but she doesn't know what it means.

"I believe you," he says when she finishes. "It's the conclusion I came to when I fell down this rabbit hole. I figured out it was probably Vinny Tranh who killed her. What I couldn't understand was why you set the fire. You could have just called the police."

"And then what?" Paris asks. "The police start looking for Vinny? What if he found me before they found him? Mae hid the drugs and cash in my apartment, in a spot nobody was supposed to know about. What if Vinny thought me and Mae were in on it together?" She looks away. "I had the cash. I saw a way out. A chance at a new life. I took it. Honestly, I didn't think anyone would miss me."

"Not even me?" Drew asks.

"Especially not you."

A short silence.

"How much cash was it?"

"A hundred grand. Combined with my savings, I had enough to get where I was going."

"And where did you go?"

"Everywhere, but nowhere special."

"And you settled in Seattle?"

"I like it here." She frowns. "Why does it feel like you're interrogating me?"

"Because I am. I'm trying to make sense of it, why people around you tend to end up dead." Drew's voice hardens. "Think about it from my perspective. Charles Baxter. Mae Ocampo. Jimmy fucking Peralta. What's the common denominator? *You.* And you've already proven you have the incredible capacity to lie. Your entire life now is a lie. Every one of those people died prematurely from exsanguination. That means—"

"I fucking know what 'exsanguination' means," Paris snaps. "I probably knew that word before you did. And don't come at me with your Occam's razor bullshit. Life is complicated, Drew. And in case you didn't notice, I'm not a girl anymore, and you're not allowed to lecture me. Thank you, by the way, for reminding me of how self-righteous you can be. It's probably your only flaw, but you might remember it's the reason things didn't go so well the last time we spoke."

Drew sighs and puts a hand up. "Okay, look, it's been a long few days—"

"I'm not finished."

Paris stands up, puts their plates in the sink, and leans against the counter, trying to stay calm. She thinks carefully about what she wants to say to him now, because this may be the only opportunity she has to say it before she throws him out.

"You always came across as this self-aware, sensitive guy who was willing to listen," she says. "And I know you've apologized, but even your apology comes with an agenda. Telling me you're sorry is just your way of manipulating me into letting my guard down, so that I'll talk to you. But the truth is, you were the person who judged me more than anyone else ever did. My mother never had expectations for me. She thought I was nothing, and that was an easy standard to meet. But you? You had all these hopes for what you thought I could be, which were really just expectations disguised as optimism."

She looks down at him, her breath coming fast.

"And when I didn't turn out the way you hoped, when you decided that I didn't meet your definition of what a good person was, when you couldn't *fix* me, I became *less than* to you. Even now, all these years later, you're expecting me to apologize to you for the choices I made when I was twenty, that had nothing to do with you. I can say that I'm sorry I left Toronto with you thinking I was dead—I agree that was a shit move. But I won't say I'm sorry for anything else, because you don't know what it's like, Drew."

Paris is heaving.

"You don't know what it's like to be born into a life of cruelty and abuse, and you don't know what it's like to have to claw your way out in order to have any sense of self-worth. There's probably a long line of people who will always wonder if I actually did kill my husband, and there's nothing I can do about that. They're allowed to think whatever they want. But not one of those people is allowed in this house, because I decided a long time ago that I'm done being everyone's toilet. You no longer get to shit your opinions on me. So if you're going to sit there like the king of perfect, you can take your Raptors hat, go back to Toronto, and go fuck yourself with it."

She gets up and walks away. If she stays in the kitchen, she doesn't know what she'll do. She plops down on the living room sofa and puts her head in her hands.

She's so tired. So tired of the journey she took to get here, and already exhausted just thinking about the thousand more miles she still needs to go. It doesn't matter that the murder charge was dropped. There will always be whispers, questions, doubt.

And she hasn't even dealt with Ruby yet.

A few minutes later, Drew takes a seat beside her on the couch. He hands her a fresh beer. He's gotten himself another one, too.

"I deserved that," he says quietly. "Joey—"

"It's Paris now."

"It feels weird to call you that," Drew says. "But you're right. You're Paris now. I'm sorry, okay? In another life, you and I were best friends. I don't know where things stand now. I do know I want to understand. The last time I saw you, you were on a stretcher under a tarp, being moved into the back of an ambulance. I saw your body. I saw the burns. If not for the tattoo and your necklace . . ."

"You saw the burned body?" she asks, hearing the anguish in his voice. He nods. "It was bad."

She slumps into the sofa. For nearly two decades, she hadn't allowed herself to think about Mae, who was so vibrant, the kind of girl who could instantly change the energy of a room just by walking into it. She had loved Mae. Just like she had loved Drew.

Paris leans her head back against the sofa. She's completely wiped out. Drew looks at her. "I should go."

"Stay," she says, and it surprises them both. She reaches for his hand. "Just stay. Please. We can talk about the rest of it in the morning, if you still want to. But you're the one person who knows me, Drew. So just . . . stay."

He doesn't say anything, but he doesn't move, so Paris leans into him and rests her cheek on his shoulder. They stay like that for a while, and as she listens to him fall asleep first, she wonders what Drew would think if he knew the truth about Charles.

Because Drew doesn't know her, not really. If he did, he would leave.

In the end, everybody leaves.

CHAPTER FORTY-TWO

When Paris wakes up the next morning, the doorbell is ringing and Drew is gone.

She sits up, the sofa blanket falling off her. At some point in the night, he must have covered her with it, which is something he used to do whenever she'd fall asleep in front of the TV in their apartment all those years ago. He was only here for maybe fourteen hours total, but already she feels his absence.

He didn't even say goodbye.

She pads upstairs to retrieve her phone, and sees that she has several texts and emails, many from people who've been silent the past couple of weeks. The press release from the DA was released the evening before. *The underlying cause of Jimmy Peralta's death has been ruled undetermined. The District Attorney's Office has withdrawn the first-degree murder charge against Paris Peralta.*

Henry texted her a link to a local news station's website where there's a video of Sonny Everly's response, which appears to have been filmed earlier that morning in front of his law office. "Jimmy Peralta's death has not been ruled a homicide, because there's simply no evidence to prove that it was," her lawyer said to a dozen or so reporters, looking rather respectable in a suit and tie. "Even so, my client, Paris Peralta, has been cleared of all wrongdoing, and she respectfully requests that you all give her time and space to grieve her enormous loss."

Henry has also texted, *Don't read the comments!* which of course is a surefire way to make her want to read the comments. She scrolls down, and the first one she sees says *Paris Peralta got away with murder!* She puts her phone down immediately. In a lot of ways, it doesn't matter that the murder charge against her has been dropped. She's already been tried in the court of public opinion, and been found guilty. Sighing, she pads to the window and chances a peek out from behind the shades. Other than the usual sightseers across the street at Kerry Park, there's nobody there.

It's really over. Life can go back to normal. Except she has no idea what normal is now, without Jimmy.

The aroma of fresh coffee hits her when she enters the kitchen, and she's surprised to see a half-full pot in the coffee maker. Somehow, the kitchen is clean. All the food from the night before has been stored away neatly in the fridge, dirty dishes in the dishwasher. She wonders if Zoe is here somewhere, because this is the kind of thing the assistant always did. But it's not Zoe. Outside on the patio, Paris sees a man in one of the lounge chairs with his legs up, typing on a laptop.

She swallows. It's Drew. He didn't leave. When she opens the glass doors, he looks up with a grin.

"Good morning." Drew closes his computer, and then stands, stretching his arms up over his head. He's dressed in swim trunks and a damp tank top. "You slept ten hours. You must have needed it."

"You're still here." Paris is thrilled to see him, but tries not to let it show. She moves aside as he steps through the patio doors and into the kitchen. "How long have you been up?" The stove clock tells her it's ten a.m.

"About three hours. I'm still on East Coast time. I didn't want you waking up alone." He places his laptop on the counter. "Don't worry, I had things to do. I made coffee, went for a swim in your pool, and fixed myself a plate of leftovers for breakfast. I figured if I was going to overstay my welcome, I might as well go all the way."

She grins.

"And you're lucky that I didn't know you still had one of these lying around, or else I would have brought all my old mixtapes." He points to Jimmy's old Sony stereo. "You know I have songs on those tapes that aren't available on iTunes, that I haven't heard in two decades? I might have to go on eBay and find myself an old boombox."

Even after nineteen years, he's still so . . . *Drew*. It feels exactly right for him to be here, to cover her with a blanket, to make himself at home. She doesn't know where they go from here, but in this moment, she's never been more certain about one thing: she wants her best friend back.

His phone pings, and he grimaces when he reads the message. "Shit. I forgot to check into the hotel last night, and they just canceled my reservation. And now the hotel is fully booked. Any recommendations? I thought I'd stick around for a couple of days."

For me? she wonders, but she doesn't dare say it out loud.

"I have a bunch of recommendations, but I'm not giving them to you." She pours herself a cup of coffee. "You can stay here."

"I don't think that's a good idea." Drew hesitates. "Don't you think that might, I don't know, raise some eyebrows?"

"Since I married Jimmy, my entire existence has been one big raised eyebrow," she says dryly. "I have two perfectly good unused guest bedrooms upstairs, and you already know the food and the pool here are better than at any hotel. Just stay, okay? It's . . ." She pauses. "It's nice having you here."

They make eye contact. Paris looks away first.

"All right, you're stuck with me for a while longer." Drew rubs his face. "I could use a shower and a shave, and of course a razor is the one thing I forgot to pack. Any chance you have one I can borrow? Otherwise, I can run back out."

"I have a Venus disposable I can lend you." Paris snorts when he makes a face. "Kidding. I'm pretty sure there's a pack of Gillettes upstairs. I'll find them for you."

The doorbell rings. They exchange a look.

"Want me to hide?" Drew asks.

While he says it in a joking tone, they both know it's a legitimate question. A houseguest so soon? And a man, to boot? There'll be questions. And judgment.

"No," Paris says, sounding more decisive than she feels. "You're my guest. You don't have to hide from anything or anyone."

The doorbell rings again, and then there's a muffled knock, as if someone is using an elbow or a knee to bang on the door.

"You sure?" Drew says. "I can make myself scarce. Although my rental car is parked in the driveway."

"I'm a free woman now, and you're my friend. I don't owe anybody an explanation." Paris pads toward the front door, and Drew follows. "Although, there's no reason to give specifics if anyone asks how you and I know each other. Let's just keep it vague."

She unlocks the door. Zoe is standing on the porch, her hands full. She's got her laptop bag over one shoulder and a large cardboard box from the post office in her arms. Piled on top of the box are several unopened packages she must have also picked up. The box is more of Jimmy's fan mail, of course, a reminder that Paris is going to have to deal with Ruby, and soon.

Not that Ruby would ever let her forget. By now her mother must be well aware that Paris is inheriting everything Jimmy left her, and she's betting that Ruby will push even harder for her money now that the murder charge has been withdrawn.

Paris is a millionaire now. As is the frizzy-haired woman standing in front of her.

"Why didn't you just let yourself in?" Paris reaches forward and takes the packages off the top of the box before they can slide off. "You still have your door code."

"I didn't want to assume it was okay to use it again," the former assistant says, stepping inside. "And is that a rental car in the driveway? I saw an Avis sticker—" She stops when she sees Drew. "Oh. *Hello*."

"Let me grab this for you." Drew reaches out to take the box from Zoe's hands, and then flashes her a charming smile. "I'm Drew. An old friend of J—" He coughs. "Of Paris's."

"I'm Zoe," she says, appearing not to catch the near blunder. She gives him a once-over, and Paris stifles a smile at the slightly breathless tone in the other woman's voice. "Great to meet you."

"Can I put this somewhere for you?" Drew asks, his smile widening.

"Anywhere is fine," Zoe says, still staring up at him.

Paris points down the hallway. "Jimmy's office is good, if you don't mind," she says to Drew with a small smirk. "Thanks."

When he's out of sight, Zoe takes the packages back from Paris. "Where did *he* come from?" she asks. "And is he single? I didn't see a wedding ring."

"He's . . . actually, I don't know. We haven't had a chance to catch up fully yet, but the last time we saw each other, he was in a serious relationship." It's the truth. Paris just doesn't bother to mention that this was nearly twenty years ago. "You want some coffee? And you know you didn't have to stop by the post office, right? You're not on the payroll anymore."

"Yeah, about that," Zoe says, following her into the kitchen, where she places the packages on the table. "What if I was? I know I said I was planning to move on, but I don't feel right leaving you to deal with all this. There's stuff I've ordered for Jimmy that will still be arriving that needs to be sorted and returned. There's his fan mail—"

"I can help with that," Paris says quickly.

"—and I have to make updates to the website. Also, Jimmy was involved in a lot of charities. He was always talking about starting a foundation, and I thought I could—" Zoe hesitates. "I was going to propose that we honor him by starting it on his behalf. If that's something you're interested in. There's already money earmarked for it in his will, and you wouldn't have to do much, as I could—"

"Do it," Paris says immediately. "I'll kick in ten million. I'd like to be involved, of course, but only behind the scenes. You should be the one to run it. Why don't we talk more about it after the funeral?"

"Sounds like a plan." Zoe smiles and squeezes her arm. "Speaking of which, Elsie should be here soon. She wants to help with the arrangements. My advice? Don't let her take over. Because she will. She thinks she knew Jimmy better than anyone."

"Well, in fairness, she did."

"Maybe," Zoe says. "But the problem with going that far back with someone is that they have a hard time letting go of the old versions of you. Jimmy worked really hard to evolve. But whenever Elsie was here, all they did was talk about the old days. I always thought their friendship kept him stuck in the past."

Paris nods, thinking of Drew upstairs. "Do you think it's possible for old friendships to evolve but stay close, even if both people have changed?"

Zoe's eyes flicker to the ceiling, as if she has some sense of what Paris might be getting at. "I don't know. But I do think good friendships are worth fighting for."

The doorbell rings again. It's starting to feel like old times. There was always a lot of activity around the house when Jimmy was alive, people coming and going. Even when he was retired, his presence created a certain kind of energy.

"I'll get it," Zoe says. "Remember, Elsie is here to help, not make all the decisions. You get to decide whether we celebrate Jimmy big, or small."

"What do you think he would have wanted?"

"Jimmy always seemed happiest when he had all his friends around." Zoe's smile is gentle. "But he's not here. His celebration of life is *about* him, but it's *for* us. You should do whatever you feel comfortable with."

The last thing Paris wants is to mingle in a house full of people she barely knows, many of whom she won't know at all, but Zoe is right that it would have made her husband happy. When she and Jimmy got married, Paris stepped into Jimmy's world. Soon enough, she'll step back out, and back into the quiet life. After all the things Jimmy has done for her, she can do this for him.

The doorbell rings again, followed by an impatient knock.

"All right, you better let Elsie in," Paris says. "Drew needs to borrow a disposable razor, and they're in Jimmy's room. I haven't been back in there since . . ."

"It's okay to go in. His room is pristine, like nothing ever happened. I checked myself after the cleaning crew left." Zoe touches Paris's arm again. "I promise it will be fine."

"I can see why he loved you," Paris says with a soft smile. "You really are a gem."

"I could say the same about you."

It's not exactly a fresh start, but it's safe to say they've turned a page.

CHAPTER FORTY-THREE

Paris takes a deep breath and opens Jimmy's door. Before she can chicken out, she crosses the bedroom quickly, heading straight for his private bathroom. The scent of bleach hits her, not strong, but not faint. As Zoe promised, everything looks as it should. The white tile is white, the bathtub is shining, the glass is wiped clear.

She opens the first vanity drawer and pokes around, looking for the disposable razors she bought her husband months earlier. Oh, the drama over *shaving*. As she searches through the random dental floss picks, combs, hair pomades, colognes, and the electric shaver he always forgot to charge, their last argument comes back to her. They'd ended it on a compromise.

"Just give me the damn razor," Paris had snapped. "If you're going to insist on a straight shave, then at least let me do it for you."

The suggestion worked. Jimmy had finally calmed down.

"This is the beginning of the end, kid," he'd said with a dramatic sigh. He was sitting on the edge of the tub, facing the tile with his head tilted back, his face and throat slathered in shaving cream. Paris stood behind him and worked slowly, being sure to keep the exact right amount of pressure on his skin. It was her first time shaving anyone, with a straight razor or any other device. "Today, I can't shave. A couple of years from now, I probably won't be able to take a piss. My balls are already creeping down to my knees. I'm on the downward slide to dead."

"Don't you dare make me laugh, or I might accidentally cut you," Paris told him. She leaned over to give his forehead a kiss. "You're lucky I love you, you stubborn, cranky old man."

She pulls open the second drawer now and sees his small collection of straight razors. Four of them, all folded to protect the blades, lined up neatly on a soft microfiber cloth. It reminds her that the police still have the one that Jimmy used on himself, and she wonders if they'll ever return it. Jimmy owned five razors, each one with its own little backstory.

Would it be weird to have Jimmy's straight razor collection framed? He'd cherished these razors. He was so old school in the things he loved.

"If you don't follow the trends, you can never go out of style," he used to quip.

A thought niggles at Paris then, and she stops. Something's not right. When the crime scene forensic team was here, they'd photographed the bathroom extensively, including the contents of the drawers. Sonny had insisted she look at all the pictures so she'd understand the full extent of the evidence the prosecution had against her. Unless she's misremembering, didn't the crime scene photos show one straight razor, presumed to be the murder weapon, lying on the bathroom floor by the tub, and only *three* razors in the drawer?

If so, that would mean that on the day she was arrested, one razor from Jimmy's collection was missing. And now it was . . . *back*?

She shakes her head. That can't be right.

Opening the bottom drawer, Paris finally sees the unopened pack of Gillette safety razors that Jimmy never bothered to use. She grabs it and heads out of the bathroom.

"Hey," Drew says from the bedroom doorway. He's changed into regular shorts and a T-shirt. "Great water pressure in that guest bathroom. Any luck with the razor?"

"Here." She hands him the pack of Gillettes.

"What's the matter?" he asks. "Your face is doing a thing."

She doesn't answer him.

It's possible Jimmy misplaced one of his razors. In fact, with his memory issues, it's likely. But still . . .

She moves past Drew and jogs down the stairs to the kitchen. She passes Elsie sitting in Jimmy's office, who gives her a small wave. The lawyer appears to be on a work call. Zoe is at the kitchen table, sorting through the contents of the opened packages as Creedence Clearwater Revival plays on the old Sony stereo. *I wanna know, have you ever seen the rain . . .*

Paris grabs her phone from the counter and heads back upstairs. Somewhere in her Gmail is a PDF file Sonny sent her after their first meeting, which includes the crime scene photos.

She finds the email as she enters Jimmy's bedroom once again, and opens the attachment. She scrolls past the numerous pictures of Jimmy's body, the blood smears, the area on the tub's edge where Paris hit her head. Finally, she finds what she's looking for.

In the crime scene photo, there are one, two, *three* straight razors in the drawer.

She scrolls back up to the close-up shot of the razor the police still have, and confirms that it's the one with the ebony handle that Jimmy bought in Germany. Which means the razor missing in the photo—which has since been mysteriously returned—is the one Elsie gave to Jimmy. Paris had used it to shave Jimmy that morning. She remembers because when she was finished, she had rinsed it, careful to ensure there were no bits of shaving cream or hair stuck in the inscription. IT'S A CUTTHROAT BUSINESS, BUT YOU SLAYED IT. LOVE, E.

And then she had left it on the edge of the sink to dry.

So who had taken it? It had to be the same person who put it back in the drawer. Considering how few people have been in the house recently, the list of possibilities is short.

Drew meets her in the upstairs hallway, his face freshly smooth. "Want to tell me what you're thinking about?"

Again she doesn't answer, and he follows her downstairs to the kitchen.

Still at the table, Zoe has sorted through the packages and is now on her laptop, printing return labels for the items going back. Drew walks over and picks up an eight-pack of Maxell cassette tapes sealed tightly in clear plastic wrap.

"I can't believe they still make these," he says, delighted.

"Right?" Zoe glances up at him with a smile. "And thank God they do, because Jimmy used them to record himself practicing his jokes. He ran through the last eight-pack in about two weeks."

"Hey Zoe, quick question," Paris says. "Did you happen to take one of Jimmy's straight razors out of his drawer? Before he died?"

"Hmmm?" Zoe continues typing.

"You know, the one that was engraved, from Elsie? It wasn't in the drawer on the day the crime scene unit was here taking photos. But it's back in the drawer now."

Zoe's gaze remains fixed on her screen as she answers. "Did I ever tell you about the time Jimmy and I were traveling here to Seattle, and he tried to put his straight razors in his carry-on? TSA caught it, of course, and you should have seen their faces. If he wasn't Jimmy Peralta, they probably would have arrested him. I was able to get it into his checked luggage." She rolls her eyes. "Typical Jimmy. So smart in some ways, and so clueless in others."

"Zoe." Paris does her best to stay patient. "The straight razor. The one from Elsie. Did you take it, maybe to have it sharpened, before Jimmy died? And then put it back, sometime after the house was released back to me?"

"I have no idea what you're talking about. I never touched Jimmy's razors."

"When were you last in his bathroom?"

"I told you, I gave the bathroom a quick look after the cleaning crew left. But I didn't actually go inside." Zoe looks up again, and this time she sits back in her chair. "What's going on? Why are you interrogating me?"

Paris crosses her arms over her chest and waits. Drew is leaning on the kitchen counter, pretending to browse through Jimmy's cassette collection.

"The last time I was physically inside Jimmy's bathroom was the night of his charity gig," Zoe says. "Remember I told you he was upset with his performance? When we got home, he wanted to practice in the bathroom so he could see himself in the mirror."

Paris nods.

"When he got upstairs, he called down and said the tape in the deck was full, and he asked for a fresh one. We only had one tape left, so I brought it up to him, and then filed the other one in his office." Zoe holds up the package of Maxell cassettes. "And then I ordered him another batch. Right after he told me to go home."

"Wait." Paris stares at her for a moment, then turns to Drew, who's still pretending he's not paying attention. She turns back to Zoe. "Are you telling me that the cassette in the tape deck was *new?*"

"Yes."

"And you put it in at what time?"

"Nine thirty or so, right before I left." Zoe is exasperated. "What are you getting at, Paris? I feel like you're accusing me of something."

"The police confiscated the cassette that was in the stereo as part of their evidence." Paris speaks slowly, trying to process this new information. "That cassette had Elsie's voice on it right at the end. It wasn't anything much, something like, 'Did you forget we had plans?' And then Jimmy stopped the recording."

Drew is looking at her, nodding. He seems to understand exactly where this is going, even though it's clear Zoe does not.

"But when the police asked Elsie about it—" Paris stops abruptly.

Elsie has entered the kitchen, finished with her work call. In her hand are several return shipping labels that she grabbed from the printer in Jimmy's office, and she hands them to Zoe.

"When the police asked Elsie what?" she says to Paris. Then she turns to Drew, looking him up and down. "Hi. Elsie Dixon. And who might you be?"

"Drew Malcolm." He shakes her hand.

"What is it?" Elsie looks around. "What are we talking about?"

"Elsie." Paris works to control her voice. Internally, she wants to scream. "When was the last time you saw Jimmy?"

CHAPTER FORTY-FOUR

If not for Jimmy's old stereo playing a Fleetwood Mac song, the kitchen would be completely silent. It feels like everyone is holding their breath, and all eyes are on the petite lawyer. *Thunder only happens when it's raining . . .*

"Elsie," Paris says again. "I need you to answer the question, please. When did you last see Jimmy?"

"You already know when I last saw Jimmy." Elsie tucks a lock of silver hair behind her ear. "The detective asked me that during your first interview, remember? It was a few days before he died. Tuesday. I came here to the house to pick him up for breakfast."

"And that's how your voice got on the tape," Paris says. "The one Detective Kellogg asked you about. The one of Jimmy practicing."

"Are you telling me or asking me?" Elsie looks around the kitchen, aware that everyone is staring at her. "Yes, that's how my voice got on the tape. Now, why don't you just say what you're actually trying to say?"

Zoe's gasp is sharp and loud, and they all turn to her. She finally understands what Paris is getting at, and her eyes widen as she stares at Elsie.

"Oh my God, you lied," Zoe says, a hand over her mouth. "You fucking lied. That cassette with your voice on it wasn't from Tuesday morning. It was from the night Jimmy died. I put in a new tape at nine thirty, before I went home. Which means that you were here, at the house, in his bathroom, after I left. Why would you lie about being here that night unless you . . ."

"Elsie, what did you do?" Paris's voice is soft. She can hardly believe this is happening. "Did you kill Jimmy? Did you kill Jimmy and set me up?"

Elsie's face is bright red, and she glares at them both. "You two have some nerve accusing me—"

"Nobody's accusing you of anything, ma'am," Drew says. "They're just catching you in a lie, is all."

Elsie throws her hands up. "This is ridiculous. You are all out of your goddamned minds. We all know Jimmy killed himself." She turns to Drew, her voice shaking. "And I don't know who the hell you are, but you can shut the hell up."

"Then *why lie?*" Zoe cries. "It was you who disabled the smart home system and wiped all the data usage reports, wasn't it? You didn't want anyone to know you were here. What, did you use Jimmy's facial recognition to get into his phone after he—" She chokes. She can't finish the sentence.

"Did you take the straight razor, Elsie?" Paris asks. "The one you killed him with? It was lying on the edge of the sink. Did you switch out the razors to make it look like he used a different one to commit suicide? All those blades are pretty much the same size and shape, and there were three in the drawer the morning I was arrested. There are *four* there now. Did you take the murder weapon and then put it back at some point over the past few days? You've been here more than a few times."

"You hateful, conniving bitch," Zoe says, not bothering to wait for Elsie's answer. "You let Paris get charged with murder."

Elsie's face is white. She's standing against the wall of the kitchen, her shoulders curved inward like a cornered animal, her eyes darting from Paris to Zoe to Drew and then back to Paris. "I don't have to listen to this. After everything I've done for you—"

"I wasn't supposed to come home that night," Paris says, taking a step toward her. "You weren't trying to set me up, because how could you if I wasn't due home until the next evening? But *you* were here."

She takes another step forward. It's all she can do to not wrap her hands around Elsie's throat.

"You killed him, didn't you?" Paris says. "And then you tried to make it look like a suicide. You knew people would believe that because of his history. The fact that I came home early fucked up that plan. It made everyone think I murdered him. And you never said anything, because if anyone was being charged with murder, it was better me than you."

Elsie shrinks back even farther against the wall.

"So was it an accident?" Paris asks her. "Or did you stab him on purpose? And what did he say to you to make you so angry? And if it was an accident, why the hell didn't you call an ambulance?"

"Because it was too late!" Elsie shrieks, and then bursts into tears. "I was never going to get him back, so I was supposed to, what? Watch him be happy with you? I was so close—*we* were so close—and then out of nowhere, there you are, sweeping him off his feet."

Elsie is sobbing so hard, she can barely get the words out.

"Jimmy and I had so much history, but all he wanted was to be with someone who knew nothing about the person he used to be. And then six months ago, he asks me to change his will. He wanted to leave the majority of his money to you. I told him he was out of his goddamned mind. And he literally *was* losing his mind, wasn't he?"

"He left you money, too," Paris says. "And Zoe."

"But I didn't want his money, I wanted *him*," Elsie says. "I loved him. Don't you get that? For fifty goddamned years, I loved that broken, selfish, arrogant man, and half the time he couldn't even remember when we had plans. I came over that night after the charity gig because we were supposed to have some time together, and he *forgot*, because he *always* forgot when it was *me*. I went upstairs, and he was in the bathroom rehearsing his jokes, and the new will was sitting on his nightstand. I saw the amount he was leaving you, and I told him he was crazy, and he told me—"

Elsie is heaving, and she stops to catch her breath. "He told me it was none of my business and to *get a life*. Can you imagine? After everything I've done, that he would say that to me? I didn't mean to do it. But the razor was right there, and I snapped." Her knees give out, and she crumples to the floor.

"He was angry," Paris says softly, looking down at her in wonder and horror. "Because he really did forget, Elsie."

The song is over. A few seconds later, the cassette ends, too, with an audible *pop.*

Jimmy didn't kill himself. Despite all the tech in all the world, Elsie is going down for her oldest friend's murder over an analog Maxell cassette tape with no time stamp, no backup, no iCloud.

Jimmy was right.

Technology sucks, kid. Always best to go old school.

CHAPTER FORTY-FIVE

The celebration of life is a lavish affair, with friends from Hollywood and all over the world flying into Seattle to pay their respects to the funniest man most of them had ever known. There are some tears, but mostly there's laughter. It's exactly what Jimmy would have wanted.

The only person who isn't at the celebration is Jimmy's oldest friend.

After she was arrested, Elsie gave a full confession to Detective Kellogg, explaining what happened the night she killed Jimmy. They were arguing, and Jimmy said something cruel. Elsie grabbed the straight razor on the counter and waved it in his face, but only to make a point, she said. She reminded him of the day she gave it to him, and their decades of friendship, and told him that she was sick of being taken for granted.

Jimmy laughed at her, and she lunged at him. He grabbed her wrist and they struggled for a bit, until she wrenched her arm away and the razor sliced his inner thigh. He fell back into the tub and bled out in less than a minute.

His death was an accident, Elsie said. It was not her intention to kill him, and the only thing she felt she could do was make it look like a suicide.

She plugged the bathtub and filled it with warm water. Using a washcloth, she carefully removed a different razor of an identical size and shape from his drawer, dunked it in the bloody water, and then put it in his hand so it could fall to the floor naturally. Using Jimmy's phone, she wiped all the data usage from the smart home app. And then she wrapped the straight razor she had killed him with and took it with her, along with his copy of the new will.

She was afraid to dispose of the straight razor because it was engraved. Instead, she bleached it, and then put it back in Jimmy's bathroom drawer once his underlying cause of death was officially ruled "undetermined" and the charge against Paris was dismissed. With the case closed, she figured nobody would question why there were three razors in the drawer before, and four now.

No one was supposed to be accused of murder.

Nico Salazar wanted to charge Elsie with second-degree murder, tampering with evidence, and obstruction of justice. On the advice of her lawyer, Sonny Everly, she agreed to a plea. Seven years for manslaughter, but with good behavior, she might be out in four. Due to her age, and with no history of violence, they agreed to send her to a small, medium-security women's prison.

Elsie Dixon will be seventy-two when she gets out.

There's a FOR SALE sign outside the house. Zoe is taking care of Jimmy's estate sale. Everything is up for grabs except for Jimmy's old boomboxes and his cassette collection, the only things Paris wants for herself.

Drew stayed for the memorial service, and now, like so many years ago, they say goodbye in the driveway.

"So I never asked you," Paris says as she walks him to his rental car. "What happened with Kristen? And did you have a son or a daughter?"

"*Kirsten*," Drew says, giving her a look, and they both chuckle. "When I got back to my mom's place the morning after the fire, she was waiting for me on the porch. Before I could say anything, she said she thought the wedding was a mistake, and all we'd do is end up resenting each other and messing up the kid. We're good co-parents. Kirsten got married a few years later, and Sasha has a half brother and sister. Everything worked out the way it was supposed to."

He pulls out his phone and shows her a picture. Sasha is beautiful, because of course she would be. She has Drew's smile.

"And you never wanted to get married?" Paris asks.

"Not really," Drew says. "It turns out I've got some of my own stuff to work on. My mother says—" He cringes. "I never thought I'd be a guy that starts sentences with 'My mother says.'"

"Belinda is an amazing woman. Tell me."

"It's been *suggested*," Drew says, sticking his hands in his pockets, "that the reason my relationships don't progress to the serious stage anymore is because they don't measure up to the relationship I imagined I would have had with you."

"Oh." Paris feels her face flush. "Do you . . . agree with that?"

He looks down at her. "Now that I've seen you again, I probably do."

For the first time, she realizes it's possible to feel devastated by grief and elated with happiness, all at the same time.

"I'm not ready," Paris says, but she doesn't look away. "I may never be ready."

"We can talk about it when you're back in Toronto." Drew grins. "We'll go to Junior's."

"How do you know I'm coming back?"

"Because of Ruby," Drew says. "You have unfinished business with your mother."

A brief silence falls between them.

"How much does she want?" he asks.

"Ten million."

He lets out a low whistle. "You want my advice?"

"You know I do."

"Don't pay her a dime. There's no proof that you killed Mae, because you didn't. You set a fire. You're not a murderer."

He gives her another hug, and kisses her forehead. She remains in the driveway until the taillights of his rental car disappear.

She didn't murder Jimmy. She didn't murder Mae.

But she is a murderer.

* * *

After Zoe finally leaves and the house is quiet, Paris opens the cardboard box of Jimmy's fan mail. It only takes a couple of minutes of digging until she finds it.

My dearest Joey,

Congratulations. You've been exonerated. Quelle surprise.

    I have to tell you I'm losing patience. I appreciate you've been busy, but there are still ashes in an urn that aren't yours. And we both know what you did to Charles.

    Ten million. This is my last letter. Which means this is your last chance.

All my love,
Mama

Paris finds a pen and a blank piece of paper. She scrawls a quick note, which she mails right after she writes it.

Be there soon.
J

PART SIX

I'm only here to witness the remains of love exhumed

—BARENAKED LADIES

CHAPTER FORTY-SIX

She can't go into the Golden Cherry, and she can't go into Junior's. She's supposed to be dead, after all. As she sits in Drew's Audi in the parking lot behind both buildings, she gets a text.

Lineup. 10 minutes. Jerk or curry?

Both, she replies.

He sends her back a pig-face emoji. She sends him a picture of her middle finger.

The back door to the Cherry opens, and she sees a man come out. Six five, thick, naturally tan complexion. His jet-black hair now has a sprinkling of salt to it. She finally looked him up on LinkedIn—private browsing, of course—and learned that he's been Cherry's business partner for the past ten years.

She watches Chaz for a while as he moves things out the back door and into a van. After he's finished, he reaches around and rubs at a spot on the right side of his lower back. That spot always did bother him, and it's weird how familiar that gesture is to her, even after all this time. Then he stops and turns around.

He always did have that uncanny ability to sense someone watching him. Her instinct should be to hide her face, but she doesn't. Instead, she rolls the window down so they can see each other better.

Chaz freezes. Recognition slowly lights his face, and he breaks into the widest grin she's ever seen on him. They look at each other across the parking lot. He doesn't approach. She doesn't get out of the car. Instead, he puts his hand over his heart, and she does the same.

Thank you, Chaz.

Drew jumps into the driver's seat of the car at the same time Chaz goes back inside. The smells of jerk spice and curry fill the car, and her stomach rumbles in response.

"Heard that." Drew puts the car in drive. "Where do you want to eat this?"

"Take me home," she says.

* * *

Twenty-five years later, 42 Willow Avenue does not look exactly as she remembers it.

It's brighter. The old brown brick has been painted a cream color, and the rusted balcony walls have been replaced with wrought-iron railings. The building lobby has been renovated with new doors, new tile, new everything. It actually looks like a nice place to live now, and the park across from the building is clean, with two new play structures for children that weren't there before.

She looks up to where apartment 403 is, wondering who lives there now. There have probably been many tenants over the past nineteen years, all with different stories to tell. Hers was just one. Being here brings up vivid memories of Ruby being taken away that night, and while she's worked hard not to think about it, it isn't really possible to forget something that changed the entire direction of her life.

But with time, she can remember it less.

A plume of smoke catches her eye, and she spots a man barbecuing on his fourth-floor balcony. Barbecue grills used to be forbidden, but maybe they allow them now. He flips his burgers while chatting on his cell phone, and she realizes it's Mr. Malinowski, the building superintendent who used to live on the first floor. Is he still the super?

The glass doors to the lobby open, and she watches as a woman wearing colorful nursing scrubs holds the door open for an elderly woman with a walker. She recognizes Mrs. Finch immediately; her old neighbor from down the hall must be in her eighties now. Her housedress is stained and hangs off her bony frame, her white hair so thin that the pink of her scalp shows through. In the end, the woman had done the right thing when she finally called the police, even though the years that followed were hard.

Paris gets back into the car. As she and Drew drive away, she mentally says goodbye to the girl who lived in Willow Park, the one who survived her mother. All the memories here are painful, but they belong to a life that's no longer hers.

And over time, she will remember it less.

CHAPTER FORTY-SEVEN

Maple Sound looks so different in the daylight, serene and pretty, a picturesque small town someone might want to settle down in if they wanted to escape the city.

Ruby must loathe it here.

They make the long drive up the hill toward Tita Flora's place, and Drew cuts the engine when they reach the top. They sit in silence for a moment, staring across the pond at the exterior of the two-story house that she lived in for five long years. It was too dark to see much of anything when she was last here, but now, in the late-afternoon sun, she can see the effort that's been made to keep it up. The siding has been painted white to match the porch, and the flowers along the front of the house are in full bloom. Tita Flora is retired now, and with Tito Micky gone, she must have a lot of free time to maintain the place. It looks better than it ever did.

There's a shape moving in the kitchen window. She doesn't need to see a face to know who it belongs to. She would know that silhouette anywhere.

"How long, do you think?" Drew asks, breaking the silence inside the car.

"An hour," she says. "Which is fifty-five minutes longer than I'd prefer to be here."

"Do you have the cashier's check?"

She pats her pocket.

"I still can't believe you actually went to the bank." He shakes his head. "Want me to come in with you?"

"No, I need to do this alone." She gives his hand a squeeze and opens the passenger door. There's no way to predict what Ruby will say, and however this meeting goes, there are things she will never want Drew to hear. Ever. "I'll be okay."

"I'll be waiting right here," Drew calls out before she can shut the door. "Don't, you know, kill each other."

"Can't make that promise." She sees the alarmed look on her friend's face and rolls her eyes. "Drew, I'm kidding."

"With you two, it's not funny."

She shuts the car door and stares at the house for a few seconds more. Slowly, she walks toward it, passing the pond, which for now is silent. She heads up the porch steps, but before she can lift her hand to knock, the door opens.

After twenty-five years, she is now standing face-to-face with her mother.

They stare at each other from two feet apart on opposite sides of the doorway. Neither woman offers to shake hands or hug.

The first thing she notices is that Ruby's signature long, lustrous black hair has been chopped to her shoulders, its natural shine dulled due to age and cheap hair dye. There's a slight papery texture to her skin, highlighting angles in her cheekbones that never used to be there. Though her mother is still a couple of inches taller than Paris, she seems to have shrunk. She's wearing loose jeans and a yellow T-shirt, and there are new slippers on her feet.

"You look like me when I was your age," Ruby finally says. There's a tinge of jealousy in her voice. It's as good a compliment as she can offer.

"And you look like Lola Celia now," Paris says.

There's a long pause. Paris makes no attempt to enter the house. For all she cares, they can do this on the porch.

Ruby opens the door wider. "Come on in."

Paris steps inside, and as if on cue, the frogs by the pond begin to croak.

* * *

The house is cleaner and quieter than it ever used to be.

"Where is everyone?" Paris asks, even though she already knows the answer.

"Your *lola* is in Cebu," Ruby says. "She left right before I arrived, but she'll be back in a month. And your Tita Flora went to Toronto for the weekend."

"And you didn't want to go with her to the city?"

"She's staying with friends. I wasn't invited." Ruby takes a seat at the kitchen table and gestures for her to do the same. "Is that Drew I saw in the car outside? When he asked if I was available today, I assumed he was coming to interview me for his podcast, which is going to be all about me. He didn't mention he'd be bringing you."

"There is no podcast about you," Paris says. "I asked him to kill it."

"And he agreed?" Ruby raises an eyebrow. "Just like that?"

"Amazing, isn't it?" Paris allows a small smile. "And to think, I didn't even have to sleep with him."

"So you're sarcastic now." Her mother's lips flatten. "Nice way to talk to your mother."

"Would you rather I hit you?" Paris asks. "Smack you? Put cigarettes out on your neck? Would that be more polite?"

"Oh my God." Ruby's chair scrapes as she pushes back from the table. She goes to a cabinet and pulls out two mugs, and pours them both a cup of coffee from the pot on the counter. She dumps powdered Coffee-Mate into them, which is no different from how she used to drink it back in the nineties. "Are you still upset about all that? That was so long ago. It's time to move on. You're an adult now, *Paris*."

"I was a child then, *Ruby*."

Her mother sighs, placing both mugs down on the table. "Are you here to talk about the past, or are you hear to pay me so *I* don't talk about the past?"

"Both," Paris answers. "You're getting your money."

"Good," Ruby says, her shoulders relaxing. "You owe me. I deserve that money. I did twenty-five years in prison for you."

"*For* me?" Paris forces herself to stay calm. "Is that what you tell yourself?"

"You know I did." Her mother sips her coffee and leans back in her chair. "I never told anybody what you did to Charles."

"Because you know they wouldn't have believed you," Paris says. "His blood was all over your dress, and your prints were on his knife. You stabbed him sixteen times."

Ruby cocks her head. "Was it that many?"

"Sixteen times," Paris repeats. "And I was only thirteen. You would have made yourself look even worse if you accused me of anything."

"You fucked me over in court, testifying that Charles never touched you. All you had to say was that one thing. That one *true* thing." Ruby's lips flatten into a hard line. "No jury would have convicted a mother for protecting her daughter."

"Holy shit, you're still doing this." Paris stares at her in disbelief. "Bending the truth to make it fit what you want it to be. I heard you and Charles, okay? I heard you fighting with him in the other room. You accused him of using you to get to me. And you were right about that, because that's exactly what he did, because that's what men like Charles do. And then I heard him laugh and say that you were ugly when you were jealous, and that you'd never be together because you had no class."

Ruby's eyes narrow, her cheeks turning pink. "That is not what he said."

"Oh, Mama," Paris says, which will be the last time she'll ever call this woman by that name. "I've always envied your ability to deny any reality that doesn't serve you. Allow me to jog your memory."

She takes a long sip of the terrible coffee. Then she takes them both back to the night she thought she'd never have to revisit again.

* * *

Joey was in a dead sleep when Charles got into bed beside her. Though she often couldn't fall asleep when she knew he was nearby, he'd seemed so preoccupied with her mother all evening that it had felt safe this time.

It was her own fault for assuming. It made no difference to Charles that this was his house, his family home, and that his daughter's bedroom was on the other side of the wall. There were no boundaries with men like him. They were only built one way.

She felt a hand on her stomach, and woke all the way up. Her eyes flew open, but there was nothing to see, because the room was dark. Instinctively, she tried to scuttle to the other side of the bed, but he got on top of her and pinned her down with his body weight.

"Shhhhh," Charles whispered, his breath acidic from the red wine and cheese he'd been eating earlier. "Just relax. Your mom can be a lot of fun, but I've missed you, Joey."

She wriggled violently underneath him, but like the last time—like every time—it was useless. He was bigger, smarter, and more powerful than she could ever hope to be. It was never a fair fight. All she could do now was close her eyes, remain still, and allow the darkness to take over.

She didn't know how much time had passed—it could have been one minute, or ten—but she heard the *swoosh* of the door opening, and then all the lights in the room flicked on. The mattress bounced with the sudden absence of Charles's weight as he quickly rolled off her, his feet landing on the floor with a heavy *thump*.

Joey opened her eyes and blinked at the bright room. Her mother was standing in the guest bedroom doorway, her eyes darting from Charles to Joey and then back to Charles again. She looked furious. Joey sat up, the bedsheets falling away, and was relieved to see that she was still dressed.

"What the fuck were you doing?" Ruby's voice was hoarse. Her eyes were focused with laser precision on the man now stumbling around the bedroom, adjusting his clothes. It was amazing to Joey that her mother would even bother to ask a question she already knew the answer to. "Were you *touching* my daughter?"

"No, darling, no," Charles said. His face was bright red. "I got up because I thought I heard a noise, but I've had too much to drink. I seem to have ended up in the wrong bedroom." He forced a laugh.

Ruby turned to her daughter. "Joey? Is that true?"

Joey couldn't bring herself to answer. Instead, she stared at Ruby, willing her mother to hear her anyway. *And now you know, Mama. You saw it with your own eyes. Please make it stop.*

Ruby turned to Charles. "You asshole sonofabitch. Am I really not enough for you?"

"Now, Ruby—"

"Don't you dare *Now, Ruby* me," she hissed. "She's thirteen. Were you trying to fuck her?"

Charles stepped forward and hit her.

Ruby staggered backward, her head smacking the doorframe. Joey could see a red welt forming on the side of her mother's face.

"Ah, shit," Charles said in disgust. "Look, this is all a misunderstanding, okay? Let's all calm down. There's no reason to be upset. Right, Joey? Tell your mom everything's fine. And then we'll all go back to bed. In the morning, I'll make breakfast and take you girls out shopping. How does that sound?"

"We'll talk in the bedroom," Ruby snapped, turning on her heel, and Charles followed her out.

A minute later, Joey heard them arguing, the two of them hurling vicious insults at one another. Ruby called Charles a sick fuck. Charles called Ruby a jealous, gold-digging bitch. The irony was, they were both right.

Joey slipped off the bed and went straight into the connecting bathroom, where she used the toilet and tried to straighten herself up. She stayed in there until the shouting stopped, only venturing out when it had been quiet for more than a minute.

When she opened the door, she saw that Ruby was back, and she was horrified to see that her mother's summer dress was splotched with blood. In Ruby's hand was the long, thin knife Charles had been using to cut their cheese and fruit earlier. The blade of the knife was also covered in blood.

"Mama?" Joey said, alarmed. "Mama, what happened?"

"I killed him." Her mother's eyes were glassy with shock. "Oh God, I killed him. Charles is dead. You have to help me . . . oh God, Joey, you have to help me. I don't know what to do."

Just as she would testify in court a few months later, Joey told Ruby to change her clothes and go get the car. Then she headed down the hallway toward the master bedroom to clean up after her mother.

But unlike what she'd said in court, Ruby never did come back to finish the job.

As Joey was taking one last look around the master bedroom and bath-room, trying to make sure that everything her mother had brought with her was now in the garbage bag, she heard a moan, and jumped. Heart racing, she turned slowly and looked down at the carpet where Charles lay. His eyes, which had been closed before, were now open. Ruby had said he was dead. But there he was, staring up at her from the floor.

The monster her mother was supposed to have killed was trying to *speak* to her.

Joey looked around wildly, terrified to be alone with him, certain he was going to stand up and come for her. But Charles remained where he was, lying on his side on the floor.

"Joey." He managed to lift his head an inch off the carpet. "Joey, help me."

At the sound of his voice, Joey backed up until she hit the wall, hold-ing the garbage bag out in front of her as some kind of useless shield.

"Joey . . . Joey, call 911 . . . Joey . . . please . . ."

Charles's breathing was shallow, but he *was* breathing. What was she supposed to do now? She had offered to clean up her mother's mess . . . but for what? Even if Charles died, and they somehow got away with this, there would eventually be another Charles.

It was Ruby, after all. There would always be another Charles.

The knife was somewhere at the bottom of the plastic bag, covered in Ruby's fingerprints and Charles's blood.

Joey was surprised at how easy it was to make the decision.

Setting the garbage bag down on the floor, she walked down the hall to Lexi's room to retrieve the ice skate. She brought it back with her to the master bedroom, where she took a seat in the chair in the corner, filled with calm certainty about what was going to happen next. She slipped her foot into the smooth leather boot, and laced it up.

And then she stomped on Charles's neck, feeling the muscles and ten-dons split apart under the blade with a wet crunch, driven by the force of her thirteen-year-old rage and fueled by years of abuse and helplessness and shame.

Joey couldn't slay all the monsters, but she could slay this one.

CHAPTER FORTY-EIGHT

When Paris finishes speaking, her mother's coffee mug is empty.

"You don't regret it, do you?" Ruby says softly.

"No," Paris says. "But I paid the price for it, just as you did."

Ruby opens her mouth to say something, then closes it again. After a few seconds, she finally nods. "Just wire me the money," she says. "And then we can be done with each other, which is what we both want anyway."

"I brought a cashier's check." Paris leans back in her chair. "And I'll give it to you once you give me what I came for."

Ruby gets up and walks into the living room. Paris watches as she removes the decorative screen in front of the fireplace and reaches for the urn, which is sitting right inside the hearth. Paris's flashlight had passed right over the fireplace screen that night; it never did occur to her to look behind it. Ruby walks back to the kitchen table with the urn and stands near her, holding it up so the name on it is visible.

The urn is plain, about nine inches tall, and made of plastic. JOELLE REYES is stamped into the tarnished metal plate across the front.

But inside it is Mae Ocampo. Paris stares at it. To think, an entire adult human body can be reduced to ashes that fit inside a container this size.

Oh, Mae. I wish you were here.

She reaches for the urn, but Ruby moves it out of her reach.

"I want my ten million," her mother says. "And then you can take the urn and get the fuck out."

"*Ten* million?" Paris cocks her head. "Who said it would be ten million? Your original demand was one million, so that's what I brought."

Across the small table, Ruby's lips flatten again, her eyes darkening into twin storm clouds. Twenty-five years ago, this slight change in her mother's facial expression would have struck terror into Joey's young, soft heart, turning her insides into mush as she braced herself for the imminent explosion. This face meant a beating was coming. This face meant slaps and punches and kicks.

But she's not Joey anymore. She's Paris. And all she sees when she looks at Ruby is a miserable old woman who's mad she's not getting her way.

"That's not what we agreed." Ruby's voice is low.

This, too, used to be scary. The drop in tone, a decibel above a whisper, was worse than any shriek or shout. Not anymore. Once you understand how the magician does their tricks, they no longer dazzle.

"I never agreed to anything." Paris moves her chair back and stands up. "When did I ever say I'd give you ten million dollars? One million for the urn, and also your life. I could have just come here and killed you, you know. Trust me, I gave it serious consideration. Who'd even care if you were gone?"

She reaches into her back pocket and pulls out the cashier's check. Unfolding it, she holds it up. Under PAY TO THE ORDER OF, the name RUBY REYES is typed and clearly visible, as are the words ONE MILLION DOLLARS AND ZERO CENTS in the line where the amount is specified.

It looks legit, because it is. The bank manager in Seattle questioned her need for a paper method of payment, suggesting that Paris move her money via wire transfer instead. Should the cashier's check be lost or destroyed, it would be an arduous process to reclaim the funds, and could take months. Paris thanked her for her suggestion, and said she'd still take the check.

"I'm not you," Paris says to her mother. "I'd rather pay you than be you."

"Oh, get off your moral high horse." Ruby barks a laugh. "You think we're so different, you and me? We're exactly the same. We're survivors. Look who you married. You gave yourself the life I wanted Charles to give me. I taught you well, you ungrateful little grasshopper. You owe me, and I want my ten million. Don't be greedy. We both know you can afford it."

"You know what? " Paris says, as if something has just occurred to her. "I actually don't have to do this with you. In fact, I've changed my mind. No deal. Tell anyone you want about the urn. Nobody will believe you, because no matter how you got out, you're still a convicted murderer."

The look of shock on Ruby's face is almost comical. Paris slips the check back into her pocket and walks calmly out the front door, bracing herself for a push or shove that might send her flying off the porch. But Ruby doesn't follow.

Paris heads toward Drew's car, still parked in the same spot on the other side of the pond, and then finally hears footsteps coming up fast from behind.

In the grass, she whirls around to face her mother. She knew Ruby wouldn't let her leave without a final negotiation. Paris is aware that her back is to the pond, a little too close to the edge for her liking. But if this is where their last conversation has to happen, so be it.

The frogs have gone silent.

"Just take the urn," Ruby says, thrusting it toward her. "And give me the check. I can work with a million. It's fine."

"It's *fine*? You can *work* with it?" Paris stares at her in wonder. "Do you even hear yourself? How is it that you came to believe you deserve things that aren't yours?"

"Give me the check, and we'll never see each other again." Ruby gives the urn a quick shake, her arms still extended. "It's a small price to pay in the scheme of things, isn't it? You tried to get rid of me once, when you helped put me in prison. Just give me the check, and you'll be rid of me forever. I promise."

She promises? When has Ruby Reyes ever kept a promise that didn't benefit her?

Paris finally takes the urn.

"Well?" Ruby holds out her hand.

Tucking the urn carefully under one arm, Paris reaches into her back pocket for the check.

And then she rips it in half.

She does it so quickly, it takes Ruby a second to grasp what just happened. Only when Paris tears it again does her mother scream in fury, a sound so intensely satisfying that it was worth a million dollars just to hear it.

"*Tanga kaayo ka,*" Ruby spits. "You always were a stupid girl. I was glad when I found out you were dead all those years ago. Now we might as well make it true."

Her mother charges at her, full force.

The edge of the pond is slippery, and when Ruby makes contact, Paris is propelled backward into the pond. She instantly goes under. She feels the lid of the urn lift off, and sees the ashes—Mae's ashes—float out and dissolve into nothing.

In a panic, Paris lets go of the urn and tries to stand, but the pond is shockingly deep, just like her aunt always insisted it was. She tries to kick her way back to the surface, but it's no use. She can't swim, she never learned, and as the pond water enters her mouth, she hears Tita Flora's voice screeching in her head. *Stay away from the pond Jason you can't swim you will drown!*

Oh, the irony, Paris thinks. But before she can sink any deeper, she feels strong arms grab her under both armpits and pull. She can't swim, but Drew can, and he heaves her out of the water, stumbling backward with her into the grass.

From somewhere nearby, Ruby is still screaming as Paris sputters and vomits. The pond water tastes exactly like it smells.

"The urn," she manages to say, before she coughs up more water.

Drew helps her sit up. He points to the urn, which is now floating too far out in the pond to retrieve without swimming for it. As relieved as she is, it makes Paris sad to look at it. Of all the places she thought she might spread Mae's ashes, it wasn't here, in Maple Sound.

Goodbye, my friend.

In the distance, they hear the sirens. Drew called the police as soon as Paris came out of the house.

"Did you get it?" she asks him, still trying to catch her breath.

Ultimately, it probably doesn't matter. For her mother, being stuck in Maple Sound would be as bad as prison.

Drew shows her where the video he made is saved.

"I got it," he says.

* * *

The shove that Ruby gave Paris is all on video. Ruby Reyes has violated her parole and will be going back to Sainte-Élisabeth to serve out her sentence.

Her life sentence.

There are two patrol cars and four officers at the house, which might well be half the entire Maple Sound police force. As two of them lead Ruby to a car, she thrashes in her handcuffs, hair flying everywhere, her eyes wild and desperate.

"That's my daughter!" she shrieks. "She's not who she says she is! She's a liar!"

It takes both of the officers to push her into the police car, and even when the door closes, Paris and Drew can still hear her screaming.

"So that's the infamous Ice Queen," says the officer taking down Drew's and Paris's statements. "I was just a rookie when she was on trial, and I remember the story well. She is not what I expected. At all."

His partner, young enough to look like a rookie herself, could not seem less interested in Ruby Reyes. Instead, her gaze fixes on Paris as she hands Drew's phone back.

Both officers watched the short video twice. Drew captured Ruby following Paris out to the pond, where she seemingly forced Paris to take the urn. With Paris's back to the camera, the cashier's check is not visible. All that's shown is Ruby screaming and impulsively pushing Paris into the water.

From inside the police car, Ruby hollers again.

"Do either of you understand what she's talking about?" The senior officer looks back and forth between Paris and Drew. "What's this about her daughter?"

Paris is rubbing her wet hair with an old towel Drew found in his trunk. She shakes her head.

"We honestly don't know," Drew says. "I was supposed to interview

Ruby Reyes today for my podcast, and I brought my friend along. Ruby must have been triggered when she saw her, because she started going on about her daughter being alive. But if you're familiar with the story, Ruby's daughter died nearly twenty years ago, in a house fire."

Drew points to the empty urn, now floating in the middle of the pond. "Unfortunately, those were her ashes. Her daughter's name is on the urn."

Both police officers nod.

"This might be a weird question," the young officer finally says to Paris, sounding hesitant. "But . . . aren't you Jimmy Peralta's wife?"

She exchanges a look with Drew, then nods. "That's me."

Paris braces herself for a comment about the murder charge, or maybe something about her inheritance. But the officer merely nods and gives Paris's arm a light squeeze.

"I'm sorry for your loss, ma'am," she says. "Your husband was a really funny guy. I loved the first special."

"Terrific stuff," her partner agrees. "The second one is coming out soon, right? What's it called again?"

"*I Love You, Jimmy Peralta,*" Paris says, and saying the words out loud makes her smile.

Because she does. And always will.

ACKNOWLEDGMENTS

Every book is hard to write, but with the pandemic and my son in virtual school, it took several drafts to get *Things We Do in the Dark* to a place I felt comfortable showing my editor. (It's trippy to write about murder when your six-year-old is two feet away learning how to count by fives).

Keith Kahla, thank you for your patience and willingness to talk through all my ideas, even though I changed the structure of the novel at least four times. You bring out the best in me.

Victoria Skurnick, I'm forever grateful for all you've done, and continue to do. A million times, thank you. And huge thanks to the gang at Levine Greenberg Rostan for always looking out for me.

The team at Minotaur Books and St. Martin's Press is an absolute dream. Kelley Ragland, Andrew Martin, and Jennifer Enderlin, thank you so much for your kindness and encouragement. Martin Quinn and Sarah Melnyk, you two are the best marketer and publicist an author could hope for.

Macmillan Audio produced a fabulous audiobook, and I'm so grateful to Katy Robitzki, Robert Allen, and Emily Dyer for all their hard work. Carla Vega, your gorgeous voice and compelling narration was the exact right fit for this story.

It's always exciting to see translations of my books in different countries, and this couldn't happen without an amazing foreign rights team. Kerry Nordling, Marta Fleming, and Witt Phillips, thank you for getting my stories out into the world.

Ervin Serrano, huge thanks for creating the most striking, captivating cover for *Things We Do in the Dark*, which gives me chills in the very best way.

There were many sets of eyes on this book before it made it into readers' hands, and I don't envy the difficult job of a great copy editor. Thank you, Ivy McFadden, for catching all my grammar mistakes and smoothing out the awkward phrases.

This book was the first time I've ever asked for sensitivity reads, and I'm glad I did, as it can be challenging to write a psychological thriller that doesn't touch on triggering topics. Yasmin A. McClinton, I'm so grateful for your detailed notes on the importance of language when describing sensitive issues. Marie Estrada, your thoughtful perspective on our shared Filipino culture was so appreciated.

It turns out that the folks who read and write the darkest stuff are also the world's nicest people. Ed Aymar, you know how much you mean to me, so let's not be mushy about it. Hannah Mary McKinnon, thank you for untangling my plot knot, and you were absolutely the inspiration for Sgt. McKinley. Sonica Soares, thank you for thinking I'm cooler than I actually am. Chevy Stevens, thank you for sharing your accountant with me. Samantha Bailey, Natalie Jenner, Dawn Ius, Angie Kim, Shawn Cosby, Gabino Iglesias, Alex Segura, Mark Edwards, Riley Sager, Alex Finlay, and Joe Clifford, you're all rock star authors I'm lucky enough to call friends. Todd Gerber, thank you for being smart in all the ways I'm not. Shari Lapena, I'm so grateful for your generosity.

Thank you to CWOC, ITW, SinC, and MWA for providing resources and guidance in an industry that can be tough to navigate.

Librarians and booksellers are the literary world's angels—thank you for all you do to put books into the hands of readers. Huge thanks also to the bookstagrammers and influencers who shout out what they love every day, especially Abby Endler (IG @crimebythebook) for the constant support, and Sarah (IG @things.i.bought.and.liked) for the Instagram story that unexpectedly changed everything.

Shell, Lori, Dawn, and Annie, thank you for the decades of friendship, and for always being my safe space.

To my family in both Canada and the Philippines, *salamat kaayo.*

Special thanks to my Uncle Alex for helping me with the Cebuano translations in this book that Google (and me) messed up. Tita Becky, thank you for being my biggest fan from the beginning, you are forever missed.

I'm blessed to have such kind in-laws. Ron, thank you for being my unofficial Green Bay, Wisconsin publicist. Kay, you were a wonderful grandmother to Mox in the short time we had together, and you will live on in our hearts always.

To my son's teachers—and all teachers—I'm deeply grateful for everything you've done to keep the kids engaged and learning through such a tumultuous time. To the doctors, nurses, and frontline workers who've made the world safer for the rest of us: THANK YOU.

Darren, my love, we've been in each other's personal space every day for over two years now, and we haven't killed each other. I think that qualifies as a successful marriage. It helps that I love the shit out of you.

Moxie Pooh, you are such a good, kindhearted little human, and you make Mommy proud every day. I love you so much.

And lastly, I am incredibly grateful to my readers. I get to do what I love every day because of you. Thank you, thank you, thank you.